THE
EARTHER
EQUATION

KENNETH TAM

ANDROS GRIEVE
GENERAL, EARTHER MARINE CORPS

THE
EARTHER
EQUATION
THE FOURTH EQUATIONS NOVEL

KENNETH TAM

Published in Canada by Iceberg Publishing, Waterloo

Library and Archives Canada Cataloguing in Publication
Tam, Kenneth, 1984-
  The earther equation : the fourth equations novel / Kenneth Tam.
ISBN 978-0-9865017-4-6
  I. Title.
PS8589.A7676E27 2010   C813'.6   C2010-900086-2

Iceberg Publishing
55 Northfield Drive East, Suite 171
Waterloo ON N2K 3T6
contact@icebergpublishing.com
www.icebergpublishing.com

First pocket paperback printing: July 2005
Special international edition: January 2010

Cover Artwork: Wesley Prewer
Cover Design: Kenneth Tam

For Vulcan,

My first dog and the one who
taught me about the silly things
in life — idealism, responsibility,
and the philosophy
of dogs...

Rest well old friend.

KROGG SPACE: CORE SYSTEMS BLOCKADE

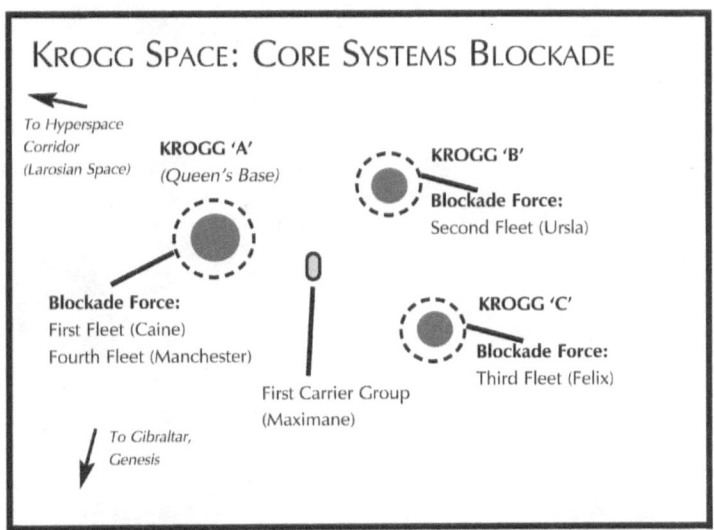

To Hyperspace
Corridor
(Larosian Space)

KROGG 'A'
(Queen's Base)

KROGG 'B'

Blockade Force:
Second Fleet (Ursla)

Blockade Force:
First Fleet (Caine)
Fourth Fleet (Manchester)

KROGG 'C'

Blockade Force:
Third Fleet (Felix)

First Carrier Group
(Maximane)

To Gibraltar,
Genesis

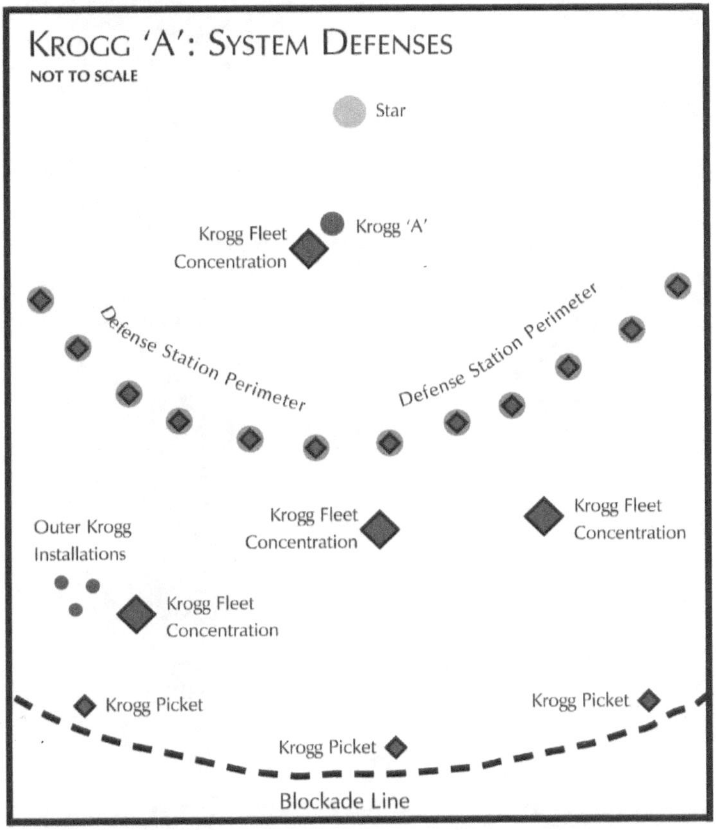

KROGG 'A': SYSTEM DEFENSES
NOT TO SCALE

Star

Krogg Fleet
Concentration

Krogg 'A'

Defense Station Perimeter

Defense Station Perimeter

Outer Krogg
Installations

Krogg Fleet
Concentration

Krogg Fleet
Concentration

Krogg Fleet
Concentration

Krogg Picket

Krogg Picket

Krogg Picket

Blockade Line

FOREWORD

I've studied wars for a number of years, taking an interest in them long ago when my grandfather, Dick Barron, told stories of his experiences as a Royal Canadian Engineer in the Korean War. As a combat engineer, Dick's job was to build bridges, blow up bridges, clear mines, and do any number of other jobs that required ingenuity, guile, and the ability to solve problems. He had many great stories.

One night in Korea, Sergeant Barron needed to run a cable across a river so that stranded troops on the other bank could pull themselves across the water on rafts. Chinese volunteers and Korean troops were moving in fast, and there was no time to waste. The Canadian engineers didn't have the required cable for the job, but the United States engineers did, so my grandfather's Captain distracted his American counterpart... then my grandfather went in to acquire the materials from the U.S. camp. An American Lieutenant tried to intervene, and my grandfather punched him out cold. The troops were rescued, and Sergeant Barron was busted down to Corporal... later to be promoted right back.

That was the sort of man my grandfather was, a good man who did what was needed to save lives and get the job done in some of the most horrible conditions imaginable. There have been many other men and women like him throughout history, and the decisions they have been forced to take in the course of war stagger me every time I learn more about them. Because I write a lot about war, and the decisions taken during hostilities, it's a subject I've become quite familiar with.

So when it came to the Earthers, humans and Larosians trying to find a way to end the war against the Kroggs, I remember clearly knowing what had to be done — or, more specifically, how it had to be done. The choices made by the Earthers in war are different than the choices made by many of the people I've researched over the years. They are decisions that reflect the Earther way — the alien philosophy that's survived some tough times through the war, and which the humans and now even the Larosians find difficult to accept.

The simple summary is this: the Earthers make no decisions out of fear.

They do what they believe is right, even if it is hard. Even if the smart and cynical say it's short-sighted, or naive, or foolish. The Earthers believe firmly that they must remain true to themselves, no matter the cost.

Now, 'no matter the cost' is an easy platitude, and in human examples it's often recited by individuals who eventually prove to be disingenuous, or perhaps insane. Rarely these days do we see such clarity of purpose portrayed as constructive — compromise is usually said to be necessary, and death for an idea is frowned upon.

Will the Earthers be like this, or will their determination hold when all hell breaks loose? Well, if you've been reading these special edition forewords throughout the series so far, you'll know that my open-ended questions about Earther character usually end on a skeptical note, and then over the course of the book, the Earthers defy common expectations and demonstrate once again that they are 'too good to be true'.

Don't bet on this book being any different.

In this final battle against the Kroggs, the Earthers hold many of the cards, and they use them to compel compliance from their allies. They take the war to their foes, and they suffer, but in the course of all this, lessons are solidified in their minds — they come to a final understanding of their collective character. They learn in the hard forge of combat what sort of people they are.

My grandfather learned the same sorts of lessons in Korea. He found he was a good man, despite some of what he had to do. And there are few challenges in life that can undermine such hard-won realizations, though some might try.

So what the Earthers learn in this book — the clear and resonating lessons they draw from the final battle against the Kroggs — will stand for forty years. And then the real test will begin.

As the war winds down, the thanks must continue to escalate.

Cody Herauf originated the Kroggs and the Larosians, and granted me the privilege of bringing their war to an end. His rich understanding of both cultures proved indispensable in making this particular story work, as the moods and cultures of both species are at the heart of this book. Thanks to him, yet again.

Keeping with the pattern, I must next extend my thanks to Wes Prewer. On the cover, you can see *Orion*, *Agamemnon*, *Engadine*, and a horde of other Earther ships and gunboats menacing one of the Krogg worlds, and that image is the result of his tireless work, endless refinements, and his perpetual patience. Wes is a fine fellow, and I'm lucky to count him as a friend and collaborator.

Wes' characters Ami Cairn and Barty Stowt (the latter, as I learned a year after we published *Retaliation*, is an homage of a kind to stories about a certain wizard!) have a cameo in this book, and will increasingly figure in the books to come. Many, many thanks to Wes. There are many more fine contributions to come from him.

Next up is, of course, my fine friend, Peter Caron. The privateers don't figure in this story, but, well, without his contributions, the simple fact is we wouldn't have been able to get to this place. What's most interesting about Peter's involvement in this book isn't so much what he contributed to the final battles, but what he gathered from them. Because beginning in the next volume, his keen and very perceptive strategic analysis of how the Earthers and humans wage war is going to have a profound effect on the universe. I won't elaborate any further, just trust me when I say Peter's brilliant at this, and I'm damned lucky to call him my friend. I'm very much obliged to him.

My parents yet again come next in the thanks, because I can never not thank them. They are business partners, supporters, and firm reminders of reality all at once. It's an incredible combination of qualities to have in any friends, and I was lucky enough to get this combination in my parents.

Though my friend Atlas never went to war, his philosophies are still well at home in the Earthers here. This story is about their identity, and that means it's also about his identity. We haven't come to the final lessons he taught me just yet — those continue to emerge in the four remaining books — but this is one of the most important stops along the way. To my bygone dog, thanks once again.

The war is about to come to a brutal end. Let's get into it...

PROLOGUE

Commodore Fox Magnus sat silently on the bridge of *ENS Atlas*, his 74-gun Third Rate ship of the line. Lying at anchor in deep space with six other 74s of similar construction, *Atlas* seemed almost lost in the void — there was no celestial body of note for lightyears in any direction. Only the great ship's grav anchors held it in place at this designated rendezvous point, and now as it waited, its sensors searched the surrounding space.

But there was nothing out there to see, and that tried Fox's patience.

The small-statured red fox tended not to be an impatient fellow — he could handle waiting, he could handle doing nothing... Usually.

But he'd been worn down by these last eleven months of campaigning. The Kroggs had attacked Gibraltar exactly 331 days ago, and Setter Caine, First Lord of the Earther Admiralty, had crushed a second loosely concentrated Krogg Fleet in the brilliant Battle of Cartenga Sun fourteen days after that. In the interceding months, Fox's 186th Battle Squadron, originally of eight ships but recently reduced to seven with the loss of *Jupiter*, had been out of port, working with the First Fleet and driving straight into Krogg space.

There had been no further counterattacks of the caliber seen at Gibraltar, but there had been numerous pockets of resistance along the way, and more than enough entirely dead worlds to leave a bad taste in the Commodore's mouth.

Kroggs — the undisputed bane of the universe — *infested* planets like a plague, destroying all life, using biomatter as compost to feed their ships and soldiers, and to perpetuate their war craze. They reveled in killing, and they made no attempt to conceal that fact.

Moreover, they were damned good at murdering and pillaging. Preliminary scientific analyses of the dead planets indicated that some amongst them had been captured by the Kroggs as many as *nine* centuries ago — at a time when Earth was in the grip of the *Napoleonic Wars*. The Kroggs had stormed through other galaxies for another 300 years before finally meeting a force that could stop them — the Larosians.

Once-feudal aliens from another galaxy, with a society structured around honor and duty, the Larosians were a complete opposite to the locust-like Kroggs, and they had proved the only power capable of standing against the destructive tide. Where Kroggs were masters of genetic manipulation — breeding living warships and fighting with genetically engineered blades, spines, and neuro energy weapons — the Larosians depended on logic, telepathy, machinery, and honor to secure victory. They were perfect antitheses of each other, and in centuries of war they'd very nearly canceled each other out.

The Larosians had forced the Kroggs back, but hadn't defeated them, and the Kroggs had recruited a young alien race to help them in their fight: the humans of Genesis...

That was precisely where Fox came in, because the humans of the Genesis Colony were the Earthers' allies, and had been for the past two and a half years. These humans were the sole survivors of an intelligent 'Omega Virus' that had been created by their ancestors. It had destroyed their species on Earth, then had created the Earthers from wolves, cats, and bears in order to fuel its existence. The plague had vanished before it could harm the Earthers, but it had left highly evolved humanoid creatures like Fox Magnus in its wake.

In fact, by some great comic coincidence the Earthers had been created just when the Larosians and the Kroggs had begun their titanic struggle... and now they were proving to be a decisive factor in that clash. In honoring their alliance with the Genesis Navy, the Earthers had been compelled to go to war against the Kroggs, first seeing action in the Battle of Genesis — a fight surrounding a massive trap set by the Kroggs for the Larosians. There had been no looking back after that; the Earthers had sided with the humans who in turn had fought against the Kroggs and *with* the Larosians.

That had been twenty months ago. Since then, the Earthers and humans had collaborated to create a second front of battle far from their native worlds, while the Larosians withdrew their strength and maintained their primary front in another galaxy. The forward Allied Base of Gibraltar had been established — and almost lost — and the Krogg Fleet had been ultimately routed.

Now the enemy had withdrawn to its home star group, three planetary systems known to Allied planners only as Krogg 'A', 'B', and 'C'. In fleeing they'd consolidated themselves into quite a formidable force and had made prospects of an Allied victory very bloody, but that was a detail Fox would worry about later...

Because right now he was worrying about waiting. And while he could recall a time when waiting didn't bother him *that* much, he'd lost some of his tolerance over these last eleven months of hard-fighting, bloody war.

Earthers, like their predatory ancestors, were disinclined toward needless killing, and even though they accepted that death was sometimes necessary, they still hated to inflict it.

Worse, they were *good* at killing.

At times better than the Kroggs.

The thought made Fox sigh and he suppressed an instinctive shiver — Earthers melded the reason of the Larosians with the instinct of the Kroggs and blended that with their native predatory skills. In war they were formidable fighters and strategists, so much so that their successes against the Kroggs had been unmatched by the humans.

While the Earthers were beginning to feel some concern over that inherent ability to destroy, the humans were increasingly *envious*. Genesis crews watched the Earthers' unparalleled success in this, their first war, while humans died in futile fights that they often lost. The war was going very badly for the Genesis Navy, and while the Earther Navy was ready to compensate for any difficulty faced by its counterpart service, the fact that help was required embarrassed the humans. And taking up the slack required the Earthers to use more of their 'dark' side... to kill more often, and more skillfully.

Yes, but we're no dark race. We do this well, and we do it because we must, so get off the bloody subject. Thinking like this will drive you mad if you don't.

With that minor revelation, Fox closed his eyes for a few seconds to clear his mind. More and more, lately, he'd been having thoughts like these. They crept up on him, and he didn't like them at all. Part of him said his resistance to them was just a denial of sinister truths, but his instincts held fast in assuring him of his own moral position.

He had a job to do. Even if he wasn't sure what it was *doing* to him, he had given his oath as an officer, and he couldn't break that.

And for all his killing skill, he still wouldn't cross certain lines; his squadron never killed needlessly, nor did any Earther squadron. Humans often went into furious rages and demanded revenge, angered by the death of their comrades, but Earthers simply couldn't.

Wouldn't.

Fox took a reassuring breath and pressed himself back into his chair, drumming his fingers on its arm. Where were these people...?

"On scope, skipper."

Fox blinked, distantly registering the voice of *Atlas'* Cruising Master, Mister Gunth, "They're closing now."

"Very good, squadron stand by drives. Let me know when we have a signal," Fox pushed himself stiffly out of his chair and paced forward to the bridge's main battle tank, frowning as twenty silver icons appeared in the holographic display.

Larosian Warcruisers.

"Hail coming in, sir," the Signal Officer reported in low tones.

Fox nodded, "In the tank."

Inhaling deeply, Fox laced his arms behind his back and straightened slightly to improve his view of the battle plot.

A gray alien face with unsettling silver eyes glowed to life in the three-dimensional projection, and offered Fox a nod, "I am Admiral-of-a-Fleet Narosh, of the Larosian Star Navy."

Fox nodded to the Larosian, "Commodore Fox Magnus, Batron 186. I'm here to lead you to the rendezvous with First Lord Caine."

The Larosian tilted his head, "Very well."

The screen blanked suddenly — just as Fox was opening his mouth to speak.

Right, the Larosians could be a bit... *abrupt* in their dealings.

"Mister Gunth, mark course for the rendezvous," Fox avoided another sigh as he looked to his Master.

"Aye, sir," the veteran shiphandler nodded in reply.

"Squadron to follow in battle order." Returning to his chair, Fox continued his orders, "Let's go, Master."

Mister Gunth nodded again, turned to the helm and put a gentle hand on the pilot's shoulder, "At 2,600 pls, prepare Wyndhymns."

Atlas began to hum softly as its main drives spun to life, and then as the Cruising Master nodded, the 74 collapsed into a ball of energy and sprinted away from the meeting point. The rest of the Allied ships followed quickly.

CHAPTER 1

Admiral Andra Ursla walked slowly down the hall, one foot moving steadily ahead of the other in a somewhat lethargic process that dragged her methodically through the bowels of the ship. She actually hadn't slept for four days... or was it five... and she was tired.

Three meters of kodiak bear, friendly on her normal days and agreeable on those rare days when she was out of sorts, Andra commanded the Second Fleet from the 150-gun *Agamemnon*. One of the Alliance's best tacticians, she'd held her post for almost two years and in that time she'd watched her fleet collapse from its original 600 vessels to 300 after the Battle of Genesis. After the Battle of Gibraltar, though, large numbers of newly-built ships had been sent up from Sol to reinforce her, and over the past few months the Second Fleet had ballooned to total about 700 vessels.

Logically, that last number should have pleased her; her fleet had grown.

But exactly 211 of the original Second Fleet ships remained — only one third of the ships that had been with her at Genesis had survived this campaign, and many of those had been extensively rebuilt at least once. The balance of the force had been constructed since Gibraltar, in the rapidly expanding yards of Earth and the recently-established shipyards at the New Halifax base.

Thus, Ursla's Second Fleet was large, and even with all its new ships it remained veteran and formidable. Still, many had been lost along the way. Many good Earthers had been asked to serve and had willingly given their lives...

That fact didn't bother Andra Ursla.

Or so she liked to tell herself...

More accurately, she pressed on in spite of it. Her blockade needed to be maintained, the Kroggs had to be held in their systems. It seemed the aliens didn't like that plan, though.

Just four days ago, three days before she'd been slotted to leave the Second Fleet to rendezvous with Caine and the Fleet commanders, the Kroggs had tried to break out of Krogg 'B' — her fleet's station. She'd spent four days playing tag with 900 Krogg ships of war, never managing to force action.

Since their swift trouncing at both Gibraltar and Cartenga Sun, the Kroggs had learned not to engage the Earthers without at least a two-to-one margin of superiority, so the only result of the four-day maneuver was exhaustion, and Ursla was more tired than usual as she lumbered through the lower decks of *Orion*. She was also three hours behind schedule — a remarkably timely appearance, considering — but since the Larosians hadn't arrived yet, she wasn't technically *late*.

Well, that's the way her tired brain was calling it, and it seemed agreeable enough.

The main briefing room was just ahead now. Trying to straighten herself a bit and tugging at her uniform to make it marginally presentable, she stopped in front of the tall door and keyed it open.

The briefing room was dim but not dark, the central holo tank deactivated while the three occupants waited for their remaining guests.

Ursla greeted each of them with a weak smile — Admiral Savanna Felix of the Third Fleet, ArcGeneral Sarah Manchester of the human Fourth, and Caine himself, of the First. They were all best friends, and months ago this would have been a jubilant gathering.

But today Ursla just labored into the room and dropped into a chair next to the main table.

"Greetings all," she uttered as she flopped heavily back against the seat, which respectfully didn't groan under her massive weight.

Felix nodded first, "Nice to see you, Andra."

"Though you look like I feel," Sarah said shortly, rubbing her eyes.

The young woman with the clipped British accent was perhaps the most battered of the three, having been posted with her fleet alongside Caine and the First, surrounding Krogg 'A' — the strongest of the bases. Between the 926 ships of the First and the 1,412 human ships of the Fourth, the Allies had only a third as many ships as the Kroggs in the system they were blockading.

It made for stressful days.

Ursla could empathize, and despite her harrowing fatigue she did, "We're all beaten bloody, I think."

Sarah and Felix nodded. The latter tiger's Third Fleet rounded out the Allied forces with 654 ships, and blockaded Krogg 'C', the third of the Krogg homeworlds and the one with the smallest Krogg garrison — only 800 vessels. Felix was thus slightly less strained than his fellow Fleet commanders, and lately he was finding himself the most energetic of the four.

Ursla heaved a sigh and met Caine's eyes, "How are you, Setter?"

Caine matched her deep sigh and tugged open the top button of his double-breasted uniform coat. He shrugged, looking down at his gray-furred hands, then took a long blink, "I'm not dead."

Ursla chuckled, "A start."

A nod was Caine's reply, his mind lumbering as much as Ursla's big body had when moving down the corridor. Caine's responsibilities as First Lord gave him two great worries: first, using his Fleet and Sarah's to bottle up 7,000 Krogg ships in a solar system, and second, figuring out how it was possible to contain some 9,000 Krogg warships in three solar systems with the Allies' total force of 3,700.

He was managing to do it by keeping the Krogg systems divided and by leading very daring raids against Krogg 'A' when its occupants appeared to be mobilizing, but fear remained. It seemed all too possible that after this entire campaign of driving to these Krogg homeworlds, the Allies had only managed to make the Kroggs stronger while weakening themselves.

The Earther and human casualties had been horrific thus far, particularly since Cartenga. Shipyards had been replacing lost ships and even exceeding the losses, but the core of the old Earther Navy was being worn thin. The fleet that had faced the Church on Pluto's Orbital Plane had been destroyed. Almost symbolically, *ENS Suffolk* had been lost on Caine's last raid into Krogg 'A'. *Suffolk* had been the first ship Caine had served in... over 100 years old and the vessel had been called up from mothballs to join the Allied Fleet.

Ships were needed, after all, and that was why the Earthers had kept some 500 vessels 'in ordinary' during all those years while they prepared their Navy to meet the Church humans. The best ships of each class from those ages past had been preserved in stasis, able to be recommissioned and ordered to join the fight. It was aboard those ships Caine had risen in rank...

And now they'd been systematically smashed by the Kroggs. As had much of the Navy that had initially met the Church.

Caine took a steadying breath against these thoughts and the abject sadness they caused — his fleets were fighting as well as ever, though attrition was wearing down their spirit. And there remained at least one last great push to victory... or perhaps even two.

That was where the Larosians would come in.

The alien veterans of this conflict had been absorbing the worst of this war in fighting on their own front, battling tens of thousands of Krogg ships and retaking territory that had been thoroughly infested. Since the Battle of Genesis twenty months earlier, Caine had received intermittent status reports and, on very rare occasions a Larosian vessel would appear.

For all intents and purposes, however, the Larosians had stuck to their front, and Caine to his.

Now, at long last, they were meeting at the home of their enemy.

Caine still wasn't sure how many Larosian ships were coming to Krogg space — communication between the two fronts had simply been too limited. The Larosian Fleet supposedly numbered in the tens of thousands, though, and if that force arrived it would make victory very probable and a much less costly proposition...

A weary sigh slid from Caine's lungs as he allowed himself to hope for that Larosian arrival. Pressure would be relieved immediately; there would be an Allied *numerical* advantage, not to mention a qualitative one.

But Caine couldn't afford to count on that much support, and he knew it. Instead he concerned himself with the situation at hand. He had to continue to make the most of his wounded, rebuilt, but determined fleet.

"So, any news?" Ursla asked heavily, forcing her head off the headrest of her chair.

Being the least exhausted of the assembled commanders — as well as the most administrative by background — Felix leaned forward at the question, "Good news, actually. The Fifth Fleet is almost entirely assembled, and the Sixth is just finishing loading up before it moves out."

Ursla blinked and straightened, "Excuse me?"

Felix frowned, "The Fifth and Sixth, Andra. They'll be joining us within six weeks."

The room remained silent as Ursla cocked a surprised eyebrow at the report, "Strengths?"

Caine held up his hand and interposed with his own answers.

"The Fifth is at 460, last count, many of them cruisers. The Sixth is only up to 390, but most of them are capital ships."

Ursla nodded slowly, easing back in her chair. The Fifth and Sixth Fleets had existed on paper for some ten months — but on paper only. Since the time of Gibraltar, the Admiralty had made efforts to establish home defense formations, even if just provisional ones. Whenever ships were detached from regular fleet work or sent home for long-term repairs and reassignment, they were temporarily given a listed designation of either Fifth or Sixth Fleet. It let the Admiralty and Genesis Fleet Command more easily keep track of vessels, and provided an organized structure for the defense of the home planets. Until now, these fleets had never actually been assembled.

The Earther Fifth and Genesis Sixth had begun to evolve into organized combat units some two months earlier, when containment of the Kroggs had become a reasonable certainty. At rally points situated in Earth and Genesis space, the ships coming freshly from the yards and those recently repaired were being held and reorganized, creating two fresh, essentially state-of-the-art battle forces.

Withholding all these ships from immediate forward deployment with the existing fleets had been a risk on the part of Caine — one he'd been hesitant to take after knowing the effects of dividing his forces before Gibraltar, but one that had ultimately been required. Ships on blockade duty invariably wore down and required yard time. When it came to attacking the Krogg systems, Caine wanted a core of fresh ships to lead the assault.

So far the chance seemed to be paying off... and now they were ready...

"We got a cutter in this morning from Earth," Caine interrupted Ursla's thoughts. "Varnon will be taking the Fifth out this afternoon."

Ursla nodded slowly, glancing at Sarah, "And the Sixth?"

"Cutter from Genesis came yesterday, Liz is bringing the Sixth out here herself. She's split it into two divisions — one under Bill Wallace and the other under Graham."

Caine's ears twitched, "I hadn't heard *that* part."

Bill Wallace was a fine line officer, but ArcLieutenant-General Graham Manchester wasn't a fleet man — he was an excellent system commander, but he'd never led *ships* into action.

"Just goes to show how strapped we're getting for officers, eh?" Sarah said dimly. "No offense to Graham, him being my brother and such, but he's never liked fleet command."

The trio of Earthers nodded slowly in reply.

Exhaustion was widespread it seemed — not just confined to Earther enthusiasm and to the machinery of the ships of the Allied fleets.

"Anyway, the Sixth will be here in just about three weeks, the Fifth in *six*," Caine paused to offer a weak grin, "...though Varnon is promising to get it here in four."

Ursla managed a small smile and nodded — that sort of ambition was to be expected from Admiral Varnon Broadpaw, the veteran fleet commander who had once run the Third Fleet and who had lately been working with battle groups on the left flank of the front. His leadership would hopefully work that fresh fleet into a battle-ready formation by the time it got out here...

"Well, it'll be helpful to have them," Ursla said slowly, her mind turning back to the conversation at hand.

Caine nodded, "And once the Larosians arrive, we'll hopefully have what we need to finish this."

Felix cocked an eyebrow, "Presuming the Larosians are willing to bring all they have..."

Sarah harrumphed in quick reply, "They'd bloody well better bring it all, or *I'll* make them accountable."

The comment might have been interpreted as a joke, but the edge in the British tone was sharp... perhaps it was indicative of how *determined* Sarah had become since Gibraltar. Her guilt at abandoning the fleet just before the battle had consumed her in the year since that action, and she seemed now to be committed to redeeming herself... a vain pursuit, because as far as the Earthers were concerned, she'd done nothing wrong.

Even her own fleet supported her actions. It was widely and rightly thought that, had she been at Gibraltar, she'd probably have died with Caitie Hargreaves and the rest of the humans. Instead she'd followed her gut, managed a daring strike out on the flank, saved a fleet hero (and her lover) in Pat Conroy, and with intrepid and now-famous characters like Fox Magnus, Chronos Claw and Draco Maximane, blown a Krogg base to pieces.

The Genesis Public Information Ministry had spun it as a story of great heroism. Sarah was a beloved and tormented hero to Genesis society, one of the beacons for Harvey Bingham's social revolution.

There was even a movie coming out.

All there to remind her of her betrayal, and to try to convince her that something she knew in every fiber of her soul to be wrong, was actually right.

So she kept seeking that redemption, for herself and herself alone. Indeed, she was almost becoming dangerous with this quest, taking even more chances than she had before. None in her fleet dared rein her in... except maybe for Pat, but he seldom got to see her on blockade duty.

As Caine looked to his human ArcGeneral and dear friend, he wondered again if he should speak to her about it. Ever since she'd gotten back after Gibraltar, talking to her had been an awkward prospect. She'd thrown up walls, and he knew her well enough to realize that nothing in his arsenal of wisdom would be able to breach them — at least not until she wanted it to. But that wasn't now, and so in the meantime he just had to let her be.

It didn't help that he and Ursla had been so thoroughly drained by the long campaign. They weren't as sharp or sensitive as they had been a few years before — their tact and subtlety in matters this delicate had been sacrificed to keep their tactical abilities in top war-fighting form.

If this war didn't end soon, Caine could envision the drain leaving a very permanent scar. He had already changed irrevocably, how much longer could he maintain his fundamental core under the strain of this fight…?

The comm chirped abruptly — and mercifully — to interrupt Caine's thoughts. The voice of *Orion's* Captain, Labrador Forepaw, filled the room, "Setter, the 186th just came in. Twenty Warcruisers with them, and a wing of fighters with the Admiral-of-a-Fleet is on its way over to us now."

Caine looked at the ceiling speakers and blinked, "Good of them to arrive when we're all here. We'll be ready, Lab. Boats escorting them in?"

"A wing from our squadron."

Caine nodded to himself, "Good."

The comm cut as the fleet commanders exchanged weary glances, then one by one they forced their bodies to return to a somewhat presentable posture.

They had to look crisp and confident for the Larosians.

CHAPTER 2

Admiral-of-a-Fleet Narosh walked silently through the hull of the Earther flagship. Behind him, moving with equal discretion, the two forms of his fleet's second-in-command and the commander of his ground forces observed the insides of *Orion* with some familiarity.

The second figure was Admiral-of-a-Division Novash, the first Larosian officer to meet an Earther. At Genesis, his squadron had been the reconnaissance group that had nearly been decimated by the Krogg trap — but Ursla and the Earther Second Fleet had saved him. Even after two years away from the Earthers, Novash still believed in the debt of honor he owed to that bear — and indeed, to *all* members of her race. He seldom revealed that belief — personal debts of honor were generally not matters spoken of in public among Larosians.

The third Larosian in the group was Torallis, Captain-Elite of the Stealth Guard and a venerable ground fighter. He too recognized the Earther surroundings, and he watched with a familiar sense of respect as the four Earther marines detailed to escort the trio to the meeting moved with such subtle — but obvious to the perceptive Larosian gaze — caution.

With the aid of General Andros Grieve, Torallis had assaulted what was thought to be a Queen's Hive in the Genesis asteroid field. The Krogg matriarch had proved not to be on the base, but the presence of the Earthers had nonetheless been the deciding factor that had allowed him to complete the investigation of the Hive. Torallis' respect for the Earthers' skill was born of watching them handle blades and guns in action, and he looked forward to the opportunity to fight alongside the warriors again.

Especially now, as they neared the end of the war...

For Narosh, impressions of the Earthers were far more reserved. He had only vaguely begun to understand the alien allies of the Larosians two years ago, and he remained uncertain of their importance here at the Krogg homeworld... *homeworlds*.

All he could really expect was that they might fill in some of the gaps in his ranks... make up for some of the enormous casualties the Larosian Navy had suffered.

Narosh sighed in his non-terrestrial way and thought briefly of his Navy. There was hardly a Navy, now — at least not one as he'd known it. His fleet, bruised from years of conflict, was all that remained of the once mighty Larosian armada.

So perhaps the Earthers *would* prove important.

"Sir, this is the briefing room," the Earther escort's leader came to a halt and snapped smartly to attention beside a door.

Narosh's immediate inclination was to think his acknowledgement to the Earther, but he quickly reminded himself that Earthers were unable to telepathically connect with Larosians. Unique among all the species the Larosians had met, the Earth animal-humanoids simply could not achieve such mental connections with their seemingly primitive brain facilities.

Awkwardly opening his mouth, he revived his voice, "Very good."

The marine deftly keyed the door open, and Narosh, Novash, and Torallis filed into the room.

Narosh immediately recognized the assembled Earthers from his diplomatic meetings after the Battle of Genesis. The wolf, First Lord Caine, was senior, then Admirals Ursla and Felix, and the human Manchester.

They were all standing politely at seats around a long table, and as the Larosians entered they exchanged brief nods with the newcomers. Caine moved from his place at the table and came to stand in front of Narosh, "Admiral-of-a-Fleet, it's been some time."

Narosh nodded, speaking thinly, "It has, but now we seem to be far closer to victory than I could have expected two years ago."

Caine paused at the remark, unsure whether to take it as an insult or compliment. He ignored it instead, gesturing the Larosians to the table. As the aliens moved to seats, each of the Allied commanders offered them curt nods — brief reintroductions that would suffice for the meeting to come.

"Well, we should probably get straight into it," Caine said solidly, tugging at his tunic as he seated himself at the head of the table opposite Narosh.

The Larosian commander nodded, "Certainly. We must first gather information about the Krogg home systems, and determine what numbers we face–"

Caine had tapped the main holo tank to life as the Larosian was speaking, and the Admiral-of-a-Fleet's voice halted as the three-dimensional projection lit up the room, floating over the table.

"Every Krogg ship is being monitored. We're rotating sloops on surveillance duty in order to maintain a constant stream of real-time telemetry," Caine said quietly. "As you can see, our forces are less than half the number of the Kroggs, even with the reinforcements that are being brought up from Genesis and Gibraltar."

Narosh stared at the display, surprised and pleased by the thoroughness of the information. He could see ship classes, numbers, even *breeds*. Some Krogg ships were designed for fast work, others to be tougher fighters. The Earthers had been able to effectively note the differences between the groups.

"Comes from experience," Ursla offered in low tones, and Narosh blinked... well, mentally. He didn't visibly reveal his surprise.

Had she read his mind?

Irrelevant.

Narosh took a few moments to look over the figures that floated through the air. He was accustomed to reading English — the Son of Praaxus had insisted he learn to do so years ago.

The Son. The savior of the Larosian people.

A human boy, from a lost colony.

The human who died to stop the Krogg advance, and who had left Narosh as his chosen champion.

English! Narosh refocused himself quickly, examining words and numbers.

"You have only 3,714 warships on station?" he asked.

Caine nodded, "A number of them are actually on their way back to Gibraltar for critical yard time. We'll have another 850 or so arriving within the next six weeks, but that's the extent of our available forces. We've stripped our home systems bare to pull together this many."

Narosh took a strained breath.

Despite being two intact star powers, his allies had *fewer* ships than he did.

"We were hoping you'd be able to summon a number of fleets to aide the attack. Taking a system guarded by 7,000 ships with as much stationary support as the Kroggs have seems a bit of a daunting proposition," Felix added in cordial tones.

Narosh, without understanding the meaning of his mannerisms, let his mouth hang open, looking quickly to Novash and then back to Caine.

"We have only one fleet to bring, Lord Caine. My own, of some 4,736 war vessels. You may have no more than that."

Everybody stiffened.

"Not to be indelicate, Admiral, but I understood the Larosian Navy to be a bit more *weighty*," Sarah cocked a skeptical eyebrow.

Narosh looked at her as she spoke, silently scanning her surface thoughts. The humans and the Earthers had been counting on him to compensate for their own massive losses... their fight on this front had been no less vicious than his own.

"That, ArcGeneral, *was* the case. But I must report the destruction of most of the Larosian Navy... and perhaps ultimately of the Larosian people."

What?

Caine froze immediately, not needing to meet Felix's or Ursla's eyes to know the abrupt shock they were feeling before he voiced his reaction, "*What?*"

There was no attempt to be diplomatic with the question.

Narosh leaned forward in his chair, his silver eyes locking with Caine's deep amber-gray ones, "Lord Caine, since our last meeting a contagion has swept through much of Larosian space. It has crippled most of the fleet... only my own force has remained uninfected."

Caine's eyes widened. *A plague?*

After being created by an intelligent virus, every Earther had a certain dislike of any sort of invasive microorganism. Fortunately, Earther immune systems seemed virtually impregnable to venoms and biological attacks — one of the characteristics presumably built into Earther genetics by Omega to make sure they would be a stable food source.

"You aren't carriers?" Sarah's question was sharp and seemed rather badly timed, but the Larosian shook his head without offense.

"We are not. None of the ships that currently serve under my command have returned to our home system since the Battle of Genesis. We assembled to pursue Krogg vessels shortly after returning to our home galaxy, and since then we have been on the front lines."

Narosh paused momentarily, ordering his thoughts.

"Sixteen months ago, the first case was reported at an outer colony. It spread slowly at first, but then it reached a Warcruiser squadron that was rejoining the battle fleet. I, at the time, had been given control of three fleets, which I was leading against a Krogg base. We won the battle, but upon returning to the main body of the fleet, we found all vessels to be broadcasting quarantine warnings."

Caine frowned, "How many ships?"

"Some 6,000 warships, and an additional 3,000 support vessels."

The room was silent.

"We were only detached for three weeks, but when we returned there were no uninfected vessels. The plague had spread without visible symptoms until the last moments, and in so doing caught the entire armada unawares. Within a week, the crews were incapacitated."

Caine looked wearily to Ursla.

"We communicated with the home systems and discovered that the plague was slowly spreading among the outer worlds. When we departed to come here, quarantines were being initiated, but with the fleet lost, they will likely prove difficult to enforce."

"And you just went back to the war?" Sarah leaned forward in her chair and eyed Narosh closely.

Narosh's silver eyes shifted to the ArcGeneral, but Caine couldn't tell whether or not his gaze was a sign of being offended. Either way, the Admiral-of-a-Fleet did not pause before replying, "The Kroggs posed at least an equal threat, if left unopposed. And I believe the plague is something of their making, something to passively defeat us, even if we crush them in battle. In any case, they pose the lasting threat to interstellar peace — a plague may die out, but the Kroggs may only be destroyed."

Caine offered a slow nod, "You faced a difficult choice. I'd have done the same."

The remark was directed as much to Sarah as it was to the Larosian, and she picked that up instantly. With a scowl she sat back in her chair, crossing her arms tightly over her chest.

Caine breathed deeply and tried to reconcile the startling news. A plague was gutting their allies... and they had 9,000 Krogg ships sitting within hours of the Allied lines, still capable of combining and mounting a counter-offensive if left unchecked...

"I can send cutters to Earth and Genesis immediately, Admiral. We could provide you with some of our broad-spectrum anti-viral synthetics. A number were produced based on our own immune systems several months ago — for treating humans against alien viral strains. They have proved quite effective so far..."

"Though none of the viruses we've faced quite constitute an epidemic plague to begin with," Sarah's remark was cool.

Ursla was still absorbing the news herself, but Sarah's comment drew her attention. Her old human friend seemed to be growing ever more... *abrupt*...

Caine simply elected to overlook Sarah's words, "Nonetheless, we can supply you with what we have..."

Narosh held up his hand, "I appreciate the offer, Lord Caine, but as we saw during our last meeting, our sciences are generally comparable. Our most recent reports from the homeworld indicate that the plague has been incurable for us. Even presuming your drugs were compatible with our physiology, they would likely be no more effective than our own, and transporting them to our space would put your personnel and your entire *civilization* at risk."

Caine paused and gazed at the alien. He didn't feel an instinctive connection to Narosh. Earthers and humans, for all their differences, shared a birthworld, and that seemed to give them some sort of bond. But Narosh was so very alien.

And yet he was right.

"All I might ask of you, Lord Caine, is that you assist us in quarantining our galaxy. We cannot afford to have the virus appearing here while the Kroggs remain undefeated."

Felix tilted his head, "That could have been their plan. Take the Larosians out of the picture without firing a shot, then consolidate and hit us all at once when we're in their space."

Caine nodded. And if the plague infected Genesis... or if it proved capable of breaking the venerable Earther immune system...

There had been no reports of unusual illness from Genesis or Earth, but he'd send cutters with warnings to the fleets and planets back there immediately.

And he'd have to detach sizable forces to guard the two hyperspace corridors that opened near the home systems. One existed in the Genesis system, the other had recently been found only two days from Earth. Both would have to be guarded — Larosian plague ships couldn't be allowed through...

"Alright then. Admiral Narosh, I'm afraid I'm going to have to break our meeting for now. I have to get this news to my forces in the rear. If you could bring up your fleet, we can discuss strategy after your ships are safely on this side of the corridor. And if you could assign some of your vessels to blockade that corridor, that would be helpful as well — I'd be reluctant to pull any more of my ships off the blockade if it can be avoided," Caine came to his feet as he spoke.

Narosh stood up opposite to the First Lord and nodded, "I will return to my fleet and see to the deployment personally. We may meet again to discuss the strategic situation."

"Very good. If you'll excuse me."

Caine left the room quickly, the rest of the Allied commanders and the two junior Larosians rising after his departure. Following Narosh, they filed out of the room.

As the First Lord moved quickly down the hall towards the lift, he let his concern sink in. A plague. *Another* one.

Hopefully it would be significantly less virulent than the first plague of Earther history.

CHAPTER 3

General Andros Grieve was currently residing aboard *Algenon*, a 125-gun First Rate sitting in Genesis space. One of the original Earther 'super' capital ships, it had fought alongside the likes of *Orion* and *Agamemnon* during the Church attack on Earth, and remained one of the great champion ships of the Allied Fleet.

Now, with a new pennant flying from its transponder, it was the flagship of the newly-constituted Fifth Fleet.

Of course, that meant it had none other than Admiral Varnon Broadpaw for a flag officer. The highly-respected wolf Admiral had first made an impression on Grieve during the prelude to the Genesis battle, and the two had been friends ever since.

So it was natural for Grieve to return to the front lines with Broadpaw in *Algenon*, though they probably wouldn't be heading forward for another few weeks since the rest of the Fifth Fleet still needed to assemble around them.

In the meantime, the seemingly passive environment left plenty of time for preparative sparring–

A fist came at Grieve abruptly, forcing the General to dodge smoothly to the left and counter it with a low strike to the chin... but Broadpaw had slid around behind him. The wolf wasn't the strongest Earther, but he certainly was quick.

Grieve whirled with remarkable agility, his heavy fist driving aside an incoming blow. Broadpaw came off the ground with both feet, attempting an ambitious close-in kick to dislodge the bigger marine's footing...

But Grieve slid aside, throwing his knee against the striking leg. Broadpaw spun in midair and started to come down against the mat, his arms leading the way. As they made contact he flipped his legs over the top and landed squarely on his feet. He came forward again, quick blows testing Grieve's reflexes as the pair stepped lightly around the mat.

One blow was just a *bit* over-extended — *only* just a bit — and Grieve seized his chance. The General was perhaps the best Earther hand-to-hand fighter in the fleet, and elite fighters like Beckett Lupus, Ursla and even *Caine* gave him their respect. This was why.

Although he wasn't the most agile or the strongest, Grieve *always* knew how to seize the momentum in a fight, and to turn a movement that wasn't quite a mistake into a decisive error.

Broadpaw hit the mat on his back and wheezed.

"Not bad, Varnon. You get a bit over-enthusiastic at times, though," Grieve offered his opponent a friendly smile and a hand.

The wolf shrugged and took the hand, hauling himself up and grinning, "Well, it happens to the worst of us, I suppose. You on the other hand…"

Grieve shrugged, "I have to be good, it's my job."

Broadpaw chuckled, "Yes, I suppose so."

As if on cue, the intercom in *Algenon's* main gym chirped, interrupting the pair. It was midday and a number of off-duty Earthers were sparring or working out, so the comm could have been calling for anyone… But Broadpaw had a feeling it was for him.

Good old Earther instinct…

"Broadpaw here, who's this?"

"It's Cornelius, Varnon. We've just had a cutter come in from the front; ArcGeneral Hastings is asking for you and the General to meet her on *Genesis One* to review the contents."

Broadpaw cocked his eyebrow at his First Lieutenant's report, and looked curiously to Grieve. Must be important if Hastings wanted to see them both…

"Prep my pinnace, Corny. Andros and I will get changed and be aboard in a few minutes."

"Will do."

The comm cut and the two Earther officers left the gym.

"Admiral Broadpaw and General Grieve are arriving now, ma'am," an adjutant said politely, and ArcGeneral Elizabeth Hastings turned to the young officer and nodded in reply.

"Show them up here."

The ArcLieutenant nodded and turned away, leaving Hastings to puzzle over the data that she was about to open. Caine had sent an energy-hyper cutter with this information. It was dated from that very morning, and it was the only message carried in the cutter's rather large memory bank. It had to be extremely important — Caine made it his business not to overwork the fragile cutters with unimportant singular messages; their reactors were kept operational only by careful rationing of their high-stress work…

Were the Kroggs trying to stage a breakout?

That would be just about the only thing that would force Caine to send the cutter ahead of the routine daily schedule…

"What's this I hear about a cutter with only one message?"

Hastings looked up and shrugged at the question that came in a clipped British tone.

ArcLieutenant-General Graham Manchester — the junior of the Manchester siblings in both age and rank — sat facing Hastings across the desk in *Genesis One's* flag conference room. He'd worn many hats since the Battle of Cartenga Sun, first at Gibraltar, then returning home to oversee the abortive Genesis Carrier initiative, and now serving as a division commander in the Sixth Fleet.

He was *loving* it.

For someone who'd spent much of his career taking orders and sitting in lonely orbital forts, the constant movement and the chance to take the reins was truly beginning to appeal to him. Since his time commanding the boats at Gibraltar, he'd had more confidence in his ability to give orders in action, and soon he'd have the opportunity to make use of that judgment.

He was eager to join the fight.

"I haven't opened it yet — it's marked as flag priority, so I thought I should wait on you, Bill, Varnon and Andros," Hastings said quietly, frowning at the file icon on the big screen embedded in the wall.

She was as eager as Graham to know just what was going on.

For two years, Liz Hastings had coordinated the war effort from Genesis space, overseeing deployment, ship-building, and every other little detail that needed the attention of a logistical commander. She hadn't commanded a fighting force since she and Caine had ridden to Ursla's rescue here at Genesis. She'd elected to stay behind after that and keep an eye on Harvey Bingham and the Chancellery. But they were behaving — even doing well with their social reforms — and her job here was starting to make her restless.

She *wanted* to get back into action, so she was going to be taking the Sixth Fleet up to the front. Ultimately, she'd probably integrate it with the Fourth and take command of both, though Sarah might feel she was being demoted in that case. Liz would have to worry about that when she got out there.

The conference room door opened and three figures entered, the first a human and the last two Earthers. ArcLieutenant-General Bill Wallace was one of the most senior cruiser officers in the fleet, second in skill only to Pat Conroy. His half of the Sixth, composed exclusively of cruisers and Destroyers, would act as both the eyes of and the screen for Graham's capital ships.

Broadpaw and Grieve needed no introduction — both had been in and out of Genesis space regularly since the Navy's return to the system.

Now, these three took seats beside Graham, exchanging brief nods with the two already sitting humans.

"Well, what have we got?" Broadpaw tugged at his sleeves and then propped his elbows on the table.

Hastings shrugged, "Let's find out..."

She keyed the file open with her remote control and the room darkened as the AI accessed the signal files. The Earther crest, backed by white to indicate the transmission was from someone flying the white pennant of the First Fleet, flashed onto the screen. Then Caine's face appeared.

He looked a bit haggard, but as determined as ever.

"Liz... I'm assuming Graham and Bill and Varnon are with you... and Andros too... Hello all. I've just come from a meeting with Narosh. He's moving his fleet in to support us now, but he's only got 4,700 ships to give us. That's not the problem, though it does mean we'll need the Fifth and Sixth up here as quickly as possible. It seems a plague has swept through the Larosian Fleet. It hit while Narosh's force was detached, but it seems to have annihilated the rest of their Navy within *three weeks*. Apparently it's menacing all Larosian space, and Narosh is afraid it might spread."

The assembled commanders stared at Caine's face with various levels of disbelief. On the vid, the First Lord paused to let the gravity of his news sink in.

"I offered our medical assistance, but Narosh has refused... and probably quite reasonably. Our cures might be as bad for Larosian physiology as the virus itself, and we'd expose ourselves to contamination if we tried. Instead, he wants us to blockade the corridors. Nothing can be allowed to go through, nothing can come out. Any ship could potentially be carrying this thing, so we have to close the gates."

Hastings blinked a few times... They'd have to put at least one squadron on that, maybe two... Or they could tow one or two stations into position to guard the entrance...

"It's up to you how you do it, but make sure that corridor is well closed. I doubt if any Larosians would knowingly try to infect us, but if they do we have to be able to counter them. Now I've copied this message on a cutter to Earth... They'll probably have to strip some ships from your fleet, Varnon, to watch the New Halifax corridor. If they could get a few floating batteries out there it would probably be better, but that'll be up to the Second Lord and the Navy Board."

Varnon nodded and sighed quietly.

"I don't know precisely how serious this is, folks, but the Larosians think this plague is a Krogg creation, designed to cut the legs out from under us before they counterattack. We haven't been experiencing any health troubles out here, but I'd advise you to make sure everything from Gibraltar to New Halifax is in good shape. They could have already infected some of us... though based on the lack of an epidemic in the past sixteen months, my instincts tell me we're probably okay. Check anyway; we all know I can be wrong."

Hastings was already thinking through past updates she'd received. Since the *Bishop* flu eleven months earlier, she hadn't heard about any unexpected illness anywhere. That malady had come back with the survivors of *Harbinger Bishop* — a bug from the planet they'd been stranded on that had only surfaced after two weeks away from that world's ecosystem. It had given most humans an awful hacking cough, but nothing even *approaching* life threatening.

Hell, maybe that was it... Earther drugs had gotten rid of it handily... and the Earthers themselves had been immune.

"Be careful, everyone. Narosh says his ships are clean, but I'll be confirming that before we integrate. And send confirmations of health ahead of you before you get under weigh. I can't risk losing the fleet with 9,000 Kroggs out here. Good luck. I hope this turns out to be a false alarm."

The screen blanked, and the Earthers and humans exchanged nervous glances.

"So," Broadpaw said quietly, "we load our guns with chicken soup and hope the Larosians don't try to cough on us."

Hastings raised an unamused eyebrow, but Graham chuckled, "Well, it could be worse."

The room fell silent.

"Um… *how*?" Wallace turned to his fellow ArcLieutenant-General.

Graham blinked.

"Ahm. Well it could be… um… well the thing about that is…"

His voice trailed off and the room remained silent for a few minutes.

CHAPTER 4

"Sarah!"

The corridors leading away from *Orion's* main briefing room were relatively empty, the ship's crew either at their stations or at rest. The lower decks were generally reserved for conferences and the like, so few idlers happened through them off duty.

Sarah was quite happy to be walking at her own pace back to the flight deck, where she would board her pinnace and return to *Joseph Barron*. Maybe there was a raid she could lead or some other damned thing–

"*Sarah!*"

She stopped with a sigh and turned sharply on her pursuer, "*What*, Andra?" The question came with a stinging edge.

Ursla shortened her stride and came to a stop a few meters from her friend, looking down at the ArcGeneral with a concerned expression, "Just wanted to talk, I haven't seen you for a while. You seem a bit... out of sorts."

Sarah's eyes narrowed, "Do I? How thoughtless of me. How should you like me to be, then?"

Ursla frowned, "Excuse me?"

"Andra, I know we haven't talked for a while, but I've got a war to fight... and as I recall, you do too. Kroggs to kill, and all that, eh?"

"That's never stopped us from talking before," Ursla's tone remained calm, and Sarah smiled thinly.

With her eyes narrowing further, the human looked up at her friend, "You know, I've done quite enough socializing so far in this war. I'm a fighter, and I'm not going to forget that. Not again, thank you very much."

She turned on her heel and began to walk away, leaving a dumbfounded Ursla in her wake.

Taking a few steps backward, the great Admiral turned and paced off in the other direction.

Caine sat in his armchair and looked out the window of his cabin, holding a cold glass of water in one hand and a picture of his family in the other. There'd been no word of a plague at home. And cutters were now making regular runs back and forth to Earth.

Caine's thumb slid over the glass of the frame, gently touching the face of his wife and son. They were safe, then. He just had to stop the Kroggs to keep it that way.

He took a long sip of his water and closed his eyes. He'd do that, he supposed. He always managed to get the job done. Even when the curses of the universe seemed to converge to interfere with his duty...

Well he'd do it. Enough said.

Well, enough mused, actually. Just in time, too...

The door chimed.

Caine laid the family photo on the table in front of him, "Come in."

The door slid open and the large figure of Ursla stepped quietly through. Caine didn't even look, he just waved her to the couch facing him. She obliged immediately, rounding the table and collapsing tiredly onto the broad sofa.

"Talk to me. It's Sarah, isn't it?"

Unsurprised by Caine's perceptiveness, Ursla nodded, "Seems to be another turn on the downward spiral she got into after the renegade mission. She nearly decked me for wanting to talk. Not something to indulge in during wartime, she said."

Caine chuckled, taking a swig of the icy water, "I should be hung for talking, then."

A small smile was Ursla's reply as she absently stretched her neck, "She's looking more and more dangerous to me, Setter. She's itching for a fight to prove herself. She really hasn't had a big engagement since the Krogg base, and I get the sense that she thinks what respect she can get has a short shelf life. She doesn't think we have confidence in her any more."

A deep sigh escaped Caine and he stared into the bottom of his emptied glass, "That's partly my fault, I expect. I've been doing all the raiding of Krogg 'A' myself. Haven't let her go in because we need to use energy drive when we're in there."

Ursla raised an eyebrow, "So she's convinced you don't trust her."

Caine leaned forward and laid the glass on the table next to his family photo, "Aye. So my determination to lead from the front and her fears of inadequacy mix, and the blockade of Krogg 'A' gets even more stressful. Good thing Narosh is coming up."

"You need to stop beating yourself up. Exhaustion is wearing on everyone."

Caine waved a dismissive hand and stared out at the stars, "It surely has, but that's no excuse for me succumbing to it. A lot of people have already paid for the foolishness it caused at Gibraltar, Andra. And if any of us must face such misery due to my tired judgment again, it should be me. I've got experience."

He slouched in the chair and rubbed his eyes.

Ursla looked at him for a moment. He'd gotten himself past personal blame for Gibraltar... more or less... but Setter Caine was now determined to make sure he accepted all the responsibility for any other mistakes in this war.

Ursla couldn't grudge her friend his determination to lead from the front, and to take responsibility for everything, but she couldn't allow any mounting sense of grief or exhaustion to cloud his mind so completely.

Question was how to stop that from happening. Maybe a year ago Ursla could have talked him through, but now she was only scarcely less fatigued than he was...

"Setter," Ursla said slowly as she stood, "pardon me a minute."

Caine slowly began to draw his hands away from his eyes–

Ursla's big foot stomped through the alloy coffee table.

Caine came to his feet in a flash, alert, shocked, and staring wide-eyed up at his friend.

"Andra! By the Earth, what are you–"

"*Clear your head*, Setter! We've got Sarah digging herself into a pit of anger and despair, the Larosians are being annihilated by a plague, and I *haven't slept in four days!* We can't have you coming apart!"

Ursla's words were tired and more than a little frustrated, and the delivery was altogether out of character for her... but they did get the message across. There was so much left to do, and no time to worry about mistakes that might have been made — or might yet be made. There would certainly be a time for those worries later, but not now.

Grinding his jaw a moment, Caine turned away from Ursla and paced around the chair, "You're quite right. It's just... well you know how exhausting this is..."

"It's exhausting for *all* of us. *You're* just going to have to stop trying to protect the rest of us from your own fatigue. There's no way you can get away from it, so let us help you deal with it. That's what we signed on for!" Ursla had essentially lost control of her tone, which was in itself rather remarkable.

But Caine took no offense at his friend's words, instead sighing, "So many have died for my errors, Andra. It's just... *I* should be the one paying for those mistakes."

Ursla countered sharply, "You're paying in your own way. But you can't take on all the hard jobs yourself. What if you mess one up and get yourself killed? What you're doing is just foolish, and two years ago you'd have agreed with me. It's time we get our heads back to that state — neither of us can worry about what to do about *guilt* until the dead are all counted. Because we'll get more killed if we keep going this way..."

Ah yes, more. There would be many more. Caine had over nine million deaths to his credit so far. He accepted the blame for every death on this campaign, as his orders were ultimately the cause for the losses.

Such was the responsibility that came with his position, and he'd hardly shirk it.

But in appointing himself to this job, he had signed on to do just that — to give orders, and dictate fates. And he couldn't let insecurities about not being in top form jeopardize his tactical sense. When the war was done he'd deal with all that had been lost.

In the meantime he had to get himself back into the mode of strategic reasoning. He had to win this damned war.

"Andra, that picture of Elandra and Phealan that's on the table... er, the floor now…"

"Yes?" Ursla frowned.

"Keep it for me, would you? I need to… put it out of my mind, just until we finish this. And signal Pat. I'll move the 111th in to take his place on the picket line. Bring his squadron out for some R&R. He's got the best shot of getting through to Sarah."

Ursla nodded again solemnly, taking the picture from the twisted remains of the table, "I'll pass the word for the machine shop to get you another table."

Caine found himself chuckling, "I don't need one. I've got too much to do."

Ursla came slowly to her feet, "So you're all set to get back to business and win the war?"

Caine smiled, "I'm an *Earther*, Andra. All I need to do to snap out of my morose state of mind is have a friend crush a table."

Ursla grinned in reply, "Failing that, how about smashing the Krogg Fleet?"

"Several fleets and it's a deal."

CHAPTER 5

The Battlecruiser *Divine Templar* slid easily into formation next to *Pope Joseph Barron*, its engines slowly spinning down and its station-keeping thrusters firing absently. *Templar* had been on station around Krogg for just over six weeks now, and ArcLieutenant-General Pat Conroy had been with the ship for almost that entire time. He'd only been able to get back to the main body of the fleet once for a meeting a month ago, but since then he'd seen nothing of Sarah... and her messages were growing less and less frequent.

Pat was finding the infrequency disturbing.

For years Sarah had survived the Navy with no real privacy to speak of. A few friends, a bit of reading now and then, and the occasional joke — the typical life of an officer living under Crusader domination. The renaissance of her personal life had come after Genesis, when her brother had inadvertently forced her to act upon her once unrecognized feelings for Pat...

Things had been much brighter after that. Until he'd been shot down and she'd gone rogue to rescue him.

Pat ground his jaw. It wasn't so much the act that was the problem, since in addition to saving *Bishop's* survivors and Beckett Lupus' Earthers, she'd secured the Allied flank with her renegade force and the help of Fox Magnus. It was the guilt she saddled herself with after she'd gotten back.

Of course no one was blaming her. The Earthers understood and respected her decision to go after the man she loved. They also trusted that she knew what was best for herself and her ship. As for the fighting men and women of the Genesis Fleet, they loved her for surviving Gibraltar — by not being there — and for doing the movie-worthy thing and flying off to save her true love.

The hefty number of interviews with the Genesis Free Press had been startling for both her and Pat.

Despite all this positive reinforcement, Sarah's feelings of guilt and failure were entrenched. The way she saw it, no one trusted her anymore, and they were right not to — she felt she had to appease everyone around her, fix ills and prove herself all over again.

The same blind eye she'd managed to turn to her personal life for so many years, she now turned to her own popularity, and to the respect people had for her. Pat feared she was going to harm some dear friendships, her career, her very *life* — if she didn't clear her head of this mess.

But the last time he'd tried to bring that up with her, she hadn't listened to him. She said she loved him — and he certainly wasn't complaining about that assertion — but she was taking steps to distance herself from him. She wanted to make it clear to everyone that her duty was taking priority over everything else.

Even though Pat could live with that if he had to, he was worried about the harm she might be doing herself.

Ursla's call to bring him in hadn't been much of surprise, then. Pulling his cruisers off the line didn't displease him — they could definitely use a rest — but he wished it was for a less unfortunate reason.

Unfortunate? Woman you love is on the verge of collapse, man. That's a bit more dramatic than 'unfortunate'!

Pat stopped the editorial in his brain. It was bad business to remove a force from picket duty for personal reasons, but then, Pat's Posse — the rather unseemly name by which Pat's three Battlecruiser squadrons were commonly known — did need some recuperation. They were four ships under strength and had another nine damaged to varying degrees... moving them out was logical enough.

And if it gave him a chance to work on improving Sarah's state of mind in the meantime, the Admirals probably wouldn't object to that.

Either way, Pat and his ships would make the most of his recall.

So now he sat on *Templar's* bridge, absently drumming his fingers on the arm of the chair. His hail to *Joseph Barron* had just been put through... surely Sarah had received it by now...

A year ago there'd have been no delay between the sending of one of his messages and the matching reply...

"Anything?"

The Comm Officer shook her head, "Sorry, skipper."

Pat scratched his chin curiously for a moment and sighed, "Alright. Send that I'm coming over."

Turning to *Templar's* ArcColonel, *Bishop* veteran Jessica Forbes, he arched his brow, "She must be busy."

Forbes shrugged, "Quite possibly. I'll have your pinnace readied."

Pat nodded in thanks to the fellow survivor of his old ship, then left his chair.

Sarah sat silently behind her desk, ignoring the flashing red light on her console. Whoever wanted her could wait — she had a fleet to run, and if it was really important they'd call her on the ship comm.

Months ago, Sarah had loathed the paperwork necessary for the operation of the Fourth Fleet; now she was simply determined to finish it. That was her job, after all.

Especially since no one seemed to be willing to put her ships into action. She only had so much latitude in her current role as a commander — Caine was senior at Krogg 'A' and was keeping her under his watchful eye. He was also doing all the work himself.

Sarah knew exactly what that meant: he didn't trust her.

And how could he, with her ready to sacrifice her commission and the survival of the fleet because she couldn't contain her feelings? Pat was quite important — both to her and to the war effort — but so was Gibraltar. She'd made a choice in going to save him, and it had paid off almost by fluke — but now she had to deal with the stares of those who thought her a fool, and the disdain of her Earther friends.

They were trying to hide it, of course. Oh, Ursla wanted to 'talk', and Caine had 'full confidence' in her as a commander... They just didn't want her to do anything more than hold station and watch Caine's daring raids or read the after-action reports on Ursla's great maneuvering battles with the Kroggs in 'B'.

They got the action and did their duty while she got very little.

She'd just have to do her job as commander better than any of them — the Fourth would run as smoothly as any Earther fleet... even better. She'd *earn* their trust again, and she'd get herself back into the fight.

To hell with the rest of it.

To hell with the flashing light.

Sarah set her jaw and let the old determination — the decades-old ability to clamp down on her emotions — control her faculties.

Efficiently, she slid the form she'd just completed onto a pile with sixty-three others, and began working on the next one. Missile Requisition Form TB-A6. She needed more Type 98 warheads for her capital ships. Liz could get those for her.

She began filling out the paper, using ink that would allow the ship's AI to scan the requisition and send it through the system. She focused and quickly ran numbers in her head...

"A hundred... no *two hundred* million. Right. That should be enough to fill the tubes and the storeships..." she spoke quietly to herself.

The door chimed.

Blinking briefly, she looked up. Who could that be?

No one she wanted to talk to was within a pinnace ride of her ship, so she ignored it.

The chime sounded again — twice — but she continued to pay no heed. She signed the bottom of the sixty-fourth form and drew the sixty-fifth from the pile, scratching her requisition for Earther-built shield belts onto the white sheet.

The door slid open.

Surprised by the failure of her lock, Sarah looked up sharply, "What the devil do you think you're–"

Pat held his hands up with a smile, "Sorry, Sarah. A little fed up with waiting."

Sarah's mouth opened to speak but she found herself without anything to say. She laid her pen on the table and straightened herself in her chair.

"My Posse just rejoined the fleet for repairs, so I thought I'd check in. It's been a month, hasn't it?"

Sarah nodded slowly.

Pat stood curiously in the door, *"And..."*

Sarah cocked her eyebrow, "As you can tell, Pat, I'm rather busy." Her hands swept over the piles of paper in front of her, and she shrugged, "I really don't have time for a social call right now."

Pat's face was suddenly quite blank, "Pardon?"

"I'm sorry Pat, if you could come back later this week..."

Pat blinked, "Oh."

He paused and met Sarah's eyes, noting the indifference in them.

"Right. And we can talk then...?"

Sarah stiffened, *"Talk.* Indeed, and *who* withdrew you from the picket to *talk*, Pat? Setter?"

Sarah's tone was suddenly icy, and Pat worked to contain his frown, "Andra, actually."

"Typical... she can't interrupt me herself so she sends you to..."

"I've got four ships out of action and nine beaten up. I'm not here just to see *you*, *Sarah*," Pat's tone hardened in response.

"If you can't see what they're up to you really have been fooled. Excuse me, Pat, I have a call to make."

Sarah waved a dismissive hand at Pat and he just barely kept his jaw from dropping.

Turning on his heel, he left the cabin at a quick stride.

He didn't quite know *what* had just happened.

Agamemnon was coming to a stop and dropping anchor among the First Rates of the 201st Battle Squadron when Ursla, napping in her cabin, heard the intercom summon her back to consciousness. Artemis Tigar, Ursla's Flag Captain, had an urgent signal for her. From Sarah.

Sitting up wearily, Ursla ordered it relayed to the panel at her desk, and trudged heavily out of her bedroom. Sinking ungracefully into her chair, she keyed the comm to life... and Sarah's seething glare lanced out at her from the holo.

"Don't *ever* try an end run on me again, Andra. Stick to your fleet, *if you please*."

The screen blanked. Ursla was abruptly awake, and wholly astonished.

CHAPTER 6

Narosh's mind felt clouded as he sat on the silver bridge of his Warcruiser. *Lycrotar*, one of the most renowned ships in the Larosian service, now led his modest fleet of 4,700 towards the rendezvous with the Earthers and humans at what had been dubbed — rather blandly — Krogg 'A'. Already, forty of his battered Battleships were taking station at the mouth of the hyper corridor that had carried the Larosians to this galaxy, to ensure the safety of the region.

That force would suffice, presuming a larger or speedier force did not attempt to break through.

After sixteen months of plague, many unpredictable and seemingly inexplicable things had been happening among the Larosians. Narosh understandably knew little; even with Larosian technology, the communication time from the front to the homeworld was measured by *weeks*, not minutes like this new — and absurdly dangerous — energy-hyper the Earthers were using.

Narosh had heard more rumors than official reports, but there were certain indications that the Larosians on the outer worlds were being driven insane by the disease, trying to infect their fellows, trying to break the blockade. It was a disturbing prospect — the very idea that a Larosian could lose command of his or her own faculties was exceedingly *unpleasant.*

As a rule, Larosians were firmly in control of themselves.

Narosh, despite all his experience and his seemingly perpetual grief at the loss of the Son, feared most of all for his home planet. It was lightly defended with so much of the fleet away, and only one ship needed to slip through the stationary defenses to turn the cradle of all Larosian life into a madhouse of destruction…

The Kroggs must have had this planned all along. Having drawn the Larosian Fleet far from home, the menacing creatures were free to infect gallant warriors, and to compel them to bring death and insanity to all the worlds that had previously been protected. It was so quintessentially Krogg it amazed Narosh that he hadn't expected it.

Perhaps the Son of Praaxus had realized… perhaps he had foreseen such a failure. But he had been killed before he could warn anyone.

Fortunately the Kroggs had not counted on one thing when they'd hatched their plans — they were expecting uninfected Larosians to respond as coolly and logically as they always had, but today Narosh was not in a logical or normal frame of mind.

Primal emotions were guiding him ever closer to the precipice of revenge.

Yes, he was *feeling* that urge, and something within him was telling him to let it have its way.

It's the only way, Narosh my friend.

The anomalous thought didn't seem out of place in the Admiral-of-a-Fleet's mind, though it didn't feel quite like his own...

Alas, where the thoughts were coming from was of no consequence. The Kroggs would *die.*

"They're coming in at about 1,900 pls," *Atlas'* First Lieutenant looked up at Fox. "Not in too much of a hurry."

Fox shrugged, "After 600 years of fighting, I don't suppose a few hours would matter all that much to me either."

The Lieutenant cracked a smile and Fox grinned in return, letting his head fall back against the headrest. With 4,700 Larosian ships coming to join the action, the pressure on the Allied ships around Krogg was easing... at least slightly.

For some reason, Fox found himself breathing easier now that the Allied Fleet was more than double its strength of a week ago.

For some *reason? Uhh... maybe because the FLEET IS TWICE THE SIZE IT WAS A WEEK AGO.*

Fox mentally laughed at himself — he really was quite tired, so his bloody brain wouldn't stop coming up with such brilliant observations. He would have smacked himself on the forehead, but he didn't want to cause any worry among his bridge crew. He was, for all intents and most purposes, quite sane.

Or at least as sane as one could be these days.

And his job had been relatively easy. Prior to this assignment, the 186th had spent much of its time in close support of Pat's Posse, ready in case the Kroggs moved against the Irishman's picket with more force than human Battlecruisers could handle. Such attacks had already come on two occasions, one resulting in the loss of *Jupiter.* Such was the nature of blockade — sitting and watching, allowing the enemy the initiative and waiting under stress to see just what would come after you...

But that stress was soon to be alleviated. With so many new ships available to participate in the blockade, weary Earther squadrons would be rotated to the rear for rest before the final assault, and there would be far more support in the event of a breakout.

Though it seemed unlikely the Kroggs would dare try to come out to fight before being pressed into action. They were strongest with their orbital and planetary defenses backing their position; open space battle against the Allied Fleet would be simple suicide. The numbers might be close to even, but to have survived this long, almost every one of the vessels in the Alliance had a veteran skipper and an excellent crew, giving them no mean advantage over the Kroggs they'd face.

Even the new Fifth and Sixth Fleets would be quite experienced, drawing their crews from survivors of long-destroyed ships.

Hopefully things for the Kroggs were just the opposite — by now they had to be relying on a large proportion of weary ships or inexperienced ones, a combination that did little to strengthen their position. True, they were resting and consolidating during this respite, but with Caine continually harassing them in Krogg 'A' the stress on their organization's efforts had to be as perpetual as the strain upon the blockade.

And beyond that, while Earther and Allied vessels couldn't get physically exhausted, living Krogg ships could become quite tired when worked too hard. Like cavalry horses in the old days, they could only take so much.

So, Fox decided with some relief, the Allies might all be tired, but the effectiveness of their ships wasn't impaired. They were also getting regular practice while the Kroggs were cooped up, and Allied ships, though named and all too often treated as characters in themselves, were not subject to quite the same fatigue limits that plagued biological ships.

Things were beginning to take a turn for the better...

Captain Chronos Claw ground his jaw and frowned.

The Kroggs seemed to know something was going on. They probably had some sort of long-ranged detection grid that could spot Larosians from lightyears away... they'd had 600 years to prepare for the worst, after all.

But what they were doing now seemed to make little sense — even to the veteran skipper of the Earther sloop *Flame* and the 119th Scouting Squadron of sloops. Chronos had been with *Flame* since long before Fox Magnus had made that tiny ship's name a widely-known one and he'd maintained the sloop's tradition of daring with the advent of energy-hyper and the support of Pat's crashed *Bishop* crew. Now he was leading seven additional maverick vessels in deep-system patrols of Krogg 'A'.

It was by no means safe work.

Stretching energy-drive fields to over 225 percent to avoid detection and moving at laboriously slow speeds, the squadron pushed through the system in a broad net, relative top to relative bottom.

Just now, *Flame* — at the center of the wide sensor net thrown out by the squadron — was passing through the middle of the Krogg system, and enemy vessels around the sloop were suddenly moving, breaking their formations and swarming like wasps.

That meant *Flame* and the other sloops were in a bad situation. This solar system was smaller than many, and this particular area was saturated with Krogg vessels. With the sloops' fields stretched to 225 percent and greater, and reactors generally overworked since their last tune up at Gibraltar, a collision with a Krogg ship could cause significant damage.

As these problems occupied Claw's mind, he allowed himself a slow blink. Could the Kroggs be after his sloops? The aliens had never before shown any signs they'd noticed the Scouting Squadron in-system...

But if any of the Kroggs rammed the sloops from hyperspace, the wake would pose a serious problem.

Claw contemplated that possibility while he held his breath. *Flame's* Cruising Master was in the process of ordering the helm over to port, and as the small ship moved, its Captain watched the unenhanced images in the battle plot as a Krogg Dreadnought headed right for them...

Flame slid just past the big ship... passing barely a stone's throw under the Krogg behemoth's lee.

The comm chirped, "Lang here, Chronos... what are you doing up there?"

Claw activated the comm link from his chair, replying to Lang Sandpelt, his First Lieutenant and engineer, "The Kroggs are getting all stirred up and we're trying not to get into a fender-bender. Why?"

"Fender what? Well whatever you did just put a surge through the generators... like we came close to an EM field or even a wake. We nearly got a surge in one and two, and three is starting to look a bit twitchy..."

Great, the EM fields from Krogg ship drives were causing trouble in the power plants... fine, to hell with it then. He wasn't losing one of his squadron just for the sake of some close-ups of Krogg Dreadnoughts.

"Alright, enough of this," Claw ground his jaw. "Close fields and get us out of here, 400 pls."

The Signal Officer passed the orders on through energy comm and the squadron suddenly tightened its drive fields from 225 percent to 100 percent, each ship's engines driving it hard vertically up through the system. The Kroggs could see them, but none could hope to catch up, since their FTL hyper drives were hopelessly clumsy within the hyper limit of their star...

They were probably watching us anyway. No point being stealthy only to get ourselves atomized. Now we'll be fine... Oh damn. I just thought *that...*

As if on cue, a Krogg Dreadnought on their escape vector dove in front of *Match*.

The 18-gun sloop drove right through it... a rather brutal experience for both vessels.

The sloop reeled from the impact, having survived because of the tight cohesion of its nominal energy drive, but with two of its reactors overloading in their independent compartments. Its energy drive collapsed, and the energy release shattered the Dreadnought in a gory cloud.

Match spun away from the collision at barely one percent of light speed, its hull devoid of main power. Claw uttered something unbecoming under his breath, then ordered his ships to aid the maimed sloop.

"Send for backup," he said quietly, watching the massing Krogg forces swarm.

Things were taking a turn for the worse.

CHAPTER 7

It was night shift on the blockade, and having just finished her paperwork, Sarah was on the bridge of *Joseph Barron*. The big flat screen at the front of her bridge showed the telemetry coming in from Chronos Claw's sloop squadron.

The Kroggs looked like they were getting ready to make a lunge... and if she was reading them correctly, they were preparing to hit the Larosians before they could join the Allied Fleet. Divide and conquer — such an attack would certainly make sense, but if that was their plan, why hadn't they just taken out the Allied Fleet weeks ago before the Larosians arrived at all?

Perhaps they simply preferred fighting Larosians. Six hundred years of experience with them and all.

So some of the Kroggs would try to run her blockade, and she'd have to maneuver to stop them–

"Ma'am! *Match* has just collided with a Krogg Dreadnought... Captain Claw is maneuvering his ships to assist and he's requesting as much support as we can provide!"

Sarah frowned at the screen; one of the little sloops had been hit by a Dreadnought, and was virtually powerless and adrift in Krogg 'A' space. The sloop certainly couldn't be left there to be captured and Chronos didn't have a hope of getting *Match* out of there with only seven other 18-gun ships. So Sarah would have to do something. But what about this sortie the Kroggs were mounting — damn it, she couldn't save Claw and stop the Kroggs at the same time...

Though if she managed to do just that, it would be a clear demonstration of her ability...

"Send the 111th in directly, support Dran with the 167th and 192nd. The Fourth Fleet to form by division and enter the system at 3.2 cee," she said quickly. Her Genesis ships were ready for a fast deployment — she'd been hoping for one.

Commodore Dran Nightclaw didn't sleep much when he was on close picket duty, even when he had two squadrons of 74s backing him. He was an experienced panther, Ursla's hand-chosen successor to command of the 111th, and was widely and rightly known as the most brilliant cruiser officer in the Allied Fleet.

After seeing the chaos in the system, Chronos Claw's call for help wasn't unexpected — activity was simply too thick for any of the reconnoitering sloops to hope to escape unnoticed, and now with *Match* so badly shaken up, getting out would be a much more difficult prospect.

That'd be where Dran's frigates came in — or *were going in*, more precisely, as he'd already laid out a course to get the 38-gun ships to *Match's* side before Sarah's orders had reached him. Led by *Cerberus*, the eight ships of the 111th Flying Squadron sprinted from their blockade position. The Kroggs were too disorganized to intercept them, and the fifteen 74s that followed quickly to support the cruisers passed unmolested as well.

But the Kroggs had had enough time to see the Fourth Fleet shake itself quickly into battle order — the entire 1,412 ships of the Fourth Fleet formed by division, then slowly began to press towards the system edge. These ships weren't trying to reach *Match*, but were now determined to draw the attention of the Krogg forces and to give Claw and Nightclaw a few minutes to secure the damaged sloop under tow.

Caine woke abruptly, hearing the alarm. He was on his feet and out of bed before he was quite awake, and keying the comm before his eyes fully opened, "Report."

On the bridge, Captain Labrador Forepaw replied quickly, "One sloop is out of action in the middle of Krogg space. Dran's going in after him with fifteen 74s in support, and Sarah just moved the Fourth into the system to draw attention."

"The Kroggs are holding station?"

"They just started moving about — I'm willing to bet they're trying to break out to hit the Larosians before we link up with them."

Caine blinked, "I'm coming up. Order the fleet to stand by to maneuver in support of Sarah... get a warning to Fox."

The link cut as Caine began hauling on his uniform, buttoning it hastily. If the Kroggs were indeed trying to break out, it would be a desperate attempt, and one that would leave their home open to counterattack from the Allies...

Unless they were only sending some of their ships, hoping to do some damage to the Larosians and then run back to the safety of Krogg space. It was possible — ships in hyper weren't susceptible to guns, but they could be shadowed well enough, and they could be 'depth-charged' by the new jury-rigged spatial charges Ami Cairn, Zed Dune and Fleet R&D had put together in recent months at Gibraltar. That was how Caine had dissuaded them from trying to get beyond the cordon so far...

But now their objective was both more concrete and more threatening than a stationary Earther base to the rear of the war. If they were determined to break out in smaller numbers to wreak havoc in Narosh's fleet, they might get around his charges more easily than a dense fleet would...

Then again, Sarah had over 1,400 ships which theoretically could intercept them...

The question was, with her now pushing further in-system trying to help recover *Match*, would she actually be able to maneuver to intercept any ships that ran off the expected vector? The Kroggs had tied down his active scouting squadron with the collision. They knew their old foes were coming to tip the odds against them, and they suddenly had the initiative.

Did they think the Larosians would be easier to defeat than the Earthers?

Caine's mind began turning over quickly, and he went swiftly to the bridge.

"*Graf Spee* is taking *Match* in tow, skipper. They'll need about two minutes to secure the anchors for energy drive."

Claw nodded at the report, watching as the Kroggs slowly became aware of the prey in their midst. Juicy targets... nice and vulnerable — between his squadron and Dran's ships, they had only fifteen capital vessels and fifteen escorts. Bad odds against 7,000...

Well, he'd make do.

"Range to the nearest attackers?"

"About forty seconds, sir."

Once they arrived he'd have to make do for eighty seconds.

Sarah's blood was up. It always was when she managed to get her entire fleet into action at the same time...

"Second Division turn nine points starboard, First and Third continue in. Open fire at maximum range..."

She was about to use the last of the warheads she'd filed the paperwork to replace only hours before... Good, they'd have plenty of room for the new ones when they arrived.

She watched on the screen as 400 ships of the Second Division approached a cloud of Krogg vessels, "ArcLieutenant-General Anderson is opening fire. ArcLieutenant-General Nichols is closing to range..."

The screen lit up with thousands of missiles, the advanced warheads with double the hitting power and about a third again the maneuverability and range of the old ones.

Still disorganized, the cloud of Krogg ships simply spun apart, trying to slide out of the missiles' paths. It worked, but only to a limited extent. Hits were registered, and a handful of ships vanished. Not *many*, but some.

"First and Third open fire on target groups ahead," Sarah watched on the monitor as missiles separated, and felt the slight shift in *Joseph Barron's* acceleration as the ship's hundred tubes flushed.

The Kroggs were organizing fast, massing to meet her advance; their counter fire was intense and their numbers were three times hers. Two of them fell victim to the volley, the rest of the missiles smashing into an impenetrable wall of neuro pulses.

More salvoes could no doubt have broken the shield, but Sarah didn't intend to stand and fight against that many Krogg ships.

"All squadrons, reverse course and prepare to accelerate into flux."

They'd gotten the attention of the Kroggs, and hopefully they would draw a sizable chunk of them away from the wounded *Match*. She'd just have to be careful they didn't break past her ships and jump out... her forces weren't in position to respond.

Caine would have to handle it.

Without accepting fire, the Fourth began to move from the system.

"They've veered off, skipper... looks like the *entire* Fourth came out to draw them off."

Chronos Claw blinked — that was more help than he'd been expecting.

"They're reversing to avoid action, but they've bought us the time we need."

Claw suddenly froze, watching his plot. At least 1,000 Krogg ships weren't moving after the Fourth — they were moving towards the gap in the blockade perimeter where the Fourth had been...

Open space. If they get through there in good order there'll be no reaching them with charges...

"Get me a line to Caine — we have a serious problem! Warn the 167th and 192nd to reposition — *quickly!*"

Caine emerged on the bridge just as the message came in, but from *Orion's* main battle plot he could already see the situation.

"Redeploy First Fleet — all ships maneuver into position at 900 pls. Beat to quarters."

His voice was cool and calculating. By moving her whole force off, Sarah had saved *Match*, but she'd given the Kroggs a chance to get out. Her ships were quickly withdrawing to their original positions, but there was still a gap along the hyper limit...

The Kroggs could enter hyperspace anywhere in a solar system, but within the hyper limit of a system, ships in the lower layers of subspace were subject to tougher grav shears of a sun, and thus were slower and easier to hit with spatial charges. If the Kroggs could get past the hyper limit under normal drives and then enter hyperspace, breaking them up before they hit Narosh would be nearly impossible...

Caine would have to get the First into position, use his ships to stop any Kroggs trying to break out and hope no others noticed the gap he'd be leaving on the far side of the system.

This whole blockade was coming completely apart, all of a sudden.

The First accelerated hard into energy drive.

CHAPTER 8

Still well away from Krogg 'A', *Atlas* and the 186th Battle Squadron were cruising in company with the Larosian Fleet.

Fox was sitting quietly — and contentedly — on the bridge, barely twenty minutes from his rendezvous with Caine's fleet, when the frigate *Phoenix* appeared unexpectedly on his plot. Moving into formation with his 74s at an impressive clip, the smaller ship broadcast a warning.

The dapper little Commodore stiffened as soon as he saw the relatively up-to-date feed from the frigate — the Fifth Rate had bridged the gap from Krogg 'A' to the Larosian Fleet in only a few minutes, and the reason for that haste was clear enough.

The Kroggs were staging a breakout. And if they came out in force to hit the Larosians, he'd be nearly helpless to stop them. He had only his seven ships on hand, and *Phoenix*...

"Warn Narosh," he turned to his Signal Officer. "Quickly."

The First came out of energy drive at the last possible second, their guns running out immediately.

As the interference cleared from the battle plot, Caine blinked in astonishment. The Kroggs were charging towards open space faster than he'd expected, and the First had returned to a material state in their midst. It was only the skill of the First Fleet's Cruising Masters that allowed direct collisions to be avoided.

"Shields up," Forepaw nodded to his First Lieutenant, his demeanor calm and professional. "All guns fire as you bear. Helm, down angle fourteen degrees, port sixty. Master, give me 85 pls."

This was no longer a grand strategic operation. Caine's ships had moved fast, but the Kroggs had been moving faster, almost as though they'd expected this to be their opening all along. The Earthers weren't going to be able to cut them off with a neatly organized fleet action. Instead it would be a close melee as Earther ships came to grips with whatever Kroggs they saw around them...

But the Kroggs weren't stopping to fight. Almost a hundred were blasted to a halt by point-blank broadsides, and the rest didn't try to fire back. Instead, they raced past the blockade force and launched themselves into hyperspace.

Seven hundred Krogg ships were heading for the Larosian reinforcements...

"Pursuit course, all ships," Caine ordered darkly.

• • •

"I've got them, they're coming at us fast from Krogg 'A'. Looks like 700 ships, give or take…" the Sensor Chief reported quickly on *Atlas'* bridge.

"Any word from Narosh?" Fox turned to his Signal Officer.

The Earther shook his head, "None, sir."

Fox took a deep breath. What was Narosh doing? Until the Kroggs came out of hyper there was little the Earthers could do to interfere with them without severely endangering the Larosians. Spatial charges used energy-hyper reactors to significantly damage ships in hyper, but those weapons affected a wide area, and they'd surely tear the Larosians apart as easily as the Kroggs.

That would be rather counter-productive.

As far as Fox knew, the Kroggs would have to come out of hyper to engage… But then again, perhaps they could fight in hyperspace when their foe was already in there…

"The First is under energy drive, coming out after them. Looks like they have close to even numbers," the Sensor Chief continued, and Fox frowned.

Hopefully the Fourth was redeployed by now, able to contain the rest of the Kroggs in the system…

"Hang on… the Larosian Fleet is maneuvering in hyper. They're forming into some sort of broad wall…" the Sensor Chief scowled at his panel, trying to interpret the garbled readings reaching him through the layers of subspace.

"I think they're going into battle mode."

Larosian ships, just before entering action, physically expanded. Mechanically they were designed so that their components shifted further outward from the hull to enhance armor protection of ship vitals. For anyone watching the transformation, it almost appeared as if they were animals rearing up for a fight.

Narosh and his 4,700 ships were getting ready to face the Kroggs, and they had a seven to one superiority in numbers…

Fox let out a smooth breath, then turned back to the Signal Officer, "Send to *Phoenix*… return to the fleet and tell Caine that Narosh is handling the breakout."

Caine would doubtless want to get back on station as quickly as possible. With only a portion of the blockade intact and the Kroggs acting with this much guile, the First Lord would need to be there.

"Squadron to quarters, prep boats," Fox continued after a moment, "just in case some of the Kroggs decide to come out of hyperspace to pick a fight."

Narosh watched with a curious stare as the Kroggs came towards *Lycrotar*. In his many decades of battle experience he'd never witnessed such an action from his foe. This enemy force, substantially inferior to his own, had risked the security of Krogg 'A' simply to come out and confront him. It was either grossly stupid or deviously brilliant…

But these were Kroggs — 'brilliant' was seldom a word that could be associated with them. For 600 years, their dominant strategy had been 'kill', not 'think and kill'. Thought and logic, combined with a healthy amount of valor and discipline had defeated them on many occasions.

Now, it seemed that with his fleet arrayed in a wall, he would simply overwhelm the assaulting Kroggs with missile fire and wipe out part of their fleet without substantial loss to his own.

It would be an acceptable start to the campaign.

Caine frowned and drummed his fingers on the arms of his chair. Narosh didn't seem to mind fighting in hyper, as he was lining up his ships for action without making any moves to return to normal space. But the nature of this Krogg breakout was nagging at Caine — what could they possibly be trying to accomplish?

They couldn't have planned on *Match* or any of Claw's squadron being damaged when they started their movements, and even if they'd hoped to wound some of the scouting sloops they couldn't have known how quickly and powerfully Sarah would react with the Fourth...

They certainly couldn't have expected a fleet-sized gap at their hyper limit. Thus far the blockade had been solid, pinning the Kroggs and countering any attempt they made to build up strength at any one point of the Allied line.

So was this just an impromptu and incredibly futile rush to try to weaken the Larosians with whatever was on hand? Or was there more to these ships than he could see...

Caine turned to Forepaw, "Lab, send *Phoenix* back to Fox. Tell him to prepare a spread of spatial charges and to order Narosh back. I want the 186th to soften up the Kroggs before the Larosians hit them."

Fox quickly received the orders, as *Phoenix*, having returned to the echelons of the First Fleet for only seconds, turned around and again bridged the rapidly closing distance between the fleets at a good clip. The order to lay a spread of charges appealed to Fox; Caine was right, there was something *off* about this move by the Kroggs. They had something up their sleeves, perhaps...

That'll be the day, a Krogg in a shirt with sleeves...

Fox shook his mind out of its useless meandering, and the crack 74s of the 186th moved into position, ready to carry out their run.

If Narosh would just get out of the way.

"No response yet?"

The Signal Officer shook his head and shrugged.

They'd warned Narosh of their intention: each of Fox's 74's would drop a single spatial charge into hyperspace, right in the path of the Kroggs. The tactic should work easily enough since the Kroggs were coming towards him; in a stern chase scenario, getting the charges into position was rather a challenge.

The charges, which were really just small pinnaces retrofitted with energy-hyper reactors, would accelerate into hyperspace at 350 pls relative speed and collide with the nearest target.

With the additional velocity provided by hyperspace, the kinetic force of the detonation could be quite impressive.

So far these charges had been used only a few times on the blockade during counterattacks to Caine's raids at Krogg 'A', but often enough to make the Kroggs wary of them. The problem was they were only good against targets in hyperspace because the physics of that layer of subspace magnified their destructive ability. They were also very tough to manufacture, so there was no point wasting them except when circumstances demanded. Moreover, the weapons were awkward to carry; large to the point of debilitation, spatial charges could be carried only by ships of the line, and even then only one to each. Flagship First Rates sometimes carried two, but loading capital ships with gunboats had been more of a priority in the last few months.

Now, as the AI-piloted charges began to warm up their engines, Fox waited with mild frustration, hoping that Narosh would back off quickly. What was he waiting for...?

Though part of Narosh's nature continued to question the Krogg assault, he remained generally unwilling to refuse the Kroggs action. They had come to fight him — not the Earthers — and with his superiority in numbers, he had little fear of casualties.

He conveniently ignored Magnus, determined to prove the Larosians' dominance in this war once and for all–

What?

Narosh paused at the telepathic exclamation of one of his officers, and looked closely at the telepathic monitors being routed into his mind. All but a few of the Kroggs were retreating, or so it seemed. But why...

The last dozen enemy vessels began to accelerate towards his fleet, and finally he recognized that something seemed wrong about this entire situation. Most of the breakout group was retreating home as though they had been an escort or perhaps brought along only to confuse...

All ships withdraw immediately! Allow the Earthers to engage the targets!

Narosh's orders were quickly transmitted through the minds of all the Larosians in the fleet, and the silver vessels managed to hold formation as they turned hard about, moving away from the Kroggs. Unfortunately they were without the necessary speed, as slower Battleships were delaying the fleet's progress... but to break formation might risk defeat if the Krogg force came forward again...

No, the Krogg maneuver seemed too much a threat somehow — it demanded dramatic reaction...

Break formation, escape in all directions!

It struck Narosh that his sudden awareness might have come too late.

"They're coming back towards us, sir," *Orion's* Sensor Officer said with a bit of relief.

Caine released a sigh — the Kroggs had recognized reality. Seven hundred ships wouldn't make a difference out here against an Allied force of thousands, but they could prove quite useful in defense of their home system.

Unless they didn't *get* home.

There were almost 400 spatial charges aboard the ships of the First Fleet. Caine couldn't afford to expend all of them here, but perhaps forty wouldn't be missed. A spread laid out by five squadrons of 74s could knock the Krogg Fleet about quite handily...

"Get Jax Furgus on the comm. I want his 74s to lay a spread of charges over the Kroggs as they come by."

Fox experienced a moment of relief as he watched the Kroggs begin to turn away. But relief was replaced quickly with concern as a dozen Krogg vessels held course and seemed to continue with their charge. This was making less and less sense... unless these Kroggs were some sort of kamikazes...

Oh.

A dozen ships could probably have evaded the blockade and reached the Larosians, even if Sarah had been in position to try to stop them. The small, fast blockade runners could conceivably have breached even the thickest blockade perimeter... and the Larosians wouldn't concern themselves too much with such a small attack force if they saw it approaching them, having slipped through the blockade.

Then *boom*, they ambush the incoming Larosians.

Clever.

A bit *too* clever, actually, though that was unimportant just now. The Larosians were trying to evade the incoming attackers, but the Krogg ships appeared to be the new, faster Dreadnoughts bred to run with Earther ships of the line. The Larosians weren't quite quick enough...

But Fox's 74s were.

"Prepare the charges from *Dominant*, *Gettysburg* and *Fuji*. Target those Kroggs... and warn Narosh."

Narosh was just beginning to order defensive missile fire when Fox's warning came in from normal space, and this time he heeded it.

Suddenly a massive hyper wave blinded the sensors of every Larosian ship in the fleet, and three spatial charges slipped into hyperspace. Their speed multiplied by a half dozen orders of magnitude, relative to normal space, and their guidance computers paused just long enough to mark their targets.

Then, three seeming-pinnaces slammed into three Krogg Dreadnought-sized kamikaze ships, moving at over a million pls. The resulting explosions were massive, a shockwave expanding outward in hyperspace as the Kroggs exploded.

Lycrotar was thrown into a tumble by the pulse wave, its armor absorbing the blast with some difficulty. Then, the Krogg ships that hadn't been hit exploded in the shockwave–

• • •

Fox was waiting for the sensor screens to clear from the energy-hyper interference when *Atlas* bucked violently under his feet.

The 74 and its squadron-mates were in energy drive, having only paused to drop the charges, and now the wake was tossing them as though they were in a hurricane.

"We're barely holding together... recommend we go to normal drives to ride it out!" Mister Gunth, *Atlas'* seasoned old Master, looked to his Captain as soon as the 74 began to pitch.

Fox nodded immediately, "Pass that along to the squadron. All hands *hold on!*"

No spatial charges since the first test had caused this kind of shock in normal space... The weapons the Kroggs had been carrying in those ships had been *big*.

CHAPTER 9

Jax Furgus' 74s had just dropped their spread of spatial charges when the rumble went through the First Fleet. Caine frowned and cast a questioning glance at Forepaw, but the Flag Captain was already calling up a map of local space on the main battle plot. As the blue holo tank came to life the jaws of virtually everyone on the bridge dropped. They'd been hit by a massive shockwave from the area of the Larosian Fleet's location, despite the fact that they were almost six minutes away at 2,500 pls.

The energy release had not only been massive, it had been in *hyperspace*, meaning the Kroggs had hit Narosh with something. Something far more powerful than the Allies had seen from them thus far. Something that could generate a hyperspace wake of incredible proportions.

This whole breakout had been a ploy on the part of the Kroggs.

They'd had some sort of bomb ship this whole time... something that would work well against Larosians... probably a hyperspace bomb. They'd sat and waited, pooled their strength, then held their weapon until it could hit the Larosian reinforcements just before they arrived at Krogg 'A'...

Caine blinked — at least that was how it *appeared*.

Awfully clever.

The spatial charges dropped by the First abruptly began driving home. Forty disturbances in hyperspace were being registered on the blue battle plot — flashing clouds of gold that wiped out swathes of black Krogg icons.

Only about 200 alien ships would be getting home...

Caine's mind was the first to refocus as a massive explosion lit up the battle plot. He turned to the Signal Officer, "Order the fleet back to blockade stations. Have Jax take his division out to investigate that blast."

The operator nodded and the orders were beamed from *Orion*.

Vice Admiral Jax Furgus was becoming quite renowned for his handling of smaller forces. Since his time with Ursla and the Second Fleet at Genesis, he'd seen quite a lot of action, and like Varnon Broadpaw, he'd built upon his already impressive reputation within the Allied fleets.

Not that he was one to brag. He'd had half a dozen ships shot out from under him in the last two years, and he certainly didn't consider himself brilliant. In his own estimation, he was just a good and capable officer.

Sitting on the bridge of the 74-gun *Madrid*, he watched the battle plot slowly clear as his ships neared the site of the explosion. The interference was still quite remarkable — even after eight minutes, scans were nearly impossible.

Finally, a few icons started popping up on the screen — 74s of the 186th. *Lucifer* and *Vulcan*, followed by *Fuji* and *Dominant*. Jax watched quietly as that entire squadron began to reappear, scattered and a bit battered, but remarkably intact.

The interference was too thick to get signals to the ships until the range dropped, but already Furgus could see they were maneuvering themselves into some sort of order. They seemed alright.

As relieved as he was to see the 186th intact, just one squadron of 74s wasn't important just now. They had to hope Narosh's force had survived.

"Send the sloops ahead," Furgus ordered quietly, and his flag staff passed the orders on to the 195th Scouting Squadron.

The six 16-gun ships of that unit moved out ahead of *Madrid*, the other thirty-seven ships of the line that made up Furgus' Battle Group using their better sensor suites to pierce the energy currents that floated about space.

Telemetry slowly began to reach *Madrid's* main battle tank. For the most part it was more of the same — muffled readings of dense energy fields...

Then, rather abruptly, nearly 1,000 Larosian ships appeared.

Mainly Battleships, the floating Larosian vessels looked to be only lightly damaged, possibly having escaped hyperspace before the explosion. But what about the rest of the fleet?

The sloops continued to press forward, moving over the Larosian ships while scanning through layers of subspace to detect Larosian vessels adrift in hyper.

Furgus watched and waited silently, wondering whether there was anything else left.

The Larosian ships were just beginning to come alive, their maneuvering jets firing while their hulls shrunk back to normal size from battle mode. A hyper point then opened, and a slow but steady stream of Larosian ships began to crawl through it, painfully emerging into normal space. Some appeared to be heavily damaged, others merely maintaining the slow pace to avoid running down the more crippled among them.

Furgus held his breath and began to count.

One... two, three.... four, five, six, seven, eight... nine...

Narosh's head was buzzing. He'd hit something hard, and now his mind was literally in pain. However the very fact that he had survived helped lighten this pain — if he was still alive, many others should be as well.

Admiral-of-a-Fleet, are you injured?

Narosh slowly sat up, waving away the officers who had asked him the question. His mind continued to buzz in an unfamiliar fashion, but he ignored the uncomfortable feeling.

No damage of a permanent nature. What of the fleet?

Forty ships destroyed, 600 missing, possibly scattered by the blast. We are in line to reenter normal space to regroup before we proceed.

What was that explosive?

We do not yet know, sir.

Narosh tilted his head and came to his feet, straightening his silver armor and shaking his head to try to stop the buzzing. *Very well.*

As he peered about, Narosh noticed two scorch marks on the walls of *Lycrotar's* bridge. A rare sight on Warcruisers, marks such as these indicated that whatever had hit the ship had been powerful enough to overload its main power lines and cause a blast fire.

Narosh had seen such damage done to a ship only once before — aboard *Lorcraytan*, when the Son of Praaxus had used that Warcruiser's hull as a massive beam weapon amplifier. The circumstances had seemed entirely unbelievable at the time, and now again the situation seemed to defy any explanation Narosh would have accepted as reasonable, had he not witnessed the explosion himself...

The Kroggs had meant to trap and destroy his ships with a massive detonation... perhaps a salvo of warheads, or bombs carried aboard the twelve vessels that had attacked the fleet. The effort might have been a success, had it not been for the Earthers and their weapons...

Narosh thought pensively of his allies. They seemed to be able to predict, understand, and interpret the enemy's activities in a way that none but the Son might have matched. It was not a skill Narosh envied — he had in mind only one fate for the Kroggs, and it did not include understanding them.

The Earthers, however, could certainly be useful in the invasion of Krogg. Their understanding would allow for better planning, and be an asset to his mission...

The buzzing in Narosh's mind continued.

"Looks like a significant chunk of the Larosian Fleet survived, sir."

Jax nodded as his Flag Captain pointed out the long stream of Larosian ships in the main battle plot. Fox had dropped his charges just in time — they must have prematurely detonated whatever the Kroggs were launching.

The Admiral turned to his Signal Officer, "Send word to Caine that we appear to have most of the Larosian Fleet, but that we are unaware of their exact condition."

The Lieutenant nodded in reply, sending the message through *Madrid's* comm array. A slight sigh of relief slipped from Jax as he looked at the swelling cloud of Larosian silver in his main plot...

Things had just narrowly missed taking a mighty turn for the worse.

"Sir, signal coming in from Commodore Magnus."

Jax looked up and nodded, and the holo of Fox Magnus appeared in the main tank, "Hi, Jax... I take it we're not dead."

The lion grinned at the younger Commodore, "Not just yet, Fox, but you came close by the looks of it. Do you have any idea what sort of weapon the

Kroggs set off out here?"

Fox shrugged loosely on the screen, rubbing his neck ruefully, "Looked like a dozen Dreadnoughts. They seemed to be a little persistent and Narosh turned his fleet around to evade. They were running pretty damned fast — I don't know if *we* could have caught them in energy drive... so I put three charges over them. I'm guessing we hit something."

Jax nodded again, "We'll probably have to take a look at your telemetry, but I'm guessing they could've blown up a star with what they shot at you."

Fox's eyes widened slightly, "I'm *very* lucky then. But the Larosians are a lot luckier."

Furgus nodded, "I suppose so."

There was a slight pause and Fox blinked, "Let's just hope the Kroggs don't have any more of whatever those were."

Jax froze.

Oh *dear*.

CHAPTER 10

Ursla sat silently on the bridge of *Agamemnon*, eyes wide as she watched the spectacle unfolding in her main battle plot. The data had just been beamed in from *Orion*, and included all the readings taken by *Atlas* during the explosion. None of the Larosians had yet been queried for their sensor data, but Fox's telemetry was startling enough.

Sitting next to Ursla, Artemis Tigar, *Agamemnon's* commander and Ursla's Flag Captain, whistled softly.

"Hell of a bang," he offered quietly.

"They say it didn't do too much damage?" Ursla asked in reply, and Tigar glanced quickly at the written report that had accompanied the pictures.

He shook his head, "Not too much. We got *very* lucky, I think."

Ursla nodded.

A blast that could leave such a huge wake in an entirely different layer of subspace was definitely something to worry about. How had the Kroggs even gained that sort of capability? As far as Ursla knew, nothing purely matter-based could deliver such a punch.

Though she was by no means an engineer, proposals for all sorts of weapons had crossed her desk in the past few years, one of the more recent having been for a star-killer missile. A Genesis scientist had suggested that a Wyndhymn generator — one of the massive energy chambers that fueled Earther ships — could potentially be placed 'under' a star in hyperspace and overloaded. The theory held that the resulting blast, magnified by the laws of physics in that lower layer of subspace, could break through the other layers like a hyperspace wake would — just with a lot more punch. The area such a blast might affect, however, was supposed to be small.

This blast's range had been quite, *quite* large.

"A weapon like this could blow an entire fleet right off station," Tigar suggested in low tones. "If they set one off in hyperspace, we'd get blinded temporarily, and they could break out."

Ursla took a breath and nodded slowly. After the four-day posturing fight she'd just finished, a walkover like that would be even more annoying... not to mention entirely disastrous for the Allied cause.

"Well, we can't be sure they'll blow this big if we don't add spatial charges to the mix," she concluded quietly. "And if they had an abundance of them they likely would have used them the last time they tried to break out."

Tigar frowned skeptically, "What, and reveal them before they could destroy the Larosians?"

Good point. Wait until they can be truly decisive and then start throwing them around all at once before the Allies can figure out what to do about them. Suddenly Ursla's 700-ship force seemed absurdly fragile.

"And," Tigar added in reluctant tones, "what if that thing detonated in our layer of subspace? Bad business, I think."

Ursla stiffened and nodded, "I think we better make sure Savanna's thinking the same thing."

Felix's eyes widened as he reviewed *Atlas'* sensor feed.

Few things actually *shocked* the white tiger — since he'd assumed command of *Tonnant* and the Third Fleet, he'd fought many actions, and even before then he'd witnessed his share of bloody fights, perhaps most notably the slaughter of six million Crusaders in Earth orbit. That had been years ago, and he could still recall it all too clearly...

But now he had a new mental picture to tack onto the list.

Glancing from the replay in his 80-gun Second Rate's main battle plot, Felix cast a curious look at his Flag Captain. Varnia Broadpaw watched silently and swallowed, "I think we've got something to worry about now."

While not prone to the moments of wit that were her father's trademark, Varnia was quite able to deliver practical and realistic appraisals of every situation.

Felix nodded in reply to her conclusion, "Something like that could blast us right off station... the Kroggs would be free to cruise wherever they pleased."

Varnia sighed, "We'd better double the pickets. If they send something out after us we'll need enough lead time to maneuver clear of it."

Felix's ear twitched — where did that leave the blockade? If a Krogg assault on the Third Fleet's position could drive his ships off altogether, there obviously wouldn't be any chance for containment.

"I don't think we're going to be able to hold them back for much longer," Felix said quietly. "They've got leverage that can get us off their doorstep and we've got nothing to counter it with. Staying in range seriously risks our survival."

Varnia silently looked at her senior, "I'm not sure I follow."

Felix shrugged, "If we stay here and they manage to hit us with one of these things, 654 ships of the Allied Fleet could potentially be lost. Right now that's about twenty percent of the confirmed fleet strength... and even if all of the Larosians are safe and in good shape, we're still about ten percent of the fleet. Ursla's another ten percent. If they were able to do to us what they tried to do to Narosh..."

Varnia nodded slowly in understanding. By simply maintaining the close blockade, they were leaving themselves open to attack by these new weapons.

"So do we withdraw for a long-distance blockade, then?"

Felix blinked at the question. His role wasn't to determine fleet policy

— that was up to Caine — but he was responsible for Krogg 'C'. A long-range blockade would keep his ships intact, but it would allow the Kroggs to come out and seize the initiative without facing an immediate adversary.

So pulling his fleet back and leaving a screen out there to watch the Kroggs wouldn't cut it because they could slip away from him. And 800 Krogg ships prowling around the Allied rear, with such a massive frontier along which to attack... not an option.

Which meant that, in order to avoid such a breakout, both the Krogg 'B' and 'C' garrisons had to be eliminated before they could run their blockades.

Oh great.

"Sloop coming in with a message from the Second Fleet, sir."

Felix looked up from the tank and frowned at his Signal Officer, "They under attack?"

The Lieutenant shook his head, "Admiral Ursla is just advising you to be aware of possible attacks with these new bombs."

Felix smiled, "Leave it to Andra to think I'd need to be told..."

He paused, keying the main battle tank to display the contents of Krogg 'C'. Felix frowned thoughtfully at the 800 black ship icons and dozen stationary bases as they appeared. He'd long ago conceived of ways to attack this system — and he'd based his plans on the Third Fleet being down in strength to only 500 ships, just in case.

What if...

"Send the sloop back to the Second, but beam them the following message first..."

Ursla read the screen and something of a sad smile crept over her face. Then she inexplicably started to chuckle, shaking her head and ruefully rubbing her neck. The chuckle grew until she filled the bridge with laughter that seemed altogether out of place.

Tigar frowned at her, "Something you'd like to share with the crew?"

Ursla grinned at her Captain and shook her head at her longtime subordinate, "It's just Savanna."

Tigar cocked an eyebrow, "And?"

Ursla's laughter deepened, crested, and then faded, as she sauntered slowly to her chair and sat, "He has an idea."

Artemis Tigar was patient, though perhaps not as patient now as usual, "Oh stop being so *cryptic*."

Ursla almost started chuckling again, but instead rubbed her forehead and let an exhausted smile slip onto her face. Caine was probably going to have a conniption...

"Artemis, order *Surge* to carry a message to Setter, will you?"

The Captain nodded, then bobbed his head quickly to the Signal Officer.

He waited a moment, expecting Ursla to volunteer the message.

"*What* is it?"

Ursla looked up, still chuckling a bit, "Ahh. 'To Setter. Savanna is of the opinion that the best alternative for continued security of Krogg 'B' and 'C' is to capture said systems as soon as possible. He recommends a launch date of forty-eight hours.'"

The bridge was silent except for the sound of the Signal Officer's voice — that Lieutenant was repeating the words to the Signal Chief and making certain the message was sent to the sloop that would carry it to *Orion*.

Tigar's eyebrows rose as Ursla recited her message, and he immediately understood why she had found it funny.

Felix was completely *insane*. They'd been campaigning for months without end, they'd been jousting incessantly with the Kroggs in 'A' and 'B', and they were still outnumbered rather significantly.

To attack, just after the introduction of what could best be called a doomsday weapon...

Tigar tried without success to conceal a smile at the absurdity of the proposition, but his Admiral had it right. He slowly grinned too, because, although it was a positively mad idea, it was the only alternative just now. They couldn't stay on blockade and they couldn't run, so they needed to attack sooner than the Kroggs would expect... take out everything except for the Kroggs in 'A', then figure out what to do with that system later.

So Tigar briefly locked eyes with Ursla, "I'll pass that on to the fleet as well, I think. They might as well know they should start getting ready."

Ursla nodded, "Took the words right out of my mouth."

Ursla was tired, stiff, and getting ready to engage a superior, fortified force in a desperate battle.

Days didn't get much more interesting than this.

CHAPTER 11

"Well that's a great idea," Caine said brightly as Labrador Forepaw keyed Ursla's message into *Orion's* main battle tank.

For a moment the Captain thought Caine was being sarcastic, but a quick examination of the First Lord revealed exhausted earnestness in his graying amber eyes.

The Larosian ships were starting to move into position around Krogg 'A', almost all of them in fighting condition. Sarah's fleet was back on station, as was the First, but soon the Larosians would have enough of the front covered to rotate out at least one of those two Allied formations.

So if Caine could split enough force off the blockade at 'A' to help over-power the Krogg garrisons in the outer systems, the Allies could come close to evening the odds in the final battle, while securing their flanks against attack from these new weapons. And if Felix was confident that he could break Krogg 'C', Ursla would certainly be able to deal with Krogg 'B', even if it took some reinforcement from the First Fleet.

The trick would be to pull it off with minimum casualties... to get the drop on the Kroggs... to draw them out... *something.* The fleet had to remain essentially intact.

Caine turned to Forepaw, "Lab, send couriers to both Ursla and Felix, we'll need to rendezvous with them here to plan this thing properly. Send to Sarah as well..."

A thought crossed Caine's mind and he paused. Narosh was busy trying to reassemble his fleet, and frankly, Caine was confident this operation could be handled by the Allies without Larosian support. The newcomers could take a break in the space around Krogg 'A' — blockade duty with their numbers would be far easier than it had been for the Earthers and humans... especially if one Allied Fleet stayed with them.

But in order to launch against Krogg 'B' and 'C', the combined fleets were going to have to be ready to replenish whatever losses they incurred. The entire force of the two Allied Navies would need to consolidate here soon after operations against 'B' and 'C' so that Krogg 'A' could be attacked before the Queen launched any sort of counterattack.

Reinforcements from Earth and Genesis would be needed soon, then.

Caine glanced at Forepaw, "Get cutters ready for Earth, New Halifax, and Genesis. We need all ships to get under weigh immediately, rallied or not."

Forepaw nodded, turning briefly to the main battle plot and identifying three cutters from the group of six that were currently with the fleet. These tiny ships, each crewed by only six small-statured spacers, were the most fragile vessels ever built by Earthers. Their reactors were disposable, so when the strain of energy-hyper began to wear them down they could simply eject them and replace them with new ones.

The lessons from *Flame's* ill-fated adventure in search of *Harbinger Bishop* had been taken to heart by Earther engineers.

Despite their fragility, however, the cutters were perhaps the most valued asset in Caine's arsenal. Subspace physics forbade them from growing beyond a certain size, so they couldn't carry weapons or passengers, but they could carry information.

And as he'd discovered very dramatically at Gibraltar, information was probably the most important element of space war these days.

Caine silently watched the main battle plot as Forepaw began giving orders to the Signal Officer. A few days earlier, the First Lord might have agonized over such an ambitious plan... now he was just determined to see it through, whether he was entirely certain of its merits or not. It was Savanna's idea, and that cat was no fool — he was one of the most skilled line officers in the service. And if Ursla had passed on the recommendation, then she agreed with it. Or at least she, like he, knew it was the only way to secure the two smaller Krogg systems.

Caine simply couldn't afford to despair over the possibility of failure. He needed to be prudent, not fearful.

Folding his arms against his chest, he began to mentally review ship numbers.

Sarah sat quietly on the bridge of *Pope Joseph Barron*, watching the two-dimensional flat projection of Fox Magnus' telemetry scroll across the bridge's main monitor. She'd saved *Match*, and she'd been very smart about it.

But the Kroggs had ruined it for her anyway. *Bastards.*

Now her move to save one of the Alliance's valuable sloops would probably earn her condemnation from the commanders... *again.* She cursed inwardly — luck was working against her. She'd been given the perfect chance, and she'd been betrayed by the Kroggs at the very last moment.

Worse, her fleet was now running short on warheads.

And with weapons capable of causing explosions such as those Fox Magnus had faced, the Kroggs would probably try to break the blockade. They had no reason to conceal these bombs' existence now. So they'd be coming out after the Allies soon, and Sarah would have to fight her ships with old-fashioned fusion heads until the replacements came up from Gibraltar.

That was fine. It might get messy, but she'd make certain her crews made up for their lack of hitting power with sheer determination.

So long as somebody let her get into the fight...

"Ma'am, we're getting a hail from *Orion.*"

Even though the First Rate was stationed on the other side of the system from *Joseph Barron*, communication was swift thanks to Earther energy comm. Rapid bursts of energy accelerated to speeds faster than light by Wyndhymn reaction-coils were sent and received without difficulty, providing essentially seamless real-time communication over distances this short.

So Caine could scold her without having to wait on the lag.

Marvelous.

"Put it up," Sarah said shortly, sitting up in her chair and squaring her shoulders. She'd made the right decision. Nothing that wouldn't have otherwise happened had happened. A dozen bomb ships could probably have slipped through the blockade even if it had been intact.

Caine appeared on the main monitor, obviously tired but also seeming surprisingly refreshed... outwardly, at least.

"Sarah, Savanna is suggesting a big push on Krogg 'B' and 'C' to make sure we protect our flank against these bombs."

Braced for an assault on her actions, Sarah had to take a few seconds to digest the pleasant surprise.

"That sounds quite sensible," she said quickly, and Caine nodded.

"I'm gathering the commanders for a meeting and I'm sending for the Fifth and Sixth immediately. Can you come over?"

Sarah nodded eagerly — did he honestly think she'd skip such a conference? "I'll be over in an hour."

"Good," Caine offered a smile. "And well done with *Match*, by the way."

Before Sarah could reply, Caine blanked the screen. Her excitement at the prospect of action suddenly overcame any worries about her earlier performance — Caine wanted her in on the planning.

And with so many Larosian ships on hand, the Fourth — or at least *some* of it — could easily be spared for those ambitious combat operations.

Turning to ArcColonel Evan-Thomas, *Joseph Barron's* commander, Sarah spoke with genuine eagerness, "Maneuver us out of formation and to *Orion*, best speed. Prepare my pinnace."

Things, perhaps, weren't so bad after all.

CHAPTER 12

Graham Manchester stared quietly into his salmon and let his head sag on the hand that was propping it up.

"She says she doesn't think it can work, Varnon. I mean, *come on*. Sure, we haven't seen each other in four months... but it's only *four*. A bloody *year* and I could buy it..."

Graham twisted his fork in the salmon.

Varnon Broadpaw sat back in his chair and tried not to laugh.

Oh it was *so* hard not to.

But he couldn't — Graham needed friendly advice.

"So she isn't one for long-distance relationships?" the wolf asked as sullenly as he could manage.

Graham looked up from his genetically-constructed fish and shrugged, "I guess not. Strange, you'd expect a marine to be gung-ho about the whole idea. Your wife doesn't mind, does she?"

Broadpaw cocked an eyebrow, "What?"

Straightening in his chair slightly, Graham slumped, "She's alright with your long-distance relationship?"

"As far as I know. She tells me that as long as I come home she's fine with it," Broadpaw shrugged. "She's always more worried about Varnia than me — Varnia being her little girl and all."

Graham stared across the table at his Earther friend and sighed longingly, "You have *kids*, Varnon. I'll *never* have kids..."

He slumped lower and put on such a face that Broadpaw couldn't help but chuckle. Lately, the emotional atmosphere within all Alliance circles had become one of extremes. Overjoyed or devastated. Nothing in between.

And sometimes the young humans could be so misguided over rather small things.

Sitting in the infamous *Bloody Pulsar* — *Genesis One's* most renowned bar (and now an eatery serving specialized food for Earthers) — Varnon Broadpaw couldn't help but wonder how someone at Graham's stage of life could possibly be so distraught over one woman...

"What? *What?*"

Broadpaw blinked at Graham and lifted an apologetic hand... though he kept chuckling.

"I'm sorry Graham, but at a time like this you're worrying about your love life with Gillian Hodge. You've got an entire division of the Sixth Fleet... don't you already have enough on your mind?"

Graham didn't appear amused, "I *never* have enough on my mind, Varnon."

The Earther Admiral grinned at the remark, "You're always worrying about something, aren't you?"

"Noticed, did you?" Graham sighed and rubbed his eyes with the palms of his hands. "It was great until this bloody posting, and now she's off at Gibraltar running marine affairs while I'm stuck here with some bloody Dreadnoughts!"

Varnon chuckled and shrugged, "Look on the bright side, you've got all of your ships together."

Graham lowered his hands to his lap, glaring at the jovial Earther.

"That makes me feel *so bloody much better*."

Broadpaw grinned widely, "I thought it would."

Graham picked up his fork and hefted a slab of salmon, pausing to mimic Broadpaw, "Ooooh, I thought it would. Oooh."

As Broadpaw started to laugh a waiter approached the table, slowing with a frown on his face as he overheard one of the senior Genesis fleet officers in the system making fun of *the* most senior Earther Navy officer in the area.

Broadpaw caught sight of him out of the corner of his eye, "Yes?"

The waiter blinked, "Oh, sorry sir. Message from C&C that ArcGeneral Hastings needs to speak with you both."

Broadpaw nodded his thanks as Graham sulked and chewed.

Bill Wallace and Andros Grieve were already waiting with Hastings in the main conference room when Broadpaw and Graham arrived.

Hastings met them with a cocked eyebrow from behind her desk as they entered, "Making a habit of being late, Varnon?"

The Earther grinned, "Aw, just to *your* meetings Liz. Besides, Graham and I were discussing unrequited love."

Everyone in the room chuckled and Graham frowned at Broadpaw.

"Are we in a spot of lady trouble then, Graham?" Wallace asked with a friendly grin.

"Shut it, Bill," Graham settled himself into a chair. "You're no family man yourself..."

"Hmm, daughter and wife don't count? Not registered through the Church, I grant you, but I've still got to live with them when I'm home," Wallace's grin grew as Graham harrumphed.

Hastings plunged in too, "So I suppose the young fellow is in hot water?"

"Why don't you talk about that with *Mister* Hastings," Graham grumbled, then perked up in mock revelation... "Oh *wait*. There isn't one!"

Nobody actually had to say "oooooooh". It was implied.

"I still sign your cheques, buddy," Hastings said with mock-menace. "Anyway, you'll be out at Gibraltar to make amends with her soon anyhow. Caine's calling us up to the blockade. We need to get there as quickly as we can."

Broadpaw's expression sobered at the announcement, "Is he moving against something that soon?"

Hastings shrugged, leaning back in her chair, "*Sooner.* He's calling us up to support the fleet's blockade of Krogg 'A', and he's got Savanna and Andra dreaming up ways to take 'B' and 'C' without us."

Graham frowned curiously, "Awfully abrupt."

Hastings keyed the room's main screen active, hitting play and allowing the silent room to digest the data from *Atlas'* sensor feeds.

Understanding it took a moment.

Even on a flat screen, the power the explosion had released was all too clear.

"How much damage did that do?" the junior Manchester asked quietly.

"The Kroggs apparently tried to rush the Larosians with a dozen bomb ships. Fox Magnus stopped them short of Narosh's ships with a spread of spatial charges, so not many ships were lost, and most of the Larosian Fleet was reported intact."

There was a collective sigh of relief in the room.

"So we got a lucky preview without paying for it," Wallace concluded.

Hastings nodded, "And to make sure we can maintain a strong blockade of the main system, Savanna is recommending we capture the outer systems, asap."

Graham digested the explanation, "They could blast us right off station with something like that. And those two systems aren't critical to the defense of Krogg 'A'... if ships from either were able to break out they could try to hit us or Gibraltar. If 'A' has that sort of bomb, they won't need the extra ships..."

Again Hastings nodded, "You see! He's just like me — hopeless when it comes to romance but good at strategy."

Graham smiled and shrugged, "If we're shipping out towards Gibraltar, I might just prove you wrong on the first half."

Grins were tossed about quickly, and then Hastings nodded, "We will be. The cutter that brought this carried a requisition for more Type 98 heads. After the breakout this morning you can bet Sarah's almost out of ordnance, so we're going to have to pick up the stockpiles we moved up to Gibraltar. There aren't enough haulers up there now to carry them all to the front, so there'll be lots left there for us to grab."

"Are the ships already at Gibraltar waiting for us?" Wallace tilted his head as he posed the question.

Hastings shook her head, "Cutters went to all four bases — all ships are moving out on their own."

"So we'll pick up warheads when we get to Gibraltar," Grieve spoke for the first time this meeting. "What about marines? We've got about 2,000 in Gibraltar. Elements of the Heavy Division, if I'm not mistaken."

He wasn't mistaken, of course. Grieve was ultimately the controller of all ground affairs for the Alliance, Commandant Gillian Hodge — Graham's erstwhile girlfriend — being his second in command.

With so much planet-hopping going on in the past months, it had been necessary to pool a large number of marines at Gibraltar. While the troops carried by ships were sufficient for some ground assaults, rooting out the really well-entrenched Krogg installations required a longer commitment and in turn a force of Earthers not exclusively assigned to a single vessel.

Thus, for the past month about 2,000 marines back from planetary operations at Avalon and Amaratsu had remained undeployed at Gibraltar. Now that the fleet was getting ready to move against Krogg 'A', they'd undoubtedly get some work.

Hastings paused as she thought about the question. Grieve made an excellent point... "Well, I'm pretty sure there's nothing in Gibraltar space capable of ferrying them to the blockade, but we've got the transports to pick them up too... if you think they'll be needed."

Grieve locked eyes with Hastings and arched his brows in a rather amused fashion.

She got the hint.

"Right. Storming the planet. They'll be needed."

"Good."

There was a silent pause in the room, as officers exchanged glances.

"Alright then, we've got our forces assembled fairly well. Can we ship out this evening? Say... 23:00 hours?" Hastings exchanged inquisitive looks with the officers.

"Sure," Broadpaw tilted his head.

Hastings nodded, "Good. Now, we should get to our ships... and Graham needs to go buy flowers and start thinking about what to say when he gets to Gibraltar..."

The junior Manchester stood slowly, "I'm sure it'll be something about revenge against my fellow officers."

He smiled politely, clicked his boot heels together loudly, and marched from the office.

Laughter followed him out of the room.

CHAPTER 13

The addition of Vice Admiral Draco Maximane and Commodore Garvin Jardaw to the meeting of fleet commanders had occurred to Caine only after he'd sent all the summons out to his fellow Admirals. As such, the sloop that carried word to the two senior officers of the Earther Carrier service departed from and returned to the First Fleet later than the others.

The First Carrier Group was stationed in the open space between Krogg 'A' and 'B', serving as a mobile response force capable of supporting any fleet in difficulty. With a current total strength of thirty-three Carriers — and approximately 3,000 gunboats between them — Draco Maximane's unit was one of the most singularly potent forces on the front, especially when joined by the fifteen ships of Garvin Jardaw's escort group.

Jardaw, a polar bear, had originally been given eight 64-gun ships of the line to use as protection for the valuable Carriers, but in the past months Krogg attention towards them had increased sufficiently to warrant him an extra squadron of capital ships. Granted, the ships he'd been given were literally *ancient* — 58-gun ships of the line drawn from the mothball fleet — but they were quite adequate to the task of escorting the Carriers.

That was all very interesting, but Jardaw and Maximane were rather late, and as they hurried side by side through the corridors of *Orion*, their boots clicked in sync on the deck. The taller white bear ground his jaw nervously, taking a second to glance down at his senior and longtime compatriot, "We nearly there?"

Maximane nodded somberly — he'd been aboard *Orion* a handful of times, though this was Jardaw's first visit to the First Rate. Today the bear got the feeling that his visit wasn't destined to end with particularly pleasant news.

The First Carrier Group and had seen little action over the past six months, their last serious fight being against a Mothership flotilla at the Ganges Belt. They'd won convincingly and had since settled into a support role. Their present duty was to remain ready to help intercept breakouts, as they simply weren't fit for service on the close blockade stations. Stopping Krogg capital ships from jumping the hyper limit was a job for ships of the line — massive, under-gunned ships like *ENS Engadine* or the smaller *Monarch* or *Boadecia* would be a liability so close to the fight, their boats vulnerable to getting left behind if they were launched at such close quarters.

With nothing else to do, a few of the Carriers had gotten small assignments to ferry boats to squadrons within the regular fleet, but even that work had ended almost two months ago. Every ship of the line and big frigate in the Earther Navy now carried at least a *handful* of boats — a total of almost 6,000 in all, last time Maximane had checked.

That meant the fleet's 3,700 ships had only twice the striking power of his thirty-three carriers... still not a bad claim for the Carriers, on the whole.

And while the First Carrier Group stood by at the front, the Second Carrier Group was fitting out at Gibraltar, waiting on the last of the *Engadine*-class Carriers to arrive from Earth before shipping out to join Maximane in Krogg space. That force would provide another twenty-one Carriers, most of them *Engadines*. The big Carrier class had, in the brief scuffles they'd seen in the last number of months, proved to be noticeably superior to the other two classes of rebuilds being commissioned.

Engadines were purpose-built Carriers, with flight decks and launch doors planned and laid out from the beginning of construction. The *Boadecia*- and *Diadem*-class Carriers were converted from old ships of the line, and thus lacked some of the native strike abilities *Engadines* offered. When the Second Carrier Group arrived, the infusion of *Engadines* would multiply the strength of the Earther Carrier force by a significant margin...

"Here we are," Maximane slowed and gestured to the door that had appeared in the wall next to Jardaw. The polar bear nodded briefly and squared his shoulders to mask his discomfort. His job was ship command and now Battle Group command; he wasn't accustomed to tactical planning for entire fleets, but alas, today he had no option. He was needed, so he'd do his best.

Keying the door, the polar bear stood aside, and let the more senior lion lead the way into the darkened room.

Ursla, Sarah, Felix, and Caine looked up as the last two officers entered, nodding to the Carrier commanders in a friendly fashion, "Good day!"

Maximane and Jardaw returned the nods and sat, frowning at the holo plot that was glowing in the center of the table. It was showing the dispositions of the garrisons of both Krogg 'B' and 'C'.

Caine hadn't given the Carrier commanders the entire story when he'd called them both — a function of the late summons. Maximane and Jardaw had drawn a few ideas together in their minds during the cruise to *Orion*, but neither had been at all certain of what was going on.

Now it was quite clear.

"Well, let's get started," Caine said in an even tone.

Having thought more on Felix's suggestion, he was beginning to feel more confident about its chances of success. This really was the only way to secure his flanks; a gamble, certainly, but one with good odds and that could allow him to concentrate on the Queen's home system, all because his enemy had been too eager.

The Kroggs had let their proverbial second shoe drop rather carelessly. Their plague — presuming it was theirs — had caught the Larosians off guard and surprised the Earthers, but it hadn't stopped Narosh from getting here. And now their little bomb gambit had been handled badly enough to give the Allies another warning before the new weapon could be used decisively against the blockade.

It was up to the Allies to take advantage of the Krogg errors, and with that in mind Caine keyed the holo at the table's center up to full size. The tri-dimensional charts of 'B' and 'C' were expanded, the icons of Krogg ships marked in black against the light blue.

"We want to capture these two systems to secure our flanks," Caine said simply, and everyone at the table nodded. The dangers of the new Krogg weapon made the reasoning behind the strategy quite clear.

"The question then is *how*. We can't afford to incur a large number of casualties, and we need to keep one eye on Krogg 'A' in case they try to take advantage of our move. Thoughts?"

Felix leaned forward in his chair, tapping the console at his fingers to shrink the other two systems and enlarge the map of Krogg 'C', "I know how I'd take this one. I could do it with 500 ships... I *think*, but if I could get reinforced up to, say, 800 then I can pretty much guarantee it."

Caine arched his brow, "That easy?"

Felix shrugged, "They seem to have sent the runts to 'C'. I know you both–" he bobbed his head to Caine and Ursla "–have had a lot of trouble with your systems, but my Kroggs seem to be about as passive as Kroggs get. And they only have three *old* Motherships to back them up. Most of their strength is in old-style Dreadnoughts, and we're all fairly handy when it comes to dealing with *those*."

Caine nodded slowly, "Alright, so if I were to transfer a division of the First to your command, you think you could do it?"

Felix nodded, "Probably with less than five percent casualties. We'll come out of energy drive around their Motherships and work our way out. It won't take long."

Ursla and Caine exchanged brief accepting glances, then the First Lord smiled, "Alright, I'll assign my third division to you. That's easy enough. What about you, Andra?"

Taking her turn, Ursla tabbed the map of Krogg 'B' up to the holo, "Well, I'm not going to have as easy a time as Savanna over here."

Felix grinned and shrugged.

Ursla smiled and went on, "They have a *lot* of corvettes on the planet, and a strong ground installation. Planetary fortification is something 'C' lacks — and the fact that 'B' has it probably explains why the Kroggs have left the system garrison relatively light. If we get in close, they can launch and do quite a bit of harm to our flanks while the fleet comes in to chew on us. That said, there's no chance the system would stand if we went in as forcefully as we're planning to. I get the sense that the only reason they've garrisoned the place is to give us something else to cover."

"A fleet in being sitting on our flank," Maximane offered helpfully, and

Ursla nodded.

"Exactly. Now, to do this with low casualties, I'm probably going to need more punch to crack the planet... maybe double what I have in conventional ships and all of your Carriers, if you can spare them Draco."

The lion glanced sideways at Jardaw and nodded, "Good place to get back into the fight, I think."

"Good," Ursla smiled in reply, then glanced at Caine. "So the next question is how many regular ships. I'm going to need enough to completely overwhelm their mobile forces. If we can get ships of the line in large numbers and bring them into the center of the system under energy drive, they won't be able to react quickly enough, especially if we can neutralize their corvette advantage."

Caine nodded, "I'll join you then. We can split operational command if you don't mind too much..."

Ursla shrugged and grinned, "I suppose I can't be brilliant alone..."

Sarah cleared her throat.

Ursla blinked and her face sobered — she had actually managed to overlook the ArcGeneral's presence at the meeting, strangely enough.

Caine prudently responded to Sarah first, "Sorry Sarah, just a bit too eager. Thoughts?"

Sarah's expression had sunk from ambivalent through unimpressed and into offended while she'd sat listening to the discussion. Now she felt as though she was the annoying younger sibling, being paid lip service for all the effort she'd given to *show up*.

"What's the Fourth going to do during all of this?" she asked coldly.

Caine took a deep breath and glanced around the table at the Earthers, then turned his head back to Sarah, "Well, to get into the middle of the Krogg formations we're going to need energy drive, so I'm afraid that rules you out. And in terms of external fire support, didn't you expend your Type 98s?"

Sarah stared coldly and nodded, any hope she'd been nursing regarding her reputation among these Admirals fading instantly. They were going to cut her out of it *again*. No matter what they tried to tell her, they really didn't have faith in her.

Caine's instincts picked up the sudden frustration that swept over Sarah, and he quickly endeavored to counter it, "More importantly, Narosh has been fairly badly shaken. I don't know that he's ready to assume command here yet. If the Kroggs try a breakout to maul our flanks, it's going to be up to you to counter them. When I can get a hold of Narosh, I'm going to tell him he's at your disposal until we can rejoin the blockade."

As a conciliatory gesture it seemed rather pathetic to her. She got to do the same thing she'd done for months — sit and watch. Sarah was not happy at all, and Ursla and Felix immediately picked up on the increased tension brought on by Caine's words.

Maximane and Jardaw exchanged frowns — from their perspective Sarah's role was both important and logical. The attacking Earther fleets would be leaving their flanks in open space, and they'd also be removing a whole *fleet* from the present blockade… it was rather important to have a solid officer holding the gate shut at Krogg 'A'.

And since Sarah's ships didn't have energy drive or full magazines, it seemed clear enough that they couldn't go on the offense.

But Sarah wasn't seeing that logic.

Glancing at Jardaw with a skeptical expression, Maximane contained a sigh. The polar bear similarly restrained himself from showing any sign of confusion. He just didn't understand fleet commanders.

At least not human ones.

CHAPTER 14

Narosh's mind was foggy as he sat on the bridge of *Lycrotar*. His injuries from the explosion were relatively light, but the concussion he'd received when he hurtled head-first into the wall of his bridge was troublesome.

The buzzing sensation in his mind had not ceased, and it was beginning to agitate him.

Any indication yet of what caused the blast?

The question was not directed at any particular Larosian on *Lycrotar*'s bridge — those with pertinent information would report their findings. Narosh waited expectantly, keeping his growing agitation and the irritating buzz below the public layer of his mind. He wanted to know *exactly* what the Kroggs had assaulted him with — a countermeasure would have to be developed — and he wanted to know right now...

I have only preliminary information, Admiral-of-a-Fleet. I am afraid it is all we have been able to gather thus far.

Narosh suppressed any hint of displeasure — he knew his crew was working with as much effort as possible and they did not deserve his disdain because the facts were difficult to uncover.

What is it?

The Larosian officer who had replied approached his chair as he received the question.

I believe, sir, that aside from the Earther warheads, the explosions were caused and fueled by telepathic energy. A sizable amount of telepathic multi-dimensional interference was released, and the characteristics of the explosion suggest it was too far-reaching to be caused by any chemical or physical reactions known to our science — or to the science of the Earthers.

Narosh let a slow acceptance of the assessment trickle through his mind — making it visible to his subordinate. A telepathic explosion... something that had only been witnessed twice in the history of the Larosian people. In the last battle of the first great campaign — 600 years before, when the Kroggs had first invaded Larosian space — Praaxus himself, the Larosians' greatest leader, had brought about a telepathic explosion that had saved the then vulnerable and fledgling Larosian Fleet from Krogg annihilation.

Then, only a few years ago, the Son of Praaxus had done the very same — using his human mind to halt the Krogg's greatest invasion of Larosian space. Narosh himself had witnessed that event. He hadn't immediately recognized this use of the technique by the Kroggs because it had *felt* entirely different, and something within him was certain that this explosion was categorically dissimilar to the one the Son had unleashed.

The Kroggs had strong mental abilities among their elite Warlords and Telepaths, but had no such power whatsoever among their lower ranks. By contrast, every Larosian had a certain level of telepathic ability, though it was rare for this ability to reach a level approaching that of the Krogg elite. Indeed, Praaxus had been unique among Larosians with his massive reservoir of telepathic ability — enough to preserve his soul even after death, and to pass part of it through time to a human, the Son.

Recent scientific studies suggested that the Krogg Queen was a telepath of power yet unseen by any Larosian — a telepath with even more power than Praaxus himself.

If the suspicions were true, the Queen would be able to kill them all with a thought once they entered range. And the mental power of this Queen would explain a great deal — what entity could create and *deliver* a plague capable of destroying the Larosian infrastructure and also conceive of the more advanced strategies that had been employed by the Kroggs lately...

Before the ambush at Genesis, no Larosian would have credited the average Krogg with higher intelligence. The assumption had been that Kroggs acted mainly on base instincts and had only rudimentary adaptive abilities. Warlords and Telepaths, the leaders of the Kroggs in battle, were generally capable of command, but they had lacked the faculties to innovate.

Perhaps the Krogg Queen was taking steps to remedy that.

She was making smarter Kroggs... she had to be.

They were, after all, breeding special vessels to combat the Earthers. With that addition of another highly capable power to the war against them, the Kroggs would have to at least attempt to be more clever.

It made sense.

At this point, however, it seemed irrelevant. Past Larosian commanders might have been unwise in underestimating the Kroggs, but 600 years of war had given them little indication that the Kroggs were more than instinctive. Now Narosh would adapt — and he would do so with the help of these new allies.

The Earthers seem very well-equipped to understand the Krogg Queen's strategy.

Narosh forced himself to accept that notion — to accept the fact that revenge would be possible only because of the Earthers' ability to comprehend Krogg instinct.

And now this evidence, even if it was preliminary, had come to light... It appeared that any powerful Krogg Telepath could potentially cause a detonation such as the ones witnessed. The technique, as the Son had once explained it to Narosh, was simple. One's mind was like a massive storage cell for energy and could be consciously overloaded. Generally the size of the resulting blast depended on the individual telepath's power and control.

When energy was collected, then, it was as though the mind was armed, and when the choice was made to release that energy — or when the mind controlling the buildup was physically destroyed — the reaction was instantaneous and destructive.

But the explosion created by Praaxus had completely wiped out the Krogg Fleet, even from a long distance. And the Son's blast had been able to clear an entire solar system of enemy vessels...

The Kroggs, from fairly close range, and admittedly with a premature detonation, had done relatively little harm. Perhaps their Telepaths lacked the devastating mental strength of the Larosian saviors.

That was likely, in fact. It required a great deal of discipline to control energy fields with one's mind. That was not something Kroggs had ever been known for, but neither was intelligence, and the Kroggs were proving quite surprising today.

Narosh's mind buzzed louder at the thought.

It was possible that the Kroggs were capable of using far more mental energy than they were given credit for... but why in hyperspace?

The telepathic explosions caused by Praaxus and the Son had been in normal space, and they had been powerful enough to destroy everything being targeted...

Narosh quickly probed his bridge crew. *Theoretically what effect would hyperspace have on the expulsion of telepathic energy?*

The officer standing before Narosh paused for a moment.

In theory, one could harness the same relative amount of energy in hyperspace, sir. But in hyperspace, the effect of that amount of energy would be magnified on release. In the same way hyperspace accelerates our traveling speed as compared to normal space, it could magnify the power collected by a mind, and thus increase the yield of an explosion by roughly the same exponent that it increases our ship velocity.

Narosh silently digested the theory. They had attacked in hyperspace because the latent properties of that layer of space-time would magnify the effect of their telepathic explosion.

The buzzing in Narosh's head grew louder, as though in response to the thought that slipped into his mind. He looked to his officer: *Perhaps that is something we can use. If enough Larosians were to harness energy with their minds, we could cause a massive explosion — as grand as the one created by the Son. We could destroy everything in Krogg space, and never have to face the Queen in a direct battle.*

His mind buzzed louder still, and a vaguely familiar sense tweaked the fringes of his consciousness.

A twinge... a familiar twinge.

The sort of twinge that the presence of the Son had made him feel... was this the moment that the Son had once told him would come?

Considering the possibility of destroying Krogg space entirely, the officer paused and then offered what one could call a mental nod.

It is conceivable, sir. We would need the cooperation of hundreds... perhaps thousands *of our crews and soldiers, but it could succeed.*

It would cost them their lives, but even if it did, they could create a blast that would echo through all layers of space-time and eliminate the Kroggs once and for all.

The Kroggs would need to be confined to within one solar system. Even the Son was unable to spread the strength of his explosion over so great an area.

So they could defeat Krogg 'A' without difficulty... the Earthers could eliminate 'B' and 'C'. The Kroggs would be wiped from this place, once and for all.

Narosh's focus shifted instantly from consideration of merit to action — it felt as though something was driving him forward.

Perhaps it was the legacy of the Son...

The Admiral-of-a-Fleet gently cleared his throat, warming his vocal cords, "Send to First Lord Caine, I am coming to meet with him immediately. This is critical — I will not wait."

His mind buzzed.

CHAPTER 15

Setter Caine closed his eyes and leaned back in his chair as Ursla and Felix left him alone in *Orion's* briefing room. He tried to make sure his mind was focused but things just felt generally odd. It was a horribly nondescript way of explaining the feeling encompassing him, but it was all he could manage. Things felt odd, and despite his mental focus, some part of his instincts seemed to whisper to him that he was wrong-footed somehow...

And that's as specific as it gets. Great feeling...

Strangely enough, the intercom even sounded odd when it chirped, but at least he recognized it as Lab Forepaw's voice filled the room, "Setter, Narosh just jumped into his fighter. He's coming over to discuss an 'urgent matter'. I just gave him landing clearance."

Caine sighed. Something told him this 'urgent business' wouldn't do anything to allay his disturbed feeling.

"Can you get clarification on the 'urgent matter'?" he asked after a moment, and Forepaw paused on the other end of the line.

"I don't think so... no. Signal Officer is getting a bit of interference on Narosh's fighter's comm. Probably more fallout from the blast. If I get him should I tell him you'll meet him in the bay?"

Opening his eyes and delivering a second sigh, Caine shook his head to himself, "No, I'll come up to the bridge for now Lab, and then I'll meet him in a briefing room."

As the link closed Setter Caine stood and left the conference room, heading for *Orion's* command deck.

Ursla really wanted to make amends with Sarah. They'd been friends for as long as Earthers and humans had known each other, and some foolish spat rooted in Sarah's fear of inadequacy simply didn't seem excuse enough to drive a wedge between them — especially *now*.

But somehow Sarah's fast stride on shorter legs had carried her out of sight of the longer-legged and equally spry Earther bear. Now Ursla hustled through the corridors of *Orion* desperately trying to catch Sarah before she got to the landing bay.

"You might as well slow down."

Ursla was still moving fast when the suggestion came from behind, but she decided to accept the advice, turning to see Felix saunter up behind her.

She frowned at him, "How did you keep up?"

He shrugged, "Short cut. Doesn't matter anyway, if you catch her I'm willing to bet she'll be entirely inhospitable. She seems to be a lot like her brother when she's in a bad mood... or the other way round... whatever."

Ursla shrugged, "Doesn't mean I shouldn't try."

Felix tilted his head slightly and restrained a sigh, "Aye, but in time."

The pair started moving again at a slightly slower pace.

"Any idea what's eating at her? Surely she's not on the 'Earthers are too-good-to-be-true' kick," Felix asked quietly as they walked.

Ursla shrugged again. For the last twenty minutes of the meeting, Sarah had remained obstinately outside the discussion, acting as though she couldn't see the logic or significance of the assignment she had been given.

"Maybe she's worried that we don't trust her," Felix continued softly.

"I suppose... she may well think we're getting her to stay here and hold down the fort because we've lost confidence in her..."

Felix nodded slowly, "Because she left the gap for the Kroggs to get out through."

Ursla stopped, "We both know that was inevitable. The bomb ships would probably have gotten out anyway — so few ships trying to run the blockade, they could easily have slipped through..."

The cat held up a hand, "Easy there, Andra. *I* know that. We *all* know that, but Sarah mightn't know we know."

Closing her eyes, Ursla heaved a sigh, "Right."

Felix cocked an eyebrow and then followed as she continued on her way.

"You're too weary, Andra. You might not be able to help her right now," he advised quietly as they proceeded down the corridor.

Casting her gaze towards her feet, Ursla nodded in reply, "Yeah. Maybe. So you should do it."

Felix donned a sad smile, "Both Manchester siblings? I'm going to get a reputation as a therapist!"

Ursla chuckled, "No, you'll just enhance the reputation you've already got."

"Oh?" Felix glanced up as friend. "What reputation would that be?"

"The only one of us who's managed to keep a completely clear head."

With a chuckle, Felix looked back down the corridor, "Oh sure, set the bar low."

Sarah was seething and had a desire to crush something.

Grinding her jaw unhealthily was about as close as she could get, but it did help vent a bit of frustration. She'd have to go back to *Joseph Barron* and spend some time sparring with the marines.

Storming onto *Orion's* main flight deck, she ignored the salute of a Deck Chief as he approached her, and marched straight for her pinnace, walking right out in front of a gunboat that was coming through the atmospheric shield a ways down the bay.

The pilot of the boat saw the ArcGeneral and instantly hammered the emergency stop key. A signal beamed from the boat transmitter to *Orion's* landing bay computer, which automatically activated a grav-anchor net to lock the craft into a hover over the deck.

It had come to within a meter of hitting Sarah.

And, somehow *still* in her own little universe, she walked on, oblivious to the close call and the pinnace-sized boat hanging in the air near her.

The Fourth was getting sidelined. Again. Good fighters were being told to stay out of it because *she'd* made a mess of things. *Again*.

Nothing seemed to be working for her... and until something did, Caine wouldn't believe she could handle a fight. But fighting was her *job*.

The ramp to her pinnace was lowered and waiting. She had reached the base and started to climb up the grated incline when an abrupt alarm chimed across the already noisy flight deck to announce that another ship was coming in to land.

The boat that had been hovering to avoid hitting her now tried to kick its engines forward, but caught between two counter-pulling grav anchors it was locked to its spot in midair... right in the middle of the landing lane...

Sarah's eyes widened as she noticed the gunboat writhing against the grav anchors.

Why had it stopped *there* of all places?

"He received clearance from the bridge but now he's not responding... they think there might still be residual interference from that blast!" the Deck Chief roared at someone. "He's coming in *now*!"

The tech couldn't clearly make out what his deck commander was saying — the straining drive of the gunboat was too loud. But no Earther could miss the urgency that had suddenly taken over the landing bay.

Picking up on the tension the moment they stepped through the hatch, Ursla and Felix immediately rushed to the Deck Chief's side, "What's up?"

The Chief stabbed a finger at the boat, "Emergency stop to avoid hitting the ArcGeneral, and I've got the Larosian Admiral coming in! He got clearance to land about five minutes ago, but now the comms aren't getting through to him — Signal section is trying him again, but they say it's the interference from that blast..."

The pair of fleet Admirals locked widened eyes — the boat was a huge roadblock in a cramped bay...

Ursla watched as the tech the Deck Chief had been yelling at sprinted down the 500-meter length of the cavernous bay.

"They're trying to redirect him to the Secondary Bay but he's not receiving from the main transmitters... the fallout must be jamming his short-range comms!" the Deck Chief roared as the report came through his earpiece.

Ursla nodded then waved at the huge space doors, "Can you close those?"

The Chief pointed across the deck at the small kiosk that controlled all the functions of the bay... the tech came skidding to a halt at it. They were in time then–

"Look out! Incoming!"

Ursla and Felix whipped their heads around to the open space doors just as an angular, shining silver Larosian fighter came through at a reasonably high speed. Narosh...

The tech worked fast, keying the grav tractors off... the boat crew saw the fighter coming on their sensors, and the pilot immediately throttled his engines up to try to avoid the collision. But it was too late.

The nose of Narosh's fighter plowed into the rear of the gunboat, driving both down onto the deck — *hard*. Ursla grabbed the Deck Chief with one arm and Felix with the other, flinging them and herself through the hatch they'd just entered by.

Sarah sprinted the last few steps up the ramp and dove into the compartment of the pinnace, yelling a warning to the pilot. The tech at the control kiosk dove without a second to spare, a rather hefty bit of shrapnel clipping his ear as he dropped.

A split second later and he would have lost his head.

The other deck crew and techs dove to the ground behind whatever cover they could find, and then something exploded. It was either the engine of the boat or the missile chamber in the fighter's nose–

A massive fireball followed by a deafening thunder filled the air, and the section of *Orion's* hull under the two small craft was cracked by the horrendous explosion...

Atmosphere and fire erupted from the bottom of *Orion*, and on the bridge Labrador Forepaw's eyes widened as his ship bucked beneath his feet–

"Stabilize! Docking thrusters!" he turned immediately to the helm.

The Cruising Master was already trying to regain control, using the small thrusters that helped *Orion* maneuver over insignificant distances to keep the First Rate as steady as possible.

"Beat to quarters!" Forepaw turned to his First Lieutenant. "Prepare for damage control operations!"

The ship went to full alert, the rest of the squadron around it abruptly going to action stations as well.

"Signal 'Ship in distress, remain clear'," Forepaw continued, holding firmly to his chair arms as *Orion* pitched again.

"Bridge to flight deck, report!"

Felix had landed on his feet in the corridor — very grateful, at that moment, that he was descended from a cat. He hammered the intercom key on the wall nearby, "Felix here, Lab. We're just outside the flight deck. Large explosion... I'm betting a breach in the hull."

Ursla struggled to her feet and tried to key the hatch open. The computer refused her — a decompression was taking place.

"Lab," she roared, "seal this section with energy shields and let me into the deck!"

Forepaw immediately recognized Ursla's voice, and bobbed his head to the officer of the watch.

"I've got maintenance teams on the way, Andra," Forepaw answered, his tone already back to its usual, controlled pitch, "but our internal sensors on the deck are dead."

The bridge hatch parted and Caine stumbled in against the bucking hull, "Lab?"

The Captain turned in his chair, "Very bad crash on the deck. Narosh was coming aboard, but his comms weren't working properly because of the blast fallout... I'm guessing he hit something. Ursla and Felix are just outside..."

Caine dropped into his chair.

How did that happen...

"Andra's about to go in... there's got to be a breach in there, I don't know that we'll get regular teams there in time..."

Caine nodded, then pointed at the arm of Forepaw's chair, "Open comm?"

He nodded.

"Andra, be careful in there!" Caine's voice came over the rumble from the deck, just as Ursla grabbed hold of the wall against the bucking hull.

"Will do..." she roared back.

That had to be a hell of a breach to be throwing a massive First Rate like *Orion* around like this...

Ursla keyed the hatch. As it began to slide open, suction immediately grabbed her — the deck hadn't depressurized, so that hole was still bleeding atmosphere.

"Atmosphere shields?" Ursla roared to the Deck Chief as she braced herself against the rushing air. The Chief nodded and stabbed his hand at a bank of lockers a ways up the bay, near Sarah's pinnace.

The small Genesis craft had been knocked onto its side by the blast, it being significantly lighter than the still-upright Earther ships around it. Ursla caught sight of Sarah climbing out of the side hatch, raised her broad arms, and yelled as loudly as she could.

Sarah's ears were ringing as she climbed out the side of the tipped-over pinnace. She swung her legs over and dropped to the deck, landing on her knees. The shocking pain stabbed through the thick fog that was surrounding her mind as she saw Ursla point at the lockers near her small craft.

The suction was immense, but Sarah struggled to her feet and forced her way towards them. Using one of the landing feet of her pinnace as a brace, she pried the nearest one open. Shields.

Lucky she'd opened that locker first…

She grabbed two shields and swung herself away from the landing foot she'd propped herself up against… but lost her footing and sprawled on her face.

The suction grabbed her and pulled her towards the two twisted wrecks at the center of the deck.

The fire had been sucked out through the hull puncture, but now, as pieces of each ship were drawn into and *through* the meter-wide hole, the unsteady escape of atmosphere acted like an unstable thruster, pitching *Orion* at random.

Sarah knew her body wasn't nearly stiff enough to get stuck in that hole — she wouldn't have a chance of holding out against the amount of rushing air that would try to drive her out of the ship. So it was open space for her…

The tech who'd run to the kiosk steadied himself against the console and then managed to get a sprinting start as he dove into the stream of the suction. Hurtling over the deck from the direction of the Larosian fighter, he used his arm as a deflector and guided himself away from the gap.

His hand grabbed Sarah's arm and his legs wrapped around a pipe that twisted out of the fighter's wreckage.

Stunned, Sarah quickly came to her senses. No spacing for her then — if she managed to close the breach…

She discarded one of the shields she'd retrieved, watching it get sucked through the gap. The second one she pressed sideways against the deck. She'd have to use it like a patch for the cut. If she had the correct side facing down, the specially-tuned airtight field would go right across the floor and seal the breach.

Nodding to the tech, she opened the top flap of the shield's casing. The 'activate' button was right there…

The pipe that had been holding both Sarah and the tech firmly against the suction snapped, and the tech abruptly swung around, his legs spinning towards the breach. Just as he slid he used all his strength to heave against Sarah's arm, pushing her back against the suction for a split second.

Then, with nothing to grab hold of on the smooth deck, he locked eyes with Sarah a last time, nodding to her before he was pulled through the hole into the void.

Sarah almost couldn't press the activate button.

Ursla rushed to the wreckage as soon as the shield sealed the hole. Deck crew untangled themselves from whatever they'd held to resist the suction and came from all sides, one going to the kiosk to make sure the bay repressurized. Sarah lay on top of the shield box, still holding it in place forcefully with her body… just in case.

As Ursla crouched next to her, teams of medics stormed the bay.

The maimed boat's crew stumbled unsteadily out the side of its side hatch, one of the pilots missing an arm.

A more pressing worry for everyone present was Narosh, and Felix was heaving pieces of debris out of the way as he tried to find the cockpit of the demolished fighter. Ursla, the Deck Chief, and a dozen Earthers were at his side in seconds, prying things away...

The Deck Chief saw Narosh first, and pulled his unmoving body from the collapsing nose of the fighter. The alien's silver armor and flight helmet showed the impact marks of sharp shrapnel.

"We have something that can fly?" Ursla looked at the Chief, and he paused and nodded.

As the Chief rallied his crews to prep a pinnace, Ursla rushed to an intercom terminal, "I don't think Narosh is dead, but it looks like he's close. We're prepping a pinnace to get him back to *Lycrotar*. Warn them."

On the bridge, Forepaw and Caine exchanged glances.

CHAPTER 16

"We've got clearance, ma'am — can I go?"

Ursla looked up at the pilot of the pinnace and then quickly glanced back into the belly of the small craft. An Earther med team was strapping Narosh onto a gurney, scanners were humming and movements abrupt.

"We clear?" Ursla asked quickly, and the leading medic looked up and nodded.

"We're secure."

The pilot didn't need to hear the words a second time. The pinnace accelerated to nearly full speed, coming out of the field at the end of *Orion's* main bay at 95 pls.

For the past five minutes *Orion* had been maneuvering quickly to close the gap to *Lycrotar*, and the Warcruiser had been coming to meet the First Rate. Damage control teams were securing the hull breach on the First Rate's flight deck even now, using a specially designed hull patch to seal the rupture. The temporary measure would work until *Orion* could come to a stop and have the breach sealed by a compound alloy and secured from the outside with new plate armor.

Two squadrons of gunboats launched by some of *Orion's* nearer escorts came into a double-delta formation around the small craft, clearing the spaceway directly between the two flagships as the pinnace sped to its destination.

Two matching squadrons of Larosian fighters quickly swung into formation with them, the smaller silver, dagger-like Larosian vessels a stark contrast to the dull gray, broad-hulled Earther gunboats.

Ursla watched the impressive formations for just a second, deciding that escorts were not unwelcome during circumstances like this, then turned back to the main cabin, walking carefully down the passage from the cockpit to the space cleared for Narosh. The head medic was still methodically scanning the Larosian, her jaw set as she tried to figure out what she could do to help the Admiral-of-a-Fleet.

Hell, she wasn't even sure she knew what was wrong with him so trying to *help* might kill him. But based on what information the Larosians had provided after Genesis, she had to guess...

"I'm comparing with old records here, but it looks like his internal organs have been damaged. What I'd call his heart is beginning to fail... his other organs are producing a *lot* less energy than they should be."

Ursla took a deep breath and nodded, staring at the alien's blank, silver eyes. His gray skin was slowly fading to white…

"Stasis patches — give me all we have," the medic put her scanner on the pinnace deck and took a handful of large stasis patches from the outstretched hand of one of her orderlies.

"Is that wise?" Ursla asked quietly, not meaning to intrude, but wary of complications.

The medic looked up at Ursla, "I'm pretty sure he's dead otherwise. I've read the med journals we got from the Larosians last time around — they need the blood to flow too."

Ursla sighed and nodded. It was something, at least…

The patches were applied first to his neck, then as the med team pulled his armor off they laid several of the units on his chest. Hopefully, they'd freeze all bodily functions and buy the team time to get him to *Lycrotar*…

The medic picked up her hand scanner and scowled at the readings, "They're not working."

Ursla blinked, as did the rest of the team.

"Shouldn't you give them a minute to–"

The medic shook her head at Ursla, "Trust me, these things either work or *not*."

One of the team held up his scanner, "His heart's failing!"

The medic took a deep breath, "Alright. Give me fifty ccm of UDRC."

Nervous glances were exchanged between the medics, but their leader was insistent.

Ursla crouched down next to the medic now, "If his physiology didn't respond to stasis…"

"Stasis is bio-electric, this is genetic. I've got to do *something*, Admiral."

Ursla was tempted to doubt the medic, but her instincts urged her to listen to the young wolf.

"Alright," Ursla said with some reservation, and the medic injected the dose of UDRC into Narosh's neck.

Uniform DNA Regeneration Compound — UDRC — was an Earther product. Like the broad-spectrum antibios that were used to help humans combat the ravages of any alien illness, UDRC was useful in helping reverse serious injury in human patients. When employed in small doses, it utilized the active stem cells that were natural within Earthers to regenerate damaged cells without unnaturally over-growing other sections of the body.

Extended use, it appeared, might actually reverse the degradation of the human body and nearly double the human life span. That was something geneticists back on Earth were exploring, but right now, the existing compound was the only thing possibly standing between the Larosian fleet commander and an untimely death.

The stem cells were fast-acting and highly adaptive. Unlike the traditional human sorts, Earther stems had a genetically-engineered ability when it came to adjusting their own structure, and were present even in adults — working with other internal defenses to provide Earthers with their impressive immune systems. So far, no human had rejected them, even though they were coming from members of *three* separate species...

But UDRC had only been used a few dozen times so far.

Hopefully the clever little cells would prove compatible with Larosian physiology.

The medic glared pensively down at her scanner and waited to see whether she'd just killed Narosh...

"Deterioration is slowing... the cells are being absorbed and integrated..."

"I think his blood pressure is dropping," one of the other medics said quickly. "Heart rate is still dropping."

"His *immune system* is fighting the cells... he's trying to reject the UDRC. Prep fifty ccm of AB-114," the medic turned to Ursla. "The cells are starting to bond to the damaged organ, but he's rejecting. If I give him some of our antibios they should counter the immediate effects of his immune system... give the cells a chance to integrate."

Ursla nodded shortly, "Yes, do it."

The shot went in; more fast-acting Earther drugs locking into battle with powerful Larosian counterparts... the Earther cells were considered dangerous and foreign by Narosh's natural defenses, so his immune system — with an amount of control that bordered on strategy — began to target the fast-moving Earther antibodies.

Ursla watched on the medic's scanner as the two immune agents engaged each other in the alien's bloodstream... and she blinked in surprise as the Earther antibodies readily battered their adversaries. The UDRC cells were merging quickly with Narosh's damaged internal organs, and his heart rate was slowly beginning to stabilize and even climb.

"Our antibios have control," the lead medic said quietly. "His immune system isn't in any shape to fight them off."

Ursla frowned, "When he heals, won't that cause him complications — his immune system fighting our drug?"

The medic paused thoughtfully, sitting back slightly now that her patient had stabilized, "I *think* it should be alright. We engineered 114 to go dormant in the bloodstream once it's neutralized the nearest active opponent. If it remains that way, his immune system shouldn't target it."

Ursla cocked an eyebrow, "And if our cells find a bug to attack and go active?"

The medic sighed and shrugged, "We hope his immune system realizes that our drugs are helping. We designed all our antibios to be cooperative... and his immune system seemed to be pretty logical..."

"So in other words, we cross our fingers that his blood doesn't start boiling one day?"

The medic shrugged and nodded.

Ursla scratched the side of her head and slowly stood, "Alright. Good work... sorry, I don't think I caught your name."

"Celia Lazarus, ma'am," the medic offered her hand.

Ursla nodded, taking the hand, "Good work – whether his blood ends up a micro-sized war zone or not."

The wolf nodded with a sad smile, "Thank you."

Ursla turned back to the cockpit, "ETA?"

"*Lycrotar's* dead ahead and forty seconds away," the pilot said quickly. Ursla nodded and turned back to the med team.

"I probably won't be able to get through their low corridors too quickly, Celia. You and your team will have to move him out to their medics... and you should probably stick around in case there's a problem with what we did. You have samples of everything you gave him?"

The medic nodded.

"Alright. Touchdown in thirty. Brace yourselves."

Ursla sighed and turned to watch the silver hull of *Lycrotar* come up around the pinnace. No Earther had ever boarded a Larosian ship, she realized silently. Another first for her...

Worst possible circumstances for a first.

CHAPTER 17

The Deck Chief stood at stiff attention, Sarah leaned on the edge of the table, and Felix sat in a chair next to Draco Maximane and Garvin Jardaw. Captain Labrador Forepaw, despite being one of the most junior officers in the room — only the Deck Chief was of lower rank — eyed these four very, *very* angrily.

Orion was *his* ship, and diplomatic issues aside, the accident on the flight deck required certain investigation. Forepaw was not a vindictive sort of fellow — he genuinely liked his crew and his fellow officers — but he *loved* his ship.

Nobody — but *nobody* — caused something to go so grossly wrong on *Orion* without a damned good reason. Battle damage he understood, accidents related to overworked machinery he could accept... but *what* had caused two small craft to collide on his deck?

"I must take full responsibility, Captain. It was my deck. I couldn't clear it or stop the Admiral from trying to land, sir. My people cannot be blamed, and I believe one deck technician deserves special commendation for giving his life to correct my error..."

Forepaw froze, "I wasn't aware there'd been a fatality."

His voice was taut and his face strained. The seriousness of this accident had just gone up astronomically — he'd lost someone...

"Yes sir, Able Spacer deck hand Granger. He was pulled through the breach when he was helping ArcGeneral Manchester close it."

Forepaw stiffened, slowly lacing his hands behind his back, "That's Lewie Granger?"

The Chief nodded. *Orion* maintained a crew of some 3,000, but Forepaw still knew all of them. Not personally — that would be impossible — but he knew faces and at least one detail about every rating, petty officer, and officer on his ship. By human standards, such vast knowledge might seem impossible, and by Earther standards it was *very* difficult.

But that was why Labrador Forepaw was the Flag Captain for the First Lord, and he was among the most respected Earthers who had ever served. He cared about his crew even more than an average Earther Captain, and in the elite atmosphere of *Orion*, that created a strong ship-wide confidence and made *Orion* invincible in battle.

So he knew about Lewie Granger, a young tech from the African continent who had joined the Navy to help protect Earth three years before the Quest fleet had reached Sol, who had a wife and three cubs and who enjoyed rebuilding old human, wheeled motor vehicles.

"Once again," the Deck Chief asserted, "I must take responsibility, sir."

Forepaw eyed the grizzled Chief silently, trying to decide what to say.

"That's bullshit."

All eyes shifted abruptly to Sarah, who stepped silently away from the edge of the table, "I was the fool who walked out in front of a landing gunboat. The crew had to make an emergency stop–"

"I should have had someone at the overrides–"

Forepaw's raised hand stopped the Chief, "Easy there, Garth." The words were soft, soothing the veteran petty officer. Forepaw glanced down at Maximane, "Draco, on your Carriers, how many techs do you have on a deck of forty-five craft?"

The Vice Admiral frowned thoughtfully for a moment, "Forty-five boats would warrant ninety deck crew, at least. Two per boat, to make sure everything is covered."

Forepaw nodded and then met his Chief's eyes, "Now Garth, you're operating at least that many boats and pinnaces, and you've got a full crew of forty. You're making do with what we can allot you, there's no way you could have *everything* covered. Especially for a freak accident like this."

Forepaw's tone had become so smooth that Sarah almost let down her guard. She didn't know all that much about Forepaw — he was a good skipper, Caine's first choice… and this must be why.

The Chief swallowed silently, "I'm still sorry, sir."

Forepaw shook his head, "Nothing to apologize for. You were able to get a pinnace off your deck a minute after the breach was sealed, Garth. Damned good work, if you ask me. And we're going to need more from you — you've got to fix the hole our alien friend put in my ship with his fighter."

The Chief nodded evenly, "Yessir. It'll be good as new."

Forepaw nodded, letting some almost paternal pride surface on his face, "I'd expect no less from you, Chief. Now, I've got to talk fleet politics, so go take care of my ship!"

The Chief nodded, offered a crisp salute, then turned smartly and left the briefing room.

As the door closed Forepaw's face sobered and he turned to the rest of the occupants of the room. Jardaw was nodding appreciatively, "Well handled."

Forepaw bobbed his head to the side and came to sit on the edge of the table, "I could hardly blame him — he did his job quite well."

Felix's ear twitched, "I'll vouch for that. He pulled Narosh out."

"You can blame me," Sarah said with some finality.

She was still in shock. So the Earther who'd saved her life was named Lewie Granger. Hell of a name.

"Granger saved me from getting spaced, *after* I forced that boat to stop to avoid hitting me."

Her words were chilly and dejected — Felix wasn't sure whether it seemed more or less positive than the volleys she'd fired in their meeting earlier, though he was certain something had changed.

But Forepaw was already shaking his head, having calmed himself as he'd comforted his Deck Chief, "*I've* walked out in front of boats before, ArcGeneral. Stops that abrupt aren't necessarily appreciated by the pilots, but they happen. And usually it doesn't matter — if we've got a boat stuck in the grav tractors we wave off all incoming craft until the way is clear. Narosh's comms must not have been receiving clearly when we tried to warn him."

Listening to the smooth tone, Sarah tried to decide whether or not she was being handled by the kind-speaking Captain.

Forepaw continued, "We've all skippered our own ships. Strange things can happen, and all too often they can happen at the worst possible times. This is one of those occasions."

Everyone in the room nodded in understanding — it was, as Forepaw had said, a freak accident. A comedy of errors, from the placement of the deck hands in the bay to the chance appearance of the ArcGeneral at just the wrong second.

But it was the kind of accident that could fundamentally change the course of a war.

"Any word on how Narosh is doing?" Felix asked quietly, and Forepaw shook his head.

"The pinnace reached *Lycrotar* a few minutes ago, but communication still seems to be difficult out there, what with the telephathic cross-feeding."

"Did he seem badly hurt?" Maximane asked quietly, and Felix nodded.

"He wasn't looking good. If he's not dead, he's definitely out of action for some time. And he can't go home for treatment..."

A series of nods rounded the table, and Forepaw continued, "Well, you all might as well get back to your ships. I'll have *Orion* combat ready, but you'll need time to get back to yours before we strike. I'm sure Garth has your pinnaces on the line by now."

The Earthers rose and nodded, offering brief thanks before filing out. Sarah made to follow but stopped thoughtfully. She turned back to Forepaw as he sunk into one of the chairs at the briefing table and rubbed his eyes wearily.

"Captain?" she asked quietly.

Forepaw looked up, "Oh, sorry ArcGeneral, what can I do for you?"

Sarah opened her mouth but nothing came out. She frowned, sighed, and moved herself to the edge of the table again, "I don't know you all that well, Captain."

Forepaw shrugged, "I know you mainly by reputation, ma'am."

Sarah nodded, "Right... can we speak frankly then?"

A frown formed on Forepaw's brow, "Certainly. What about, exactly?"

"Me."

Forepaw leaned forward in his chair and rested his elbows on the table, lacing his hands before him, "As I say, ArcGeneral, I don't know you that well."

"That's why I'm asking. You've got no reason to spare my feelings... but you have a very nice way of saying things."

Forepaw smiled thoughtfully, "I try to be reasonable, if that's what you mean."

Sarah shrugged, then met Forepaw's eyes squarely, "What do people think of me, Captain?"

The frown on Forepaw's face deepened, "They respect you, ma'am."

Sarah narrowed her eyes, "Even now? Even after I went out to get Pat with the Freetowners? And after I let the Kroggs out? And then today?"

Forepaw cocked an eyebrow, suddenly beginning to discern the deeper meaning behind the ArcGeneral's question.

"Well, ma'am, I'm not privy to the thoughts of everyone in the Allied service, but I can tell you that everyone I know has a deep respect for you."

She looked as though that didn't quite nail it down for her, so he slowly came to his feet, his mind already shifting gears. He hadn't really noticed the ArcGeneral's undertone before, but as he allowed his instincts to recall and examine her earlier words, he recognized a definite doubt.

He'd have to deal with her as reassuringly as he had the Deck Chief.

"People like myself, Artie Tigar from *Agamemnon*, Varnia Broadpaw on *Tonnant*... even the First Lord... we don't think of you any differently than we think of Admiral Ursla or Admiral Felix."

Sarah cocked an eyebrow, "Funny how I haven't seen any action since Gibraltar, then."

Forepaw rounded the briefing table and leaned against it, folding his arms and looking quietly at Sarah, "Ma'am, there hasn't been all that much action to go around since Gibraltar. I've been in it with Setter, but he's just been handling these raids himself because he's been determined to absorb all the punishment for the fleet. He's still secretly blaming himself for the losses there, so he's essentially trying to carry the weight of the entire war all on his own, not that I'd tell him that openly. But with that being his goal, he's been leaving the people he trusts to watch his flank, and that means you."

Bringing the First Lord's mental state into a discussion was not a tactic Forepaw often indulged in, but with one of the commanders of the inner circle it seemed prudent — and important — enough.

"You mean *he's* being a martyr?"

Forepaw donned a shallow frown, "Martyr might be too strong a word, but it's close. Look, you're worried about a renegade mission that ended up destroying a Krogg base on our flank eight months ago, and a maneuver yesterday to save one of our sloops that opened a gap that would have already been there, and a crash today that could have happened any time, anywhere."

Sarah nodded slowly.

"He's had a body count in the *millions* run up on his list. He feels like he nearly lost the war at Gibraltar, and he's tired of fighting. And now he has to deal with the Larosians. ArcGeneral, he's been pretty badly mauled too. I don't know if he even realizes that yet, but he was so shocked by Gibraltar he's become protective of all the people of the Alliance. He's trying to absorb as much of the punishment for them as he can. As far as he's concerned, that's his job — he's trying to minimize the pain inflicted on his allies... and his friends. People like you."

The words stunned Sarah, and Forepaw chose to let her digest them slowly.

Finally, she eyed him, "He's trying to protect us?"

"As best he can."

"But... we can all help..."

"You all are helping, just by staying in the fight. But he's not in a state of mind where he can lose one of you to reckless action. He's got to work this one through on his own, and hopefully before he loses someone," Forepaw's quiet words drew a slow nod from Sarah.

Perhaps her mind had finally been shaken from its grim entrenchments by watching a young Earther die for her... perhaps Lab's words were connecting on a deeper level... Probably both factors were playing a part.

Because she actually believed and understood what the Captain was saying to her.

Which meant...

"And I don't have anything to prove?"

Forepaw tilted his head, "That's for you to decide. But I'll tell you that war doesn't lend itself to perfection. We do what we can, the best we can. Trust me, your actions have been no less risky than many others the Allies have taken in this war, but you've made them all work."

"But I... uhm... I..."

Sarah had seemingly lost the ability to speak coherently — which came as no small surprise to her. Lab Forepaw's eyes met hers, and his hand rested briefly on her shoulder.

"You don't need to worry about proving anything, you need to keep doing the job you're doing because Setter needs you, we *all* need you, to be with us in this. That's how it is."

Sarah blinked a couple of times at the wise, quietly spoken words. Forepaw withdrew his hand and folded his arms again, his ear twitching as he contained a sigh.

After a moment Sarah looked back to Labrador Forepaw with a slim smile, "Are all you Earthers this... I don't know... wise?"

Forepaw chuckled, "Best not to answer that, I think."

Sarah smiled, "And modest too. Captain Forepaw, you've been a great help."

Cocking an eyebrow, Forepaw matched her smile.

"You'll make a great First Lord one day."

Forepaw shrugged again, "If it's in the cards."

Sarah tilted her head, "Yes, well it seems to me that you might be dealing the hands."

Forepaw shook his head and chuckled again, "Let's not venture down the philosophical road today, ArcGeneral. I must..." he paused as his mind turned back to more pressing matters, "I must write a message for Lewie's wife."

Sarah's smile faded as she thought again of the young deck hand, "I'd like to include a message of my own, if you'd think it appropriate, Captain."

"Call me Lab, ArcGeneral, and I think it'd be appreciated. Lewie had three cubs, all toddlers, so something for them might help as well."

Sarah nodded slowly, part of her mind wondering how Lab kept such information in his brain, the rest questioning why an Earther with a family would save her as Lewie had.

"He was an Earther, ArcGeneral. You don't need to try to tell them why he made the sacrifice he made, just tell them what happened. They don't need us to add meaning; they'll know he believed he was giving his life for something important."

Sarah's eyes tracked back to Lab's.

"Call me Sarah, Lab," she offered weakly in reply.

And she realized too that Lewie Granger, an average Earther deck hand, had believed in her, died for her.

It was a sharp and personal revelation and it began to tug at her mind. She couldn't let this fellow's life have been lost in vain.

"I'll write something," she said quietly after another long pause, and then with a last nod to Lab, she slowly turned and walked from the room.

Labrador Forepaw spun a nearby chair towards him, and slid wearily into it.

Orion went on working around him.

CHAPTER 18

Ursla waited silently, sitting on the floor of *Lycrotar's* sick berth.

Celia Lazarus was discussing medical matters with Larosian doctors while Narosh lay on a silver table surrounded by instruments and his own surgeons. Thus far, no one had complained about the Earther intervention on Narosh's behalf... hopefully it would stay that way.

The Larosian sick berth was a relatively small room — at least by Earther standards — holding only a handful of beds and a limited array of equipment. It seemed that the Larosians weren't well accustomed to treating wounded; perhaps many Larosians chose death first.

Such a sentiment could be noble, Ursla supposed, but wouldn't be very sensible from an Earther point of view. You died if it was necessary or unavoidable, but you didn't turn down treatment if it was available and wouldn't disadvantage someone else...

But these were Larosians, their culture was their own — and they did seem appreciative of the Earthers' exertions to keep Narosh alive. They were continuing that effort, using their own tools to begin the slow repair of Narosh's injuries.

The Earther drugs and compounds were helping, according to what Ursla had overheard so far, and the chances for Narosh's survival were now quite good. But it would take at least a month for him to recover fully.

The Larosian Fleet would be denied its leader for that long... and all because of a strange accident.

Ursla slowly rubbed her head as she sat, both out of exhaustion and to massage away the bruises she'd gotten as she'd followed Narosh's gurney quickly through *Lycrotar's* silver hull. The corridors were oval-shaped, and only two and a half meters high at the top of their arc. She'd hit her head enough times to give herself a sizable headache.

A Larosian suddenly appeared in front of her, and she attempted to straighten against the curved wall. The Larosian stared at her with what could easily have been disapproval... or thanks...

Captain-of-the-Fleet Natosh was the commanding officer of *Lycrotar*, and Narosh's Flag Captain, to borrow an Earther term. And though the Earthers might not recognize it, he was beside himself with shock.

Accidents such as this simply did not occur within the Larosian Fleet — Larosians were so well-tuned to each other telepathically that such mistakes were not made. And yet the only remaining great Larosian leader was now fighting for his life filled with alien medicine because of an *accident*.

That was hardly the worst of it. The continuing fallout from the Krogg telepathic explosion was still interfering with telepathic communications. Most of the fleet did not even *know* its leader was near death.

Atop the chaos of past weeks, this incident was testing Natosh's control. He stared now at the Earther, remembering his protocol… or most of it.

Admiral, I am Captain Natosh. My apologies for not meeting you in the landing bay… I did not receive word of the emergency in time to reach the chamber.

The Earther did not answer him. Natosh had never met an Earther before — perhaps she was so much in shock that she was unable to respond. That seemed unlikely though — she was such a large and venerable a creature, and one bearing quite a sense of assurance…

Ursla kept looking at the Larosian, frowning at him after a moment. Was he just going to glare at her?

Admiral Ursla? He repeated his query.

She isn't telepathic, sir.

Natosh paused briefly as one of the nearby doctors reminded him of that Earther characteristic. He had, of course, known all along, but given the circumstances had simply forgotten. Quickly adjusting his mindset, he cleared his throat with some discomfort. Larosians were slowly beginning to evolve beyond the need for vocal cords — only very rarely would an average Larosian use them for communication.

Cautiously, Natosh began, "Admiral Ursla."

Ursla nodded, "That's me."

"I am Cap-tain Natosh of *Lycrotar*. My apologies for not meeting you in the bay, but the Krogg telepathic blast has greatly disrupted our communications."

As he spoke, he attempted to reproduce the normal rhythm of his thoughts in the syllables of his words, and he was reasonably successful.

"It's good to meet you, and don't worry. Believe me, niceties are the last thing we need to worry about…" Ursla nodded to the Captain. "What word of Admiral Narosh?"

Natosh quickly scanned the mind of the head doctor for information, "He will require an extended period of regeneration treatment."

Ursla looked from the Captain to the Larosian doctors, "He'll live, then?" "Yes."

A wash of relief passed through Ursla — at least they hadn't been responsible for the death of the commander-in-chief of their ally's fleet.

"I must thank you for your rapid and thoughtful response to Admiral-of-a-Fleet Narosh's injuries," Natosh said slowly.

Ursla blinked and arched her brow, "It was our responsibility — he went down on our deck."

"As I understand it, the crash was an accident borne of unexpected and un-predictable circumstances beyond the control of anyone."

Ursla shrugged, "That's true. Still, he crashed on our deck."

Natosh appreciated the Earther's acceptance of responsibility, though he hardly wished to condemn her or her people for an accident. However, to press that point now would not be prudent — verbal discussion was by no means a favored skill of his, and he did not wish to somehow offend Ursla because of his lack of experience in talking. Indeed, he had more pressing concerns to deal with...

"I must return to my duty now."

Natosh clearly wasn't well-versed in standard conversational courtesies, Ursla decided as he turned away and moved to interact with the doctors. He had likely come down to see his Admiral and hadn't expected to have to deal with the Earthers.

The Earther medical team began packing their kits, and Celia Lazarus came over from Narosh's operating table to stand before Ursla, "It looks like we made the right call when we dosed him."

Ursla nodded, "I'd gathered as much. You're done here?"

The medic nodded, "Not much more we can do. They have samples of UDRC and AB-114, and they've got facilities designed for him. I'm pretty sure they estimated twenty-five days of regeneration treatment and rehab, but they were making references in a different set of time units, so I can't be absolutely certain."

"Alright," Ursla slowly rocked herself to her feet, crouching uncomfortably in the berth. One of the Stealth Guardsmen who'd arrived to escort them to and from their pinnace indicated the exit and guided them out.

Natosh watched them go, then turned to the head doctor. *His injuries are substantial?*

They will require long-term treatment. Under normal circumstances, he would be dead. The Earther medicines seem to have reversed some of the damage done by the crash. I cannot determine whether they will be rejected in the long-term, but for the time being they are providing us with time to reconstruct his fulma-centuriosis and gangis-chaka.

Natosh nodded slowly. *These medicines are potent then?*

Indeed. I cannot help but wonder whether they would be effective against the plague. We should store these samples in case we have the opportunity to return home with them.

The thought appealed to Natosh. *Keep what you need to treat the Admiral-of-a-Fleet. I will transfer the remainder to a hospital ship so they may remain safe until this fleet returns home.*

Perhaps the large, strange Earthers could help save the Larosian species...

Ursla watched *Lycrotar* vanish behind the pinnace and then noted the gunboat squadrons dropping into a protective formation outside the windows. There was no external threat to her craft, so their presence was purely precautionary... But it was comforting nonetheless, and Ursla wasn't about to turn away comfort at a time like this.

Based on the words of Captain Natosh, it didn't seem they were blaming the Earthers for this mishap. They could certainly hold the Earthers responsible if they wanted to, but then Ursla supposed she could just as easily blame Narosh for the crash...

It seemed, however, that both races had the sense not to point fingers. No doubt there would be changes in communications frequencies, but there wouldn't be an abrupt collapse of an alliance because of an accident...

When something like this happened, such a fear was probably quite natural. But everyone involved here seemed to possess a decent amount of perspective.

Rubbing her head again, Ursla leaned thoughtfully back in her chair.

CHAPTER 19

Admiral-of-a-Division Novash had been the first Larosian ever to meet an Earther — Ursla had saved him from the Krogg ambush at Genesis. After that incident, he'd come to hold a great appreciation for the Earthers, and he considered a number of them to be professional friends. In saving the Fourth Larosian Fleet-of-War from the ambush laid by the Kroggs at Genesis, he had worked closely with members of Admiral Ursla's command, and as such he felt most strongly attached to them. The opportunity to finish this war with them seemed somehow... *agreeable*.

The Earthers had proved their skill to Novash, even though other Larosians remained moderately skeptical. Despite the fact that they could not be read telepathically, Novash had long ago decided that the Earthers could be relied upon...

Novash had been meditating on the combination of Earthers and Larosians against Kroggs when scattered thoughts began breaking through the prevailing haze of the fallout of those explosions.

They were desperate thoughts, wholly uncharacteristic of Larosians... and they vaguely suggested... an incident... an *accident*.

With such ambiguous warnings filling his mind, Novash had moved rapidly from his quarters to the bridge of his Warcruiser, *Shanavorus*. It was there that more particular information had begun to reach him, though the reports seemed to come only in brief thought bursts... the Earther flagship appeared to be damaged... a small craft supported by Earther fighters was making its way to *Lycrotar*... *Lycrotar* was scrambling its fighters.

Sensor data seemed to be coming in clearly, but no phrased thoughts were yet crossing the din of the explosion's fallout. Earther energy comms were stabbing through the haze with impunity, but the sharing of thoughts remained quite difficult...

Focusing on the sensor data, Novash first tried to extrapolate... and the conclusion was absurd. Upon first sight, it seemed as though a battle had broken out between the Earther flagship and *Lycrotar* — wings of fighters converging on a formation of gunboats in open space.

But that was dismissed instantly with a brief report that *Lycrotar* was preparing to receive a critically injured officer. This was a surprise to the Admiral-of-a-Division — while the fleet was taking up its blockade station, orders had been given for all Larosians to stay within their ships. As second in command of the Fleet, he had given that order himself.

But as Novash continued now to reflect on the report, and to listen carefully for further, clearer telepathic reports, thoughts more menacing than confusing began to fill his mind. What was going on?

It was maddening to Novash — as second in command, he was responsible for the internal workings of the fleet. In time of war, the commander-in-chief had to be able to rely on the readiness of his fleet, but the fallout was damning him to ignorance. This new Krogg weapon was potent indeed; perhaps in future the fleet should adopt a backup communications network of Earther energy comms...

A signal is coming now, Admiral-of-a-Division.

Novash sat up slightly straighter in his chair and focused his mind. *I shall take it directly.*

You will not be able to, sir. The message comes from Orion.

Novash halted his mental communication preparations. That was entirely unexpected — generally, Caine directed his business with the Larosian Fleet to Narosh, so why would he turn now to the second in command?

As Caine's face appeared on the screen, Novash mimicked an Earther smile as best he could... though he imagined it wasn't all that successful. Caine's face, however, was clearly grim.

"Admiral Novash," Caine bobbed his head shortly.

Quickly clearing his throat, Novash replied, "Yes, First Lord Caine. Can I be of service?"

Clearly distraught, Caine gathered himself and took a deep breath, "Do you have an update on Narosh's condition? I haven't been able to contact *Lycrotar.*"

The entire bridge crew of *Shanavorus* halted. As soon as the question was asked pieces began falling into place, and the crew belowdecks almost immediately detected the shock on the bridge and began to telepathically read the conclusions being drawn.

Their leader had fallen?

Novash telepathically ordered one of his subordinates to query *Lycrotar*, then forced his vocal cords to work against the shock, "We were not aware of any 'condition', Lord Caine. Our normal communications are still being interrupted by the fallout from the blast..."

Caine's brow furrowed, "Oh."

Larosians were not the sort of beings usually prone to emotional reactions, they thought and acted logically... but Novash distinctly felt as though he was beginning to panic.

"The fleet — the *Larosian* Fleet — must know, First Lord Caine, and your transmitters are the only ones operative in this din. Please broadcast that information immediately... and tell me what happened..." Novash managed to maintain command of his tone, and Caine nodded off screen to his Signal Officer.

Novash's mind detected the shift of the Earther signal to general broadcast, and then Caine looked back to the Admiral-of-a-Division, "We had a ship stuck on the flight deck when Admiral Narosh attempted to come in. He wasn't receiving our warning signals and we couldn't move the boat in time. He crashed into the back of it, wrecked his fighter pretty badly."

Novash paused, mentally observing the bridge officers as they absorbed the facts.

"Ursla moved him immediately to *Lycrotar*, but I haven't heard from her yet. Our medics were suggesting that his injuries were life-threatening."

Novash stiffened. Larosians were generally quite resilient — capable of healing most wounds with a minimum of outside influence — so the impact must have been quite forceful if it had nearly killed the Admiral-of-a-Fleet.

"You're second in command of the fleet, aren't you Novash?"

The Larosian offered a silent nod, leaving many of those receiving the transmission — those not acquainted with Earther mannerisms — confused as to his reply. Novash did not concern himself with their lack of understanding... something was coming through from *Lycrotar*.

This is Captain Natosh, we are receiving the transmission from Orion. *May I interject?*

Novash held up a quick hand to pause Caine's explanation, "I am receiving something, sir. A moment please..."

Yes, Captain, what is the status of Narosh?

Natosh seemed to pause briefly, waiting until *Lycrotar* properly integrated his mental transmission into the signal from *Orion*. The entire Larosian Fleet would hear this news, albeit through the comm of the Earther flagship.

He lives, thanks mainly to the medical substances provided him by the Earthers on his flight. He will recover, but it will take at least a long cycle.

That is good news. Novash contained his relief in the lower layers of his thought.

Yes, sir. Are you to assume command during his recovery?

Novash paused briefly, contemplating the abrupt question and its ramifications. Yes, he would have to.

Yes, until Narosh is capable of retaking command.

Very good, sir.

Natosh removed his thoughts from the communication link to *Orion*, and Novash turned his attention back to Caine.

"You heard that report, Lord Caine?"

Caine let the relief slide onto his face, "Indeed, and we're all certainly glad to hear it. What sort of time period is a 'long cycle'?"

"As I understand it, that equates to about four of your standard weeks..." Novash checked his mental math a second time, "or *three and one half*. He benefited from the compounds your people provided him on the pinnace."

Caine cocked an eyebrow, "So they injected him without complication?"

Novash nodded again, "It seems so."

Caine's expression neutralized, "That's good news, to be sure. If his case is typical, it could mean we might be able provide you with drugs to help combat your plague."

Novash again offered a slow nod, but he remained preoccupied.

"We will have to make that determination later, Lord Caine... but it is certainly a promising possibility. In any case, I'll be assuming command of our forces in Admiral-of-a-Fleet Narosh's absence."

Caine nodded, "I'd thought as much. We'll have a few things to discuss in a little while, but for now I just wanted to make sure Narosh was stable."

Novash offered a traditional bow-nod, "He is, thank you Lord Caine."

"Good. I'll signal you later to set up a meeting... I'm afraid I may be putting a bit of strain on you rather immediately."

Novash paused, "You sound as though you have a plan."

Caine's ear twitched, "Well, yes. You need to make sure your command structure is intact before I discuss it with you, though."

Novash tilted his head and attempted to furrow his brow, "It will not take long to organize this structure, as it will only be provisional. My thanks for your actions, Lord Caine."

Caine snorted a laugh, "My thanks for not declaring war on us, Admiral Novash."

Novash's face blanked, "I'm sorry, I don't follow."

Caine shook his head, "Just a shadow from human history. This sort of accident could have started a war in other times, even between allies."

Novash's mouth opened in surprise, "I always thought the humans were somewhat... quick to act."

"Not all of them, but some certainly," Caine said softly. "Anyway, I've got a hole in the bottom of my ship that needs patching, so I'll let you go."

Novash turned his head slightly to the side and bow-nodded, "I will look forward to our next contact."

Caine nodded, and the screen blanked.

CHAPTER 20

Graham stood and stared silently at his chair.

The air was heavy, the bridge crew apprehensive... Everything rested on this one single act.

Graham narrowed his eyes and edged over to the front of the chair. A pensive hand cautiously touched one arm, then slowly, deliberately, he turned and lowered himself into the seat.

Everyone held their breath.

Shifting himself back into the seat, Graham steepled his fingers and leaned back.

"Hmm..."

Everyone on the bridge stared at him.

He set his jaw and shook the chair a bit...

"Just as you all promised," he said in low tones.

Many pairs of eyes stared at Graham's face, trying to figure out what he meant...

"Comfortable!"

A single cryptic word that meant victory for the crew...

Graham grinned, "Donuts for all, somebody go get the donuts!"

There was a cheer on the bridge deck as Graham swung his chair around to face the Sensor Officer to his left, "Has the Fifth begun to depart yet?"

The ArcEnsign stopped cheering immediately and dropped into her own seat, "The first squadrons are going now, sir."

Across the bridge, a console chirped, and the Comm Chief stopped cheering as well, "Call from ArcGeneral Hastings."

"Put it on, by all means. Somebody getting the donuts yet?"

There was a fresh surge of cheering as Liz Hastings appeared on the main bridge monitor of *Pope Edgar Fitzpatrick*, Graham's new flagship.

The ArcGeneral, smiling as the channel opened, raised a questioning eyebrow, "Happy ship, Graham?"

The junior Manchester shrugged, "I made a bet with the bridge crew that my chair here wouldn't be as comfortable as the one in my office. They won."

Hastings' eyebrows went up, "Strange way to build morale, I suppose."

"Now, now, it's not just about them. It's about donuts for me too..." Graham looked back over his shoulder, "Where are they anyway?"

"Coming, sir," someone called.

"Good show," Graham turned back to Hastings. "Well, it worked better than a sappy speech about how I'm new at this but I'll give it my damnedest."

Hastings frowned disapprovingly, "I just gave that speech."

As donuts appeared on the bridge and another cheer broke out, Graham shrugged, "Donuts work better."

"Well, mister innovation, I'll keep that in mind. Meantime, I'm moving out with my squadron. Bill will move in the vanguard behind me, and your battlewagons will bring up the rear."

Graham nodded, taking a chocolate donut off a tray that was coming around and holding it up towards the monitor, "Ladies and gentlemen, a toast to the ArcGeneral!"

The bridge crew held their hastily-distributed donuts towards the monitor, twitched them appropriately, and then took large bites.

"See you at Gibraltar, Liz!" Graham grinned, taking a massive bite.

Hastings chuckled and nodded, "Yeah. Don't get fat on the way, eh?"

Graham stuffed more of the donut into his mouth and looked innocently at the screen, "Mho? Amae?"

Hastings blanked the screen and Graham, still chewing, turned to *Fitzpatrick's* ArcColonel, "Your drives warming up?"

The woman nodded between bites, "We're just waiting in line."

Graham took another donut off a tray, "Splendid. Comm, send to the division that we're in back. Order double column by squadrons, Superdreadnoughts ahead and Dreadnoughts to the extreme rear."

The Comm Chief nodded and began keying the orders into his console, holding his donut in his teeth.

For some reason Graham felt incredibly silly, but he'd been in that sort of mood since the meeting earlier that day. And when you asked the crew of a Superdreadnought to accept a new flag officer *and* to ship out the same night — at 23:00 hours, no less — you needed a sturdy icebreaker.

Graham knew he had a bit of a reputation as a Manchester. Generally, he and his sister were considered steady, serious, duty-bound officers of high quality.

Well, they were... but that didn't mean he couldn't have a bit of fun.

As the crew began to settle down at their posts — some with a stack of donuts sitting precariously next to them — Graham let his smile grow. Maybe he could handle this whole division-command thing after all.

Or, more precisely, maybe it wouldn't completely overwhelm him.

Andros Grieve was hungry. Varnon probably wouldn't let him eat on the bridge though, and since he'd been invited to *Algenon's* command deck to watch the launch of the fleet, he didn't think it'd be appropriate for him to run off to a kitchen.

Grieve wasn't a vacuum-blooded spacer — he tended to like his battles on solid ground and his weapons small enough to carry. But he was also Broadpaw's friend, and the senior ground officer with the Fifth and Sixth Fleets, so his witnessing their departure wasn't a bad idea.

He stood next to the main battle plot, just ahead of Broadpaw's command chair. The wolf Admiral was giving orders to the Signal Officer, establishing formations and looking after some of the more mundane details of his ship's operation.

Broadpaw had been behind the front for some months now, and he had to admit he was looking forward to getting back into the swing of things. His fleet was half the size of any of the Earther formations on the blockade, but he had essentially assembled it himself. He'd known most of the officers commanding his ships before they'd been transferred in, and he'd come to know the rest in their days rallying at Genesis.

He was quite confident in their abilities. And he knew he'd need to be.

While they'd be joining the fleet too late to deal with the smaller two Krogg systems, Broadpaw was well aware of the composition of the defenses at Krogg 'A'. Under the *best* of circumstances, it was going to be a long and bloody fight. One that would require the Fifth to operate with the same efficiency as the battle-hardened First.

Well, Varnon Broadpaw believed they could operate on that level.

Broadpaw settled himself down in his chair after giving the last of the orders, and eyed Grieve with a frown, "Awfully quiet there, Andros."

Grieve turned from the main tank and shrugged, "Lots of little blinking lights."

Varnon grinned, "I suppose you could look at it like that..."

He hit a few keys on his chair arm, and the main battle plot suddenly glowed and expanded, going to enhanced video. The entire Fifth Fleet was translating into energy drive in waves, and the visual effect was stunning... a cascade of energy was slowly working its way back through the ranks of Earther vessels, making them vanish into tight energy spheres before leaping away.

"Better?"

Grieve smiled slightly at the spectacle and shrugged, "It's nice."

Broadpaw couldn't help but chuckle, and Grieve turned away from the holo display, thinking about his stomach.

Algenon accelerated into energy drive.

CHAPTER 21

Silence was something that Sarah was very accustomed to, and by this point in her relatively young life, she was already quite comfortable with it.

Usually.

But her darkened cabin on *Joseph Barron* didn't offer the same comfort it had before she'd gone to *Orion* for the commanders' meeting. She was much too unsure of just who she was turning into... and she kept seeing Lewie Granger getting sucked through the hole in the flight deck.

Sarah knew how to forget losses — death was part of her business, and so she needed to be able to cope with it. In spite of that necessity, however, Spacer Granger remained firmly locked in her psyche.

It seemed cold to think of him as just a figment of her mind, but she could only reflect on the experience of a few hours earlier in terms of logic. She'd decided long ago that she wasn't allowing her emotions to come into play until the campaign was over — and logically, someone dying for her wasn't that unthinkable...

Then Forepaw had convinced her she had nothing to prove. She wasn't sure whether that assertion was going to stick or not — she was already having trouble accepting that Caine was trying to carry so much weight on his own. It was clear enough to her, after all, that the entire Alliance was ready to help shoulder the burden he'd taken on, and that he was no more to blame for their hardships than anyone else.

But that was for him to deal with. What about *her*?

It was easy for Captain Forepaw to say she was respected, but based on the way he'd comforted the Deck Chief, it seemed eminently possible that he was just sparing her feelings. And even if he wasn't, how could he know with absolute certainty that the rest of the Earthers agreed with him?

Sure, the Earthers tended to be fairly uniform in their opinions — not out of forced conformity but due to a seemingly inescapable mutual wisdom and worldview — so there was a chance he was right.

But it couldn't be that easy. She'd abandoned her post in Gibraltar, and that was totally out of character for her. How could she be trusted?

I was convinced of it only an hour ago, but now I doubt that respect exists. What does that say?

The questions were starting to pile up in Sarah's mind, and despite repeated attempts, she couldn't set them aside. Her inability to focus was getting frustrating...

● ● ●

Pat was in a less-than-stellar mood.

His Posse was nearly out of warheads, his new ship wasn't quite the same as *Harbinger Bishop*, he hadn't been in a really good fight in a couple of months, the Larosians were being aloof, the Kroggs had a super-weapon, *and* Sarah wouldn't talk to him.

Well, actually, the last one was the only thing that was really getting to him.

So he was going to fix it.

He'd had a brief talk with Savanna Felix after the Narosh emergency had wrapped up, and he'd heard about the circumstances surrounding the accident. Not only was Sarah becoming unpleasant to deal with, she was actually causing accidents that were damned near killing Allied fleet commanders.

Now, the Earthers were too sensible to tell her off, and the Larosians were probably too aloof and logical.

He, on the other hand, had an Irish temper.

And he wasn't one to take *this* much garbage sitting down.

Pat's face was thus quite red as he stormed down the ramp of his pinnace and to the lift nearest *Joseph Barron's* flight deck. A junior officer moved to greet him and escort him to a briefing room where he could wait for Sarah, but Pat left the fragile-looking ArcLieutenant in his wake.

The image of a burly, red-faced Irishman hammering through the corridors wasn't one that encouraged intervention.

For a moment Pat wondered whether they'd call the marines on him… yeah, just let them *try*…

Letting his anger off the leash, even if only briefly, was almost relaxing, Pat thought to himself as he maneuvered his way around spacers and officers. He hadn't gotten angry enough to yell at someone in a couple of years. It wasn't something he liked to do regularly, but sometimes it was necessary.

Like when Sarah had decided to meddle in the ground battle on the Antarctic Plain. He'd yelled quite a bit… but she'd still gone. Then he'd saved her from getting splattered by a psychotic Crusader Shappa who'd gotten the drop on her.

He *really* didn't want to have to stop her from doing something stupid out here.

And he did have a new card up his sleeve since then — the whole love thing.

Sarah's quarters appeared in front of Pat with surprising speed, and he took a quick breath to fuel his fire before he chimed the admittance key.

Brooding felt odd to Sarah. She generally wasn't someone who spent a lot of time thinking about how bad her life was.

But lately, she realized, it had become something of a hobby. Perhaps she was just trying to cope with the same sort of stress Caine was dealing with. He was obviously doing a better job...

The door chimed and she frowned. She glanced quickly at the clock on her desk and thought back through her day's schedule. Hadn't she marked this off as paperwork time? The bridge should've been able to screen guests for her...

Standing, she went to the door and opened it.

Pat looked like a bomb waiting to go off.

He met Sarah's eyes and she raised an eyebrow, "Pat. Your face is awfully red."

Pat's eyes bulged, "Oh, Sarah my girl, you don't know the *half* of it."

Sarah frowned in confusion, "Did you eat something bad? Would you like some water... come in, I'll get you some water."

Before Pat could get another word in Sarah was stepping quickly off to the kitchen, leaving him without someone to yell at. He grumbled and came in, seating himself on the couch until Sarah returned with the glass.

"I *don't want* a glass of water!" he erupted.

Sarah frowned, "You look like you do."

"Aw for crying out loud, can't you say something snide so that I can blow up properly? Tell you off like I came here to do and such."

Sarah's face suddenly set and she put the glass of water down on the coffee table, "Tell me *off*?"

"Yes," Pat's tone was exasperated. "You know, causing accidents, alienating your friends... all that garbage. Trying to compensate for a problem that isn't there..."

Pat groaned inwardly — he'd been all ready with that good yelling energy and she'd managed to halt his charge with a *glass of water*.

"Aww forget it, I've lost the moment. Give me that water, will you? I'm sweatin' something bloody awful."

Sarah passed the cold glass to the Irishman and he leaned back sipping it, "Well, at least it got me in the door this time."

"Hmm?"

Pat pointed at the stack of papers on Sarah's desk, "Shouldn't you be at that. I'm interrupting, right?"

Sarah shook her head and sat, "I was thinking, actually."

Pat raised an eyebrow, "Ah, gone back to that habit have we. Realized that you're brooding over nothing yet?"

Sarah blinked and looked at Pat, "That's what Captain Forepaw told me."

Pat gulped some water, "Told you *when*?"

Shrugging, Sarah glanced again at the clock, "About an hour ago."

"Sure I could've told you that eight *months* ago, but you wouldn't ask me, would you?"

"Not as such."

Pat groaned and let his head drop onto the back of the couch, "You sure have a way of doing things, don't you? Always like to strike out on your own and try to absorb *all* the grief for everyone before it gets to them."

Sarah blinked and her expression sharpened slightly, "What do you mean?"

Pat lifted his head and glared at her, "What do you mean what do *I* mean? Sarah, for as long as I've known you you've walked a fine line. You keep sticking your neck out for no reason because you *think* you have something to prove."

"Ridiculous," Sarah scowled.

"Oh *really*. Let's see, you tried to beat *Genesis* with a Dreadnought. Oh wait, first you blew up your own damned ship for 'the sake of everyone else'. And then there was that lovely series of stunts in Antarctica... do I need to go on?"

"Probably better that you didn't," Sarah said coldly, standing. "As you mentioned, I have paperwork."

"Oh sit *down*. Here's the way I see it — and I bloody well ought to know. You've been forced to prove yourself throughout your whole career. You did it when the Church was running the show, you did it when Liz made you an officer before you were eighteen, you did it to earn the Earthers' respect. You did it to prove your commitment to me. But now you don't have a thing to prove to anybody, so you're inventing garbage to use against yourself to tell yourself you're not bloody good enough!"

Sarah stared icily at Pat, but he kept pushing.

"Now Andra or Setter wouldn't say that to you because, as far as they're concerned, you're good at what you do, and they happen to be politer than me. But you don't seem to be able to accept the idea that there's nothing to prove, so you're trying to give them excuses to make your doubts reality. And mark me, you're going to give them an excuse if you keep this up."

He drained the last of the water and stood, "Now, you've got two options. You stop this nonsense and focus on winning the war, or you keep on with the self-indulgent self-pity and wait for Liz to swap you for Graham. Cause I *know* she'll bloody do it if you make her."

Sarah followed Pat with her eyes as he slowly rounded the coffee table and passed her.

"I'll let myself out. Give me a call when you come to your senses. I won't be holding my breath."

She heard the door close as Pat left but she didn't quite know what to do. Was he right?

Pat felt awful as he walked slowly back to his pinnace.

That's why he didn't let himself blow up all that often — it could be *very* satisfying to put some sense into someone's head, but it could also be so cruel.

Well, it had all needed to be said.

Pat just hoped that Sarah wouldn't continue on the road to self-destruction. She'd always had a nearly suicidal streak...

He shuddered and forced himself to stop thinking about it.

CHAPTER 22

"Maybe we should all just rent rooms here. What kind of rate do you think you can swing for us, Setter?"

Caine looked up, "I don't know, maybe your immortal soul or something like that..."

Felix winced and glanced at Ursla with a grin, "He obviously doesn't like having us around so much."

"*Us* or *you*?"

Caine chuckled and Ursla smiled broadly.

"Anyway," she turned her attention back to Caine, "what exactly is *this* meeting about?"

A night had passed since the crash, so they had only thirty-six hours left before their projected launch hour for the strikes against 'B' and 'C'. The constant traveling of fleet commanders back and forth between the blockaded solar systems was certainly becoming tedious, and it didn't smooth preparation efforts at all.

They could always try moving their timetable back... but the threat of the Krogg weapon remained. It was better to act quickly, even though pulling together two major fleet engagements in such little time was an effort that some might call overly ambitious.

It was a risk, but Caine recognized that it was one he had to take.

"Novash wants to consult with us before we launch," he explained. "His fighter is on the way now, as I understand it, and there's a new broadcast frequency. Lab is keeping up a constant chatter to make sure the landing goes safely."

The two Admirals nodded slowly and exchanged brief glances. They *really* didn't want a repeat of yesterday, but Forepaw would want it even less.

"Is Sarah coming?" Ursla asked in a more somber tone, and Caine shook his head.

"Didn't call her... Novash wanted to discuss offensive operations, not the blockade of 'A'. He can meet with her when he's ready, but I think we should give him some time to get used to his new job first," Caine leaned back in his chair.

Silent nods came in reply, and the atmosphere remained comfortable.

The intercom chirped and Forepaw's voice came over it, "Novash just landed. He's on his way up to you now."

"No problems, Lab?" Caine asked with a tiny bit of angst.

"You know better than to ask that," Forepaw's words sounded matter-of-fact.

The intercom switched off and Caine straightened himself in his chair. He ached, physically, from the copious amount of tension he'd suffered through lately. Centering himself and getting his mind out of a darkened state had helped, but his muscles still had to absorb some of his nervous energy.

"Remember when we always used to go meet the honored guests?" Ursla asked, shifting in her chair.

"Back when we were young and energetic," Felix grinned.

"A year ago?" Caine added.

"Nine months, I think," Felix tilted his head slightly. "Must be some sort of temporal thing... time added to stress and multiplied by experience to the power of number of actions, equals actual wear on the body."

"You think about things *way* too much," Ursla said just as the door opened.

The three Earthers stood and nodded to the arriving Novash, and the Admiral-of-a-Division replied with his best-practiced smile and a deep bow-nod.

"Come have a seat, Novash. We were just talking about combat stress," Felix pointed the Larosian in the direction of a chair at the briefing table, and the three Earthers retook their seats.

Novash moved to the indicated place and sat somewhat gingerly, his head angled to the side slightly, "Combat stress? I'm not well versed on the subject."

Caine held up a hand, "Don't worry about it, we're just annoying Savanna. We're *much* more interested in what you have to say."

Felix grinned, "Don't let that go to your head — they're setting the bar low. They'd rather have teeth pulled than listen to me prattle sometimes."

Novash understood that this was a humorous exchange, so he chuckled politely in reply. To the Earthers, his effort sounded more like a cough, but his nod prevented any misunderstanding. The alien then looked back at Caine.

"I have spoken with the bridge crew of *Lycrotar*, and I believe I know why Narosh made such a hurried launch. It seems we've discerned the nature of the Krogg weapons."

Caine started to open his mouth, but Ursla beat him to speaking, "The bombs?"

Novash offered his bow-nod again, "Though they are not, in fact, warheads."

The Earthers raised their eyebrows simultaneously, turning into a fully captive audience, and Novash continued, "The explosions were telepathic in nature, created by powerful Kroggs harnessing the energy of hyperspace."

To Novash, the explanation seemed complete enough — though the trio of Earthers exchanged confused glances.

"I'm sorry, a little more elaboration please, Novash," Felix linked his hands on the table in front of him.

Novash tilted his head, concluding that the Earthers were not as well acquainted with telepathy and hyperspace as the Larosians. Indeed, upon reflection that conclusion seemed logical.

"One fundamental ability of a telepath is control of energy fields," Novash began, and the Earthers nodded slowly. "Now, in the history of this war, two warriors for the Larosian cause possessed sufficient telepathic power to harness vast amounts of energy with their minds. Praaxus and the Son of Praaxus were both able to gather unprecedented quantities of energy with their minds, condense it tightly, and then release it abruptly — with great destructive force."

Indeed, they'd seen as much already...

"The result of such a release is a large explosion, as the amount of energy collected attempts to diffuse and return to its natural dispersion. The physics is somewhat–"

"Don't worry about that, we're well aware of energy's properties," Caine interrupted. "Go on about this telepathy, though."

Novash nodded slowly, "Well, most Larosians lack the sort of telepathic control needed to blow up a star system, but we each do have some ability. Usually the Stealth Guard are most highly skilled with it — they use it in lieu of traditional energy weapons. In any case, certain higher-level Kroggs have the ability to use energy with a general output somewhere between Praaxus and a Stealth Guardsman. It seems that some of these were aboard the Dreadnoughts that tried to eliminate our fleet."

So that was it. Caine looked from Novash to Ursla to Felix and back. They were facing a *telepathic bomb*.

And any higher-level Krogg with a brain could use one... that meant they had a few *thousand*, if not more.

"There is good news," Novash continued quickly. "Our scientists believe this technique must be used in hyperspace for it to be effective. You see, hyperspace energy is far less... *stable* than normal space energy. When trapped, condensed, and abruptly released, its impact is greater than that of normal energy by an exponential order of magnitude."

"That's what makes energy hyper work," Felix noted helpfully.

"Indeed. So the advantage to us is the fact that, without the benefit of hyperspace, this weapon is relatively ineffective in the hands of the Kroggs. Their Telepaths might be able to collect enough energy to cause an explosion that could damage a few ships in normal space, but our specialists cannot conceive of them reaching the power required to eliminate a fleet."

"That aside," Ursla's eyes narrowed thoughtfully, "they couldn't try this explosion thing on us if we're in among them. Not without destroying their whole fleet."

Novash tilted his head deeply to the left, "If it suits their purposes, they may well sacrifice much of their fleet. If, for instance, they could vanquish our combined fleet in an attack on Krogg 'A', they would be able to destroy our homes quite easily with the forces that remain in Krogg 'B' and 'C'. But that, at least, is not an issue. The Kroggs do not possess any Telepaths powerful enough to destroy the entire fleet."

Caine and Ursla exchanged brief glances — two years ago, the Larosians had been certain the Kroggs were a broken foe. Perhaps assumptions like this one weren't particularly safe or accurate.

"Well just in case, we're planning to hit 'B' and 'C' in thirty-six hours," Caine said simply, and Novash twitched and looked at him.

"You intend to attack them without your reinforcements?"

Caine nodded, "And we'll leave you and ArcGeneral Manchester to hold the Kroggs here in 'A'. We're willing to bet they won't risk the security of their birthworld for the sake of those planets, and if that's the case, we can secure our flanks and focus our effort."

Novash let his head drift backward towards the seat, "You do not wish our help in your assault?"

"Not this time, Novash," Ursla said smoothly. "We need two sizable forces guarding Krogg 'A', and we've got the ability to pierce deep in-system under energy drive. We should be able to storm the two garrisons without giving them much advance warning."

Novash tilted, "Ah yes, your energy drives. Very well, I will contact ArcGeneral Manchester to discuss our containment plans for 'A' when you launch your strike. I take it you will be removing the Earther First Fleet to support the attacks?"

Caine nodded, "I'll be joining Andra at 'B', and I'm giving one of my fleet divisions to Savanna for 'C'. We're reasonably confident about the prospects for success."

Novash nodded again, "I do not foresee a problem — at least, not based on the telemetry I have seen of the systems. I would suggest you press the action immediately to within the hyper limit of each system, in case they attempt to bring another explosion against you."

Felix was nodding, "Already on the cards."

"In that case, I will wish you all good fortune," Novash slowly stood. "I should contact the ArcGeneral... make sure we have our fish in a row."

Caine blinked and looked up at the Larosian, "That's 'ducks', Novash. *Ducks* in a row... and where did you learn colloquialisms?"

The Larosian approximated a shrug, "I'm telepathic."

CHAPTER 23

"We're going to have some fun with this one, wouldn't you say?"

Garvin Jardaw's eyes narrowed as he paced around the main battle plot in *Engadine's* flight briefing room. The light blue holographic display was filled with black orbs and icons, revealing the composition and strength of the Krogg forces currently holding 'B'. There were quite a few to contend with... and the Carriers would be heavily involved.

While all Earther ships of the line and some of the newer big frigates carried small numbers of gunboats, the responsibility for concentrated combat operations with small craft remained the job of the Carrier Group. The boats from the regular fleet were crewed by volunteers, and were more routinely used to escort their ships than to provide offensive support. Many were smaller and slower than the heavy boats of the purpose-built carriers, and none were able to strike-launch.

Carriers, newly-built or converted, all had specialized launch tubes, capable of quickly ejecting boats into space. Recovery was done through regular landing deck operations, just like on a ship of the line, but the ability to send large numbers of small craft into action rapidly was a decisive advantage that only the Carriers maintained.

The specialized ships could thus launch their boats before the ships of the line could open their flight deck doors... and before even the new Krogg Motherships could open their launch 'eyes'.

With all these special capabilities, the inclusion of the Carriers in a large-scale operation against well-protected and corvette-rich systems was quite important. They could do what no other ships in the Allied Fleet could... except perhaps for the Larosian Carriers and their smaller fighters.

Of course, none of that *really* mattered to Garvin Jardaw. The polar bear certainly didn't need to tell Draco Maximane how to fight — as the Commodore in charge of the Carriers' *escort*, he only needed to worry about protecting the unwieldy ships, not deploying them. Of course he did need to know what Maximane was planning in order to ensure his 64s and 58s would be safely between the Carriers and any Krogg interlopers...

And that was what he was here to find out, so he'd best stop musing and get back to more immediate matters. Looking at the seated Maximane, Jardaw nodded slowly, "And Ursla wants us to deal with the Motherships alone?"

Maximane nodded. For his part, the Vice Admiral was rather nervous. He had no experience with these Carriers in large fleet actions — there had never been an attempt by *Engadine* and its consorts to break a fortified system with a garrison, or to face such a concentration of Motherships.

But now his Carriers were going to be responsible for covering Ursla and Caine's attack — the gunboats of the group would have to take on the Motherships and then interdict against the corvettes launched from Krogg 'B's only colonized world. The gunboats from the fleet would help with the latter task, but the prospect remained daunting.

Estimates gave the Kroggs about 7,500 corvettes. With the aid of Carrier Group, the Earther fleet being deployed against 'B' could reply with about 6,000 — a disadvantage in numbers that could hopefully be compensated for by Earther skill with the boats and superiority of design. Hopefully they could narrow the odds from the outset — if they could just manage to destroy the ten new-breed Motherships in the system before they launched their corvettes.

"That's the plan, but I'm not entirely sure how we'll be able to swing it," Maximane leaned forward and keyed the center of the solar system up in a magnified cube. The black spheres representing the Motherships floated over the surface of Krogg 'B' in a net, spread all around the planet so that some were inevitably shielded from the line of sight of others.

It would be tricky to get all of them in a single strike... the Carriers would have to be separated and tasked to focus on individual Motherships. That wasn't just a little *risky*, it was patently bad Carrier policy to divide forces while closely engaging enemy vessels.

Still, they'd have to find a way to pull it off...

"Well, I can put three Carriers against each of those Motherships," Maximane said slowly, scratching his chin. "If we put one of your ships with each Carrier trio and then leave the remaining six to hammer the most stubborn Mothership, we could probably do it."

Jardaw nodded slowly, trying to decide how much work it would take for six 64s to smash a Mothership. Probably a fair bit, though if they got the drop on the Kroggs, they might be able to put enough fire directly into the Mothership's main flight bay to put it out of action. But for the ten Krogg vessels being assaulted by Carriers it would probably come to a gun duel; boats could swarm all around a Mothership, focus their fire, and ultimately be more efficient with the gunpower they had. Against the large corvette-carriers, that would be a fairly decisive advantage.

But then it had to be remembered that these were new Krogg Motherships, well armed with anti-ship weapons — spines and heavy neuro pulses. They could beat his 64s into rather messy wrecks given a chance, even without their corvettes. Well, they could do that if he *let* them.

Slowly, Jardaw nodded, "Alright. We'll make sure no Motherships gets to launch. I'll keep six 64s for that task, put the 58s and *Warden* with your Carriers. We'll still have to deal with the corvettes coming off the ground, though."

Maximane leaned back in his chair and nodded. More than half the corvettes in the system were based at the main military installation on the surface of

Krogg 'B'. With the boats out dealing with Motherships, Carriers would be quite vulnerable to attacks from the surface-craft...

"Well, we'll just have to make sure we take the Motherships out quickly. And perhaps if we start bombarding planetary installations while we're waiting, we could knock out some of their corvettes on the ground..."

Jardaw nodded — they certainly had that option. Thus far in the war, the Earthers had rarely been forced into firing upon the surface of a planet. Over the course of the campaign it hadn't been a very popular option — the collateral ecological damage it could cause was rather unappetizing.

But here at Krogg 'B' there was no ecology to worry about — apart from Krogg installations. They could scan the surface for the corvette launch banks and take them out. Indeed, they might even neutralize the entire ground-based force with a concerted strike.

Of course there would still be hundreds of corvettes floating about in the system — on patrols, maneuvers, or based on small asteroids — but the main concentration could be crushed swiftly. The Kroggs had put all their eggs in one basket, and they'd have to pay for that.

Jardaw paused and frowned, "Isn't it a bit convenient that they've stacked their corvettes in one nice concentration? They have to know we can pounce right on them... shouldn't they have them divided throughout their fleet?"

Maximane sighed briefly and narrowed his eyes, "It's almost as though they want us to come right in. A trap?"

Jardaw nodded slowly, "It can't be this easy. Not when they've been so clever in the past months."

Maximane matched Jardaw's nod and slowly keyed the Motherships into a larger frame. They seemed perfectly normal, each laden with twice as many corvettes as *Engadine* had boats, each well-armed against capital ships. The Kroggs had to know that was expected...

"No," Jardaw leaned towards the holo slowly, "no, the Motherships are right. It's the *planet* that concerns me."

Maximane blinked and keyed up the image of Krogg 'B'.

There were a host of energy signatures, definite indications of corvettes... What could be wrong with the planet?

"All I see are a few dozen corvette bays," Maximane glanced curiously at the bear.

Jardaw tilted his head and examined the planet's holo closely, "I have a feeling that's exactly what we're *supposed* to see."

Maximane looked up at Jardaw and met his eyes. Instincts flared for a brief second, and Maximane abruptly recognized his former First Lieutenant's caution. The Kroggs had used old Motherships as bait to spread Caine out before Gibraltar... could they be baiting the Allies again now?

"I think we should get some *very* close recon. I'll ask Caine for a sloop."

Jardaw nodded slowly, "Good plan."

They wouldn't walk blindly into a trap.

CHAPTER 24

"Déjà vu."

Lang Sandpelt's ear twitched and he looked at Chronos Claw, "I might be wrong, but I don't think any one sloop has reconnoitered as many key systems as we have. Genesis, the Krogg base, Krogg 'A', and now 'B'."

The Captain of *Flame* ground his jaw, sighed and shrugged in reply, "Price of being the best, I suppose."

"There are 400 sloops with the fleet, Chronos. Why is it *always* us?" Sandpelt tapped his fingers on his leg.

Claw looked at his friend and smiled sardonically, "Because we probably need the stories to tell our cubs more than anyone else."

Sandpelt grinned and nodded, "You'll need to find me a wife for that argument to hold any water. But anyway, I'm going down to the engines."

Claw nodded, "Keep them together."

The Lieutenant half-shrugged, "That's what I do."

The bridge of *Orion* was tense as *Flame* slid into energy drive, opened its field, and began a run into Krogg 'B'.

"So they're convinced this is a trap?" Ursla looked into *Orion's* main holo plot and Caine nodded behind her.

"The planetary set up is so *neat* — it's as though they're setting up their corvettes to get destroyed."

Ursla shrugged and straightened, turning to Caine and Forepaw, "They could just be deploying against expected Larosian assault tactics. They do have a solid force on the hyper limit — they could be keeping their Motherships back until they know where to commit them."

"But *you've* been the one blockading them, Andra," Caine said skeptically. "And they had the demise of the Larosians well planned."

Forepaw frowned and moved to the plot, "Could they be planning to use their telepathic bombs? Try to get our Carriers in close and then blast the space surrounding the planet?"

Ursla and Caine paused thoughtfully, then the latter shook his head, "I'm inclined to agree with Novash. The blasts are probably quite impotent in regular space, otherwise they'd have used them by now."

"Planetside batteries then?" Ursla suggested quietly... though that didn't quite make sense either. A planet wasn't particularly maneuverable, and any weapon fixed on the surface would only be able to target a given percentage of its sky at any given time. That was precisely why the Allies relied on semi-mobile defense stations — they could move around a planet to bring firepower to bear.

But planetside weapons were a possibility, nonetheless.

"*Flame* is moving in-system, sir. Coming to the planet in 'B' right now..."

"Feed telemetry directly to the plot," Forepaw replied to the Sensor Chief, who nodded quickly.

As the veteran sloop slid to sublight speed in the space around Krogg 'B', images and information began to fill *Orion's* plot. The planet was the focus of the scanning, but again it showed no unique or unusual signatures. It had 3,000 corvettes sitting on it, but aside from that it seemed to be unremarkable enough.

"Order *Flame* to make a complete orbital scan. I want to be sure," Caine said slowly, and the Signal Officer sent the veiled burst-message to the sloop.

"A complete survey," Claw said to himself quietly. Fair enough.

He keyed the comm, "Lang, everything alright down there?"

"Fine. We doing a full orbit?"

Claw smiled, "You called it. Can we keep the field out long enough?"

There was a brief pause, then, "Of *course*."

"Good. Helm, at 12 pls, make it an easy orbit. Sensors, keep an eye on all the Kroggs around. I don't think we want to get immobilized out here."

"Interesting how *Flame's* always in the thick of it, eh Andra?" Caine's remark seemed to come out of nowhere, but Ursla nodded immediately.

"Lucky ship."

"There still seems to be nothing out of the ordinary," Forepaw frowned at the plot and laced his hands behind his back. "Most curious."

Flame was doing as admirable a job as ever, and yet none of the deep-piercing Earther scans were showing anything but corvettes hidden in regularly spaced subterranean caves ringing the planet's equator.

Caine didn't intend to discount the concerns of the Carrier commanders, but he had nothing to substantiate those worries. The attack needed to go ahead; they'd just have to be very prudent and cautious about their work.

Ursla folded her arms over her chest at Forepaw's remark, "They're sitting there ready to deploy... but they're just *sitting*. I suppose we could be lucky... they really could be this naïve..."

Caine and Forepaw looked at each other and then looked up at Ursla. She exchanged glances with both of them and shrugged, "No, I wasn't buying that either. Caution then?"

"It'll have to be. We'll go with Maximane's preliminary plan to hit them, but I think we might want to have heavy support standing by in case they try anything."

Nodding, Ursla turned her back to the plot and leaned carefully against it,

"A fleet division?"

"I'd say Jax's in that case," Caine frowned thoughtfully and eyed Krogg 'B' again. "He has a way of making his ships count."

"Will his twelve squadrons be enough?" Forepaw asked quietly, glancing between the commanders again. "They could have a significant number of Kroggs coming down on them."

Caine took a breath and nodded, "We'll keep the rest of the First on standby, I think. A strategic reserve. I'll put us into it wherever we're most needed…"

"I'd recommend limiting the size of Maximane's force anyway," Ursla turned back to the plot and poked a big forefinger into its representation of a planet. "The trap could be completely unconventional — another telepathic bomb or something such. We'll have to be able to get our forces out of the blast range quickly, and that's easier if we limit their numbers."

Caine 'hmmed' and nodded. There was no way to know exactly what was in store for the attack — desperate to save themselves, the Kroggs seemed to be trying new and disturbing tactics at every turn these days.

Well, were he in their position, he would be equally desperate. For now he had to find a way around their evident craftiness… and without the ability to go into their minds and listen to their plans, he'd have to rely on his intuition.

Admittedly, the circumstances could be worse, but right now he almost longed for an old-fashioned, stand-up fight. The Earthers *never* lost those — their predatory legacy allowed them to kill, and to kill efficiently, when the situation called for it.

That talent might come into play in this attack, but no amount of forethought would guarantee it. So they'd storm the system, see what was waiting for them, and then deal with it. There was nothing more to do.

"We'll keep it simple enough," Caine said with some finality, and Ursla nodded. "We can't be sure of what's going on down there, but whatever it is, we'll face it when it reveals itself."

Ursla took a deep breath, "I hate it when things get this uncertain…"

Caine shrugged, "If it comes to it, I'd bet on our improvisational skill over their planning — any day."

Ursla's eyebrow cocked and she half-smiled, "You're quite optimistic."

A short laugh came from Caine, and he rubbed the back of his neck, "I don't think that's the word…"

Then again, maybe it was.

CHAPTER 25

General Andros Grieve sat quietly in a chair in *Algenon's* officer's mess. The First Rate was still in energy drive, only a day out of Genesis with the rest of the Fifth and Sixth Fleets. Despite the inevitability of the upcoming battle, the daily routine of the ship was relaxed and efficient, the crew moving smoothly back and forth from their posts to their quarters, the messes, and the gyms.

Grieve, however, was starting to feel tense — there was something not right about the mission. The whole siege of Krogg was beginning to seem like a bad idea to him, and he couldn't put his finger on why.

Jitters?

No, not likely at all. Andros Grieve was the most experienced officer in the Earther Marine Corps — he'd led the action on the Antarctic Plains from the front with rifle and bayonet. He'd led a few companies against a Krogg base in the first ground encounter with the aliens at Genesis, and then he'd gone with Torallis into what they'd believed was a Queen's Hive — the hive had long since been abandoned by the Queen, but it had been teeming with soldiers nonetheless.

He'd been on a forward planet during the Battle of Gibraltar, leading a brigade of marines in an effort to force the Kroggs off without demolishing the local ecosystem in the process — and he'd managed to do just that with only sixty-four fatalities in a force of 2,000. Many, *many* severed limbs among his marines, but not many deaths...

Grieve was, quite clearly, good at his job. The best according to some, and he didn't argue with them.

So his tension was almost becoming self-perpetuating — why *was* he so anxious?

"I was thinking, maybe we should bribe our bridge crews with fish cakes."

Grieve nearly jumped as Varnon Broadpaw, holding a tray generously laden with brunch, dropped into the seat facing him.

"Isn't it a bit early for all that food?" the General frowned in response.

The wolf looked up at the bear while shoveling the first load of food into his mouth, "Awfully odd thing for *you* to say–"

Grieve's eyebrows went up, "How do you mean?"

Chewing happily, Broadpaw poked his fork at the pair of empty trays in front of the bear. Grieve looked down and frowned, "Oh."

"Mmhmph," Broadpaw kept chewing.

The General paused, then vaguely recalled taking two trays of food... sitting down, eating... well go figure, he'd eaten all of it.

"Must've forgot," he said slowly and leaned back.

Broadpaw frowned and swallowed, preempting his next food load, "Something wrong?"

"No."

Broadpaw's eyebrow arched, "Why don't I believe you?"

Grieve shrugged, "You could be dumb as a post."

Varnon's eyebrows shot up and he leaned back, "Now I *know* something's up. You're smokescreening."

"I'm doing nothing of the sort," Grieve persisted, but Broadpaw was already shaking his head.

"Don't even try it, I'm married remember."

Grieve paused and eyed his friend, "Now I'm lost."

Broadpaw frowned in a friendly fashion, "You look it. Anyway, I can read past that 'I'm fine' garbage. So, I say it again, don't even try..."

Grieve scowled, not exactly in the mood for psychoanalysis.

"Oh come on, you're worried about something. Let me in on it — I'm worried too..." Broadpaw let his voice trail off, electing to quietly continue with his meal while the General collected his thoughts for a moment.

Apparently it took a long time to collect those thoughts, because Broadpaw emptied half his tray during the ensuing silence.

"Well?"

Grieve sat back in his chair and eyed the smaller Earther opposite him. He wasn't even sure whether he had anything to talk about, let alone whether he would want to talk if he did.

"Fine, I'll start," Varnon leaned forward and propped his elbows on the table. If nothing else he was persistent. "How do you feel about charging off into battle against an unquantifiable superweapon backed by clever Kroggs fighting dirty on their home turf?"

Grieve hid the abrupt flare of concern that seemed to blossom with the question.

"Fine."

Broadpaw looked up at his friend over a forkful of potato, "Right. I'm the Queen of Argentina, by the way. Nice to meet you."

He began chewing and Grieve simply arched his eyebrow, "I read in a book once that 'you can't get blood from a turnip'."

Broadpaw stopped chewing for a moment, dropping his fork to his plate, "I know geneticists who could change that. Talk to me."

Grieve shook his head, "Nothing to say really. Bit of a bad feeling about this one, but nothing I can put my finger on."

Broadpaw frowned, "A bad *feeling* is turning you so morose?"

Shrugging, Grieve shifted in his seat, "I'm not used to it. Didn't have one at Antarctica, didn't at Genesis, and I didn't on Avalon."

Broadpaw tilted his head at the last one...

"My brigade action, we named the planet Avalon."

Broadpaw nodded slowly, "We have a flare for the dramatic names, don't we? Alright, so you're a bit worried. Happens to all of us. We just move on..."

Grieve nodded, "I figured that much. It's just uncomfortable, that's all."

"You don't say. Here I was thinking it was *peachy*."

The remark was meant to brighten the table... and maybe it started to work, as Grieve cracked a half smile, "Yes, well, if you don't want me to mop the floor with you next time we're on the sparring mat..."

"How can you mop the *floor* with me if we're on a *mat*, hmm?" Broadpaw lifted his fork and started stabbing a piece of frosted cake.

"I'll find a way."

"Mmm..." Broadpaw sampled the white cake, "this is really good. Maybe it'd be a better bribe than fish..."

Grieve reached over the table and lifted the rest of the piece off the plate, popping it quickly into his mouth and chewing happily. As his jaws worked he offered an exaggerated nod, "Mmm-hmmm!"

Broadpaw threw his fork onto his tray, "Typical."

Grieve shrugged, and Broadpaw stood and went back to the chef's counter.

CHAPTER 26

The chronometer was ticking down awfully slowly.

Two... one... and *zero*.

Felix let out a breath and leaned back in his chair, looking across at Varnia Broadpaw as she sat next to him.

"One hour to launch," she said quietly, and he nodded.

Despite his better judgment, Savanna Felix was moderately excited about the prospect of action today. It would be good to get the Navy off its laurels again, and to make sure the Kroggs didn't hold any of the initiative after revealing their new weapon...

But it would cost lives. It always did. So that tempered the cat's enthusiasm, though not entirely.

The Third Fleet, joined by 200 ships of the First, sat at its regular blockade station around Krogg 'C'. Thus far the squadrons weren't forming up into vanguards, rotating capital ships to the front, or running an abnormal number of scans. They were doing what they always did... except in forty-five minutes the whole fleet would beat to quarters and clear for action. Fifteen minutes after that they'd launch, every ship rushing to the center of the Krogg Fleet and coming out around the old, vulnerable Motherships that floated lazily next to a tiny, useless asteroid.

Krogg 'C' was itself a fairly unremarkable system. It had a star without any major celestial bodies, and aside from the hyper limit protection it offered against Larosians and the presence of artificial grazing stations for ships, it lacked any stationary presence at all.

But strategically, it was important. The Kroggs had many more ships than the Allies, and by sending the oldest of them to 'C', they both concentrated their best ships in the two systems of value *and* put a threat on the Allied flanks.

Well, presuming that the Allies remained badly outnumbered and without the initiative.

Felix was about to change that — and at the same time Ursla and Caine were going to do similar in Krogg 'B'.

Hmm... he'd been thinking for a while. Maybe a lot of time had gone by...

"How long now, Varnia?"

His Flag Captain paused as Felix looked at her, then turned her head slowly, "A minute less than the *last time you checked*."

Felix blinked, "Oh."

He looked away sheepishly.

"Forty-five minutes to go," Forepaw settled himself into his chair next to Caine as he spoke. "We're sitting steady, no indications to tip them off."

Caine nodded, "Good. Any word from Savanna?"

Forepaw shook his head, "He's keeping to regular signal traffic hours. We won't hear from him before we launch unless there's a problem."

Caine nodded — an abnormally high volume of comm chatter between the two solar blockades would doubtless be suspicious.

"And Andra?"

Forepaw shook his head again, "No word. *Agamemnon* is on regular station, and we should be far enough back to be out of sight of 'B'."

The First Fleet had departed from 'A' on what had looked like — or what Caine *hoped* looked like — a routine rotation. With fresh ships coming in, it would make sense to withdraw the battle-weary First to repair and restock, so they'd drifted straight back away from all the Krogg systems until they were safely out of detection range.

Then it had only been a matter of moving down towards 'B' and staying away from Krogg sensors.

So far things were going according to plan. No signs that the Kroggs were expecting anything out of the ordinary, and the First's ships were positioned just how he wanted them for quick deployment.

He took a deep breath. Not too long now.

Ursla stood at the main battle plot on *Agamemnon's* bridge. Thirty minutes to go.

The ships of the Second were steady on their blockade stations, the frigates only slightly closer in than usual. She kept wondering whether the Kroggs somehow knew what was being planned.

Well, even if the aliens did know, some 1,200 ships of the line, frigates, and sloops were going to come barreling down on them... not to mention the Carriers and the boats. The aliens would have a tough time dealing with that much firepower, no matter how ready they were.

At Gibraltar, the Kroggs had been able to gain a numerical margin of superiority in excess of two-to-one. Here, the Earthers had numbers on their side.

Logically, then, things should go well for the Allies...

Yes. Certainly...

Ursla nearly laughed at her own efforts to convince herself of the viability of the plan as Artemis Tigar came to stand next to her at the plot. The veteran Captain of *Agamemnon* looked up at his Flag Officer, "Remember when we were still wondering how tough the Kroggs would be?"

Ursla looked down, "Before Genesis, you mean?"

Tigar nodded, "Yep. You said things could be much worse, if I remember correctly."

Recalling slowly, Ursla nodded, "Yes, why?"

Tigar shrugged, "Well, either this *is* worse, or there's still worse to come."

Ursla frowned, "Was that supposed to be a pep talk?"

Tigar shrugged, "I'm not sure it even made sense, actually."

"It didn't," Ursla smiled.

"We're at fifteen minutes... *now*."

"Beat to quarters, send to squadron to clear for action."

The bridge of *Highlander* darkened and reddened as the ship went to general quarters. Built in an older day, the 64 featured such novelties as red battle lighting and a decorative nameplate on the bridge, features that newer ships didn't have. Garvin Jardaw appreciated it somehow... it added a little to the character of his ship.

"Comm call coming in, skipper. Vice Admiral Furgus... on a three-way with Vice Admiral Maximane and Commodore Magnus."

Jardaw straightened in his seat, "In the plot."

The 64's main tank shifted its displays, and the heads of Jax Furgus, Draco Maximane and Fox Magnus glowed into being.

"Garvin, we're all set. You?" Maximane spoke as the image stabilized.

The polar bear nodded, "We're cleared for action."

"I hate to tell you your job, Garvin," Furgus put in, slowly beginning to smile, "but I've decided to attach a squadron of 74s to you — I'm actually going to inflict Fox Magnus on you..."

Fox nodded with a confident smile to Jardaw. For his part, the dapper little fox wasn't worried about this fight — *Atlas* had been through a lot in the past years, and he knew the 74 and the entire 186th Battle Squadron would do fine. It was generally being seen as a sign of good luck that they'd stopped the Krogg telepathic bombs, and that they'd been able to shrug off the blasts without too much pain... good luck that would hopefully carry over to today.

"It'll be good to work with you, Garvin," Fox said. "I'll follow your lead."

Jardaw didn't know Fox well, but he did know some of the maverick Commodore's friends — the Freetown Privateers. They were as sensible beings as any he'd met, despite their humanity, and they'd liked Fox a lot. Somehow, Jardaw felt comfortable having someone with that sort of reputation fighting at his side.

"We'll be glad to have you, Fox. I take it I can signal the rest of you directly if I need you, Jax?"

Furgus nodded, "As soon as you need us, we'll come out of energy drive. Until then, we'll sit back and keep a lookout for plays against your flanks."

Jardaw nodded, "Very good."

There was a pause among the four officers. Maximane was the first to break it, "I think luck is in order, my friends."

The Earthers nodded, repeating the sentiment.

Then the link cut.

"And... one minute."

"Cruising Master, stand by energy drive. Course plot 144 by 219 by 107. Stand by 400 pls..." Varnia Broadpaw's smooth voice launched *Tonnant's* bridge crew into action, and Felix quickly supplemented the orders.

"Signal all ships, stand by drives. We follow the plan until circumstances demand a change..."

Felix spoke with assurance as he watched the ships of his fleet come to action stations in the main battle plot. This would work.

It had to.

"Ten... nine... eight... seven... six..."

Well. Here we go.

Caine watched the clock.

Five. Four.

Ursla let out a last breath and settled into her seat.

Three.

Fox steadied himself on the arms of *Atlas'* command chair.

Two.

Garvin Jardaw narrowed his eyes slightly and watched the last number turn on the main chrono.

One.

The Earther Navy went into energy drive.

CHAPTER 27

The three Motherships protecting Krogg 'C' were of the old type. Veterans of the Larosian war, they were massive, each maintaining some 700 corvettes behind giant eyelid launch doors. In combat, they could fill space with corvettes and then withdraw to the protection of their escort groups.

As with all Motherships from the Larosian war they were bulbous, thinly armored, and slow. When fighting the Larosians, there was never a fear of such Motherships being forced into close action against capital ships — the Larosians, like the Kroggs, were confined exclusively to slower-than-light drives for most space combat. There was no way a Larosian squadron, no matter how determined, could break the Krogg escort quickly enough to catch a Mothership before it escaped to hyper... and hyper was not precise enough to allow the Larosians to jump in past the escort.

So the veteran Motherships were well suited to the Larosian battles. They carried twice as many corvettes as the new battle-Motherships, and they could literally overwhelm the Larosian Carriers and their *puny* fighters.

But this was no longer just a Larosian war.

The Earthers had energy drive and it gave ships of the line the ability to arrive *between* the Motherships and their escorts. Old Motherships, thin-skinned and unarmed, were merely floating targets to Earther guns.

So these last three, the largest vessels stationed at 'C' and the potential flank threat, were quite a rare sight on the front lines. Or anywhere, for that matter.

Somehow, that almost made Felix feel guilty.

Of course, 'almost' was the operative word.

Tonnant was the first out of energy drive, and Felix ground his jaw against the abrupt deceleration. The 80-gun Second Rate dropped from many times the speed of light to a dead stop in the course of a few seconds, and then the port broadside ran out smoothly.

"We're run out, ma'am," the First Lieutenant called quickly to Varnia Broadpaw, who was ready for the report.

"Fire."

The first broadside of the action was appropriately *Tonnant's*, and it was directed at the leading Motherships in the formation around the asteroid.

Following their flagship, the ships of the Third Fleet came out of energy drive quickly; most of them had detailed their guns to the destruction of the old behemoths. Their supporters from the First came out of energy drive next and slammed into the formations of Krogg capital ships and Destroyers. The Motherships would die quickly.

Felix watched dispassionately as the first Mothership literally came apart, the guns of over 100 ships of the line slicing it to pieces. The second began to spiral out of control into the asteroid as he watched, leaving only the third to try to open its launch doors.

"Focus fire on number three," Felix said quickly, then listened as the Signal Officer repeated his orders to the fleet.

Ships turned fast, the broadsides of numerous 74s coming to bear on the reeling Mothership. As the great beast made a last attempt to open its eyelid and spew its corvettes, the guns overwhelmed it and it too came apart.

And that was it for the Motherships... easy enough.

Felix was tempted to think it *too* easy, but that wasn't something to worry about just now–

"Rear Admiral Peregrine reports good incursion by the First's division," the Signal Officer reported quickly. "Light damage; they're facing old Krogg ships..."

"Turn us about and launch our boats," Varnia ordered quickly to *Tonnant's* Master, as Felix turned to the Signal Officer.

"Fleet to launch boats and turn about," he ordered. "Engage Krogg capital ships from the rear."

Tonnant was not as handy at the helm as a 74, but the longer 80-gun ship of the line was still fast. Its flight bay doors opened and fifteen gunboats erupted, launching without any particular finesse as they compensated for the great ship's fast turn and then angled out towards the fight.

The rest of the Third Fleet launched simultaneously, their boats forming small deltas and accelerating into the unprotected flanks of the Krogg battle fleet. As *Tonnant* chased them, the main battle plot filled with images and icons of Krogg ships simply flying apart under the fire. They didn't even seem to be making a fight of it anymore — the division of the First that had been detailed as a diversion was abruptly tearing them apart.

The Kroggs had a numerical advantage of four-to-one against that single Earther formation, and yet Kylie Peregrine's ships were still dominating the day...

Felix turned quickly to *Tonnant's* Sensor Chief, "What's going on here?"

The Chief, looking up from her screen, offered her own look of confusion. Felix got out of his seat and leaned into the plot, watching black icons disappear. The Third and the First's division had lost exactly four ships.

Four.

And the Kroggs were dying by the bucket load.

"Are these decoys?" Varnia came from her chair too, pausing as *Tonnant* rolled hard and delivered a broadside under the direction of the First Lieutenant.

Felix looked back at his Flag Captain and arched his brow, "Decoys for what?"

Varnia shrugged, "It can't be this easy."

The Sensor Chief was shaking her head, "They're Krogg ships... they're old, that might be it. Some of them look to be *very* old."

Felix frowned, "We knew that... we still expected them to put up a fight."

"Maybe they get to a certain point in life and they can't fight any more..."

Felix frowned at the thought and turned back to the plot as *Tonnant* led the Third straight into the rear of the Krogg 'C' garrison.

Coming in at oblique angles to keep their broadsides engaged, the Earther ships of the line were easily crossing through ranks of Dreadnoughts and Superdreadnoughts — very little counter fire was reaching them...

Felix half expected a sudden increase in the intensity of the Krogg attack, but none came. The alien ships slowly lurched around as if there were attempting to counter the Third, but they were both outnumbered and outflanked.

"They're doing this for a reason," Felix turned to Varnia. "We just have to keep shooting and be watchful."

She nodded, "Very good."

Stepping back to her chair, she nodded to the Master, "Down angle 163, port 110. Prepare starboard broadside against the Dreadnoughts ahead."

Felix turned to the Signal Officer, "Order all ships to break fleet vanguard and finish it by squadron. Be watchful and keep drives ready. This may still be some sort of trap."

The orders were repeated smoothly, and Felix peered back into the blue holo. Both Earther fleets came apart in what seemed a chaotic dance, squadrons of 74s being guided by squadrons of frigates and sloops. They zigzagged through space at high speed, laying broadsides against every Krogg ship in sight.

Tonnant bucked once as a piece of a shattered Dreadnought slammed into the shields near its engines and overloaded part of the shield grid, but nothing damning seemed to be happening. The 301st Battle Squadron followed its Admiral closely, and Dreadnoughts all around simply evaporated with little resistance. The old Krogg ships seemed to lack the will to fight...

Had they been this weak all along? If they had been this unable to fight, what would the point be in leaving them out here?

Felix slowly let his mind wrap around the question — with a fleet in being at 'C', the Kroggs had tied up his ships and kept them from aiding in the blockade of 'A'... Yes, but they'd done nothing to take advantage of their superior numbers at 'A', and they'd had many opportunities...

Tonnant rolled hard to port and delivered a volley of energy shot into a Superdreadnought as Felix watched the plot.

What else did keeping ships in 'C' do for the Kroggs...

In relation to 'A'?

Or 'B'?

Felix shook his head in an attempt to order his thoughts.

With two smaller systems — 'B' and 'C' — to cover, the Earthers could never risk attacking only one and allowing the other to launch a counter-attack on the flank. They had to commit the whole fleet to take both simultaneously, or they risked getting sandwiched between two forces. That was why the plans had called for both 'B' and 'C' to be struck today.

But they would have had to take 'B' even if 'C' hadn't been occupied... and they would have had far more ships to do it with...

It didn't *quite* fit...

Felix turned his mind back to the plot. A few of the Kroggs were resisting, but a few weren't enough. Only eleven Earther ships had been destroyed, and by the looks of it the crews from all of them had managed to escape. Usually the Kroggs liked to pick off lifeboats.

Little more than 200 Krogg ships remained.

This was always meant to be a decoy... but why? Decoy from what?

CHAPTER 28

Fox watched Krogg 'B' appear under *Atlas* from the 74s' bridge.

"Mister Gunth, starboard eighty, up roll thirty-four. Port broadside to bear on the Mothership on that bearing."

The veteran Master of *Atlas* didn't reply — instead, the ship moved, and the port guns ran out. Slightly to the rear, *Vulcan* and *Fuji* followed their flagship's course, and within seconds a sizable energy salvo tore into space, then rammed into an unsuspecting Mothership.

Unlike the Motherships in 'C', the Motherships of 'B' were state of the art, heavily armed and armored models. Though they didn't seem to be expecting an attack.

As the first broadsides slammed into them from the Allied escort vessels around the planet, the Motherships made no move to launch their small craft — nor did they try to return fire. Granted, they were given a relatively short time in which to act, but there was no reaction whatsoever.

Fox wanted to dismiss that lack of response, but he couldn't let it go. Something felt wrong about this level of inactivity.

Nothing felt right about it, in fact.

"We've got the Motherships — send to Maximane that he should hold his boats."

Fox didn't technically have the authority to stop Maximane from launching, but this bad feeling was too much to deny, so he'd send the warning...

He didn't like this at all.

Nor did Garvin Jardaw, as *Highlander* and three other 64s laid waste to a Mothership that should have been able to smash them — or at least done a great deal of damage trying. The Carriers were hanging back slightly as the escorts cleared the way for them — they could launch at a second's notice in response to any corvette activity, but to put boats without energy drive into space without knowing exactly what was going on would be negligent. Were this a trap, all those boats and their crews could be lost in a rout, so they should only be deployed with good reason.

And now, it seemed that there mightn't be such a reason...

"Send to *Engadine*, hold boats until otherwise notified."

Draco Maximane watched in silence as the Motherships came *easily* apart under the guns of only three smaller Battle Squadrons. He'd faced new Krogg

Carriers before, and they'd never been simple ships to beat. In a gun duel, one had destroyed a 64 before the boats of *Ark Royal* had overwhelmed it.

But now the formidable Krogg ships were just sitting there, accepting whatever punishment was being handed to them...

"Sir! To the rear, we've got at least a hundred Dreadnoughts closing! Forty seconds out!"

Maximane blinked. The Carriers were sitting in normal space just off Krogg 'B' watching the cleanup being led by *Highlander*. They were without protection just now — their boats were the only armament they could really call on.

But something was telling Maximane not to launch them yet, despite the Dreadnoughts coming up behind him...

"Signal Jax to intercept."

Jax Furgus didn't need to be asked twice. As he watched the tide of Dreadnoughts turn back on the Carriers, he ordered his ships of the line and frigates out of energy drive to respond.

Appearing in squadron vanguards all around the Kroggs, his division of the First Fleet opened up on the racing Dreadnoughts as they closed range. And unlike the Motherships, these Kroggs didn't seem the sort to simply accept fire without answering.

The hundred-odd Krogg vessels broke into their own squadrons, and began to weave in matching patterns with Furgus' ships. Enough Earther squadrons were on hand to intercept them all, but as *Madrid* began lobbing energy shot at a Dreadnought running down on it, the first 74s started to come apart under Krogg fire.

"Looks like more are headed in after the Carriers. Could that be their trap?" Forepaw looked at Caine through the holo tank on *Orion's* bridge.

The First Lord frowned at the readings — the Krogg Motherships seemed to be immobile. Perhaps they were bait, designed to lure the Carriers in to meet them, then to be overwhelmed by the Krogg forces in system...

There could be no escape for the Kroggs fighting that far in-system — the hyper limit was so far from them now that they'd never be able to get past the Earthers to reach it. But the Kroggs must have known the loss of the Carriers would seriously limit the Earthers' strength in boats.

Clever.

"Ursla moving in now?"

Forepaw nodded.

Caine paused for a second and then turned to *Orion's* Signal Officer, "Send to the fleet, we're going straight to the planet. Make speed 400 pls."

Madrid bucked hard as another salvo of spines tore into it. On the bridge, Furgus tightly held the arms of his chair and watched the battle unfold on the main plot. His division was getting battered — fourteen ships completely gone, over thirty heavily damaged...

After only a few minutes.

He'd seen much worse — Gibraltar had been a nightmare of corvettes that had destroyed hundreds, and the Battle of Genesis had been a hard capital ship fight...

But this *felt* worse.

The ships of his division were close to being overwhelmed, even though they were giving better than they got...

"Send to Maximane, why doesn't he launch?"

"ETA on planet's corvettes?" Fox turned to his Sensor Chief.

The Chief frowned briefly, looked up to the supervising Sensor Officer, and then to Fox, "Skipper, they aren't launching."

Fox looked away from the plot.

"*What?*"

What were the Kroggs playing at — 3,000 corvettes in position on the planet and they weren't going to use them?

The Chief shrugged and the Officer leaned over his shoulder, eyeing the panel and nodding, "Nothing, sir. They're still in their caves. The energy readings are up... but nobody's coming out."

Fox frowned and turned to the plot, watching almost half the Krogg Fleet double back against the planet...

"We've waited long enough," Ursla said quietly to Tigar.

They'd held the Second Fleet back to watch the progress of the Carrier Group, and now they'd have their chance to hit the body of the Krogg Fleet while it was in turmoil. Some alien ships were going back towards the planet, others were repositioning to try to fill the gaps... But they weren't concentrated or prepared to deal with an entire Earther fleet dropping in.

"All ships, fleet vanguard," Ursla turned to *Agamemnon's* Signal Officer. "Move in *now*."

The First thundered from energy drive almost on top of Jax Furgus and his division, *Orion* firing as soon as the broadsides ran out. Seventy-five guns on the massive First Rate's port beam drove shot through a Dreadnought, and then the starboard guns added to the fury.

The First Fleet, minus the ships attached to Felix's command, was all together now, and Furgus' beleaguered squadrons found themselves at home with dozens of others to protect them. The Kroggs moving to attack the Carriers were suddenly outnumbered.

Caine watched with some mild satisfaction, listening as Forepaw fought his ship and offering a few orders for the fleet as he noted the weaknesses of the Krogg counterattack. The Earthers had this one well handled...

The holo tank chirped and changed maps as Ursla and the Second Fleet barreled into the hyper limit front of the Krogg defense, catching most of the aliens unaware and disorganized. The trap for the Carriers hadn't worked then — the Kroggs had baited it with mock Motherships, and now the jaws of their snare were being forced open by Earther squadrons.

"All ships prepare to launch boats," Caine turned to his Signal Officer.

They'd held the boats back until the situation had clarified itself... now the small, heavily-armed Earther strike craft would help make short work of the Krogg remnants.

And then something struck Caine — the Carriers hadn't launched.

Nor had the escort squadrons.

"Belay that," he turned again. "Send to the Carrier Group requesting boat instructions. Also send to *Agamemnon*... suggest withholding boats until otherwise notified."

Ursla hadn't actually thought about gunboats by the time the signal from *Orion* reached her, so she accepted the recommendation and passed it on. They didn't need to risk the valuable small craft now anyway — her ships were meeting Krogg warships on even terms, there was no need to bring the gunboats into it.

Agamemnon danced through space with the 201st Battle Squadron, its mighty broadsides batting aside smaller Krogg opponents. The Second Fleet was paying — almost thirty ships destroyed now, and twice that many damaged — but the Kroggs were getting the worst of it by far. Their front was close to breaking...

"They're falling back to the planet," the Sensor Officer on *Agamemnon's* deck reported abruptly, and Ursla nodded.

"Pursue."

Atlas was scraping the atmosphere, rumbling angrily as its shields deflected gas particles of a higher-than-usual density. Above the 74, *Vulcan* and *Fuji* held station, watching to make sure nothing tried to run down on their squadron flagship when it was skimming the atmosphere in that vulnerable position.

"Sensors now at maximum, skipper..."

Fox frowned into the main battle plot as the deep-piercing energy pulses that made up *Atlas'* active sensor grid shook themselves through rock to find the corvettes. The images arriving in the holo were garbled and not particularly revealing — the Krogg corvettes were hiding something in those caves...

And he had a feeling the real trap was waiting for them down there.

"Are we going to launch, sir?"

Maximane shook his head at Captains Ron Hobbes and Farley Karr, the former with him in *Engadine* and the latter in the holo plot.

"We're not necessary until corvettes show up, and I don't want to chance our boats until we're needed," Maximane's words were even.

"The corvettes still haven't launched from the surface?" Karr frowned through the holo tank.

Maximane shook his head, "Fox is checking it right now. But we can't leave as long as they're a potential threat."

"They're falling back right into us, and Ursla's coming with them."

Caine nodded at Forepaw's observation. Both First and Second Fleets had suffered relatively light casualties thus far — just about five percent now, with a maximum projection of ten percent for the operation. Most of the crews were getting out alive.

Now, with the Kroggs in rough shape and being routed, the Earthers had a chance to finish the fight with less than ten percent...

"This can't be right."

Fox turned to the Sensor Officer, steadying himself as *Atlas* again bucked against the atmosphere of the planet, "What?"

The Sensor Officer glanced to the Sensor Chief, then nodded and looked up, "We've got readings of corvettes traveling *into* the planet... have a look."

The main holo glowed with the sphere of Krogg 'B', where small black icons were working their way through caverns. Like ants through a colony...

"How long until they get to the core?"

The Sensor Officer frowned but the Chief had already plotted the aliens' course, "A little over forty seconds."

Fox's mind wanted to freeze, but at the same time his instincts told him exactly what was going on. These crafty alien bastards–

He was already whirling to the Signal Officer, "All ships disengage and get *out of here*! The planet is rigged!"

The Signal Lieutenant did freeze for a split second, but then the signal went out... garbled through the atmosphere of 'B'.

"Mister Gunth, get us out of here *fast*!"

Maximane frowned as a static-laden transmission from *Atlas* came through *Engadine's* system.

"...ll ships dis... et out o... net rigged."

"*Atlas* just cleared the atmosphere and went into energy drive," someone said with mild surprise.

Rigged. Ships out.

"All ships, break action and get out of the system —*fast*."

He didn't know precisely what the threat was, but it was formidable and it was immediate.

Engadine leapt into energy drive, followed by the escort force.

Orion heaved broadsides into more Dreadnoughts, and the space around the First Rate filled with blood and gore.

As the ship continued its mauling of the Kroggs, Forepaw looked at Caine,

"Should we launch, Setter? We'd make it cleaner that way."

Caine looked up at Forepaw.

Nothing wrong so far.

"Yes." He turned to the Signal Officer, "All ships, launch–"

"Sir, the Carriers just withdrew from the system!"

Caine's head snapped around to the Sensor center on *Orion's* bridge, and his mind ticked over...

If Maximane was leaving something had to be very wrong.

"All ships disengage and exit system at maximum speed. Pass the warning to Andra."

Orion went into energy drive as quickly as its guns would come into their ports, leaving angry Krogg ships alive as it withdrew.

Agamemnon and the Second Fleet were driving hard in-system, their guns firing as soon as they charged. The Kroggs were running quickly, and Ursla was determined to get most of them before they could reach their comrades.

The amount of gunfire coming from the Second Fleet — still united in a massive vanguard and firing chasers in squadron order — blocked out the readings showing the withdrawal of the First Fleet, and the same interference was garbling all signals trying to reach the flagship.

Ursla sat quietly next to Tigar and watched her ships at work.

Deep within the planet of Krogg 'B', a corvette carrying a Telepath dove into the planetary core then released a sizable amount of telepathic energy. A dozen more made it to the core in the following seconds, and the combined release of their telepathic payloads ruptured the world, causing it to *explode*...

"Wait a minute, ma'am, the First has withdrawn..."

Agamemnon's Sensor Chief leaned closer to his console and then transferred the readings to the main battle plot. Ursla frowned at the blue holos as they came up...

And then everything seemed to stop for a second as the planet in Krogg 'B' shattered in a massive explosion.

Ursla's eyes widened. The Second Fleet wasn't far from the planet now — its chase of the retreating Kroggs had brought it right into the path of the shockwave. So this was the perfect trap and it had drawn the Earthers in close. It was a miracle someone had warned off Caine... and hopefully the Carriers...

"We have *incoming debris!*" the Sensor Chief roared, but Ursla was already turning to the Signal Lieutenant.

"All ships *move!*"

Tigar was well ahead of her, and as she roared the Master was already sending *Agamemnon* into crash energy drive, forcing the great ship's massive hull to groan as the translation from 12 pls to 2,600 pls hit hard with the guns run out.

The ship could handle it, but it didn't accept the punishment without a few heaves for good measure.

The rest of the fleet wasn't necessarily so quick...

Ships either saw the explosion themselves or heard the warning, and they made their own crash translations into energy drive, withdrawing from the system as fast as they could manage.

But many were too late or too badly damaged. Throwing all their available power into their heavy shielding at the last possible second, they were smashed by the shockwave and rained on by massive chunks of rock.

Brilliant and brutally effective. Krogg 'B' *had* been a trap.

CHAPTER 29

"Sir... I'm getting a large energy spike from Krogg 'B', looks like something massive detonated."

Felix paused in his pondering — 'C' had been a decoy. Somehow the Kroggs were using it as leverage to make 'B' a better slaughterhouse...

Tonnant was suddenly hurled through space.

Felix, standing at the plot, was flung painfully into a nearby wall, "Report!"

A second salvo of spines slammed into the Second Rate, and Felix abruptly recognized the sensation.

"About a hundred active Krogg ships, all here at the center of the system..."

So they'd been hiding amongst the cripples, playing possum while the older ships had been destroyed. Or perhaps the older ones had simply been meant as bait to keep drawing the Third Fleet into the system...

"They blindsided the 132nd. It's gone, and the 398th and 360th..."

"Reorganize by squadron and engage — quickly!" Felix growled the orders and forced himself back to the main plot, the 100 active Krogg vessels appearing rapidly as they weaved around his ships. They'd managed to destroy twenty in a single volley...

A broadside slammed into one of the alien vessels, followed quickly by many other salvoes. The Kroggs had struck hard with surprise on their side, but they still had to deal with ten-to-one odds.

Tonnant's starboard broadside thundered with the flagship's first reply to the clever Kroggs, and the Second Rate pressed in close to nearest Super-dreadnoughts. Carronades and guns fired quickly, viciously carving up the attackers as the range came down.

A dozen more ships of the line came apart, bursting under heavy fire from unexpected angles. As *Tonnant* rolled into the center of the Krogg formation, its guns blazing, a few 74s came to join it, their guns beginning to pay off against the heavy infiltrators.

"The Kroggs are running back down towards their star," the Sensor Chief offered quickly.

Felix frowned at that prospect. What were they doing making that sort of run? The hyper limit was the other way...

Of course, going towards the hyper limit meant forcing their way through most of a *very* angry Third Fleet, and an equally vengeful division of the First. The Kroggs might be trying to sprint past the star and exit the system on the far side. If they were fast enough they could get away with it.

He should chase them, but chasing them had 'trap' written all over it — they could have reinforcements hiding in close orbit of the sun, just out of sight of the routine patrols that cut through the system.

"I need sloops ahead — check the star for their reinforcements. And recall all boats... I don't like the smell of this."

The orders for reconnaissance found their way to *Flame*, the one sloop that got all the fun work in this galaxy — or so it seemed to Chronos Claw.

Claw keyed the comm, "Lang, we're going out ahead to run recon. Everything alright down there?"

There was a huff on the speakers, "Close enough to. How many we have with us?"

"Just *Flower* and *Smoke*, the rest I've sent back for repairs."

"Lovely."

The line cut and Chronos Claw took a deep breath. His sloops had been attached to the Third Fleet for the attack on 'C'. Things had been going so well until those Kroggs hiding in the ranks of the catatonic had gotten into it, and now he'd lost one sloop entirely, and three others were banged up enough to order them out.

But despite the losses, someone had to see just what the Kroggs were trying to pull, and what ship better than *Flame* for that duty...

The sloop rocketed out ahead of *Tonnant*, both ships veterans of the Battle of Genesis. Now, the former and its escorting pair of sloops went to light speed and a little beyond, using energy drive to pass the large number of Krogg warships that were trying to flee the wrath of the Third Fleet. *Flame's* high-powered sensor net was carefully probing the star, piercing the corona of the small sun as the range ticked down...

"No ships or stations detected yet..." Claw came out of his chair as the Sensor Chief spoke, "Hang on..."

Claw turned to the Chief and waited as the readings from the enhanced detection suite slowly processed in the computers.

"Well?"

"Not sure, skipper, but it's like I'm reading *two* stars out there, one big and one awfully small. It might be a focusing problem on the sensors — we did get banged up a bit."

Claw nodded — that much was true. He turned across the bridge to the Signal Chief, "Request *Flower* and *Smoke* confirm that. Pass the telemetry on to *Tonnant*."

Still under normal drives while the boats returned, *Tonnant* led the Third Fleet in pursuit of the remaining Krogg ships, but Felix was feeling more and more like this was what his enemy wanted him to do.

He glared uneasily into the plot as they neared the star, and he watched *Flame's* telemetry with suspicion. This wasn't right.

Well, whatever was there, the Third Fleet had the advantage in numbers — that was a certainty. There was no way the Kroggs could hide enough firepower around that star to do more harm than his forces could... but he still might want to move some ships around to attack them on their flank.

"Send to Rear Admiral Peregrine, take the First Fleet division around the star at 400 pls and stand by to engage from that flank."

Something in *Tonnant* suddenly 'banged'.

Varnia was on her feet as soon as the abnormal sound resonated through the Second Rate's hull, "Report."

The Master and the First Lieutenant both rushed to the ops consoles and began checking systems, but after a moment they no longer needed to.

Tonnant's power flickered, and the ship's engines died.

"Looks like damage from that second salvo we took," the Master reported quickly, checking with sensors throughout the ship.

The First Lieutenant nodded in confirmation, "The reactors just shut down on safety protocol — there was a feedback loop that wasn't on the panels... the detectors must have fried after that shield overload."

Tonnant still coasted through space on momentum, it just lacked the ability to speed up or decelerate. Impacts of small space particles began to angle the ship's bow down slightly, pointing it away from the direction the Third Fleet was traveling in, and at the same time that minor friction began to slow the Second Rate so that the rest of the fleet started passing overhead.

"Damn..." the Master wasn't usually one for coarse language, so his comment drew Felix's gaze. The grizzled ship-handler looked to the Admiral and shook his head, "Engineering says it'll take two hours to get the mains up... they say they can give you drives in ten if we skip the startups."

Varnia cast a questioning glance to Felix and he nodded. The backup generators still provided *Tonnant* with power for light, gravity, and comms. The ship just lacked the ability to fight.

"Order the next squadron by to detach a ship to cover us," Felix ordered quietly.

He didn't like being aboard a crippled ship, even if it was only temporary.

"*Sultan* is approaching... and *Carolina*. Both coming into escort positions, sir."

A 64 and a 36-gun frigate — a reasonable guard in case something abrupt happened.

But was something happening?

Flame slowed as the grav well of the sun thickened, and the sloop's sensors dove deeper into the atmosphere of the burning ball of gas. So far there wasn't a thing to repo–

"*By the Earth!* Skipper, we've got a large vessel of some sort sitting low in the atmosphere. It's generating a *lot* of power..."

Claw came out of his chair again, "On the plot."

The main holo changed from its system map to an image of the star, showing a black dagger-like ship sitting low, just as the Chief had said.

"It looks like it's getting ready to go *in*..." the Chief looked up from his panel. "Do you think they'd..."

Claw's face slowly drew taut. Those crafty *bastards*...

"Send a warning to all ships, we've got something here that appears to be tampering with the star. Prepare energy drives..."

"Would they do anything while their own ships are still in-system?" the Chief frowned, and Claw shrugged.

"Their ships have no way out as it is. They're better off taking most of us with them..."

"Hang on... it's moving. Looks like it's going in..."

Claw watched in the main plot as the dagger-shaped ship dove straight into the sun... whatever it was, it was surviving long enough to actually reach the surface, and probably to get a bit below it...

"It knows we've seen it. Warn all ships to get out of here," Claw turned back to his seat. "Master, up speed to 2,400 and set bearing 230 by 190 by 110."

Flame veered away from the star, *Smoke* and *Flower* following closely.

"They're going to supernova the star," Felix said grimly. "Order all our ships out."

If Felix hadn't sent Claw ahead the Third Fleet would have been dragged straight into the shockwave — and not even Earther construction and shielding could survive that...

Oh.

Oh *damn*.

"Engineering, we've got a bit of a problem. Can you get our drives online?" the First Lieutenant was well ahead of him.

"Ten minutes, bridge. We're already cutting all the corners we can."

"Fleet is exiting system now — we've still got *Sultan* and *Carolina* with us," Varnia observed quickly. "We can recall someone larger for a tow."

There was always that. While a 64 couldn't hope to haul an 80, a First Rate or another Second might be able to handle the job... even a 74 in a pinch.

"Get a signal off — volunteer ships to tow us–"

"Sir!"

Felix was looking down as he spoke, and now he glanced at the main battle plot as the star of Krogg 'C' came apart. It wasn't a smooth explosion — whatever had been carrying the telepathic bomb hadn't made it all the way to the center of the sphere, so the blast had gone off about a third of the way down. A large chunk of the star hurtled off the side first, and the rest collapsed quickly thereafter.

Of course, the big chunk was hurtling right for *Tonnant*.

"We just lost long-range comms, sir. That's more interference than we can handle..."

Felix nodded slowly, turning to the Sensor Chief, "How long until we get the shockwave?"

The Chief keyed things into his panel — the speed at which *Tonnant* was coasting, the speed of the shockwave...

"About six minutes."

Felix closed his eyes and nodded, turning to his chair and the intercom, "Engineering, Admiral Felix here. The star of this system just blew up. We're dead if we aren't out of here in six minutes.

There was a pause on the other side of the line, "We hear you, sir. We'll do our best, but we're looking at eight minutes."

"Anything helps. Cut whatever corners you can."

Felix turned to Varnia, "Evacuate the crew to *Sultan* and *Carolina*. Just in case. Use the life pods and the pinnaces, standard drill."

Varnia nodded slowly and turned to the Master, "All hands evacuate. Nearest exit points."

"Looks like all ships are clear, a couple of damaged 74s had to get towed out."

Claw nodded at the report, "Pass on our scans of that ship to *Tonnant*. They're going to want to have a look at it... whatever it was."

"Yes sir."

Claw sat back in his chair and sighed. Job done — they'd managed to neutralize the effects of the Krogg trap.

Good work–

"Skipper, *Tonnant's* not on scope. Its squadron says it experienced engine trouble in-system... they haven't seen it since."

Claw stiffened.

"Find it... Admiral Felix will need a tow, so find a bigger ship too."

"We can't see anything in-system, skipper — the shockwave is–"

"Don't tell me we *can't!* Find them!"

"Two minutes."

"All crew except the engineers are now off ship... *Carolina's* picking up the last of them."

Only Felix, Varnia, the First Lieutenant, and the Master remained on *Tonnant's* bridge.

Felix nodded, "Very good. That just leaves you three to go. Take one of the bridge pods."

The three *Tonnant* officers exchanged glances and stood stoically in place, "We stay with you and this ship."

"No, not today. Go. If the engineers get things running, I'll maneuver us out of here. You don't have long, so I'm ordering you to go," Felix's voice was firm.

The First Lieutenant stiffened a bit and then nodded slowly, the Master opened his mouth to object but the Lieutenant's hand on his shoulder stopped him.

"Good luck, sir," the latter said in low tones.

They headed to the rear of the bridge, where three lifeboat ports lay behind the bulkhead. They keyed one of the ten-person pods open and slid in, leaving the door open for their Captain.

Varnia looked stubbornly at Felix, "I'm not leaving my bridge."

Felix cocked an eyebrow and looked at the clock, "Eighty seconds, you *go*. Your father would never forgive me if I let you stay."

"My fath–"

Felix held up his hand, "Go, Varnia. You know how this always works — Earther timing. They'll have the drives online. But it's less dramatic if I'm not the only one up here."

Varnia Broadpaw saw right through the façade of confidence. She extended her hand and Felix took it, "Good luck."

Felix nodded, "Thanks. See you soon."

Slowly, Varnia turned and marched to the pod. As the hatch closed she exchanged a last, brief glance with her Admiral, and he smiled and nodded.

With a minute left, the pod shot from *Tonnant's* bridge, and straight into a waiting grav tractor from *Carolina's* launch bay. As the pod drew in, the frigate turned and accelerated away from *Tonnant*, heading into energy drive as soon as the bay doors closed.

Sultan followed, leaving a 'good luck' transmission in its wake.

Felix left the plot and came to sit in his chair. He keyed his panel into the helm controls and plotted a course away from the shockwave.

With thirty seconds to go he keyed the intercom, "Ready yet?"

A five second pause, "We can try it, sir. But it may just fry the power grid."

"You've done all you can. Find yourselves the best protection you can…"

"Aye sir. Good luck."

Felix swallowed and looked at the clock. Twenty…

He had plenty of good luck… now he just needed it all to pay off…

On his panel, he keyed the energy drive controls to life.

At ten seconds to go he hit the 'Activate' key.

At nine he realized nothing had happened and hit it again.

And at eight, seven, six, and five.

At four he looked up at the holo tank, and saw a large diffusing ball of flame coming at his unshielded hull.

At three he smiled to himself.

So this is how it'll end. How very sad. Who'd have thought.

"Good luck, Setter, Andra, Varnon, Varnia, Fox, Chronos, Graham, Sarah, James, Audrey…" his words were soft.

If I can't use the luck, I transfer it to them.

They'll win.

At one Admiral Savanna Felix closed his eyes.

What's this I see…?

At zero, *ENS Tonnant* shattered.

CHAPTER 30

Something in Caine suddenly shuddered, and he frowned.

"Massive power spike from 'C'... the *sun* just went nova!"

Caine blinked a few times... "The Third Fleet?"

"I'm picking up a large number of our ships outside the system... I can't get pennants for them yet, but it looks like all of them are there."

Caine nodded slowly, but something — something inexplicable — felt wrong.

"Casualties from the Second?" he asked quietly, his conscious mind overriding the unpleasantly eerie feeling with some difficulty.

"About 150 got caught in the blast... it looks like a dozen managed to survive."

"Send squadrons in to tow them... they'll have to be on the lookout for fast-moving debris," Caine moved from his chair back to the plot and keyed it to show the system he'd just evacuated. A few ships remained more or less intact within the wreckage of the destroyed planet. The force of the blast had scattered the remains of Krogg 'B' throughout the system.

So the Kroggs had baited the Earthers with fighting ships. They'd drawn the entire attacking force into close proximity of the planet, and they'd committed suicide for the chance to wipe out the Earther Navy.

If it hadn't been for quick wits on the part of Draco Maximane and Fox Magnus, the Krogg plan would have worked to perfection. The aliens must have tried the same at 'C' — just using the star there instead of the planet.

These Kroggs weren't only clever, they were *vicious* and cold-blooded.

And now something about that strategy made Caine want to kill them all.

Yes, *kill them all.* Caine wanted to do that, at least for a brief few seconds.

The very thought made him shiver — that was *not* what Earthers did. They did not annihilate.

Funny, until now he hadn't really focused on what to do at that next stage — when the Kroggs in 'A' had to be dealt with. Now he wondered whether they'd let themselves be defeated or whether they'd go out in a massive explosion of their own making...

Caine took a deep breath but felt no more comfortable. There was something *very* wrong.

"*Agamemnon* coming up alongside, sir. Signal coming from Admiral Ursla."

Trying to clear his mind, Caine turned to the battle plot as Ursla's head appeared. She looked drawn and unsettled as well.

"They blew their own planet to kill us," she said quietly. "They killed 150 of my crews doing it."

Caine nodded slowly, "Not the kind of war we fight, is it?"

Ursla shook her head.

"You have the feeling that something else isn't right?" Caine asked after a moment.

Taking a deep breath, Ursla frowned and nodded, "Did I hear something about a supernova in 'C'?"

"Yes. The Third appears to be intact... but both systems were traps."

Ursla slowly rubbed the back of her neck, "For the most part, we managed to evade them today. But I can't help but wonder if 'A' is a trap as well."

Caine shrugged, "We'll have some time to figure that out. There's no way we try to hit that system until we get reinforced."

Ursla nodded, "Indeed. For now we should finish recovery and get back there, just in case the Kroggs try anything."

"I'll send a sloop to call Savanna..." there was a twinge in his stomach and he suddenly felt like his blood was burning. Ursla twitched too... "...and get the Third to come in," Caine finished with some difficulty. He didn't know what was happening to him.

"See you at 'A', then," Ursla cut the link almost gingerly.

Flame sat in stunned silence, as did the Third Fleet and Kylie Peregrine's Division of the First.

The nova had swept the system clean. Cleared it entirely. Obliterated everything...

And as the interference slowly began to fade, the absence of *Tonnant* became glaring.

There was no sign of it anywhere on scopes, it wasn't sending out distress signals, and there certainly weren't any life pods...

Chronos Claw tried to come to terms with the implications of that, but he wasn't able to. The Earther Navy was no stranger to losing officers, but Admiral Savanna Felix was one of the elite. A Fleet Admiral. A brilliant fighter. A respected leader. And one of the most energetic and innovative...

Claw closed his eyes for a moment and let his chin sink to his chest.

"Sir, sloop coming in from Krogg 'B'."

Raising his head slowly, Claw turned to his Sensor Chief, "Do we know who's in command of the fleet now?"

The Chief shook his head, "The interference is too thick for me to identify most of the fleet... though I do see *Gargoyle*."

Gargoyle was Kylie Peregrine's ship, and thus was the flagship of the division of the First assigned to this attack. That would have to do...

"Pass on those coordinates to the sloop."

Orion slid out of energy drive in the blockade formation around Krogg 'A' and sent out a general flagship assembly signal. *Lycrotar, Agamemnon*, and *Joseph*

Barron slowly edged into formation with the First Rate — moving from their respective posts around the blockade. The First and Second Fleets deployed to positions in support of the already posted Allies.

Pinnaces began to cruise between ships, *Agamemnon's* being the first to approach *Orion's* side. The flight deck had handled the strain of the battle well enough, and as the Deck Chief personally waved Ursla's ship to its slot, the kodiak Admiral attempted to suppress a burning in her blood. It was something she didn't remember feeling before and it was all but impossible to describe.

Time passed in a blur as she slowly came down the ramp, nodded to the Chief, and paced across the deck to Caine, who waited near the hatch to the corridor. The scorch marks from the explosion were gone. The Chief kept a clean deck...

But Ursla's mind barely registered this as she approached Caine. The First Lord stood silently, looking up at her with a frown.

She stopped a few meters in front of him. There was something wrong — all her instincts, her very *blood* was telling her so. And he didn't have to say a word for her to know he was feeling the same...

Nodding in agreement to a statement that Caine hadn't actually made out loud, she followed him into the corridor and towards the briefing room, walking unsteadily through the halls.

Then Caine stopped and his frown deepened. He turned to Ursla, "It's Savanna, isn't it?"

She blinked and nodded.

Caine's eyes roved quickly back and forth across the deck, and his brow softened and saddened.

Neither of them could be sure of what their instincts were telling them... and yet they both *knew*. And the tragedy of the loss, the *presumed* loss, perhaps, escaped neither of them.

"He was the most energetic of the lot of us," his voice was low and crisp.

Ursla nodded. She couldn't think of anything to say, so as Caine gently patted her on the back, the pair simply walked on.

CHAPTER 31

Sarah came cautiously down the ramp of her pinnace, looking in every possible direction to make sure there were no airborne craft waiting to land. Convinced she wasn't about to cause a crash, she crossed the flight deck and offered a short nod to the Deck Chief, who nodded back kindly.

She didn't feel as though he blamed her, and she appreciated that. She knew she was at fault for the crash — Pat had made that brutally clear — but at least she wasn't being condemned. Not by the Earthers...

An alert chime sounded across the deck as the doors at the far end of the bay stopped closing and began to open again before the field that maintained deck pressurization had been deactivated.

A silver fighter slowly climbed into sight outside the field, and as they opened sufficiently it eased its way into the bay. The Larosian craft moved with certain caution as it made its way over the deck, then began its form change into a walking robot for landing.

Coming down on two feet with sword and gun weapons in its mechanized hands, the craft looked rather unpleasant, but that was soon remedied by the opening of a hatch from the underside, and the lowering of a disc on which the Larosian Admiral stood.

Sarah slowed her stride and stopped before the hatch, watching as Novash stepped off his fighter's lift and sent it back up. The Larosian then cautiously crossed the deck himself, tilting his head and offering a bow-nod to the Deck Chief as he slowed before him.

"You operate this flight deck, sir?" Novash asked courteously, and the Chief nodded.

"Ah good, I missed you on my last visit. I should tell you then, sir, that none among us hold you responsible for the accident involving Admiral-of-a-Fleet Narosh. And he will recover."

The Deck Chief nodded evenly in reply, "Thank you, sir."

Novash bow-nodded again, then left the Chief and sighted Sarah. Slowing before the ArcGeneral, he took what one might consider a deep breath.

"Do we have any indication yet as to what went off in 'B' and 'C'?" he asked softly, and though he read the answer directly from Sarah's surface thoughts, he politely waited for the vocal reply.

It often seemed intrusive, he found, when he pre-read humans, so he tended not to publicize the practice.

"None, I'm afraid. You saw the same spikes I did, and it looks like we have quite a few battered ships to deal with."

Novash offered a slow nod and then gestured to the corridor, "We should attend. After ladies."

Sarah smiled, "Ladies *first* is the traditional way of putting it. But thanks for the sentiment."

Leading them into the corridor, Sarah kept a steady pace that Novash easily matched, and forgetting her company, she let her mind wander a bit.

Well, a lot.

To Pat. To all he'd said. To her supposed need to prove herself. To her carelessness...

Being here again reminded her of Lewie Granger — that innocent Earther would haunt her for a long time. So visible, so personal... such a disaster.

Her fault.

Pardon my intrusion, but I assure you it was not.

Sarah came to an abrupt stop in the hall, then whirled on Novash, "What are you doing in my head? We talked about this before *Genesis*..."

Her tone was low and sharp, and the Larosian came to a stop and met her blue eyes with his silver ones. *I'm trying to be discreet and helpful, ArcGeneral.*

"Well stop it."

I can assure you that you are not blamed for the accident of the Admiral-of-a-Fleet. We do not blame you.

I was bloody-well at fault, Novash. Back off.

Novash tilted his head slightly. *Your hostility is unnecessary, I seek only to help you. Yours is an unenviable position... you are afraid that you do not understand yourself as well as you believe you do.*

Sarah's eyes widened slightly and her hand leapt to the Larosian's throat, driving him back against the corridor wall in a surprising and forceful gesture, "Do *not* analyze me, Novash."

A quick-sliding hand from the Larosian dislodged her, and Novash freed himself easily from her experienced grip, "I understand you are upset, ArcGeneral, I am merely trying to help. You need not explain anything. Though I would advise you against making such random physical attacks in future."

"I don't *want* help. Get it?"

Novash straightened slightly. *Perhaps Pat is right then.*

The Admiral-of-a-Division stepped past Sarah and continued down the corridor. *My apologies for the intrusion.*

Sarah angrily watched him go. She was furious and afraid. And one intensified the other and caused her a great deal of angst. She'd just physically accosted a Larosian...

Sarah closed her eyes and took a deep breath. She had to stop making excuses for snapping... he must have hit a nerve. Oh, so very easy to say that...

Why was she feeling so defensive?

Sarah took another breath, trying to collect herself. She'd get over it. She had to. She had a job to do...

And, she recalled somewhat reluctantly, a life to live.

Maybe she'd have to mend some fences.

Caine sat opposite Ursla as they read the signal packet sent on by Kylie Peregrine from *Gargoyle*, including the report on the destruction of *Tonnant*.

Neither Earther was surprised, and both were trying to come to terms with the eerie knowledge that they'd felt something had happened as *soon* as it had happened from lightyears away.

Savanna Felix, one of the fleet commanders... *Savanna*.

Gone. In the jaws of a Krogg trap, just a few minutes short of safety, and refusing in the end, to leave his ship. Refusing to leave *Tonnant* in a bid to save it at the very last second. But what Fox had called 'Earther timing' hadn't been able to intervene at the right moment this time.

It felt like a bad omen, but to Caine that was overshadowed by the grievousness of the loss. He and Felix had been friends for years — they'd both been in the administration of the Navy for decades before the humans had arrived, and Caine had been the one to commission Felix as line officer. In fact, he'd handed *Tonnant* to him with a mandate to stop a rogue group of violent Naval officers...

To Caine's recollection, Felix hadn't gotten a chance to see home since.

And, of course, at Gibraltar, it had been Felix who had kept Caine's determination from unraveling, who'd dealt with Graham's anger, and Caine's grief...

He was a pillar of the Earther Navy. One now gone.

Ursla hadn't been quite as close to him, but she had still been his very dear friend. Felix had saved Narosh with her. He'd shown up to help her at Genesis. He'd helped win Gibraltar.

He was a hero.

He had been.

Caine sat back in his chair and rubbed his eyes a bit ruefully. He had lost so many already, but none had been such a dear, close friend. They had always been strangers or reputational acquaintances, or more distant friends like Kella Felar.

The First Lord's mind tried to find the last moment he'd actually spoken to the Siberian tiger, but his memory seemed locked shut. He needed to pull out of this mental quagmire... he couldn't be dwelling on dead friends when they still had 'A' to deal with, though they would inevitably have to wait for the Fifth and Sixth to arrive to mount an attack.

And he'd need to spend some time finding a commanding officer for the Third. Kylie Peregrine and Jax Furgus from the First were two options...

No. He could decide later.

Now his head felt numb beyond reason...

Ursla's mind felt little better.

She let her chin rest in her hand, her elbow propped on the arm of her chair.

Things seemed abruptly different, and she lacked the will to think or do. For so long there'd been an air of invulnerability surrounding the fleet commanders. They were the champions, the veterans, the *best*.

And then to lose Savanna. Perhaps the brightest of them. A talented and charismatic, *thinking* leader.

To lose him to bad engines and a trap.

It was saddening... maddening... senseless in so many ways.

Just like every other thing this war yielded up when examined carefully enough.

She was tired of it.

And as she met Caine's eyes, she knew exactly how he'd been feeling for months... how he had to be feeling now.

Caine frowned as he looked at Ursla.

"I know how tired you are of all this," Ursla said grimly.

Felix almost seemed to appear before Caine's eyes — almost. Just enough for him to have a glimmer of hope that the tiger was back, even if he was only haunting the lounge.

Don't worry about me, you've got a job to do... he seemed to be saying.

But Caine was beginning to see in his mind everything the Kroggs had done. This last pair of traps had cost the Allies so very dearly and had almost destroyed them all...

"We end this quickly," he said in a hard tone. "And we end this whole war with that Queen. She's been behind this. All of it."

Caine's voice had steeled over with determination, and Ursla sat up slightly at the seeming strength in it.

"You sure?"

"They get smarter as we get closer to her. She wants to stop us at all costs. And while I won't exterminate all the Kroggs, I *will* see this war end with her. We finish it here."

Ursla leaned slowly back in her chair as the door to the room opened.

CHAPTER 32

Novash heard Sarah's footsteps as she followed him down the corridor, but he didn't slow his pace — she'd catch up to him if she wished... And she did want to catch up, though she wasn't sure what to think or say, whether to be angry or to apologize. Her head was filled with so much superfluous information she couldn't focus.

I understand. You do not need to apologize, your mind reveals your trouble quite clear–

The door parted in front of Novash just as he was thinking his consolation to Sarah, and neither needed to be telepathic to recognize the dread that filled *Orion's* briefing room.

The pair entered, their previous discussion and argument forgotten...

"What's happened?" Sarah asked anxiously.

Caine, who was leaning forward in his chair with his back facing the door, slowly turned. His eyes met Sarah's abruptly, and a jolt of sadness seemed to flow through the gaze.

"There were traps waiting for us in both 'B' and 'C'," Ursla said sadly.

"*Traps?*" Novash vocalized with some awkwardness. "*Krogg* traps?"

Caine nodded, "Even more clever than what we've been seeing. They drew us into the space around Krogg 'B' and then blew up the planet, and they did something similar with 'C's star."

Sarah was edging her way to a seat, "Gods wept."

She slowly dropped into a chair one down from Caine, while Novash moved to sit on the far side of her from the First Lord.

"The losses were serious?" the Larosian asked in a low tone, and Ursla nodded in reply.

"We lost 150 ships of the Second, and many more were damaged... and that doesn't begin to describe the loss of life..."

Ursla's voice trailed off as Caine keyed the main briefing room holo to life, "And this."

Tonnant sat there, in the path of a nova shockwave. The holo portrayed it as the sensors of *ENS Sultan* had seen it. The image vanished with less than a minute to impact, as *Sultan* escaped to energy drive. But on the star map of Krogg 'C', the blue dot representing *Tonnant* collided with the blue-white shockwave and burst.

Sarah stopped breathing.

"They got off?"

Caine slowly shook his head, "Not all of them. Some stayed behind to try to save their ship."

Sarah's face, already grim, seemed to further darken. *Tonnant* had been a fine ship — to lose a flagship was terrible, even if Savanna did escape the–

"Savanna was aboard."

Sarah's mind refused the information.

He couldn't have been aboard. He was a fleet Admiral. He couldn't... be...

Her own problems suddenly seemed so trivial — here was a truly cruel loss to crown the many brutal losses on the part of the Earther Navy today.

It was a harsh thing to admit, but this somehow hurt more than thousands of dead.

And it suddenly made her ashamed — in a way she couldn't quite fathom.

"It's all that much more real all of a sudden, isn't it?" Ursla asked quietly, and Sarah found herself nodding painfully.

She had lost a dear friend... Sarah's shame at focusing on her own woes was beginning to turn to self-loathing. All she'd been thinking about was her petty vendetta to prove herself and bolster her ego while this was going on all around her. It was all about her, never about anyone else.

Easy there, you are able to recognize your troubles — you aren't self-absorbed to the point of delusion.

Sarah blinked at Novash's somehow still discreet intrusion and wasn't entirely sure what to feel.

"Don't beat yourself up, Sarah," Caine said quietly, gently rubbing his forehead. "You couldn't have done anything even if you'd been there. And you know that."

Sarah realized she was staring at her boots under the table so she looked up. Caine turned his head to meet her eyes again.

"He's dead. He died relying on the luck Earthers can usually count on. He was taking a big risk, but he didn't really have a choice," Ursla offered in a wise tone, and Sarah again nodded slowly.

Novash didn't quite understand — even the insight he drew from Sarah couldn't quite make sense of Ursla's words for him, "Perhaps you could make that a little clearer for me?"

Caine cocked an eyebrow at the alien, "He died needlessly for something as trivial as an 80-gun ship of the line. But he believed he could get *Tonnant* out of that system, because he'd never really failed. We've never failed... so he just *had* to try."

"He failed, and, forgive me for my bluntness, he died a useless death," Novash slowly shifted his gaze from Caine to Ursla.

The two Earthers silently peered back at him, Caine gently shaking his head, "He–"

"He gave us perspective," Sarah said quietly, looking between her fellow officers as she did. "He died and put all our internal demons to rest by doing it.

Because my ego or Setter's martyrdom or Andra's fatigue — none of it compares now to the price he paid."

Novash tilted his head, "It is a price we are all willing to pay, is it not?"

Caine nodded slowly, "If we must. But what burns more than the fear of death, Novash, is the loss of such a friend. We're much, much less now than we were before."

Novash slowly leaned back, beginning to understand the situation in more Larosian terms, "It seems, Lord Caine, that you are all more complete now, in a way."

Caine's eyes drifted down to the desk and he tilted his head. Novash was right — he now knew what he had to do, and why he was going to do it. His time for brooding was over.

He'd lost one friend and he might well lose more in the weeks to come.

But in losing them he'd save others. And he'd fulfill the commitment made by the Earthers years before — to help the humans defeat the Kroggs.

Sarah felt tears beginning to form, but she blinked almost angrily against the sting in her eyes as she stared down at the floor again. So much time spent focusing on so little, and it was a death close to home that had to shake her out of it.

She hated herself.

Don't...

"We've all been in a bubble, Sarah."

Ursla's voice drew Sarah's eyes, and she frowned at the great bear.

"We've all lost some of our perspective because we've had to deal with so much. Now we're stepping back from that..."

"And," Caine said in a very low tone, "ignoring what we've learned in favor of self-punishment would do nothing to honor Savanna. We have a war to win."

Sarah thought about the words as they reached her, and in a way she believed that the friendly, adept tiger named Felix had died specifically to help his friends find their way again.

And then, of course, there was the issue of the Kroggs having killed him.

That thought finally got through to her — he wasn't just dead, he'd been murdered in a typically cheap play to save the Queen from her fate...

Well the bitch is still going to die.

"I hope I speak for everyone here," Caine straightened in his chair, "when I say I intend to *finish* this fight. We'll wait one month, let reinforcements arrive and allow Admiral Narosh to heal, and then we'll end this."

Novash, Sarah, and Ursla all nodded at the resolute words.

"It will be Krogg annihilation, then?" Novash pressed. "Death to the last of them?"

Sarah felt a familiar determination beginning to float into her veins — one based on a cause greater than self-righteousness.

"I certainly hope so," she said as she restrained an icy grimace.

Caine looked quickly to Ursla and then thought of Felix.

And for just a moment he thought too of his son.

"We'll sort that out later," he said in quiet tones. "For now, we make sure we have the Kroggs tightly locked in 'A'."

There were nods around the table, and with Felix on their minds, the commanders set about planning the containment of his killers.

The Queen would fall — they only needed to wait a month.

CHAPTER 33

Algenon slid smoothly from energy drive and slowed as it entered Gibraltar space. After a nine-day run from Genesis, the First Rate took some relish in pausing to rest its drives however briefly before it got back on course for another ten-day trek to Krogg. On the bridge, Varnon Broadpaw and Andros Grieve were both literally itching to get off the ship...

Well, Grieve was; Broadpaw was just humoring him.

There was a cutter waiting for them as they came out of energy drive, but there'd been no word from it since its computer had acknowledged their arrival — the crew was off the small ship while its engines were being refitted, so only the vessel's computer had responded to regular transponder queries for identification. The messages carried by the vessel had already been downloaded by *Gibraltar One*, but some were eyes only, and so a request had come in for Broadpaw and the other flag officers to go aboard the station to view them.

No one complained about *that* request — never hurt to change scenery for a few hours. Indeed, some flag officers had been even more eager than Broadpaw to get aboard *Gibraltar One* — the pinnace from *Edgar Fitzpatrick* was just ahead of *Algenon's*, though *Pope Gerald Windsor's* was in the cue behind.

"We're coming in now, sir," the pilot reported over the intercom, and Broadpaw blinked.

"Thank you, pilot... anybody waiting for us?"

There was a pause, "Looks like a couple of Commodores out there on the deck... that's it."

"Karl... and Ami, I'd guess..." Varnon said to himself quietly, and Grieve, sitting across from him frowned curiously.

"Karl Kandam's been with these stations since they were built. Good fellow," Varnon clarified. "And Ami Cairn... well, you ever read the Genesis Free Press? She's Dran Nightclaw's nearest rival for title of best cruiser officer out here..."

"She's the one always being written up," Grieve nodded as he looked out the window.

"Exactly. Her squadron's joining us. I've only met her once, and she was a bit somber then..." As he assessed Grieve's apparent disinterest, Broadpaw's smiled, "But *you* wouldn't know anything about being *somber*, would you Andros?"

Grieve cocked an eyebrow, "I know more about keeping annoying small Admirals quiet."

"Touché."

The pinnace glided gently down towards the deck as the witty jabs continued to fly, and only the popping of the outer hatch saved Broadpaw from a particularly glib remark about his ancestry...

But as the pair of Earthers slowly descended the ramp to the deck, a grim feeling struck both Admiral and General. It moved from striking to consuming them as they came to the ground and rounded the pinnace where they saw the two Commodores speaking to Graham.

The junior Manchester's face had fallen.

Varnon led the quick march to Kandam's side, extending his hand to Cairn and Kandam in turn, "Ami, Karl, good to see you both again... what's going on?"

Karl Kandam was known for being amiable and calm — he was a very good commanding officer for a station where things could get unfortunately hectic, and he was damn near unflappable. But now he seemed rattled as he took Broadpaw's hand.

The reason was revealed immediately, as the Panda looked between Broadpaw and the General, "The attacks on 'B' and 'C' were traps."

Cairn concurred with a nod, then her sad eyes met Varnon's, "We lost 219 ships, sir..." Her words halted awkwardly for a moment, "It's Savanna. He's dead."

Varnon Broadpaw stopped breathing for a moment, and his eyes shifted to stare at Graham. Grieve stood very still.

"Dead?" Hastings stopped abruptly behind Graham, having just come from her own pinnace, and he turned back and nodded quickly.

"*Tonnant* was lost when the Kroggs detonated the star of 'C'," Cairn's soft words made it sound almost as tragic as it must have been.

Grieve's hand found Broadpaw's shoulder before anyone else present quite realized the implications of what that meant...

"All hands?" the wolf Admiral asked in a rasp.

His daughter was the Captain of that ship. His only daughter, the one his wife fretted over–

"The Admiral ordered most of the crew off before he tried to escape with *Tonnant*, Captain included," Kandam's rich voice provided the good news.

But Broadpaw still didn't breath because no one had bluntly said 'Varnia is alive'. Finally it processed, and he let out a very long breath as Grieve patted him gently on the shoulder.

Savanna is dead... my daughter isn't...

The Fifth Fleet's commander looked from Kandam to Cairn, "What's that mean for our orders, then?"

Kandam met Varnon's eyes, "I can't say for certain. The dispatches from the First Lord are marked for your eyes. I *have* been ordered to pack up four of our mobile yards to ship out with you, though, and the marines here are ready to ship as well."

"And I've got the Second Carrier Group and three squadrons of frigates collected for you. We've reduced the local picket to minimum strength," Cairn added.

Varnon managed to nod in reply, but despite having asked the question, he quite honestly was having a tough time listening to the answer. His daughter was alive; his dear friend was *not*...

Grieve let out a long, growling sigh. "We better read the dispatches."

"So it's straightforward enough," Graham said in a sad tone.

The assembled commanders nodded at the simple statement — they were to pack up four mobile repair yards and the 2,000 marines in Gibraltar space and move them to the blockade station. With the Fifth and Sixth Fleets, of course, and the Second Carrier Group which had been waiting for them at Gibraltar with Ami Cairn's frigates.

These reinforcements would arrive in Krogg space in a rather weighty wave, and then Caine would launch against Krogg 'A' with them bolstering his forces.

So that part was easy.

But the shock over what had happened in 'B' and 'C' still hadn't worn off — nor would it, at least not for some time.

The death of Savanna Felix... the last thing they could or would have expected... People always *could* die... but the likes of Savanna never did...

Broadpaw, at least, had a certain consolation. If he'd had to choose between Felix and his daughter, he would have had no option but to choose the latter. She was his *daughter*, and somehow Varnon knew that Felix had been thinking of his old friend when he'd ordered her off *Tonnant*.

He wasn't sure whether that made the cat's death easier to cope with or harder.

For his own part, Graham was deeply shocked. A year prior he'd accused Felix — and all Earthers — of not paying dearly enough in this war, of not being willing to make the ultimate sacrifice, of being idealists.

And Savanna Felix had told him he'd be willing to die, along with every Earther, to see their word fulfilled.

At the time, Graham had never really conceived of the death of the wily cat Admiral. And even in his darkest moments of confrontation with Caine, when it had been Felix who had put him in his place, Graham had still... *appreciated* the Admiral's intervention. Deep within, he'd recognized the cat's goodwill.

"Well, there's nothing we can do to honor Savanna from here."

Graham didn't even realize he was speaking until everyone looked at him.

Then he stood — on auto pilot, it seemed — as the Manchester fighting genes kicked in. The immediate shock was wearing off, and the resolution that was replacing it favored payback.

"I'm going to go see Gillian, get her marines squared away. Andros, you should probably see Beckett Lupus. Liz, Varnon, you should sort out the yards.

Ami, Bill, if you could get a cruiser screen ready for the run to Krogg. We'll need to keep alert… these bastards are getting *particularly* fiendish."

Graham finished and paused with a set jaw. Everyone looked at him in mild surprise, and he took a breath.

"Right then. Let's get to it."

As he turned and walked out of the briefing room, Hastings and Broadpaw exchanged glances and shrugged, "I suppose we do what the man says."

They nodded and stood, almost glad to have someone so resolute give the orders.

CHAPTER 34

Graham walked at an even pace through the familiar corridors of *Gibraltar One*. The station had been his base of operations for many months, and it still housed Commandant Gillian Hodge, the senior Allied human ground officer in the system.

He'd left Genesis space most worried about patching up their tattered romance, but the news of Savanna's *death* had pushed his mind into a different gear. He wasn't so inclined to worry about his personal life; he could fix broken links after the Kroggs were dealt with.

Perhaps it was unthinkable that the many thousands of deaths up to this point hadn't had the same effect... perhaps he'd become desensitized. Whether he was or wasn't seemed irrelevant now. He had work to do.

So Gillian Hodge, once Pat Conroy's marine commander on *Harbinger Bishop* and successor to command of the Genesis Marine Corps', was now no more that a fellow officer in Graham's eyes. And he wasn't precisely sure why.

Graham had always been amazed when his sister overlooked the obvious chemistry with Pat during their earlier days — he'd been young, idealistic, and mildly motivated to find true love... That was all before the war, when he'd been in command of a bunch of orbital stations in Genesis, with very little to do but look busy for the Church and keep the welds tight.

He really hadn't had much in the way of combat experience in the fleet. He hadn't watched people die, he didn't have the benchmark of personal tragedy that seemed to add perspective.

And now he was thinking with words like 'benchmark'.

Bugger hell, you've gone loopy old boy.

Graham tensed his jaw against such thoughts and rounded the last corridor to the Commandant's office. The decks of the Earther-built station were plain, so the only identifiable marking next to the door was a simple sign saying 'Commandant Hodge, GNMC'.

He barely skidded to a halt in time to key the door open before he slammed into it, and inside the marine clerk at the reception desk looked up with certain surprise–

"Good day ArcLieutenant-General... Uh... the Commandant–"

"Stand down, Boothe," Graham vaguely remembered the clerk from the days he'd frequented the office before his reassignment.

He walked right around the reception desk and through the open door to Gillian's office, finding the tall, fine-lined marine with her nose buried in a report of some sort and her heavy sky-blue tunic dangling over the back of her chair. She looked up abruptly as he came in, laying the report on the cluttered desk.

"Graham... hi."

Her tone seemed inappropriately awkward — as though she was still concerned with their relationship history. History that was, as far as Graham was concerned, not relevant just now.

"We'll be shipping out within twenty-four hours. You've heard about Savanna?"

She blinked twice at the businesslike tone and nodded slowly. All things considered, she'd really been wanting to make amends with Graham since she'd broken off the long-distance relationship. It had seemed a good idea at the time, but as the end of this war drew near, Gillian Hodge was beginning to realize what she'd decided to give up.

Still, the prospect of being in a close relationship which could be abruptly destroyed by the Kroggs wasn't sitting well with her at all... and she had a stark reminder of the ramifications now that Graham was standing right in front of her. She was probably better off alone...

Slowly she came to her feet and nodded, "We've known for six days. It's horrible news."

A very business-like Graham continued, "It most certainly is. Your marines ready to move out?"

"I have four full regiments ready, if you have the ships. That's about 4,100 troops," she said softly, tugging uncomfortably at her uniform shirt.

Graham nodded, "We've brought plenty of haulers. Andros Grieve is probably talking to Beckett Lupus right now about the Earthers. Order your regiments to get themselves ready to board. I'll send the transports to pick them up in–" he glanced at her desk chrono, "–four hours."

Gillian nodded again and slowly rounded her desk, "We'll be ready... will you want me to go on a transport or should I travel with your flagship?"

"Is that supposed to be a suggestion?" Graham's eyebrow arched as Gillian came closer to him.

Frowning, Gillian shrugged, "I was just thinking..."

Now certainly wasn't the time for such things, and the very suggestion that he might focus on *such things* just now seemed fundamentally wrong. Too much to do...

Ah, I'm starting to see the utility of Sarah's attitude at last.

"Lovely idea. Next time one of our leading Admirals and my very dear friends hasn't been killed in a bastardly Krogg trap, I'll mull it over. Meanwhile, you should travel wherever you bloody please. Be ready, four hours."

Graham turned on his heel to leave but Gillian's hand gently held his shoulder from behind, "Graham, are you alright?"

The junior Manchester paused, grinding his jaw against his abrupt anger — it was equally inappropriate for the moment.

"Very little is *alright*, Gillian. On the whole, I'm fairly awful. Thank you for asking."

He pulled away from her grip and stormed past the clerk, leaving a confused Gillian Hodge behind. That behavior was not what she was accustomed to from him... worlds apart from the Graham she knew, really.

Graham didn't dwell on whether he was like himself or not. He stepped quickly through the corridors seeking Beckett Lupus, determined to do his duty.

Colonel Beckett Lupus was training with his sword against Sergeant Major Howler, the veteran member of his old recon squad. The two were parrying and launching attacks with the kind of speed and economy of movement that demonstrated their extreme skill.

Long before the humans had arrived at Earth, then-Sergeant Major Lupus had been renowned as an excellent hand-to-hand fighter, he and his squad hailing from Ursla's *Cerberus*. They'd escorted Pat and Sarah during the Battle of the Antarctic Plains, joined Grieve's attack on the empty Queen's Hive in Genesis, and pulled Pat from the wreckage of *Bishop*.

That latter action — and a heroic near-kamikaze effort by Lupus to save human survivors — had seen the seasoned soldier promoted to Major and placed in charge of the marines in *Atlas*. After commanding the entire 2nd Battalion, 54th Regiment of Foot in action with General Grieve, he'd been raised to Lieutenant Colonel, and after the promotion of the previous Brigadier of the Guards Brigade of the Second (Heavy) Division, he'd been bumped up to full Colonel and given command of the elite four-battalion formation.

Of course, the Guards Brigade had been out of circulation since that time, their friendly rivals from the equally elite Guards Brigade of the First (Light) Division getting the more recent assignment of securing the New Brisbane theatre. So, for now, Lupus' command was serving as Gibraltar's semi-fixed garrison of Earther troops. Both Battalions of the 2nd Guards Regiment gave the Brigade its illustrious name, though only the 1st Battalion of the 4th Guards had joined the unit, leaving the last slot in the 2,000-Earther formation to Beckett's own renowned 2/54th.

Altogether, the Brigade was the best in the marine corps, at least as far as Beckett was concerned. Mustafa Bengal, Lieutenant Colonel of the 1st Battalion of the 1st Foot Guards in the Light Division, tended to disagree. But that was to be expected.

Anyway, all that confusing organizational prattle for those interested aside, the Guards Brigade of the Heavy Division would be getting into the fighting again soon...

Because someone unexpected but instantly recognizable stepped onto the gym deck.

Noting the presence of that foreign but familiar figure, Cadmus Howler bounced back off the sparring mat and quickly sheathed his sword. Lupus halted his rapid attack and turned to face his old comrade, greeting the General with a friendly smile.

"Beckett Lupus, you been looking after my Heavy Brigade?" Andros Grieve came to a halt at the edge of the sparring mat, and Lupus smiled.

"You know better than to ask — we're all fat and complacent now."

Grieve chuckled, "I can see that. You slowing down, Cadmus... or wait, sorry, I meant are you speeding up?"

The Sergeant Major grinned, "You can find out the hard way, any time you like, sir."

With an approving nod, Grieve looked back to Lupus, "So I take it you've heard as much as I have about what's left for us out there?"

The Colonel waved them both to the benches against the wall near the mat, nodding as the two paced to the seats, "As I understand it, all we've got left to take is Krogg 'A'."

Lupus was the first to sit, and Grieve replied as he followed, "Looks that way, which means a landing based around our marines and the Larosian ground forces Novash has."

Lupus nodded, "We have two brigades of Genesis marines — four regiments that are well trained and properly fitted out... relatively. And aside from being fat and complacent, the Guards Brigade is up to strength and ready to ship out as soon as the transports dock."

That was good news and it made Grieve feel much better somehow. The Second and Fourth Guards and 2/54th had (rather confusingly) started their history with him as part of the First Division on the Antarctic Plains. Since then, they'd been united into the Guards Brigade of the Second Division, and he'd had elements from at least one of their battalions with him at every ground action he'd fought so far. And the entire brigade had been with him at Avalon and after at Amaratsu...

"Well," Grieve said after a pause, "that's what I wanted to hear."

Lupus smiled. He was finding himself eager to help finish the war — after all the fighting they'd done, from the Antarctic Plains right through to Avalon and Amaratsu, he was determined to see the end of this conflict. He wanted to go home, find a nice lady wolf, settle down and relax for a few decades.

That would all be possible, as soon as he finished this last, most important landing of the war. And he'd get to fight alongside his friend Andros Grieve yet again. It felt good, and somehow, it felt right that the last battle would be under his charge and the General's.

Grieve came to his feet, extending his hand to Lupus again, "Will you ship out with your troops, then, Beck? Or do you want to come aboard *Algenon?*"

Lupus frowned, "We should all probably take the same ship — we can start laying out preliminary plans. Whichever one you'll be on, then."

Grieve nodded, "I'll let you know when I do... it'll probably be *Algenon.*"

"Very good," Lupus took Grieve's hand again. "I suppose it'll only be a few hours then."

"Indeed. Finish your match in the meantime, though. Cadmus is looking like he needs to be taken down a peg or two," Grieve felt his spirits climb and he smiled.

Howler's ears were too good to miss the remark, and now he grinned too, "You take down any of my pegs and I'll grab them from you and beat you over the head with them, General sir!"

Lupus chuckled and stepped back to the mat, his atom-chainsaw-bladed sword coming from its sheath and humming to life. He then keyed his personal shield.

Grieve didn't leave immediately — it was calming to watch a good bout between skilled Earthers like Lupus and Howler. With them next to him on Krogg, he could deal with anything.

CHAPTER 35

Graham felt more than a little confused about his intense determination and sudden eagerness. His way of coping with Savanna's loss, he supposed. The strategy that let him deal with the death of a friend and his own impending confrontation with mortality. The horizons were all darkening–

"Oh *Gods*. If I'm going to turn into a bloody drama king, I can't be one with such bloody cliché phrases!"

The actual verbal statement in response to a series of musings rather unsettled Graham. Oh well… he was what he was. And at least he was being civil with his fellow officers and friends.

More or less.

Before Graham's mind could snap him out of a momentary wishing about whether he'd ever actually mend fences with Gillian, a hand tapped him on the shoulder–

"Gods!"

He came four inches off his seat in surprise and his head whipped around at the unexpected interruption.

"Gods, Andros, you shouldn't do that!" he said in an agreeable enough tone, and the big General smiled pleasantly and shrugged.

"I have to wait on Varnon to finish up before I head back to *Algenon* — we shared rides. I thought I'd wait up here."

Graham turned back to the glass in *Gibraltar One's* Observation Lounge, "Suppose we had the same idea then."

"Yep."

The pair enjoyed a comfortable silence, Grieve pacing up to the glass wall in front of Graham's chair. The taller General laced his hands behind his back and watched the deck crew scurry about, running fuel lines and refitting the mixed small craft in the bay. He felt better and more confident after his reunion with Lupus and Howler in the gym.

He had four crack battalions from the best Earther brigade he'd ever fought with ready to back him up, wherever he went. That meant the job would get done, and he could do his part in stopping the Kroggs before they trapped another good fellow like Felix, or killed hundreds more…

Grieve's eyes narrowed as his instincts began to pay closer attention to the unsteadiness under Graham's visibly calm exterior… well, he wasn't exactly unsteady, just *different*. Not the Graham Grieve was used to.

"So," the big General turned to the human, "you're coping well enough?"

Graham looked up and shrugged, "I've got a job to do, coping comes later I think."

Grieve smiled, "You can just flip a switch, turn off the emotion?"

There was a pause as Graham looked up at the General, "You know, I'm not sure. I've never had to try. So I'm just doing what comes naturally..."

A short chuckle escaped Grieve, "Natural to Manchesters, is it? Going to go hunt a bunch of Crusaders in an underground ice base?"

Graham grinned, almost loosening his strange resolve in the process, "I don't think I'm *that* far gone. It just seems to make sense, you know. To take action to honor Savanna instead of simply mourning him."

Grieve nodded with a smile of his own, and turned to the table at which Graham was sitting. Pulling out the chair opposite the ArcLieutenant-General, he lowered himself into the seat, "That's a very Earther-like sentiment, actually. Tends to be the way we do things."

"Really? I honestly hadn't thought about that," Graham hadn't considered it in such lofty terms, but as he did so now, and remembered what Savanna had told him all those months ago in the corridors of *Orion*, he conceded that Grieve was right.

He was dealing with Savanna's death the way Savanna had dealt with the deaths of so many of the crews who were close to him at Gibraltar.

"When someone dies," Grieve repeated the wise sentiments quietly, "we can't really do anything about it. We're less than we were, but eventually we stop grieving and keep going. Honor the lost by completing the mission, and such."

"*Exactly*," Graham nodded evenly. "Otherwise it's a waste — they died for nothing."

Grieve smiled, "Yes. I'm glad you've got a handle on it."

"I wouldn't go that far," Graham leaned back in his chair. "I'm a bit off the rocker, I think. I'm giving orders to people senior to me, damn near bit Gillian's head off..."

"We don't mind, and she couldn't really expect you to be great friends after she broke it off with you..." Grieve's tone slowly edged from wise to amused.

Graham shrugged, "I suppose... maybe I'll fix that later. But for now... well, this seems more important. It's something I have to do... fulfill my obligation to Savanna. You know how it is."

Grieve nodded slowly and glanced back to the deck. That quest to honor one's friends and one's word seemed to be an almost ineffable truth about being an Earther. It could get shrouded by the vast battles they were fighting, but in the end it was at the core of what drove them. And Felix's death had helped Graham get back on the track to finding that truth...

"Andros?"

Grieve blinked and looked back at Graham, "Yes?"

"Can you analyze this whole 'honor the fallen' thing without using bad-sounding clichés, because I sure as bloody hell cannot."

Grieve grinned, "No, I don't think I can."

Graham nodded with a thoughtful face, "Good. Then I'm not stupid."
"I didn't say *that*."

Hastings and Broadpaw walked to *Gibraltar One's* main flight bay together, both worried about their commands and the action to come...

And Varnon had to admit that he was seriously preoccupied. Felix's death could be accepted, but the near loss of his daughter was grabbing at the back of his mind. She was still alive, and healthy for that matter, but she'd been unpleasantly close to death. Felix had saved her — something for which Broadpaw would be forever thankful — but she'd still been caught out.

He'd thought he was prepared for such dangers to his family, but the threat to Varnia, and the loss of his good friend amplified the dread of this war more than Varnon had realized was possible. Despite years of fighting, he hadn't been as prepared as he'd thought to deal with the real gravity of his profession.

He'd have to use this experience to his advantage...

"Uh, fishcakes?"

Varnon barely heard Liz Hastings' admittedly awkward question as he was lost in his pondering. His lack of response drew a frown from the ArcGeneral.

Liz was having her own problems with Felix's death, but not the same sort that so many of her colleagues seemed to face. She'd been off the line for years, but before that she'd been the leading combat officer of a fleet that routinely got slaughtered in action against the Larosians, their Church-dictated 'enemies' of the time.

She'd known back then that the Genesis Fleet was being used by the Kroggs through the Church as a pawn in a bigger war. Instead of throwing in the towel, she'd simply decided to increase the pawn's armament.

But even when well-trained and well-armed, the Genesis Navy never won fights on its own, and she had gotten used to watching friends die. So she could handle it, even if she still didn't like it — she had no other choice. She was finding now that she had to resurrect the old steel in order to set her mind against grief, and more importantly, to turn it away from fear.

The Kroggs had killed *Savanna Felix*, after all. He had been damned near untouchable, by all accounts...

Hastings, now deep in her own pondering, almost didn't hear Broadpaw's reply.

"*What?*" the Admiral's sharp question managed to pierce the din of her mind, and she blinked.

"We're both thinking about things too much," she said immediately, and Varnon slowly nodded.

"It's hard not to," Broadpaw said with a bit of a forced smile. "We'll just have to win the war. Nothing to worry about then."

Hastings smiled, "Let's see, there's death... and then taxes. In that order."

Broadpaw chuckled and the pair turned back to the corridor.

"Move to Earth," he said. "We don't much worry about either."

CHAPTER 36

Pat's Posse had rotated to the rear, having been pulled back from the front line of the blockade while squadrons of battle-hardened Larosian Warcruisers took its place. The Warcruisers had to cope with the hyper limit, but their standoff missiles were more powerful than the Type 92s that remained in Pat's Battlecruisers' magazines.

Pat had been feeling uneasy since his confrontation with Sarah, and hearing about Felix's death had done nothing to help his disposition. Even now, over a week after the fact, he regretted that the Posse hadn't been there to help the Earther, to catch the jaws of that trap before they closed on *Tonnant*. His Battlecruisers might not have made a decisive difference, but that didn't stop Pat from wondering if there was anything they could have done to change the outcome.

All the same, his resolution to win this war was even more cemented than it had been. He'd been a fighter with a cause before; now he was a fighter with several causes.

And yes, he admitted to himself, one of them was Sarah.

Felix's death had been a stark reminder of what could happen if officers — no matter how capable and high up on the chain — took chances. It wasn't that Pat disagreed with Felix's decision to stay with his ship, especially when there was a good possibility he'd save it; the Irishman simply acknowledged that the plague of death that had spread over the lower ranks in this war was climbing higher up the organizational pyramid.

Sarah would inevitably put herself right into its path, too, with one of her trademark stunts. The thought made him shudder, because he knew — *knew* — she'd find a way to attempt one of those. Some installation she'd attack alone, or a squadron of Superdreadnoughts she'd attack with her pinnace... or *something*.

She had a way of picking fights she could only finish dead, relying on her luck and her friends to pull her out. Earthers could do the same — though they were arguably luckier — but Felix's loss showed how even their attempts could backfire.

So Gods only knew what Sarah was going to get herself into now, with an enemy homeworld to take and numerous ways to get herself killed. Death would come seeking the fleet during the upcoming attack, that was inevitable. But it would be better if people didn't go *looking* for the bloody grim reaper, and tapping him on the shoulder and tugging his robe, for that matter.

You're thinking about interactions with the grim reaper... again. Best stop it.

Indeed, all these grim thoughts couldn't be good for Pat's mental health. So he was doing what he could to resist them.

And that was one of the reasons why he was in *Agamemnon's* lower officer's mess, orchestrating this 'wake' for Savanna Felix.

The mess of the First Rate was big enough to hold Earthers of all shapes and sizes, including Ursla, Caine, Fox Magnus, Chronos Claw, Lang Sandpelt, and many of the survivors of *Tonnant* as well as a handful of human officers.

Pat was hell bent on *not* brooding any more. Grim reaper be damned...

He almost certainly is. Drop it.

Setting his black-robed preoccupations aside, Pat moved between groups of talking officers and crew, greeting and meeting some of Savanna Felix's best friends and most loyal subordinates, offering his own memories of the Admiral and laughing at jokes which he only sometimes understood...

He'd only known Savanna for a few years, after all.

Caine was floating about in Pat's wake, absorbing the atmosphere in the light-hearted mess. *Tonnant's* crew had some exciting and amusing tales of Felix's first time out with the fleet; Ursla had described a few of the days at Antarctic Base. There were drinks and snacks to be had, and at the head of the mess, a holo of Felix with a friendly smile stood waving at everyone.

It was strangely uplifting and helpful, at least for Caine. He had to hand it to Pat, for an Irishman 700 years removed from his island, the man knew how to drive grief aside. That, Caine had read, was an Irish thing to do... grieve and *celebrate*.

Earthers held little ceremony around death; they remembered the fallen everyday as they went about their business, and pressed on with their lives and goals. But as Caine was all too aware, pressing on had become more difficult of late, and so Pat's wake was... well... serving the purpose the Irishman had hoped it would.

People were remembering the Felix who'd become a fleet-wide hero, who'd saved Fox Magnus and the crew of *Flame*, who'd set up the Gibraltar stations in record time, and who was an all around good character.

The blackness that filled Caine's soul was slowly evaporating...

He had been noticing its disappearance since he'd arrived; it had lifted almost entirely by the time he stopped in a crowd of humans surrounding Fox and Chronos. The latter two officers, both of *Flame* during Felix's breakout mission, were regaling the Genesis officers with the tale of *Tonnant's* rescue of the stricken sloop in the system near the future site of Freetown.

Fox Magnus remembered telling that same story to a group of humans in the *Bloody Pulsar* with the help of Felix himself, scant weeks after it had happened. The Genesis bar had been grimier and not particularly tailored to Earthers back in those days, but the human crowds had been intrigued by the young Commander Magnus and the seasoned, but lively Vice Admiral Felix.

There was no way Fox couldn't feel sad about Felix's loss. The cat had been a mentor to the maverick, red-haired Earther fox — he'd saved him from certain death, then given him a Captaincy followed by a detached pair of 74s and ultimately the recommendation to Commodore.

He hadn't been there to help Savanna Felix at the last moment, and that hurt deeply, but at the same time he knew Felix had gone out in a blaze of glory that suited the battleship Admiral. Fox wanted to write books about Earther timing one day, and he'd be sure to record the illustrious life of his mentor.

And the spectacular bang he went out with. It did take an *exploding star* to get him, after all.

So with pride and reverence he told the stories of his days with Savanna Felix, and let the positive atmosphere slowly begin to diffuse throughout the mess. Hopefully it would spread to the fleet.

Pat watched with a note of pleasure. The wake was helping, as he'd known it would.

Then Sarah walked into the mess.

The room went silent — well not really, he just *perceived* the room to be silent despite the fact that the noise remained. One more 'mourner' — no matter who she was — didn't draw too much attention in this company.

As she paused just inside the mess door and scanned the crowd for familiar faces, Pat locked eyes with her for a second, tried to gauge her mood, but failed as she turned away slowly and walked towards Ursla. The elder Manchester looked somewhat shell-shocked... as though she was still uncertain of herself despite ten days of reflection on her predicament.

'Shell-shocked' was exactly how Sarah felt, actually. She was desperately tempted to pick apart her life in a bid to understand the motivation behind her actions, but it would be hard to say whether such investigation would help or hurt her. It felt as though she'd have two battles to fight if she did try — one external and one internal...

She'd decided she didn't want to stir up the wasps on the internal front just yet — she'd have ample time to deal with it after they beat the Kroggs. Her focus was thus external, and if she died, then she wouldn't have to worry about any of this complicated internal mess.

Her relationship with Ursla needed to be mended though. Sarah still hadn't quite patched things up, as she'd been too busy in the last days trying to get her fleet reorganized, refreshed, refitted and ready to tie in with Liz's Sixth. It was a lot of work to fit that many ships into a new order.

Admittedly, the distraction had been appreciated...

Pat watched Sarah ignore him, and he felt a bit of ice slide around in his lungs. So she wasn't ready to talk to him yet... yes, well fine. That wasn't important just now...

Turning towards the door, Pat banged straight into Novash. The Larosian took a steadying step back as the burly Irishman slammed into him, looking somewhat surprised at the impact of the large human.

"Oh damn..." Pat stepped back. "Sorry about that, Novash. Didn't see you there... you slipped in awfully quietly, didn't you?"

Novash approximated a shrug, "I must admit I feel a bit out of place, being among so many who knew Admiral Felix so well."

"Ahh that's garbage, *man*," Pat turned and put his arm around Novash's shoulder. "You knew him too — come have a drink."

Ursla couldn't help but grin as Novash was forced more or less against his will to the refreshment table. Pat wasn't chancing alcohol on the Larosian, but the Admiral-of-a-Division didn't seem to be particularly craving *Agamemnon's* crisp, cool water just now.

Still, Novash took it in stride, settling down a bit as Pat took him aside to talk about campaigning on the Larosian front...

Caine was mingling, Fox was regaling, and Ursla was starting to feel a bit superfluous.

"Andra."

Ursla's head dipped instantly as Sarah came to a stop before her, "Sarah."

Swallowing, Sarah turned and glanced across the mess towards Pat, "How are things?"

Ursla followed her line of sight to Pat and listened to the troubled tone of her voice, "Things are fine, you?"

Sarah heaved a sigh, "I'm about to be superseded in command of my fleet, my ships don't have Type 98s, we're getting ready for a suicide battle, Pat won't talk to me, and Savanna is dead. I'm doing pretty badly, actually."

Ursla 'hmmed', then looked down, "You want to talk about it?"

Sarah paused and looked at Pat a moment longer, "Yes. That would be nice."

Novash enjoyed 'joking' — he lacked the faculties to laugh completely, but he had a sharp wit and a quick mind, once he got a hang of the structure of humor. Now Pat and he could go three rounds easily, and come to a stalemate. And Pat had been practicing...

It was almost enough to make Pat forget *all* his troubles.

There was a 'but', of course, because Pat was human, and Novash knew sorting human issues wasn't that simple. Doubt, fear, anger... there was always something lurking unforgotten.

In this case it was Sarah.

You don't have to worry Pat — she's coming around.

Pat was in the middle of a joke, but he stopped as the telepathic interruption entered his mind.

You sure? He knew he couldn't mentally send the question, but he could think it for Novash to read.

I think so. Admiral Felix's death seems to have put some perspective into her life again. She hasn't had that since the Church stopped threatening her.

"Or before," Pat nodded and spoke in low tones.

Novash bobbed his head towards her abruptly, "Look."

Sarah was talking with Ursla.

That was good.

Actually, that was very good.

A small smile spread on Pat's face, "We better win this war fast, eh Novash? I can't wait for *my* apology."

Novash's head tilted in uncertainty, "You will apologize?"

Pat looked back at the Larosian quickly, "*No, she* will. For Gods' sakes, you can read my bloody mind can't you?"

Novash did.

"Oh."

Pat nodded, "Damned right."

They laughed again.

CHAPTER 37

"Well, time flies when you're having fun, doesn't it?" Caine asked in a friendly tone, trying to open the meeting on a lighter note than one would expect after the events of the past days.

Novash frowned questioningly at Pat, who shrugged in reply. Sarah cocked an eyebrow at Ursla, and the bear rolled her eyes. Garvin Jardaw glanced curiously at Draco Maximane, who in turn looked questioningly at Jax Furgus. Fox Magnus scratched behind his ear and avoided eye contact. The room remained silent.

"I think the point to the awkward silence is a general lack of levity," Pat offered.

Caine paused and looked over the assembled officers, "I'm trying to be optimistic, folks. But suffice it to say the time's passed quickly."

"There you go," Furgus nodded.

"Better? Good." Caine keyed on the briefing room table's main holo, "Now, we've got a war to win, and six days until the Fifth and Sixth arrive to make that possible. I know we've been thinking about this for ages, but we're going to have to get a plan finalized today, organize our resources, and be ready to fold in the reinforcements as soon as they arrive."

Slow nods came from around the table, and Caine activated the main holo with detailed scans of Krogg 'A'.

"Here it is."

Everyone at the table shifted in their seats and leaned forward, carefully eyeing the plot as it filled with black icons representing ships and planets. Nothing was said as the images blinked into existence, though a few of the assembled officers exchanged quick glances.

The commanders here were the very best available, representing all Allied forces. Caine had picked them for their expertise, rank being a non-issue when the planning was so critical. Just because an officer wasn't senior didn't mean he or she wasn't smart enough to provide valuable input.

But even the best minds in the fleet were a bit stymied by the promise of Krogg 'A'.

"That's about 7,000 ships of war, my friends. With exactly 914 stationary weapons platforms or facilities of one sort or another. And that doesn't count the planet itself. For now we need to plan to secure the planet; we can figure out what to do with it once General Grieve arrives with the marines from Gibraltar. We may need to land a large number of troops, so that'll be his department…"

Pat cleared his throat and leaned forward, *"Land?* Pardon me there Setter, but shouldn't we just blow the bloody thing wide open from orbit?"

Caine looked to Pat and paused. He then exchanged glances with the other Earthers at the table, each of their eyes reflecting precisely what Caine felt. Earther policy was not to be questioned in this matter, and Caine had to make that clear right now.

The Krogg homeworld was not to be destroyed.

It wasn't something that had been easy for him to decide, and for quite a while he'd been considering capitulation on the subject, but in the end he couldn't. Felix would never have accepted complete annihilation of another race or its world... *no* Earther ever would. And Setter Caine wouldn't. He'd go home with the same morals he left with, casualties or not.

Making eye contact with Ursla last, Caine keyed off the holo and looked at the non-Earthers in the room.

"I should make this clear now, Sarah, Pat, Novash..." Caine straightened his posture as his eyes moved between them. "We will *not* bombard the planet from orbit. We will *not* attempt to nova their star, irradiate their atmosphere, wipe them out with a plague... *nothing.* Is that understood?"

Sarah's eyes widened slightly in surprise, Pat frowned and leaned forward expectantly, and Novash tilted his head. Just now the Larosian very much wished he could read Caine's mind.

"We'll end this war by killing the Queen herself. We all know the theories that she's the head of the Krogg race and controls all their actions. If we kill her, they should become passive, or at the very least, disorganized enough to contain."

The Earthers at the table outnumbered the other terrestrials and the Larosian, and the trio certainly felt the moral weight of that presence as they absorbed the announcement. Fox watched with some particular interest, noting Novash's seeming lack of reaction and Pat's deepening scowl.

"Setter, I really must ask, *why?"* Pat's tone was confused to the point of uncertainty — he'd never greatly considered the manner of this war's ending. He'd assumed a crushing victory, an end to this chaos by the destruction of the single most threatening race that had existed within recorded history.

If they didn't get rid of the Kroggs, what the hell had this all been for?

Caine's wise amber-gray eyes settled on Pat's troubled brown ones, and the Irishman peered deep into them for some hint of explanation.

Somehow he got one.

Hundreds of years of manipulation and oppression by the Kroggs and the Church regimes they'd supported had jaded Pat. He knew that, though he'd never thought the Kroggs worthy of saving so he'd neglected to worry about being unfair to his enemy. He had other concerns — the Kroggs were simply there to be killed after all.

"That's exactly how the Kroggs see the galaxy," Caine confirmed, somehow in tune with Pat's thoughts. The Irishman nodded slowly.

Caine shifted his gaze from Pat to gauge Sarah's reaction, and noted that she seemed equally confused. It was, Caine supposed, a difficult thing. Hell, there was no 'supposing' about it. To let one's most mortal enemy live after it had manipulated society and sent millions to die in its stead... it made very little sense. Mercy in this case could easily be called foolish and idealistic.

A small part of Caine didn't want to spare his foe. But that was the least Earther part of him.

His predator forbearers would never have *dreamed* of entirely wiping out a species of competitors. Ever. They would fight off attacks and compete, but they would never completely annihilate their foes. Such wholesale destruction would do more harm than good, no matter who the enemy was.

While the associated threat would therefore always remain, the Alphas of the wolf packs that had given Caine life would choose to live with danger instead of destroying it completely.

It was simply who they were, who Caine was, and who the *Earthers* were. Universe be damned.

"Maybe we'll end up paying for it in the long run, but we don't make this choice lightly. I intend to commission Krogg as a permanent Earther station after the war, with at least a division here to keep an eye on the goings-on. We'll confine them to the ground, and make sure they don't get vengeful."

The Earthers at the table slowly nodded, and looking deep into Sarah's eyes, Caine concluded, "We will *not* do what they do."

Sarah's mind slowly wrapped around that last statement... the ultimate proof of superiority, she supposed. Enlightened, risky, but right?

It was slowly dawning on her now, as she listened to Caine and thought about her duty here, that there was no doubt left at this table — about her, about the mission, about the way to achieve victory. She was the only one still nursing her own uncertainties, which meant she was the only one she needed to prove herself to.

So that's what she would have to do.

She would help defeat the Kroggs, but she would not seek to annihilate them. And that measured, thoughtful victory would prove to her that she didn't need to kill just to give herself credibility.

Sarah offered a slow nod to match Pat's, and Caine took a breath and turned to Novash. The Earthers in the room tensed ever so slightly. Here was the non-terrestrial, the alien with no bond to Earth, no eyes to peer into aside from silvery, seemingly empty ones.

A telepath who could not read Caine's mind.

"What about it, Novash? Do you agree?"

Novash tilted his head a bit further, then he approximated a smile.

"I was quite confused at first, but after being rather impolite and thefting thoughts from Pat and Sarah, I think I understand. It is an honorable objective you suggest, Lord Caine, though it is risky."

Novash looked at the resolute faces of the Earthers around him. They were unlike Larosians in most ways, but he could see one resemblance that drew the races inexorably together.

Turning back to Caine, Novash vocalized, "My people want to end this once and for all, but we cannot necessarily afford to do so. If we were all to die here, trying to destroy all Krogg life, we could potentially destroy our own race. We would leave our homes without help against the plague, and the Kroggs would ultimately triumph."

A few nods punctuated the agreement of those assembled, and Novash looked back to Caine, "Still, many Larosians will not quickly accept that. The want of revenge is deep and true. I have it myself..."

Another pause and Novash looked at each of the Earthers around him.

"What my people will understand is the nobility and determination with which you are acting. You are staying true to what you believe, as much as we are, and we cannot fault you. We will not disagree then... I will see to that. So long as I command, we will abide by your decree, and perhaps we will come to agree with your solution."

Caine nodded slowly, "We very much appreciate that, Novash. And trust me when I say we will see honor served."

Novash bow-nodded, "I do believe you, Lord Caine."

And he'd see to it that the Larosians believed Setter Caine as well.

There was a very long, thoughtful pause at the table, the Earthers releasing relieved breaths at the neutralization of the more genocidal sentiments in the room. They all knew they could well end up paying a bitter price for this decision — somehow, some day, what they did here in sparing the Kroggs would likely cause them problems. But they'd face those consequences if and when they came, the same way they always dealt with problems.

That was the Earther way.

"Alright then," Caine keyed the holo back on, "let's get to it. We have a *very* tough system to take..."

Philosophy disappeared as the overwhelming onslaught of objective tactics began.

CHAPTER 38

It took only two hours before a room full of the fleet's best needed a break.

Facing a system as tough as the Krogg homeworld, it was quite easy to fall victim to pessimism. Conventional attacks hammering in from the hyper limit were risky, and the Kroggs' recent preference for large-scale traps made a direct energy drive attack against Krogg 'A' seem rather unwise.

Novash was certain there would be no major traps in Krogg 'A', and Caine had to admit there was some logic to the Larosian's statement. The Queen had doubtless been orchestrating the traps from 'A', and it seemed unlikely that after all this effort, she'd be willing to kill herself.

Of course, that was just an obvious assumption — Caine could be dead wrong about it...

Stop.

The First Lord was no longer in a mood to over-analyze. His instincts were telling him what to do, and he was willing to listen. Even if the opposition did seem as though it was going to be near-impossible to overcome.

To freshen minds and get new ideas flowing, the meeting had broken up into three smaller ones, each headed by a fleet commander and sporting a third of the other assembled persons. Caine sat in the briefing room with Novash and Pat, while Ursla, with Garvin Jardaw and Fox Magnus, held court in the next room down the hall. Draco Maximane and Jax Furgus were with Sarah two doors away.

"Well I don't recommend trying to walk straight in. Good way to die, I think," Pat paced around the perimeter of the table and winced at the glowing holo.

Novash tilted his head, "In that case, it does reveal a certain noble death."

Caine and Pat both set eyes on the Larosian, who shrugged absently, "I know the notion is not popular among your people, but it holds a certain credence with mine."

"I think we're all a tad more battle effective when we're alive, wouldn't you say Setter?" Pat responded.

Caine drummed his fingers on the edge of the table, "That's how I've always thought of it. Hard to get the dead to crew their guns."

Pat grinned, "So it's not a good plan, eh Novash?"

"That may be the case, but it is a noble alternative. And right now, there's not a particularly broad range of strategies available."

Caine and Pat 'harrumphed' simultaneously.

• • •

"We could always try a coordinated strike on all the installations," Fox suggested through the tank to Ursla, and the Second Fleet's Admiral frowned.

"I don't think we'd be able to do it safely. We'd be divided into ten-ship groups... not ideal for facing equal numbers..."

"Mmm," Fox nodded. It was never a great plan to divide forces in the face of such a massive enemy, and to divide into such tiny formations would literally negate the tactical advantages associated with eliminating the stationary defenses around the star system.

Garvin Jardaw leaned in closer to the plot, his white hair reflecting the light, "Perhaps not *all*... what about these? Blaze a trail straight to Krogg from one side, and then work outward?"

Ursla frowned and nodded, "Concentrate on one point and push through?"

"We could hold the corridor that we carve, giving the Larosians and the humans a safe escape vector if it comes to it."

Ursla took a breath, "Well, I tried a focused attack on Crusaders at Antarctica, and I did it again against the Kroggs at Genesis. Both times I got flanked and surrounded."

Jardaw raised an eyebrow and nodded.

"We won't have a gunboat advantage, so I suggest we keep the fleet consolidated," Maximane said as he keyed a few boat and estimated corvette numbers up into the plot.

Sarah and Furgus nodded slowly.

"We maximize our gunboat cover if we stay together?" Furgus asked smoothly, and Maximane nodded.

"You know better than most how rough corvettes can be on capships."

Furgus certainly did — he'd had a division of 64s at Gibraltar, and they'd been punished badly by the Krogg corvettes that had survived the destruction of their Motherships.

"All the same, I don't like leaving my ships to maneuver without an umbrella," Sarah said quietly. "Do you think there's a way to engage the corvettes away from the fleet... keep our ships out of it?"

Maximane carefully looked over the Krogg positions and shook his head, "They've got corvettes spread out over *200* Motherships. We'd never be able to concentrate enough boats against all of them."

"What about piecemeal?" Furgus suggested quickly. "We hit from one side and you take out the corvettes from that side, then turn to engage either flank?"

Maximane paused for a moment, "On paper..."

"We pretty much know we have to put marines on the ground at Krogg to get the Queen, right?"

Caine looked up at Pat's question and then glanced at Narosh. The Larosian nodded, "It's been what's required to kill Queens in the past. The Queen the Son destroyed was far too well protected to be struck down from orbit."

"Hence our landing at the Hive in Genesis," Caine added. He looked back up to Pat, "We've got the Guards Brigade from Heavy Division coming out of Gibraltar with Grieve — the 2/54th and the Second and Fourth Guards."

A smile crept briefly onto Pat's face, "You Earthers sure do history right, don't you? Do you have any idea what sort of heritage those regiments have in human armies of the nineteenth century?"

Caine nodded, "They have an excellent heritage, I do know. Just as there were 74-gun ships of the line fighting at Trafalgar. I suppose we learn from history... but we do add other things to the mix, I think."

Pat grinned, "You do at that. And maybe now you'll give history even more to record... we know that the Queen's on the ground and that we have to put troops down to kill her. How the troops do that is Andros' business, not ours. Question is what we need to deploy into that area of space to secure the orbit for him, isn't it?"

"If we want to land and attack, we're going to need a decent force in orbit, aren't we? We'll have to establish a zone of control..." Jardaw glanced from Fox to Ursla, and both nodded.

They'd witnessed the near-destruction of the expedition against the Genesis Hive years before — neither needed to be reminded of how close the ground forces had been to being left without orbital aid in that instance.

"At least a fleet," Fox said a bit dismally. "Two or three if I had that option."

Of course *Flame* had been one of a handful of ships that had been detailed to that first Hive strike, so he was a bit biased.

"And they can only be Earther fleets," Ursla reminded both him and Jardaw. "We're the only ones who can get in there safely under energy drive."

Jardaw nodded, "So we have to commit to the planet if we want the Queen. Do we want to go in hard and fight all the way to the planet, or go in easy and fight our way out?"

"I've been toying with using boats to attack the Queen's Hive," Maximane commented after a period of silence.

Sarah frowned, "Well, the one in Genesis was too tough to take from orbit... I'd imagine it'd even be hard on boats from closer range."

Maximane nodded slowly, but Furgus raised a thoughtful eyebrow, "What about air support? You were on the ground at Antarctica, Sarah. Would close cannon support have done any good?"

Sarah's brow furrowed thoughtfully, "Had the place not been made of ice, quite probably."

"And that'll be up to us, since the Larosians have no way to rush their Carriers in. We need to put Carriers into action around Krogg 'A'," Maximane scratched his chin. "If we want to concentrate our forces under a boat umbrella, it has to be established there."

"Easy for you to get there," Sarah tapped the arm of her chair.

"Hitting the front would be a very Larosian thing, wouldn't it?" Caine looked to Novash and the Admiral-of-a-Division nodded. Caine persisted, "Alright, what if you did, and we backed you with the Fourth, Fifth, and Sixth Fleets? Follow me on this one Pat... we start by slamming them from three sides with what looks like everything. We force them to commit to the outer front where we can spread them out... then First, Second, Third, and the Carriers go straight in on Krogg. We'd have them in a tough spot once they committed... you wouldn't be badly outnumbered on the hyper limit and you could keep yourselves back enough not to suffer major casualties."

Pat frowned, "We keep them occupied and keep them away from Krogg, then? What's to stop them from turning right around and crushing you?"

Caine shrugged, "Your dogged determination to kill every last one of them, maybe."

Novash bow-nodded, "That seems logical enough. And if you include an Earther unit in our force, it may appear to be an attack by our entire force."

"The Queen's probably smart enough to buy that... the question is whether she'll weaken her home defenses in response."

"A defensive pocket around the planet would *not* be easy to hold," Fox frowned at Krogg 'A's black icon. "We'd have to deal with their home fleet and a significant number of stationary batteries."

"It'd require us to draw their fleet out to the hyper limit..." Jardaw's voice trailed off and his eyes wandered about the system. It seemed unlikely that any of the facilities there were sufficiently important to draw the thousand-strong home defense fleet from anchor around its homeworld.

Ursla nodded thoughtfully.

"But if we were to concentrate our boats around the planet, we could turn the thing into an iron ball. They wouldn't be able to get to the surface, so they'd have to try to break us there... and if the rest of the fleets are coming down on their positions at the hyper limit..." Maximane offered the suggestion and Sarah started to nod.

"I could take the Fourth against their hyper limit defenses... with Novash's ships and the reinforcements. We could give them a good fight so long as we didn't press it too far... draw them out and give you an opening to get in," she was picking up on that idea.

"Problem is," Furgus leaned in a bit, "*what* could get the Krogg defense away from the planet they're duty-bound to protect unto death?"

Maximane frowned and leaned back in the chair.

•••

"We have to lose."

Pat and Novash looked straight into Caine's eyes as the words came from the First Lord's mouth, but the wolf held up a hand to preempt their questions.

"Not *really* lose. But just imagine the Queen's delight if we *break*. We get driven back off her front lines at the hyper limit. We act as though we've been scared off by the potential of a trap. If we make it look *really* good... if we break by squadrons and run in all directions, she won't have enough ships to go after us all... or at least she won't think she does."

"You think she'd risk her own life to track us down and annihilate us?" Pat leaned on the back of a chair. "Seems that'd be awfully convenient."

Novash tilted his head, "It might actually fit her character. She very much likes killing us — and you. Her traps have casually sacrificed thousands of ships to date."

"None have been so close to home though. And even if she does, what the merry hell do we do when the Kroggs catch us when we're in squadron order? We'd be flattened," Pat wasn't the sort to wear a sign marked 'bait'.

Well, not without a better chance of success.

"You'll have surprise, even numbers, and they can't afford *not* to go after all of you at once. If they're willing to chase you off their defense stations, they'll have to keep the pursuit up. Otherwise they leave the system unprotected," Caine explained.

Pat scratched his chin.

"We can't be sure they'd chase us," Fox frowned. "They could just as easily hold station and force us to act."

Ursla shrugged, "That would be a bit out of character for them, don't you think? Never the passive types, the Kroggs."

Jardaw tilted his head, "What makes you say that?"

"Both traps could have been completely passive... instead, they fight us right up until they flip the switch. They like fighting, I think. They always have. If we offer them the chance to get back at us after so long..."

"The trick would be rallying the fleet again. We'd need to be well mapped out in our vectors to make sure we could reform to at least division strength. We could start hunting them then..." Furgus leaned back in his chair thoughtfully, and Sarah's eyebrow arched.

"We could use the Sixth to buy us time. If we kept them back the Kroggs wouldn't be any wiser, and they could have their divisions hunting while we reform," she nodded to herself thoughtfully. That would give Liz a taste of the action she'd been craving for almost three years.

"And when the Kroggs try to reform against the Sixth's counterattack they'll fall back to find the First, Second, Third, and the Carriers on their doorstep," Maximane's eyes narrowed.

The room paused, and Sarah smiled, "We have a plan, don't we?"

• • •

"We should tell the others," Caine stood, and Pat and Novash joined him at the door.

Ursla stepped into the hall and almost slammed right into Caine. Sarah came up behind and the three exchanged surprised glances.

They talked for five minutes and concluded that this near-telepathy was becoming *very* strange. Their plan was essentially set.

CHAPTER 39

Caine sat in his chair and looked absently at the place on the table where the picture of Elandra and Phealan usually sat. Ursla was still keeping the small portrait for him, and despite his new resolve, withholding reminders of home continued to seem like a good idea. Yesterday the best commanders in the Allied service had finalized the risky plan to be used in the attack against Krogg 'A', and they still had four more days to wait for the reinforcements to arrive.

After that, there'd be another thirty-six hours to orient those ships before they could begin the attack.

It had been decided that it was best to launch as quickly as possible after the arrival of the reinforcements — the longer the additional ships sat without action, the more likely it was they'd be noticed by the Kroggs. Caine wanted to keep them a surprise until the very last minute...

This whole plan was risky enough as it was. There was no way to be rationally sure the Kroggs would give chase to running Earthers — the aliens could just as easily sit back and watch the Earthers break and run. It would be less dramatic, but so long as they stayed on the defensive, Krogg 'A' remained reasonably secure.

But then it had been suggested that the Kroggs wouldn't want to chance collateral damage if the action closed to the space around the planet — a lucky broadside or a kamikaze Larosian Battleship could potentially wreck the Queen's ambitions if it managed to hit her palace.

The aliens would do everything they could to drive their foes far away from their sovereign. The chances of her accidental death seemed nearly non-existent, but there was no way a thinking Queen could even provide the Allies with an opportunity to get close. So maybe there was a mildly tenuous means of explaining the supposed Krogg desire to give chase.

That explanation was secondary, though, to Caine's instincts.

Now he'd just have one more challenge to face before they set about campaigning. Narosh was coming out of the regen tank on *Lycrotar* tomorrow, and he'd heard none of the briefings or plans. Caine was honestly unsure how the Larosian would take the news the Kroggs weren't going to be eradicated, and Novash had been reluctant to offer a comment on the expected reaction.

When an ultimately forthright Larosian Admiral didn't want to comment, Caine got a bit nervous. Essentially, Caine could understand the *principle* of genocide. One's enemies gone for eternity — no more threat, no more danger...

No more Kroggs.

But every time he tried to step into Narosh's shoes, to understand the death of a *savior* and the hundreds of years of war, he could think only of how much the Earthers had paid thus far to fulfill their commitment to the fight. He also kept wondering what he'd tell his son if he went home with the extinction of a race on his conscience.

For him, ultimately, it was very simple: he could not and would not accept the destruction of an entire race. Novash said the Larosians would respect the noble honor of that sentiment because the Earthers were making this decision not out of stupidity or greed, but because of morality. By and large, Caine imagined the young Larosian would be right.

But something told Caine that Narosh — who'd put so much of himself into his quest for revenge — would be less inclined to accept the Earther model of this endgame.

And despite his disagreement with the Larosian's position, Caine certainly couldn't blame him.

But first they had to win.

That would mean Grieve on the ground, relying on his marines to actually kill the Queen. Somehow, part of Caine almost longed to go down there with them to handle the Krogg monarch himself... but something a little more forceful in his blood seemed to say it wasn't right. Not his time.

Again, he'd have to rely on his instincts. And Andros Grieve would be sent down to deal with the Queen, supported strongly by gunboats in orbit and as many marines as he needed. Though it seemed unlikely that more than the elite brigade he was bringing would be required.

The more marines that landed, the harder it would be to get them down and back safely. And 2,000 Earthers, properly supported, should be *more* than enough to cut through Krogg lines and get into a Hive. Caine was by no means a marine officer, but he had read the after-action reports by the likes of Beckett Lupus and Grieve himself — the dispatches that detailed their crushing ground victories.

Apparently, when Torallis of the Stealth Guard had been informed of those victories, he had been quite impressed — the Kroggs were tough to beat, even for the experienced and well-honed Larosians. The Earthers acquitted themselves particularly well, it seemed.

But Caine knew those achievements had come at higher cost than the casualty numbers suggested; it had forced the Earthers to operate with far less reason and conscience than was their custom. Something, perhaps, that this action would again demand of them...

Generally speaking, the Earthers seemed to be the perfect balance of aggression and reason — powerful enough to meet the Kroggs in hand-to-hand combat, but with enough latent *irrationality* to understand the ways of their foes. Or something to that effect. That ability seemed to slightly unsettle the Larosians — even Novash — and to be honest Caine almost feared it himself.

He could think much like the Krogg Queen seemed to, if necessary — he could conceive of things evil, murderous, and self-serving. It seemed the Earthers had the potential to become as evil as the Kroggs, and with their inherent rationality, they'd be far more dangerous.

If for no other reason than to confirm Earther moral identity, then, the Kroggs had to live. If the Earthers were forced to wipe out the whole race, Caine couldn't help but fear that it would be the unleashing of something horrible in Earther nature.

A lust for killing, perhaps?

It was not something Earthers were necessarily fond of — their desire to make a fight — but it was something hardwired into their predatory minds. It was controlled and restrained by the so-called 'higher level' mental processes that made the Earthers themselves... but it was there.

Because of it, Caine had reason to fear for his race. And the Earthers, he knew, all feared the possibility of such an evil genesis among themselves. Ursla had felt a pang of it after she'd single-handedly destroyed a Crusader company on the Antarctic Plains, and most of the Earther marines and naval crews had felt it similarly after the slaughter of humans in Earth orbit and on the ground.

It had been displeasing at the time, but it had been written off as a move to protect Earth. There was no way, however, to justify mass slaughter of Kroggs...

Caine gently rubbed his eyes and tried to pull his mind out of the tailspin. He could do his job. He could live with many, many dead. He couldn't survive the destruction of a race.

And all he had to do was convince Narosh of the merits of that choice... or at least force him to accept it. Caine had his doubts, but there was one thing that gave him the most bargaining power in the galaxy just now.

Turning away from the empty spot on his desk, he tapped the desk holo on and scrolled quickly through the current ship totals of each of the Earther fleets present, as well as through the size of the Fifth now on its way in.

No one else could do what the Earthers did in war, especially against the Kroggs. And if that ability gave Omega's creations the opportunity to become a universal evil, it also gave them the opportunity to do right. They'd be the ones around the Queen's planet, the Larosians couldn't get so close so fast, no matter what they tried.

So long as the Kroggs remained irrational, the Larosians would never be able to defeat them as completely as the Earthers could.

So while it disturbed Caine, his greatest leverage was that the Earthers were sufficiently similar to the Kroggs to become indispensable in defeating them. The Larosians had to follow his directives if they wanted the Earthers' help, and they needed the Earthers' help to win.

Caine closed his eyes and hoped Narosh could be swayed. If he couldn't...

"Tomorrow. Deal with that tomorrow."

Slowly coming to his feet, Caine made his way to bed.

CHAPTER 40

Andros Grieve silently squinted at the main holo in *Algenon's* briefing room. The bright blue display, usually reserved for depictions of space craft and system maps, was showing a battlefield.

Or more precisely, a *potential* battlefield.

During the last number of months of blockading Krogg 'A', the Earther sloops passing through space around the planet had done some superficial scans of the surface. While none had gotten close enough to get a clear look at the underground networks that Grieve knew *had* to be there, they did show the façade of the Queen's Hive citadel, and the land surrounding it.

Jutting out of the top of a large plateau, that citadel occupied one end of an egg-shaped rock layer 600 meters above the valley surrounding it. The plateau had sheer cliffs with a total area of two square kilometers — and only a square kilometer of clearing safely away from the perimeter of that Hive. To land, Grieve would have to put all his troops down in that area, then move against the citadel on foot.

He could hopefully expect some gunboat support on that front — he'd been talking occasionally with Captain Trax Earon, the gunboat commander for the entire front who was moving up to the blockade with the Second Carrier Group. The coyote had assured him that the boats could come in reasonably close and lay Mark XV shot on a target within three meters.

It would make for an interesting fight if it worked — but Grieve couldn't formulate a plan that depended on it. Boats weren't as experienced in ground support so there could be unforeseen problems, or corvettes could tie them up. And, for that matter, Larosian fighters couldn't be expected in support either — Grieve got the feeling that Earther ships would be making this drop on their own.

So he needed a way to use the Guards Brigade, and perhaps reinforcements from Torallis and Gillian Hodge, to cross almost a kilometer of plain and reach the citadel.

Getting into the palace was an entirely separate issue... work for energy charges, no doubt. Bombs that gathered energy from the surrounding area and then released it abruptly, energy charges could blast through strong fortifications. They just needed time and space for set up.

Somehow, Grieve expected both would be in short supply when the Guards hit the ground.

If they hit they ground, he supposed. He mightn't even be assigned to this...

"You're sure we'll be going down too, eh?"

Grieve turned from the holo tank to the briefing room door and watched Colonel Beckett Lupus step through. The wolf, only a year ago a Sergeant Major, carried the officer rank well on his shoulder epaulettes.

"I am. You had a look at this yet?" Grieve waved a hand at the plot, and Lupus nodded slowly, approaching.

"It's not *quite* the same as Antarctica, but it's an open-field attack against a well-fortified target. This time we're seriously outnumbered, but they can't possibly deploy *everything* they have in that Hive at once."

Grieve nodded slowly. The plateau did appear to suit a landing strike in numerous ways. A smaller force on the plateau couldn't simply be flanked and overwhelmed — so long as the Earthers covered the 750-meter width of ground effectively, the ends of their line could be secured by cliff sides. Still...

"They could simply stack Queen's Guards in front of us. We'd have a hell of a time cutting through them. Torallis thought there could be thousands at the Hive in Genesis. This is probably *much* worse."

Lupus nodded, keeping his eyes on the tank, his mind quickly turning over options. He'd faced the Kroggs on a number of fields, he'd killed many dozens. He knew how to beat them, and Grieve did too. The menace here was the total numerical inferiority, and their inability to do anything about it.

As long as they fought on the plateau, they could only land so many troops without overcrowding their own landing zone. So they'd have to be surgical, but even that was difficult against the Kroggs. Regular Krogg soldiers were not that venerable when it came to fighting crack Earther troops. They could, generally, be handled.

But Queen's Guard soldiers were supposedly massive, brutal creatures, somewhat in line with Krogg Warlords — the powerful if seldom seen Generals of Krogg infantry. And there'd be *thousands*.

"They'll come straight on and try to overwhelm us, won't they?" Lupus looked up at Grieve and the elder General nodded.

"That's exactly what they'll do. They've got no reason to be fancy — they certainly haven't tried to hide this citadel. It's an open challenge — if we can get close enough to attack, they mean to finish us the hard way."

Lupus ground his jaw and nodded. He'd seen that sort of resolve when the survivors of *Bishop* had been clinging to life. The Kroggs were incessant fighters, and this open terrain gave them little choice but to come out swinging.

With four — or perhaps *six* — blades on each arm, that made for a menacing mental image.

"Any ideas?" Grieve asked quietly, and Lupus again thought carefully. They'd need a way to use sheer brute force to push the Kroggs aside and back. A line perimeter wouldn't work on its own... they could establish one to guard the landing site, but there was no way it could advance against a determined sea of Kroggs.

"What about getting some Larosian fighters into ground mode to cut paths for us? They're well designed for anti-soldier work," Lupus looked up at his General, but Grieve slowly shook his head.

"We'll likely be going in with Earther transports only. I doubt if we could support a big enough squadron of fighters to make a difference down there, and that aside, I don't expect they'd last long on the ground with that many Kroggs to swarm them. My impression is it'll be up to us and Torallis to try something with swords..."

Grieve's voice trailed off and he punctuated his silence with a huffed sigh.

Blade-to-blade melee fighting was not at all efficient for pressing a strategic goal with any sort of tactical order. If the entire brigade simply charged into the Kroggs, few — if any — would survive to reach the citadel.

They'd need to organize an assault column, a vanguard of some sort...

Lupus briefly frowned to himself, his memory trying to drum up old images of a human tactic from pre-omega history...

It was something he'd read as a pup — something he'd thought was fascinating and highly appropriate at a time when bladed weapons were the norm and humans of inferior sizes were trying to combat those who were significantly larger.

It would require shields — and not the Earther type. Larosian energy shields worked essentially like shields of medieval times. Instead of being made from wood or metal, however, they were comprised of an impenetrable energy wall growing from a forearm-mounted generator, which presumably could be shaped to fit the needs of the wearer. The Earthers had the blueprints on file somewhere, they'd just never seen a use for them...

"Andros, I might have an idea," Lupus looked up at the General again.

As the Colonel explained it, the pair quickly came to agreement about the potential usefulness of the thought.

Sitting in his cabin, Varnon Broadpaw reacted to the chime of the door with some surprise. By ship chronometers, it was well past 23:00 hours — few tended to disturb Fleet Admirals at such a late time. Problems always got relayed via the intercom, and visitors were usually only by appointment after 22:00.

Not that Broadpaw really minded the interruption. He'd been reviewing ship specs in hopes of maximizing the effectiveness of his vessels when they integrated with the rest of the fleets. They were only five days away from reaching the blockade lines now, and while it could seem like a long time, it wasn't.

In any case, the door opened to reveal a tall, bright-looking Andros Grieve stepping into the room. The General almost had a smile on his face, and as Varnon looked up over a stack of papers at his friend, the wolf frowned.

"You're up to something."

Grieve shrugged, "I've been trying to figure out what to do if I'm ordered to attack the Queen's palace. It's not a very friendly place to land."

Broadpaw's brow arched, "No, *really?*"

Grieve cracked a grin and walked across the cabin to his friend, holding out a book-bound volume of *Garnan's History of Pre-Omega Earth* — one covering a reasonably early period. A page of the classic book was marked with a red slip of paper, and Varnon took it with a frown and opened it to a picture.

Broadpaw looked up at Grieve, "Borrowing from these guys is going to win the war?"

Grieve shrugged, "Borrowing is probably what won Antarctica for us. We don't *usually* advance in a Napoleonic battle line, remember."

Varnon nodded, "I suppose you don't. What can I do to help?"

"I need to manufacture at least 250 Larosian-style personal shields to a modified pattern by the time we get to Krogg 'A'."

Broadpaw's ear twitched, "*Come again.*"

"I already worked this out with Beckett Lupus and one of his techs to get the pattern ready. I just need your machine shops to start turning them out. It's only fifty a day — one per ship per day, if you like."

Broadpaw looked with some disbelief at his friend, "You really need these?"

Grieve pointed at the picture.

Broadpaw sighed, "As I recall, you needed to manufacture quite a few swords for the last foray against a Hive. Now you've got those and you want *shields*?"

Nodding, Grieve shrugged, "Easier to live if we have both."

Broadpaw looked down at the picture again and let go a second sigh.

"Alright then. Pax Eartheria, or whatever..."

CHAPTER 41

Admiral-of-a-Fleet Narosh's mind had been lost in a dark place for what seemed like an eternity. He could not touch any other minds, nor could he fully exorcise his memory of what had happened. It had been a period of almost subconscious self-contemplation — in other words, twenty-four days of waking nightmares.

And then, finally, something had changed, and the tank that held him in a cushioning field of energy slowly began to shut down. Healing particle fields had partially replenished the resources of his defeated immune system, and the Earther additions had made up for the rest. The two forces, perhaps inexplicably, had seemed to merge.

The combination returned Narosh to his feet a day before predicted, and left an odd feeling in his chest as his feet came down slowly on the floor of the Regeneration Tank. He couldn't explain — to himself or the doctor — precisely what it was. It just seemed that his body was a little more than it had been while also being a little less.

It mattered not. His mind regained full control of his body and began reaching out as the door to the tank swung open. The surgeons stood before him, watching him with measured caution.

I am in good condition.

You are certain, Admiral?

Narosh scanned himself somewhat tentatively to confirm his conclusion, and when nothing appeared wrong he made his confirmation.

Yes.

Nonetheless, Admiral-of-a-Fleet, I believe we should test the changes made to your immune system... the Earther medicines might have side effects that we cannot yet understand.

Narosh stepped from within the tank. *Earther medicines?*

He didn't wait for an answer, instead reaching out with his mind to the Larosians around him, drawing from their knowledge of what had occurred. His memory suddenly surged into life, and as he learned of the traps in Krogg 'B' and Krogg 'C', he realized with more certainty than before that it would be necessary for the Larosians to use the Kroggs' own technique against them.

Prepare a fighter for me at once. I must see Caine.

But–

I will not be delayed now. Novash hurried from the bay. *This time I'll just have to be a bit more careful.*

• • •

"You're sure he's coming in?" Forepaw frowned at *Orion's* Signal Officer, who nodded in reply.

Lab Forepaw sighed and shook his head slightly, turning to his Second Lieutenant, "Alright, alert Garth to nail *everything* to the deck. I'll inform the First Lord."

It wasn't so much fear of a repeated crash that concerned Lab Forepaw — he knew the Earthers had learned the lessons of the last incident. He'd seen to that... *they'd* seen to that. But to have the Larosian Admiral simply demand clearance again, and to cruise in alone...

Forepaw turned away from the signal station and paced to his chair, keying his comm as he did.

Caine looked up at the ceiling as he heard the comm chirp, "Caine here."

"Lab from the bridge, Setter. Narosh just announced his arrival. He'll be here in... four minutes."

It took a few seconds for Caine to process the words, and then he slowly laid his papers on the desk, "You're sure?"

"I am, Setter. You'll want to get to the flight deck."

Caine sighed and nodded as though Forepaw could see him...

"Right."

As the comm cut, Caine came to his feet. He wasn't much looking forward to this... then again, that seemed to fit with the times. He'd be psychotic if he could say he looked forward to what was going on.

Narosh was probably the closest thing to a fanatic Caine had dealt with since Harvey Bingham, though he was far more logical and justified in his actions than the human. But Bingham had mended his ways and was governing Genesis at the head of the Chancellery.

Maybe Caine had a sanifying effect on people.

Yes, he was very *sanifying*.

"Maybe if I start by *not* making up words..."

He exited his cabin at a quick step, ignoring the fact that he was talking to himself.

The Deck Chief watched the Larosian fighter glide into the far end of the bay and then took another sweeping look at the entire chamber to be certain nothing was in the air or in the way. The approach of the silver dagger-like vessel was slower than it had been during the collision, and there wasn't a writhing leviathan of a gunboat locked to a piece of air over the deck either.

So two bits of good news thus far...

Narosh's fighter followed the landing markers to his slot without difficulty, and from within he activated its conversion to battle mode. The vessel's fuselage twisted down and legs emerged, allowing the craft to land on the deck upright in the shape of a semi-humanoid robot. The Admiral-of-a-Fleet then lowered the embarkation lift, and stood on the departure disk as it lowered him to the deck.

This was already quite an improvement over his last visit...

As the Earther deck filled his vision, he recognized Caine's shape as the First Lord came through the deck hatch on the far side of the bay. The Earther nodded to the Deck Chief, and then began making his way across the open flight lane to Narosh's ship.

Narosh came forward from his fighter to meet the First Lord, both commanders slowing to a stop in the middle of the landing lane.

"Good to see you well, Admiral," Caine said with a kind smile.

Narosh bow-nodded, "I've been told the quick treatment by your doctors proved decisive in saving me. My thanks. I've also heard of the tragedy that befell Admiral Felix and I must offer my deepest condolences."

Two abrupt, matter-or-fact acknowledgements that nearly startled Caine — it surprised him that the Larosian, alone in a regeneration tank for nearly a month, already knew so much.

"I believe I have a solution that will satisfy all concerned now, Lord Caine. A way we can destroy all Kroggs and spare as many innocent lives as possible."

Caine looked up with a slightly worried expression at the seeming *eagerness* in Narosh's voice... was this the big 'kamikaze' speech, or did he really have a good idea?

"We should talk in the briefing room," Caine began to gesture to the hatch, but Narosh held up a hand, "It is rather simple, Lord Caine. We simply use the Kroggs' tricks against them. I will infiltrate with my fleet to their homeworld and then detonate a large telepathic blast that will doubtless eliminate all life in the system."

Caine had been turning, but now he froze, "We *seriously* need to talk, Narosh. With me, if you please."

Novash emerged on the bridge of *Shanavorus* in something of a bad mood.

Why was I not informed at the awakening of the Admiral-of-a-Fleet?

Apologies, sir. He awoke and then immediately departed Lycrotar — *we only found out from Captain Natosh a moment ago.*

Novash approximated what humans would call a scowl and tilted his head. *He has arrived safely on* Orion?

Indeed, sir.

Blocking his mind from those of his crew, Novash took a breath.

Good luck, Lord Caine.

"What do you mean when you say *no*?"

Caine sat across the table from Narosh, the latter having just taken a seat at the opposite end. The length of the table separated the pair, but somehow the quarters felt very close as Caine delivered his decision. He wasn't particularly afraid of the Larosian from a combat standpoint, but he was well aware of the sort of friction he was about to cause.

Was causing, actually.

"I mean we will not allow you to wipe out all the Kroggs, nor will we allow all of you to die in such an attempt."

Narosh's shock was deep. What in the *Son's* name was Caine talking about? It was their destiny — it was what was demanded by the codes of retribution that anchored Larosian honor in this instance.

Six hundred years. Over forty billion Larosians dead, including Praaxus at the beginning and the Son only a few years ago...

And the Son had been Narosh's friend. His dear friend.

The day he'd watched the Queen's Hive in Sashtas explode under the influence of the Son's mind — the day he'd watched a human die for all Larosians everywhere — Narosh had committed himself to the destruction of those who would kill all things.

He would annihilate all Kroggs.

And Caine was saying they would show *mercy?*

"I *cannot* accept that, Caine," Narosh said forcefully, and Caine leaned back in his chair.

"You have to. I'll remove you if I must, but I will not let you all throw your lives away for the sake of revenge... and I will not be party to genocide."

Caine's own words were filled with a sort of conviction that differed from Narosh's. His words were a defense against a fear of lost identity — a fear he'd failed to completely grasp until he'd really reflected on what Savanna had died for.

Any attack on Krogg was a grizzly prospect, but it could not be reduced to genocide. Not if the Earthers wanted to remain true to who they were, not if they wanted to retain their society based on the morals they held so dear.

Felix would never have accepted such mass murder, nor would any of the Earthers who had fallen in this war. The Earthers had always fought for their way of life — that was precisely why they'd spent so much energy preparing to defeat the Church.

That determination to remain true to their character had brought them to a place that forced them to decide the fate of the Kroggs.

And now Caine had made that decision.

But Narosh was not ready to accept it. As his glassy, silver eyes peered at Caine's deep amber-gray ones, the Larosian tried to comprehend what the First Lord was demanding — aside from making threats to the Alliance. He couldn't get into the Earther's mind, he couldn't see the underlying truth.

All he knew was that what Caine was saying went completely against the essence of what he was. He was a Larosian, and his honor depended on stopping for all time those who had murdered so many of his people. Those who had killed his friend... his savior.

"If you will *not*, we will complete this task on our own, Caine," Narosh's voice sharpened. "And you have no control over the workings of my fleet."

Caine let his head tilt slightly, "If you try to destroy them all, I *will* stop you Narosh. Don't force me to."

The threat appalled Narosh, "What gives you the impression that we can be stopped! You may be formidable, but we remain the more experienced! You cannot simply come into this war at the last minute and take control for your own purposes–"

"Novash accepts my decision," Caine really hadn't wanted to bring Novash into this... "And the humans do as well. Narosh, we *will not* massacre the innocents among the Kroggs."

Narosh came forward in his chair and slammed the table, "*What* innocents? What do you really know of the Kroggs, Caine? Praaxus himself died at their hands. They all kill, none have pity. Their Queen is a terror, their soldiers are a plague, they cannot be taken lightly — they must be wiped from the cosmos."

"Their *Queen* must be. But you've never actually investigated the rest of Krogg civilization, have you? Can we hold them all responsible for the actions their Queen commands of them?"

"*Yes!*" Narosh thrust himself to his feet. "You don't understand them as I do!"

A sharp pain was beginning to lance deep into Narosh's chest. It had nothing to do with the recent regen treatments... it ran far deeper.

Because he could *see* the death of the Son in his mind's eye, and he could see the loss of so many in his fleets and now at home.

Because the Kroggs would never stop, with their plagues and their murders and their attacks. It was *what* they were.

"No, I don't see it the way you do," Caine remained seated and looked down the table at his counterpart. "And that's why I'm making this call, Narosh. Because I haven't had 600 years to lose my way. Because after three I'm damned close to losing it, but I *haven't*. And I won't let you execute all the Kroggs for revenge."

Narosh's head swung slightly to one side, his eyes attacking Caine's, "You have lost *nothing* compared to what we have lost. We have the right to retribution. To kill them all–"

"And to *die* yourselves? To leave your home to be victimized by the plague, to never see your worlds again? Is revenge worth that much to you?"

"*Yes!* If I know that I am saving my home in my death, then I have died with nobility and honor," Narosh began to edge down the side of the table, and Caine stood slowly at the approach.

The Larosian didn't want to budge, but Caine would never back down. Not when Felix was gone, not while he had a son to go home to.

"You die with *honor* today, Narosh, and tomorrow your planet could well fall to the plague. You can't be so selfish as to ignore the well-being of your race," he said coolly, stepping aside from his chair to face the Admiral-of-a-Fleet.

Narosh slowed slightly, his mind overcoming the challenge, "I can still send some back. But the Kroggs *die*."

Caine's eyes narrowed as Narosh came to a stop just in front of him, "No."

Narosh couldn't believe the impudence, "You *coward*! You cannot handle the thought of death, can you? You've bled so little, and now you don't have the courage to finish this! There is no middle ground, Caine. Realize that!"

"*You* are the coward, Narosh!" Caine's voice boomed now as the First Lord felt his anger beginning to marshal beneath the surface of his skin.

He didn't suffer fanatics well, and right now Narosh was acting the part of one.

"I am no–"

"You want to hide behind genocide!" Caine snarled, taking a step towards Narosh. The Admiral took a quick, surprised step back as the First Lord's eyes swelled with darkness. "You can't handle a threat, you're afraid of a *challenge*. So you want to destroy the entire race, just for revenge and peace of mind. Is *that* what your *Son* would want, Narosh? For you to cower behind the annihilation of a race?"

Narosh tried to reverse the momentum, "They are the *Kroggs*. They've *earned* extermination, and I mean to give it to them."

"No one can *earn* death, Narosh. We cannot *become* what they are by killing them — *that* would be cowardly. We need to face them, and to face them for as long as they choose to oppose us. We cannot destroy them to escape our fear of defeat."

Narosh's head tilted and his mind screamed, searching for a way to crush the words of the First Lord, "You'd leave them to pillage *your* planet, to kill *your* family?"

The harsh question hit the wrong button.

Narosh didn't actually realize Caine's fist had gone through the metal tabletop until the First Lord slowly drew the gray furry hand back through the jagged hole in the alloy. Caine, for his part, hadn't even known he'd been so close to the briefing table.

But he didn't particularly care.

"My *son* will not grow up with a murderer for a father, Narosh. Not any more of one than he *must* have."

Narosh tilted his head quickly in confusion and stepped back once more as Caine closed his bloody hand before him. The blood began to mat in the gray hair as the hand balled into a fist, and both commanders watched it slowly ooze through the wolf's fingers.

Caine's anger was so deep, so exhausting. It had remained below the surface, waiting and growing as Felix and thousands of brave Earthers like him died. But the First Lord could not turn that anger and exhaustion into genocide.

Narosh stared at Caine's bloody hand, and his mind withdrew for a moment and thought of the Son, just as the First Lord had suggested.

"Don't become them."

It had been the last thought the Son had sent to Narosh before the end.

He hadn't understood it then, but perhaps now it made sense.

Caine was ready to die before he changed who he was at the core... and once that had been Narosh's way too. But he'd been through so much, he'd lost that clarity. Here was a reminder of how he had once been. The Earthers, it seemed, had a wisdom beyond their age.

Far beyond.

Narosh would *not* become the thing he most hated. He would have mercy, and he would remain vigilant in case the Kroggs resurfaced. That was noble; that was *honorable*. What the Son had reminded him of, and what he had forgotten as the grip of the plague had closed around the Empire.

Narosh's hand slowly reached up to Caine's fist, and he locked eyes with the First Lord. For the first time in all his meetings with Earthers, Narosh *understood* what was behind those foreign eyes. The wolf's bloodied hand opened, and Narosh took it.

The red liquid smeared over the Larosian's hand, and the Earther part that was now inside him seemed to twitch in recognition.

Caine, his rage quite literally bleeding off, felt as though he'd stopped breathing, and he stared into the silver eyes of his fellow commander.

For the first time, he too thought he saw something recognizable there.

"You do your people great honor, Lord Caine," Narosh's words were suddenly even and resonant. "You are right. And I agree."

Caine straightened slightly, the pain in his hand fading.

"You do your own people far more credit," he said quietly.

Their hands parted and they stood facing each other in silence.

"I think you'll have to meet my son someday, Narosh," Caine turned away then, waving to the table. "For now, strategy."

Narosh nodded slowly and took a seat. It was time to plan this... this... *redemption*.

CHAPTER 42

Sarah wasn't feeling all that lively — she was more herself than she'd been in a while, but she still wasn't quite *right* as far as she was concerned. It was good that Liz would be around to take over the fleet in another day. Sarah was fairly confident she could handle the Fourth in its little withdrawal feint, but she'd want some significant support when she did.

The final mission of the Fourth and Larosian Fleets was simple — they were the decoys. The Earthers would go in and do all the messy fighting around the planet; it would be up to everybody else to keep the Kroggs occupied in the meantime.

Sarah could handle that well enough. She'd just have to coordinate with her commanders and make sure there was a resilient pattern to the formations when they broke, despite the fact that they would need to appear chaotic. Narosh could handle his ships however he liked — the Larosian commander knew far better than Sarah how to deploy them.

The Genesis ships would be without boat support, though. There would probably be a few Larosian fighters fluttering around them, but Narosh would have to commit most of his small craft to the protection of his own ships. Since the Genesis Carrier Program — Graham's erstwhile baby — was still only in its infancy, that left Sarah's Fourth and Liz's Sixth open to swarms of corvettes.

They'd just have to be careful, keep the Larosians between themselves and corvettes... do what they could.

So she could handle it.

There had been a time when a statement like that was a given. Of *course* she could handle it. But now what had been egotism and a need to prove something was being revealed as self-doubt — was she really as good as she made everyone think she was?

It seemed that life just didn't get simple for her. Why was that *not* surprising.

Well, in sixty-odd hours they'd launch against the Kroggs. Then it'd be done with — the war would be over, she could go home, apologize, and live however she wanted to for the rest of her life.

Only three more days — less, even.

Pat sat back in his bridge chair on *Divine Templar*. He still missed *Bishop* — he'd served from the bridge of that old Battlecruiser for half a decade all told, and he was still having a bit of trouble letting go.

The new, squeaky-clean, fully-loaded *Templar* was nothing to shake a stick at, but *Bishop* had been a ship you couldn't have even found a stick to shake at in the first place.

"Oh Gods, my brain's stopped making sense again," he muttered to himself as the strange stick-shaking cliché entered his mind. He was tired and wanted to be done with the war, and in a couple of days, Gods willing, he would be.

Then Sarah wouldn't be able to use the damned conflict as an excuse to not think about him. She was making progress, as far as he knew, but she was still doubting herself — no longer the way she was perceived, but her actual ability to perform. She'd been certain of that ability before, just convinced that no one else recognized it. Now she knew it was recognized, but worried it wasn't actually there...

Sarah was having a lot of issues.

And Pat could understand that. She'd had a *lot* laid on her shoulders from an obscenely young age. Between a *very* oppressive and dominating regime, the Kroggs, the Quest, the Earthers, Liz, him, the renegades, and every other bloody thing that had gone on in her twenty-eight odd years, she hadn't had much time to herself.

Nobody had the constitution to absorb that much punishment without some of it having an impact.

So after the war they could focus on her recovery.

And then Pat would write books — that was always fun, or so they said. He could write history books about the war, maybe. Be like Caine's grandfather, or Garnan, and perhaps he could even work with Caine or one of the other Earthers to produce a definitive account of this war.

That would be fun too.

Yes, lots to do after the war.

As long as I'm not dead.

Pat blinked and smacked himself in the forehead. Stupid... uhm... brain.

Well, if I'm dead I guess I'll sleep a lot.

There, that's never too bad.

Fox Magnus was leaning back in his chair with his feet up on the desk. It wasn't a very professional posture, but he was alone. He'd had a long week of planning sessions and strategy discussions, and now the assault was all ready to go. He would worry about fighting the actual battle tomorrow, or more precisely, in about fifty-eight hours — in the meantime, life could pass by with his boots on his desk. Because for the moment, that was a simple enough pleasure to keep him happy.

That was the sort of character Fox was — he was the maverick, dapper, crafty fox who kept near the front and always charged to the rescue. He was a bit dramatic and he liked being on the proverbial edge.

But then, the Earther standards for the 'proverbial edge' probably weren't really that edgy by human reckoning.

Earther standards meant the boots on the desk — and boy-howdy, was he ever on the edge!

Wow, I'm gone. That's it, just gone. Loopy, nuts, insane, fried, out of it, gone. Good thing I don't have to lead ships into action in fifty-eight hours... but wait, I do!

Fox blinked twice and shook his head at the strange train of thought. Gently setting his hands behind his neck, he leaned back further and stared up at his cabin's ceiling. He wasn't entirely sure what he wanted to think about — he could review tactics, dream of retirement, or maybe think up titles for books he wanted to write.

"*Earther Timing: Damn It's Good...*" Fox paused, "Well I suppose Savanna took that one with him."

He'd lost a friend — his mentor, his old commander, his comrade. It was something he still found himself brooding over and it was something he'd remember when his 74s were hurtling into battle around Krogg 'A'.

I wonder if Savanna left any luck with us when he went.

Fox was certain of the plan they'd crafted and of the power the Allies could project into the system, but he never minded having good luck on his side.

Here's hoping.

Garvin Jardaw's cabin on *Highlander* was not small, but it felt somewhat cramped just now. He wasn't really sure why... he just felt as though things were closing in around him. He was a group commander in the Earther Navy, and usually the responsibilities that came with such a position were enough to control his nerves...

But Jardaw had never thought of himself as a great leader. He'd been a good First Lieutenant, a competent Captain, and *Highlander* had always treated him well, but he was still relatively new at command. With this large action before him, prudence, not stress, was demanding that he question his abilities to lead his ships into action.

Granted, he'd come out of 'B' with every ship. But 'B' had been a trap that had nearly gotten him. Fox Magnus had saved him, and now he had to wonder whether he had the ability to do the same in return if it became necessary.

He sat in silence, pondering that very question.

Draco Maximane wanted the rest of his Carriers. The Second Carrier Group would give him more than enough power to protect the defensive bubble around Krogg 'A', and with that bubble established he'd be able to lend his support both to the ships in orbit and the marines on the ground.

It would all fall into place then.

The Second Carrier Group was on its way with Varnon Broadpaw and the Fifth Fleet, and the *Engadine*-class Carriers that filled its squadrons were loaded with well-trained and well-armed boats... Maximane just wanted them to actually get here.

Once both forces were united under his command, he'd feel a lot more useful to Caine and the Navy. His Carriers now were literally a tiny percentage of the Earther force... and he supposed the addition a couple of dozen wouldn't change that.

But the boat advantage...

It was tactical thinking based on a doctrine that Maximane himself had pioneered. It was thinking that served to almost comfort him... and thinking he hoped would pay off when the time came.

Graham felt like a proverbial basket case.

You couldn't see it on his face — indeed, people around him kept telling him he was the most assured they'd ever seen him. But they were bloody liars...

Or not.

Maybe they were telling the truth, and the way he looked was significantly different than the way he felt. He hoped so.

Graham just didn't know. Sarah dealt with all this somehow... though she also had a slight tendency to go insane and charge the guns. She was blessed with enough luck to live through such *glorious* acts. But Graham doubted he was.

No, he'd worn quite a few hats in his days as a Genesis Naval Officer, but this one — command of the battleships in the final fight — wasn't one he was sure he could handle. He doubted himself, plain and simple... though people didn't think he did.

Felix had gotten killed, and Felix — beyond just being a friend — had been the best.

Graham was certain he had reason to worry.

And he knew he would, at least for another day. Then they'd get to Krogg 'A' and presumably be attacking soon after. He'd coordinate with Liz, Bill and Sarah, do his job, and then go home.

Maybe he'd start thinking about a family then too...

Ha! If Gillian wants anything to do with me.

So Graham wasn't a great Lothario.

"More like bloody *Romeo*," he muttered to himself. "Chances are we'll both end up dead."

Oof, that was rather grim.

Liz, despite herself, was getting a bit... well, *excited*.

She'd been behind a desk for far, far too long. At the beginning of this whole mess, she'd been one of the key players upon whom the success or failure of the Quest would rely. Then the recovery time for her leg combined with a gaping hole at the top of the new civil administration installed by Harvey Bingham at Genesis had kept her from rejoining the war effort proper.

She'd become sometimes irritable, irrational, and quite unfriendly — fighting was in her blood, and she didn't like having the fleet she'd done so much to construct out there without her.

Liz had been an officer for almost twenty-five years. She'd spared Genesis

Fleets from total destruction when the Kroggs had sent them against Larosians, she'd led a fleet into the sprawling Battle of Genesis... albeit arriving near the end.

Now she'd be at a battle from the beginning, with excellent subordinate commanders and Allies she could count on.

She was finally going to get to do her bit.

Though she wasn't a glory-seeker, Liz Hastings did relish the chance to make a visible contribution to the war effort. She'd be in the right place at the right time, and she wouldn't have the bloody Church breathing down her neck.

And that was something too. While she *liked* commanding, she *loved* doing it without Crusaders and Shaspas and Shappas and Chancellors all trying to keep her 'faithful' as she gave orders. She fought hard and well, and to hell's gulags with the lot of them...

Well, she wasn't so sure of Harvey Bingham's guilt any more, but him aside, the Church be damned.

This war was a few days from its end, and she'd finally be an important part of it.

Varnon Broadpaw was finally feeling a bit more comfortable.

His thoughts on his daughter and on this war had finally come to a closing point: the war was three days from over and he'd be damned if he'd let himself or his little — *not-so-little*, actually — pup get killed in that time.

The wife would slaughter me if I did.

Rubbing his eyes, Broadpaw rolled around in bed, trying to settle himself for some sleep. He wanted to be awake when they arrived at the blockade, so now was the most logical time to get some rest. It'd probably have to last him a while, too.

All things being equal, he wasn't so badly off. He'd take a nap, wake up refreshed, arrive, and find his daughter. Then he'd help win the war.

By the *Earth*, he was tired...

Broadpaw rolled over and tried to sleep.

Beckett Lupus stood opposite Howler and demonstrated the sword technique that Grieve was recommending for the battle on the ground.

"Simple thrusts?" Howler frowned at his old Sergeant. "Our blades aren't well suited to point fighting."

Lupus nodded, taking a look at the blade in his hands. It was the same blade that had been with him on the *Bishop* planet — he'd managed to keep it despite being blown up down there. The katana-like weapon had a single bladed edge and a slight curve. The chisel point was sharp, but it had never been intended as a thrusting weapon.

"We'll have to make do... and actually, I doubt if we'll be the ones going through the shield to use them. Andros is only taking 250 volunteers out, with the Larosians probably. The rest of us keep them occupied on the line. We might have some of the new shields in case we need them, but I expect it'll be business as usual for the brigade, if you take my meaning."

Howler nodded slowly.

The first functioning model of the new Larosian-style shield sat on Grieve's desk. Much like current Earther shield-belts, it operated from a simple physical platform: an arm band with a long silver plate meant to face the enemy.

The wearer simply keyed the red button on the top of that silver plate and a wall of impenetrable energy expanded from the shield, taking on a rectangular shape sized to suit the wearer. For the most part, it was Grieve's understanding that the Larosians used shields in a simple circular pattern — good for defense but not too cumbersome when it came to quick offense.

Such shields added an exceptional layer of protection to a melee fighter, and if used correctly they would never fail and would stop every Krogg blow. Thus far the Earthers had preferred their skin-like shields for combat — though vulnerable to weakening the shield belts had allowed a freedom of motion that favored Earther martial arts.

But for this particular operation, Grieve knew such arts would be useless — at least until they got into the Hive.

Crossing the floor of his cabin, Grieve unsheathed his long military-issue blade and keyed the atom flux along its edge to life. Returning to the shield, he carefully activated a rectangular energy wall. The light blue-green shield field expanded to a significant two meter height and one meter width, the small Earther power source built into the armband easily handling the output of energy.

Stepping back, Grieve poked the shield with his sword.

The blade and barrier crackled as they came together, and Grieve drew his sword back and quickly examined the shield for any indication of weakening.

The display on the arm band still read at full strength.

Krogg blades were sharp, but being high-density bone, they lacked the piercing value of the atom swords. By the looks of this, though, the shield could likely handle both bone and energized steel...

But just in case, he started poking the shield again.

Andros Grieve was going to be leading a fight unlike any he'd experienced on the ground. He'd be ready when it came to it. As his blade crackled repeatedly against his shield, he was sure of that.

Narosh and Novash sat in silent conference aboard *Lycrotar*. The latter had just arrived aboard the Warcruiser, and now they were beginning their first — and probably only — exclusively Larosian strategy meeting for the battle to come.

We are both aware of the plan assembled by Caine and the Earthers. Narosh began.

Indeed, sir. I assisted in its formulation.

Good. In that case, my decision will not be unwise: I plan to give you command of one half of the fleet — the Battleships supported by some Warcruisers. The balance of Warcruisers will be under my command, and during the battle we will endeavor to operate independent of each other.

The details of the plan were provided to Novash through a quick telepathic note-comparison. Keeping the Battleships apart would improve the pure maneuverability of Narosh's Warcruiser force.

When it comes to the battle, we will collaborate but operate as separate units. If things go wrong, Novash, you must retreat. You must escape to our own galaxy, and help protect our home.

Novash, his mind still halfway into Earther speech configuration, nodded and spoke, "I understand."

It was that simple for the two warriors.

The end of their long journey was at hand.

And then there was Caine, sitting on his couch and gingerly flexing his hand. He *really* shouldn't have put a hole in that table — Forepaw had scolded him about it for an hour, and the last time he'd talked to Ursla he could tell she'd been itching to do the same.

She'd been wise enough to stay quiet — she'd put her foot through his table, after all.

Well, that aside, things seemed to be coming together. He was feeling some of the old confidence — that understanding from the days of the Church incursion. There was an ultimate goal at hand now… a purpose easy to recognize and to keep in perspective.

The door chimed and interrupted musings.

Caine looked up, "Come on in."

As the hatch slid open, Ursla took a slow step through, "Hello, furniture smasher."

Caine cracked a grin, "*I* didn't *smash* it. I just put an easily-fixable hole in it. *You*, on the other hand, did *smash* my table."

Ursla chuckled and eased her way into Caine's cabin, taking a seat in the big chair facing the couch, "Well, we've both set bad examples. I guess we have to start being responsible members of society again."

Caine paused thoughtfully… "Nah."

Ursla smiled, "Well, good that we're both in better spirits. Only a couple of days to go now… then we finish it. Almost hard to believe we've come so far, isn't it?"

Caine shrugged, looking briefly down at his hand again, "I suppose… ups, downs… we've been through quite a lot."

"And it's not over," Ursla said in a more sober tone.

Looking up, Caine offered a nod, "True enough."

Ursla sighed and looked blankly at the table for a second.

"We've got a lot of people coming together here. Think they're all as ready?"

Caine's eyebrows arched, "I hope they are."

"You think we'll win?"

Caine looked over at his big friend as she asked the question. Well, who did they have with them...

Sarah.

Pat.

Fox Magnus.

Garvin Jardaw.

Draco Maximane.

Graham.

Liz.

Varnon Broadpaw.

Beckett Lupus.

Andros Grieve.

The Larosians.

And Ursla and himself, among many, many others.

The only one thinking things through for the Kroggs was the Queen.

"I think we just might," Caine met Ursla's eyes. "In fact, I'm fairly certain we will."

Gods save the Queen.

Because she'll need all the help she can get to stop us now.

CHAPTER 43

"Strange reading on the plot, sir."

Labrador Forepaw looked up from his pad at the report from the Sensor Lieutenant, "What sort?"

The Lieutenant frowned, "Not sure. For a moment I *thought* I saw something in hyperspace, but I'm not getting consistent readings."

Forepaw frowned and came to his feet, "An attack?"

The Lieutenant slowly shook his head, still frowning over his Chief's shoulder at the display, "Can't say, sir. Could be nothing... I'll try running a few recalibrations and see if I can clear it up."

Forepaw nodded slowly, then turned away to his First Lieutenant, "Get a spatial charge ready and open the doors to Bay Three. Just in case."

Appropriately, *Algenon* was the first ship out of energy drive as the Fifth Fleet arrived near blockade space. Carriers aside, the 125-gun First Rate was one of the largest ships left with the Earther Navy, and the builders had certainly laid it down to serve as a fleet flagship.

Now Varnon Broadpaw guided the huge vessel towards *Orion, Agamemnon, Joseph Barron,* and *Lycrotar*; all those flagships were already together so their commanders could conference as they awaited the arrival of the reinforcements.

Behind the lone *Algenon*, hundreds more ships abruptly appeared — echelons of 74s and frigates, massive vanguards of warships that, while less numerous than the rest of the fleets, still offered an ominous sight.

Behind them and to one side, the Sixth Fleet finished its deceleration from flux. The Genesis ships weren't as handy at the helm as the Earther vessels, but they certainly could place themselves into a small window when it came to deceleration. They came to a halt just abreast of the Fifth, and *Gerald Windsor* and *Edgar Fitzpatrick* both came ahead to rendezvous with the flagships as well.

Almost immediately, the seven leading flagships of the fleets had assembled in a compact formation and begun exchanging pinnaces.

Caine and Ursla stood next to each other, watching as the officers began to gather. Narosh and Novash were first to arrive, both landing their fighters with a small measure of hesitant caution. They weren't the sort to repeat mistakes.

As soon as the Larosians came to a halt next to Ursla and Caine, Sarah's craft came to a stop in its slot. She came quickly down her ramp, and, looking both ways, crossed the landing lane. Exchanging short, sober nods with all present, she thought a polite greeting to the surface of her mind for the Larosians' sake, then took her place next to Ursla.

The pinnaces began arriving from the other ships within minutes. *Algenon's* small craft was the first to cruise through the field, finding a slot with some difficulty — the gunboats were now taking up most of the room usually reserved for additional guest ships.

Nonetheless, the Deck Chief parked the pinnace in a gap, and the Earther ship touched down and lowered its ramp. Varnon appeared at the top and descended quickly, crossing the deck at a trot to approach the assembled commanders.

Caine smiled in a friendly fashion as the Fifth Fleet's commander covered the last few meters, extending a hand to Broadpaw as he slowed, "Good to have you here, Varnon."

Broadpaw matched the smile and took the hand, "Glad you waited for us."

He withdrew his hand from Caine's grasp and took Ursla's, then Sarah's, and finally each of the Larosians, "Good to see you both again."

The Larosians bow-nodded in turn, and Novash approximated his own smile, "I think we're all a bit better off now that you're here."

Varnon grinned, "Ha! Glad to see you've all still got a sense of humor..."

The sound of two closely following Genesis pinnaces coming down to the deck turned Broadpaw away from the Larosians, and the officers all straightened again.

Liz appeared at the top of her pinnace ramp first, and Caine, Ursla, and Sarah all immediately moved to greet her as she crossed the deck to the cluster of commanders. None of them had seen her in about fifteen months...

"Whoa, whoa," Liz slowed as the trio edged forward. "One at a time, eh?"

She took Caine's hand first, "Good to see you, Setter."

"Better for us to see you, I think," he replied, stepping back to give Ursla room. The bear Admiral grinned at her oldest — that is to say *first* — human friend.

"How are you keeping, Liz? The leg alright?" Ursla's great paw extended and Liz took it with practiced caution.

"Really good. I'm all set for the fight, I think..."

Ursla nodded and stepped back as Sarah approached slowly from the side, "Hi Liz."

Hastings grinned and put her hands on Sarah's shoulders, "I've been hearing great things about you."

Sarah smiled sadly and didn't meet her old mentor's eyes, "Just *don't* hug me."

Liz chuckled, "Don't worry, I wouldn't embarrass you that much... that's for him to do."

Sarah looked up and frowned, following a subtle bob of Hastings' head.

"Sarah sister, how *are* you?" Graham was smiling, because as much as he could brood in his cabin, right now his mind was on his big sister.

She barely had a chance to brace herself before the more-heavily-built sibling caught the smaller, stunned one in a hefty hug. Giving up, she hugged back, "I'm alright, I think. You?"

Graham slowly pulled back and shrugged, "I'm rather out of sorts, actually. Barely even recognize myself in the mirror."

Sarah frowned at the… joke?

"We'll talk later," he assured, and then pointed back to the assembled officers. Sarah turned as Caine and Ursla went aside to speak briefly with Broadpaw, and the Larosians approached to talk with their human allies.

"Almost have something, sir. I'll put it in the main plot."

Forepaw and the First Lieutenant approached the holo tank and frowned into its blue light. There was nothing identifiable, just a red wireframe diamond inserted by the computer to surround an area of unusual energy readings in hyper.

"Try to clear that up," the First Lieutenant ordered.

Forepaw looked at the presumably empty space of the diamond…

It could just be an anomaly.

"We received word about 'B' and 'C' at Gibraltar," Broadpaw looked between Caine and Ursla. "You're alright?"

Caine nodded slowly, "We're okay. Been better, but you know how it is."

Broadpaw replied with a similarly slow nod, then looked again between his two comrades, "So… where's Varnia?"

"She's bunking on *Agamemnon*," Ursla met Broadpaw's eyes. "She's quite alright, and I'm pretty sure she'll be wanting to see you in the next while."

Broadpaw brightened a bit, "Let's get down to this, then…"

Novash shook the hands of each of the humans, scanning their minds subtly to make sure he had all the details of the last few years.

"Well, everybody, the briefing room awaits, and we'll want to get to it quickly. War to win, and all," Caine approached the group and Graham grinned, rounding Sarah to extend his hand to the First Lord.

Caine smiled at his young human friend, taking the hand, "Up to no good again, Graham?"

The ArcLieutenant-General shrugged, "Donuts."

There were friendly greetings going on in the landing bay, but on *Orion's* bridge Lab Forepaw wasn't so sure things were as good as they seemed.

"Anything on that anomaly yet?" he was standing with the First Lieutenant at the main battle plot, frowning at a flickering semi-icon that seemed to hover around the flagships.

There was a pause, and the Sensor Lieutenant shook his head, "I can't get a good reading on it, skipper. It looks like it's in the hyper layer, but I can't quite make it out."

Forepaw frowned, "Is it a bomb ship?"

Again a pause, then, "Seems unlikely, sir... the energy readings are virtually nonexistent... but it is in hyper, and it's floating nearby. Maybe an observer."

"Who just watched our secret reinforcements show up," Forepaw turned to the Signal Officer. "Hail *Agamemnon*."

Artemis Tigar's head quickly appeared in the battle plot, "What's up Lab?"

Forepaw frowned at his fellow Flag Captain, "Check 133 by 252 by 321, relative vector north. I think we have a snoop."

Tigar turned away from the holo screen for a second and then looked back, "I see it. You think it slipped the blockade?"

Forepaw tilted his head, "I don't know... but we can't chance it. We've got all the eggs in one basket here... signal *Joseph Barron* and *Lycrotar* to get their defenses up. I'll warn *Algenon* and the rest. I've already got the bay doors open, I'll drop the charges."

Tigar nodded and vanished.

Turning back to the plot, Forepaw knew he could be overreacting, but he wasn't about to risk the fate of the battle tomorrow by waiting for more certain confirmation that might never come...

"Signal Officer, send warnings to all local squadrons that we're rolling a charge. Mister Coyto, prepare one please."

Caine sat at the head of the briefing table with Ursla at his right and Varnon Broadpaw at his left. Liz and Sarah faced each other across the short side of the rectangular table, and Graham was next to Sarah. Narosh and Novash were seated next to each other beside Liz.

"Alright. We have a plan that we hope will give us a shot at landing marines on Krogg 'A'. Our objective is to establish a zone of control in orbital space, then put Andros on the ground to kill the Queen," Caine tapped the main battle tank to life. "I'll have to talk to Andros about what he needs in the way of ground support, but here's where we all fall into–"

The intercom cut in abruptly, "Briefing room, Lab here on the bridge. We have an unidentified signature in hyperspace, I'm about to drop charges. Hang on..."

The comm muted again, and Caine exchanged abrupt glances with all present. Quickly, the First Lord tapped the briefing room display to tie in with the main sensor grid, and the flickering black icon appeared in their screen...

Forepaw took a single deep breath and turned to his First Lieutenant, "Beat to quarters. Shields up."

The Lieutenant repeated the orders and *Orion* suddenly leapt into life. The output of the reactors climbed as the guns charged and crews rushed to the targeting platforms.

Guns wouldn't likely be of any use in this situation, but it never hurt to have them ready…

"All ships in local space have their defensive systems online, skipper."

Forepaw nodded, "Very good. Mister Coyto, on my mark."

Caine frowned as the flickering icon made an abrupt turn and started running in-system. The small vessel must have escaped the blockade…

Orion shuddered slightly as a hyper point shifted the gravitational quotient of the local space, then the charge erupted from the tertiary landing bay. The fast energy-hyper kinetic missile slashed through the spatial layers and drove right into the icon.

The explosion was nowhere near as forceful as those the Kroggs had attempted to use against the Larosian Fleet, but was strong enough to indicate the destruction of a regular Krogg vessel.

On the bridge, Forepaw let out a breath, then keyed his comm, "We got it. Doesn't look like it was a bomb."

In the briefing room, Caine nodded, "But it saw us."

Forepaw's voice was quiet over the intercom, "Yes it did."

Caine took a breath, "Alright, Lab. Good work. We'll have to watch for more of those."

"Aye, we probably wouldn't have seen it if we weren't on heightened alert for *Algenon's* arrival. I'll pass the readings throughout the fleet. Bridge out for now."

Maybe the ship had been destroyed before it could report… maybe it hadn't.

Maybe there were others that *hadn't* been caught.

"I think the plan just changed," Sarah said in quiet tones.

Looking through the plot at his fellows, Caine ground his jaw, "No, we just push the schedule up. Don't give them time to redeploy or guess what we're up to."

There were a few slow nods — no one had expected quite so quick a fight.

"We go today, then," Ursla finished Caine's thought, and he nodded.

"Ten hours."

Everyone in the room stared silently at him.

"We better bloody get started then," Graham leaned forward. "A lot to do."

CHAPTER 44

The pinnace to *Agamemnon* slid from *Orion's* deck a little over three hours later, leaving less than seven hours for its occupants to get their commands ready for action. Dran Nightclaw's 111th, Ami Cairn's 141st, and Pat's 444th were already deploying forward at the heads of the blockades, keeping close eyes on the shipping in Krogg 'A' to make sure no preemptive strikes erupted.

There was no way to be sure what the Krogg scout had seen, if anything, but the very prospect of a preemptive attack against the Allied forces on the hyper limit called for urgency. The Allies had to hit the Kroggs before the Queen could figure out just what was going on.

Ursla, in a way, was almost glad of the accelerated schedule. Waiting another day or more would have been arduous, and she knew seven hours was more than enough time to get her crews ready for action. For the past week, the entire Allied Fleet had been gearing up for this fight. They'd doubtless been thinking about it for far longer than that...

Sitting across from her on the pinnace and tapping his foot in time with the engines, Varnon Broadpaw wasn't so much worried about the upcoming battle right now. His daughter was on *Agamemnon* and he was determined to see her. The reality of how close she'd come to death had very much sunk in — he wanted to see her to help relieve it.

His good spirits were dimmed, so he sat in uneasy silence and watched the gunboats swirling around beyond the window.

Sarah sat across from Liz in *Orion's* lower mess and clinked her icy glass of water against her mentor's. Liz was smiling, enthused about the plan Caine had just finished laying out. She'd been away from the fight for so long, forgotten from the war books and essentially lost from the front. Now she'd return with a bang. Literally.

Because when Sarah and the Fourth Fleet pulled back, it would be Liz's ships that would meet the pursuing Kroggs. And Liz was the best one for it, absolutely.

"We'll finally get to fight an action together," Liz grinned as she sipped her water, and Sarah nodded through a gulp. It was true — absurd as it seemed, Sarah had never fought a fleet action as a commander with Liz involved...

Now the combination would almost certainly be striking, so long as she did her share. This fight would be the grandest of them all. The Earthers were all here — all the remaining great heroes of the wars to date — as were all the surviving human officers.

And at the head of the latter would be Liz and Sarah.

"Should be quite a spectacle," the promise of this battle, this ultimate opportunity to cleanse her mind and get back on track, made Sarah's voice resonate.

Liz smiled at her young friend and nodded.

She'd see to it.

As the main holo tank on *Engadine's* bridge glowed to life, Draco Maximane's eyes met those of Commodore Tom Locke, "Good to see you again, Tom."

Locke had been Captain of *Monarch* only months earlier during the period around the Battle of Gibraltar. After distinguishing himself in command of that converted Carrier, Maximane had recommended that he lead the Second Carrier Group — his other senior Captain, Ron Hobbes, being too important in *Engadine* to be sent to the rear to collect the new ships.

Now Locke nodded to his old commander, "And you, sir. I hear you did some great things while I was in the rear."

Maximane shrugged and nodded slowly.

"I believe we call that false modesty," Locke smiled. "My ships are at your disposal, sir."

With a grin, Maximane nodded, "Glad to have you back, Tom. I'll send the plan over immediately."

Garvin Jardaw stood beside Fox Magnus at *Highlander's* main plot. Opposite them, Jax Furgus squinted into the blue holo and pointed at icons around a projected sphere.

"We'll want to hit these first... the stations, that is..."

Fox cleared his throat, "We *know*, Jax. You already suggested that. A week ago."

Furgus looked up and shrugged, "Well, you know how I am."

"A bit nervous, that's all. No worries," Fox nodded to his CO through the glowing map. "It'll go well. All we have to do is stick close to the Carriers and let the others deal with the Krogg Fleet."

"Hmm," Jardaw scratched absently behind one ear. "Think it'll be so simple?"

Fox blinked twice, "Could be."

Narosh smoothly held his fighter's course, aiming straight for *Lycrotar* after he emerged from *Orion's* main bay. Just behind him, Novash's fighter slipped from the side of the First Rate and came up alongside him.

I'll be moving on to Shanavorus *Admiral-of-a-Fleet. I likely won't have close contact with you again until after this is over.*

Narosh acknowledged mentally: *Indeed, Admiral-of-a-Division.*

Deeper in his mind, Narosh thought briefly of his subordinate. Since this war had taken its post-Genesis turn, Novash had been a reliable and loyal deputy — to a degree beyond even Larosian expectations. As much as anyone could be Narosh's friend in these times, Novash was.

Good luck, Novash. You are a truly loyal friend, and I hope to see you at the end of this.

Novash felt sentimental for a brief second, then acknowledged with a mental smile. *And luck to you, Narosh. We must both last through this, I think, so that we can work together to save our home. Fight well.*

And you, Novash.

With that, Novash angled his fighter off Narosh's wing, and accelerated in a separate direction towards *Shanavorus*.

"How are you feeling, Graham?"

Graham looked up abruptly and put on a smile, "Setter! Bloody scared me..."

He was sitting rather still in the observation lounge, overlooking the main flight bay deep in *Orion's* belly. He liked these observation lounges, found them comforting — he could see the world but it couldn't see him.

"Well, the Chief told me your ship was the only one left on the deck. And when Liz was troubled a long, *long* time ago, she and Ursla came up here to talk. Back when they were just planning a tour of Earth..." Caine took a seat across the table from Graham, and the junior Manchester turned his chair to face the First Lord.

"Really?"

Caine nodded, "You seemed a bit troubled... despite that good show you put on."

Graham tilted his head and leaned back in his chair, "Did I?"

"You did. Like you're carrying a burden or ten."

A short laugh escaped Graham, and he slumped forward slightly, "I suppose I'm one of the gang then, eh? Just doing my bit, Setter."

"You're taking charge of your ships," Caine said in a tone tinted with pride. "You've decided, haven't you?"

Graham frowned, "Decided what?"

Caine smiled, "To do what needs to be done. To finish all this. As Savanna might have suggested you do."

Graham's eyebrow arched in reply, "*Everyone's* decided that, I think."

"You'd be surprised. It's not an easy thing to do."

"Oh Gods," Graham's hand covered his eyes. "Don't tell me I've *grown up* or something. For Gods' sake, I'm not a boy..."

Caine tilted his head, "Three years ago you were a station commander. Didn't seem all that much like a fleet commander then."

"And I am now?"

Caine leaned back with a half-knowing, half-amused look, "You've grown Graham. I know you're ready for this. More ready than a lot of us."

Graham's head dropped and he ran his fingers through his hair with a huff, "I said not to say that!"

"You'll do fine," Caine leaned forward and patted the junior Manchester's arm. "Now, can you go to your ship and get this whole thing set up? I have to pull together the marines and get the landing plans set."

Graham looked up and nodded slowly.

The pinnace landed easily on *Agamemnon's* deck and came to what seemed to Varnon to be a very slow halt.

The venerable wolf was *very* tightly strung just now, and he was instinctively, though unintentionally, broadcasting it to anyone near enough to be paying attention.

Ursla was less than a meter away from him, and his tension was almost enough to make her want to tear the arms off her chair. The poor father was coming to terms with a lot more than the death of a friend...

Varnon was on his feet before the pinnace came to a complete stop. As the last of the speed bled off, he popped the hatch and tapped his foot anxiously while the ramp slowly made its descent. He bounded down the metal gangway as it touched the deck, and then sprinted out.

Varnia had heard her father was arriving, and she'd just come to greet him when he came barreling across the deck. He skidded to a halt just in front of her and managed to get his hands to her shoulders before she quite realized he was there.

"You're alright?" his question was almost panicked, and Varnia nodded.

"I'm okay, dad."

Varnon looked directly at his daughter and took a very deep breath.

"I missed you a lot," he offered, and Varnia smiled a bit sheepishly.

"*Dad...*"

In a fatherly fashion, Varnon wrapped his arms around her and they hugged happily.

"*Now,*" he said, his voice brightening. "You're coming back to *Algenon* with me, and you're not getting out of my sight until this war ends..."

"Dad!"

Ursla caught the exclamation as she came down the ramp, and she detected the palpable relief that Broadpaw seemed to be emitting.

Well at least that had turned out happily.

Now they just had the war to win.

Ursla sighed and made her way to the nearest lift. She had orders to send out.

CHAPTER 45

Andros Grieve was rather surprised at the immediacy of the attack. He'd been expecting to launch quickly, but now the Kroggs had forced the timetable ahead. Good thing he had already done the planning. With six hours to go before Caine's desired launch, they wouldn't have had a lot of time to get things straight.

Grieve, Lupus, and Gillian Hodge coasted through space in one of *Algenon's* pinnaces, angling for *Orion's* main bay, and the General was wrapped up in his thoughts as he watched gunboats swerve through space beyond the window... he was beginning to feel uncomfortable again, and he wasn't sure why. But there was no time to dwell on such feelings.

Beckett Lupus, sitting across the aisle from the General, rested his head back against the seat and closed his eyes. He'd been preparing himself for this for a while now — he'd been sparring with Howler, practicing with the blade, and soon he'd be working on shield tactics with the Earther Guards battalions and 2/54th.

He really wasn't quite sure how to feel about the impending battle. He'd been in close actions with Kroggs *many* times before. Part of his mind was tempted to simply write this off as just another go at it... nothing to worry about. But the rest of him was sure it couldn't be that simple.

Well, he could worry about it afterwards.

That was refreshing, he decided. He knew he was coming back from this little ordeal — he hadn't known he'd survive the torpedo he'd launched back on Pat's planet. He hadn't really *known* he'd survive the Antarctic Plain. But he *knew* he'd survive what was to come.

Gillian Hodge, for her part, sat subdued and anxious in her seat next to Lupus. She was no longer worried about Graham — a good sign, she decided. Work before play, and such. She'd been doing this job from the first mutinies when she'd helped secure *Bishop* for Pat, to when she'd taken over from Commandant Falkner after everyone senior to her died on the Plain.

She'd managed to do all these things so that today could happen, and she knew, whether it killed her or not, the job was going to get done. In six hours.

Orion's main bay began to swallow *Algenon's* pinnace, but Grieve didn't really pay it any heed. He watched the flagship's flight bay appear outside his window, but his mind was already beginning to turn over what he expected to hear from Caine. They'd be landing marines on the Krogg planet, trying to get to the Queen. That much he knew for a fact now... and he also knew the terrain they were landing on.

This meeting seemed a formality. The marines of the Guards Brigade knew what they had to do, Gillian had assembled a battalion of her own to support the Earthers, and he'd meet the Larosian ground officer any time now...

He knew where this was headed, so why was he still feeling apprehensive about it?

Because the stakes were high. Because this was their all-or-nothing push for the survival of the Earthers.

No pressure, he'd fought all-or-nothing fights before...

No pressure.

Yeah. Sure.

The pinnace slid to an easy halt in its slot, and the three marine officers slowly came to their feet.

Captain-Elite Torallis and Maximane stood looking into the holo tank at a projection of the Krogg homeworld, with Caine facing them both.

"Once the orbit is secured, we should be able to launch from any place we like," Maximane said steadily, "and so should the transports. How many of those are you going to need us to cover?"

"I'm going to pull the battalions off transports and load them onto 74s, I think," Caine offered his reply in a thoughtful tone. "We'll want to keep the transports away from the fighting to use as hospital ships later on... come to think of it, I'll probably group them with Narosh's hospital squadron."

Maximane nodded and Torallis tilted his head, "May we zoom in to a view of the ground more closely, please?"

Caine nodded and tapped the holo to focus it on the landing plateau. Grieve would need to get the plans for the landing ready quickly... he'd doubtless been thinking about it for a while, knowing him, but this was rather abrupt as battle summons went.

"We will be very heavily attacked by Queen's Guards when we land, I can assure you," Torallis said quietly. "We will need to fight our way through many thousands simply to reach the palace, and then the battle through the corridors will doubtless be bloody."

"You'll have to go all the way down to set the charges?" Maximane frowned and cast a glance sideways at the Larosian, who bow-nodded.

"The Queen's Hive we encountered in Genesis was the same — resilient to unthinkable extremes. We must set the charge literally at the feet of the Queen, and then evacuate the chamber. The protection of her personal chamber can stop outside space weapons, so I must expect that we will be safe from the detonation if we can simply get outside."

Caine cocked an eyebrow, "You think you can get out?"

Torallis paused and then straightened, squaring his shoulders, "That is not an issue. If we must die, we will do so willingly."

"All the same, can you?"

Caine's amber-gray eyes met Torallis' silver ones, and the Captain-Elite tilted his head, "Even with the Genesis ore lining our helmets to scatter her telepathic attacks, Lord Caine, it is quite possible that once in her presence, all of my Guardsmen will be mentally destroyed. We are all prepared for that eventuality — our mission is simply to set the charges before we die. Escape would be acceptable, but death, if necessary, does not disturb us..."

The door slid open just as Torallis was saying the words, "I certainly hope it doesn't come to that, Torallis!"

Grieve stepped in with a small smile, and the Larosian turned to face the taller bear, "Andros Grieve!"

Torallis and Grieve had assaulted the Queen's Hive at Genesis together — only to find it empty. Now, however, there was no chance the Queen would escape this pair. As Grieve extended his hand and Torallis took it, Lupus and Hodge slid inside and nodded in turn to Caine and Maximane.

Caine rounded the table quickly and extended his hand, being vaguely familiar with Hodge from the days after Antarctica, and well acquainted with Lupus, "Good to see you both."

Maximane followed, "Good to meet you, Commandant Hodge..." he paused and looked Lupus over, "... and you look a *hell* of a lot better than when last I saw you."

Lupus grinned, "I'd just been blown up, as I recall."

Chuckling, Maximane nodded and they shook hands before he turned towards Grieve.

The General was glad to see his Larosian counterpart. They'd worked together for a relatively brief time at Genesis — only a couple of months before the two major wings of the Alliance had gone their separate ways. But they'd shared battle — against a Hive, no less — and it felt right to be going into this fight with the Stealth Guardsman at his side.

"Not a dress rehearsal this time, I suspect," Grieve finally let go of Torallis' hand, and the Larosian tilted his head forward in agreement.

Caine approached Grieve, "Which is why I've got Draco here, Andros. Good to see you again."

Grieve smiled at the First Lord and nodded, "And you, Setter. You keeping well?"

A short chuckle escaped Caine, "In an insane sort of way."

Nodding in understanding, Grieve offered his hand to Maximane, "I've heard much about you, Vice Admiral."

"And I you," the lion answered as they shook hands. "Hopefully I can help you with your problems. Some of them at least."

Grieve frowned thinly, "How so?"

"Here, let's have a look at this..." Caine gestured everyone to the main plot, and they went to work.

• • •

"I've sent the orders to the transports, they're already moving to shift their dropships to the 201st and 209th," Forepaw's voice was clear over the intercom, and Caine nodded in acknowledgement, more for the benefit of Grieve than for Forepaw, who couldn't see him.

"Good work, Lab. We go in five hours."

"I haven't *lost count*, Setter," the Flag Captain closed the line.

Caine smiled at the remark, and then allowed himself a short sigh. He and Grieve were now alone in the main briefing room, the map of Krogg 'A' still glowing over the table, icons showing the seemingly simple maneuvers Grieve had planned to use to gain the advantage on the plateau.

It was going to be bloody business.

Grieve stood silently, looking at the map, his eyes tracing the lines over and over again. Making sure it made sense. Making sure there were no flaws. Not that he could count on the plan surviving contact with the enemy...

Well, then again, they'd taught him that adage in school, but it hadn't panned out. He'd won at Antarctica. Queen or no, they'd pulled off the attack on the Hive in Genesis...

Maybe this would work. Perfectly.

Again, that ambiguous uncertainty was tugging at him, but he did his best to ignore it.

Caine, watching the General's calm face, vaguely sensed the unusual apprehension building in the bear.

His eyes widened a little and his smile faded.

"Andros."

Grieve looked up, and Caine met his eyes in a solid stare.

"You're..." Caine's voice trailed off.

For a second Grieve was confused, but only for a second.

Aha.

Taking a breath, Grieve nodded, "It's a long walk down. And a longer walk back."

Caine understood, and he rounded the table to stand before the weathered Grizzly General, "Yes, yes it is."

Grieve tilted his head very slightly, "I'll get it done, Setter."

Again Caine nodded, and this time he offered his hand, "Good luck. We'll all be with you, I think."

Grieve took a breath and nodded, the uncertainty settling into calm as he and the First Lord clasped hands.

Caine stared as the big General left the room and the door closed behind him.

This war would end awash in the blood of the brave, he decided sadly.

CHAPTER 46

"Two hours to go," Lang Sandpelt glanced up at Chronos Claw, and the Captain nodded.

Flame, in typical fashion, was already well within the boundaries of the Krogg system, scanning and checking to make sure the enemy didn't try a preemptive strike against the newly reinforced fleet.

The sloop would probably stay there for the duration, relaying important information to squadrons as the Kroggs reacted. It would be up to *Flame* and its consorts to let Caine know when the Kroggs weakened their home force.

If the Kroggs weakened their home force.

After so much punishment in battles past, it seemed, *Flame* would be delegated to watching this fight.

The thought struck Claw as amusing, and he almost smiled...

Not bloody likely.

Artemis Tigar sat across from Ursla and raised his glass in time with her, "To luck."

Ursla nodded and moved her glass to connect with his before they both drank their water. The Flag Captain was anxious, much like Ursla, but neither were really keen on admitting it.

This was the same job they did everyday, after all.

"Well," Tigar laid his glass on the table, "Varnia's got command of *Algenon*."

It took Ursla's mind a second to shift gears... Broadpaw had given his Flag Captaincy to his daughter?

"Apparently he said he wouldn't let her off *Algenon*, and it seems he's been serving as acting Captain while he's been running the Fifth. All this time, *Algenon*'s been under his direct orders."

Ursla cocked an eyebrow, "I suppose shipping them out so fast left a few gaps."

Tigar nodded, then slowly stood, "Speaking of which... I'll see you on the bridge soon."

With a nod from Ursla, Tigar turned and made for the exit... just as the door chime sounded. Tigar paused and turned back to Ursla, "Should I?"

Ursla nodded, "Please."

The Flag Captain opened the door to see Grieve standing in the corridor.

Tigar smiled and nodded to the venerable bear, "General! Your dropships boarded safely?"

Grieve nodded, and Tigar bobbed his head, "Good, if you'll excuse me then."

The General stood aside and let Tigar pass, then stepped into Ursla's cabin as she stood to greet him, "Hello Andra."

His tone was grim, and Ursla crossed the floor to shake his hand, "Andros… you're settled and ready?"

He nodded, looking up slightly to meet Ursla's eyes.

A puzzled Ursla stood still for a long moment, then a penetrating sadness settled over her like a fog.

"Just coming around to see everyone before I go," he said after a pause.

"We better drink to luck, then," she waved her arm towards the glasses on the table, and Grieve offered a small smile.

"We might as well."

Lupus stood in front of ten companies of the 2nd Battalion of the 54th Regiment of Foot, fully battle dressed and drawn up before him in smart ranks.

"Sar-Major Howler, battalion to attention if you please," Lupus' words were quiet, but the mini-microphone in his uniform collar transmitted the order to earpieces worn by every one of the marines. They each could have obeyed independently, but as was tradition for this sort of moment, they waited for the order from Howler.

"Battalion, *attention.*"

In *Agamemnon's* crowded secondary landing bay, the thunder of 500 pairs of boots snapping down in unison was daunting. The deck crews watched with silent interest and respect for the venerable 2/54th.

"Very good, Sergeant," Lupus took a step forward and looked over his command. The Guards battalions were spread over the 74s of the 290th, but 2/54th, the Larosians, and Genesis troops were all concentrated in Ursla's First Rates of the 201st. This battalion, his own through many hard fights, would stay with him in this most crucial action.

"We have just over an hour left," Lupus slowly looked from face to face, seeing many he'd known for years. "And then we'll be launching. Our drop, as you well know, won't come immediately; it'll happen as soon as the Navy can move us into position over the planet."

There was no visible reaction among the ranks, and Lupus let a sad smile creep over his face, "You're the best we've got. And we're going to need all *you've* got. You know as well as I do we're going to need everything you can give today…"

Lupus paused, his eyes drifting from face to face… Each a determined face. A knowing face.

They understood.

They were Earthers, they knew what had to be done.

And they were *willing* to do it.

That thought wasn't so much a revelation as an affirmation, and Lupus' smile filled out ever so slightly, "I know every single one of you. I can't tell any of you anything you haven't already thought of."

His voice gained a bit more strength.

"We have our objective, and we have to face the Kroggs' most elite forces to achieve it."

The Earthers seemed to stand even taller as he spoke the words.

And that sealed Lupus' confidence.

Faith. These were the most elite marines in the service, whether they had the title of Guards behind their regimental name or not.

"Whatever they throw at us," Lupus collected his voice and projected it across the deck, "we will *not fail*."

The words resonated for a moment, and then rather abruptly, there erupted a thunderous roar as the Earthers of 2/54th bellowed their determination. Lupus listened and felt the confidence they permeated slide through him.

This would be their day.

Caine stood on the bridge and watched the clock as it ticked through the nine-minute mark.

It seemed such a rushed way to end this war. He'd wanted a couple of days to prepare for this last battle, but he'd been given only half of *one*. He hadn't had time to do all he'd wanted, talk to everyone he'd have liked to talk to. He could always push zero hour back, but that would be a risk. And it was too great a risk to take.

The Allies were ready. They were organized and they were keen.

This was the culmination of many years, for *all* of them.

And when the war was done, life could go back to normal. Normal with millions dead, but normal.

Caine thought calmly about that fact as the clock struck eight.

With eight minutes left, a thoughtful Sarah sat in silence. She'd said nothing to Pat, though she had spoken with Liz for a while. They hadn't had enough time to really talk. She'd do more of that after the battle.

And this was one she'd fight sensibly.

Because she wanted to have many conversations after it was over.

Pat watched the countdown reach seven minutes and hoped Sarah would be safe. He wanted to see her again, make amends and all.

Graham's mind filled with similar thoughts at six minutes. Sarah would come through it, and Gillian would have to as well.

Narosh envisioned the Son's blazing end in his mind's eye as the time count reduced to four minutes. Revenge, and then salvation for his people, began in four minutes.

• • •

Liz watched the clock hit three minutes and turned to her ArcColonel, "Fleetcomm, Fourth and Sixth please."

The ArcColonel nodded, and the comm abruptly chirped through all Genesis ships.

"Men and women of the Genesis Fleet, this is ArcGeneral Hastings..." she paused, unsure where her words were about to come from. "In less than three minutes, we embark on the last operation of this war. This, more than any other moment, is probably the most defining for us all. We've lived with the Kroggs almost as long as we've lived with the Church. Now it's time to remove them, once and for all."

She paused again, and the fleet listened nervously to the silence.

"We all must do our duty today," she said after a moment. "Some will be lost, but not all. We *must* prevail."

Another pause, and she found her bridge crew staring at her.

"The time is now. *Now* we prove ourselves. Gods protect you all."

Liz took a deep breath.

"Hastings out."

At two minutes, Caine looked first to Forepaw, then to the Signal Officer, "All ships hail, if you please, Lieutenant."

After a brief pause, Caine's voice was transmitted to the decks of each Earther ship in the fleet. Ursla, Broadpaw, Fox, Furgus, Jardaw, Maximane, Lupus, Grieve — all eyes turned upward towards ceiling speakers.

"We've come to the end of it."

The Earther Navy listened.

Caine took a breath and then turned towards Forepaw as he spoke, "We've come far together. Farther than anyone — any*thing* — could have dreamed we'd come. We're brothers and sisters in arms, today. We're not cattle for a virus, we're not irrational or stilted. We've come this far by being who we are. *What* we are."

A collective deep breath of understanding passed throughout the four Earther fleets, and Caine smiled at Forepaw, putting his hand on his friend's shoulder.

"Now we finish what we said we'd finish. We do it the way we've done everything in this war. The same way we've done *everything* at all."

Caine's hand came down and he turned to look once more over his bridge crew.

The clock ticked into its last fifty seconds.

"We do this together."

He took a breath and straightened.

"We do this as what we are."

Forty seconds.

"We do this as *Earthers*. Let *that* be our legacy to the universe — no matter what the cost, no matter who we must sacrifice, we *do* what we say we'll do and we do it in a way that reflects us. No one, no *thing* can take that from us. And today we declare that."

Thirty seconds.

"To arms, Earthers. Today is *our* victory."

At twenty-five seconds, a roar rose in every Earther ship in the fleet, and as the comms carried the cheer through the ships, Caine closed his eyes and gently let himself down in his chair.

Savanna would agree.

Fifteen seconds. Cheers fade.

Ten seconds. Crews take deep breaths.

Five seconds. Captains steel themselves.

One second. Caine opens his mouth.

"Go."

CHAPTER 47

Sarah had been waiting, and now everything had finally been sorted out. She confidently led the way into battle...

As the countdown hit zero she nodded to the Comm Officer, "All ships, *engage*."

Despite the seemingly short preparation time, her crews were more than ready. Over 1,400 Genesis ships surged forward from their hyper limit blockade stations, moving with the same singular mind they'd used when rescuing *Match*.

That incident had proved their dress rehearsal.

The Krogg picket facing them now seemed stunned as she watched them on the plot — the small alien ships decelerated abruptly from their regular patrol runs, coming to a halt and drifting for a few seconds before turning away from the invaders.

Battlecruisers were already tearing into the space around them with lasers, seeking to kill as many as they could before the Kroggs fled in-system.

The entire Genesis Fleet surged ahead in those Battlecruisers' wake, and *Joseph Barron* led them.

Pat's Posse stuck together for this fight — Pat would be damned if he'd lose them all piecemeal. They were attached to the same group as *Barron*, and for now they were just sweeping the Destroyer pickets aside.

Divine Templar's decks trembled as the Battlecruiser made a sharp turn and spat a volley of missiles, and Pat watched on his sensor screen as the entire Fourth Fleet followed in his wake...

He checked the clock.

And... now!

Narosh's mind was focused to the point of emptiness. That was not to say he was suddenly without understanding, he'd simply cleared his consciousness to ensure that his decisions and orders were precise and accurate.

This was an occasion that would require all his skill.

As a telepathic image of what was taking place with the Genesis Fourth Fleet entered his mind, he silently counted to fifteen and then tilted his head to the side.

All ships accelerate to action. By Praaxus and his Son, victory to us this day!

Lycrotar was already in battle mode, the Warcruiser's hull bulging outward to make it appear larger and more venerable. Now the elite flagship, its squadron, and the hundreds of other squadrons lunged forward with a viciousness that was the legacy of some 600 years of war.

All ships, engage by squadron.

As they gained the range, *Lycrotar's* antimatter guns opened fire on a handful of Destroyers. Missiles slashed out.

Novash telepathically nodded to his Flag Captain and *Shanavorus* leapt forward, leading Battleships forward in a wedge towards the nearest Krogg cluster of stations. The Larosian Battleships were large, lumbering beasts, but their firepower was formidable. They would do well against the big installations laid throughout Krogg space. Novash would see to that.

Battleships by squadron, prepare to bombard.

Target range in seven minutes, sir.

Very good.

Sitting on *Flame*, Claw watched the abrupt acceleration of over 5,000 Allied ships. It was the most unbelievable thing he'd ever seen, and the Kroggs seemed as stunned by the sight as he was. *Flame* lay in energy drive relatively 'above' one of the thickest clusters of Krogg ships beyond the system's planet — some 2,000 Krogg warships were grazing around a number of orbital food stations directly in the path of the Fourth Fleet's advance.

This Krogg force was actually the closest formation to Sarah's approaching attack, and yet it was just sitting in place, watching the humans come on…

Chronos' hair was beginning to rise. The enemy wasn't reacting… was this another trap…? But wait, it had only been twenty-five seconds since the beginning of Sarah's advance. He needed to be a little more patient…

"Sir, they're deploying towards the Fourth!"

The words reached him just as the icons on the main plot changed.

No trap today.

Varnon Broadpaw glanced at his daughter in the seat beside him as she directed *Algenon*.

The crew were at action stations, the guns ready to be run out as soon as the order came…

The Larosians and the Fourth were cruising in now, meeting no resistance as yet. He had to wait until it looked as though the Kroggs were preparing to move…

"There they go, sir! Confirmation from *Flame* and *Flint*."

Broadpaw nodded, "Fifth Fleet to energy drive. Bring us out on top of them."

Varnia was already turning, "Master, mark that course and take us into energy drive if you please. Gunners, stand by your guns."

"Aye."

With the other 500-odd ships of the Fifth, *Algenon* collapsed into energy drive and surged in-system, accelerating to a quick but cautious 200 pls. Sarah was about to come head-to-head with some 3,000 Krogg ships, and that was a problem they would have to help deal with...

Sarah watched the range tick down as the large Krogg force turned slowly away from its feeding station and clouded forward to face her. The Genesis ships were outnumbered, but these weren't Earther ships they were facing. The Krogg battle record against Genesis wasn't always even... historically, the Kroggs often gave better than they got.

But that was historically.

"Optimum range... *now*, ma'am."

The vessels of the fleet had hastily filled their magazines from the storeships that had arrived with the Sixth, managing to top up their Type 98 missile stores with only half an hour to spare before action. Now, they'd expend all of them in a few hours.

"Tubes at thirty second intervals. Open fire by squadron," she ordered coolly, and as her words crossed the bridge, ArcColonel Evan-Thomas gave the appropriate orders to the gunner of the flagship.

Joseph Barron's tubes vented the first 100 missiles with a shudder.

Pat's ships whirled into a triple-vanguard spearhead with *Templar* leading, all their tubes flushing simultaneously as they closed with the Kroggs.

They were toying right now with the first screen of enemy Destroyers, and the still-disorganized Kroggs were only just shaking themselves into formation. The aliens probably hadn't expected a direct front-on attack from the hyper limit — with the Earthers being able to carry the first strike deep, it might seem foolish for them to launch an attack on the system perimeter.

Well, that was where the first fight was coming... even if it was a feint.

Destroyers met Pat's missiles head on, and he watched coldly on the monitor as a dozen vanished.

"They have a total of 5,000 ships mobilized and moving to the front, including around 3,000 that are moving out to meet Sarah. The 2,000 guarding the Krogg planet have not moved."

Claw nodded at the report and bobbed his head towards the Signal Officer, "Pass that on to flag."

Nothing to worry about just yet... the Kroggs weren't likely to weaken their home guard until the Allies backed off. Sooner would be nice, *but*.

"Where's Admiral Broadpaw?"

"On his way, sir."

Algenon appeared in the space above the lumbering Krogg flotilla with its guns running out, and Varnon simply nodded to his daughter as the First Rate glided up to battle speed.

"All guns, fire as you bear," Varnia gave her orders in an almost subdued tone, and *Algenon* shivered as its guns slid back over their heavy tracks.

Another 471 ships came with the First Rate, and in bare seconds the space above the 5,000-strong flotilla was torn with energy. The alien ships were taken by surprise, though they were not entirely unprepared. The flotilla shifted, Dreadnoughts and Superdreadnoughts rising from the center of the cumbersome cloud with their spines primed.

The Fifth Fleet laid repeated broadsides into whatever tried to present itself, but two-thirds of the Earther force was frigates, and thus lacked the weight to completely stop the Krogg replies. Spines began to retaliate...

Varnon rose from his chair and stood peering into the battle plot even as *Algenon* twisted sideways to avoid a volley. Holding the sides of the tank to keep steady, he stared into it and watched a dozen of his frigates immediately evaporate.

"Break action to energy drive and then reengage," his words were quick and he turned to his Signal Officer. "We can't give them time to count us."

The Cruising Master put *Algenon* back into energy drive.

Sarah's missiles weren't nearly as fast as the Earther broadsides — not at this range at least — but they were firing in quick salvoes, with almost 200,000 warheads in space already. They were racing through the void at the Kroggs and would be reaching attack range... now...

Neuro-energy pulses and spines lashed out at the projectiles, batting aside entire salvoes of the heavily-armed missiles. Sarah ground her jaw at the near-ineffectiveness of her first wave of 50,000... but then remembered she was supposed to lose here. Or *look* like she was losing...

The next two missile salvoes piled in against the Kroggs, the long-range warheads slowly beginning to overwhelm the point defense capabilities of the Krogg formations. Dreadnoughts blossomed — not that many, but a few dozen.

And that was *something*.

The fleets raced towards each other...

Lycrotar and the Warcruisers thundered ahead, their guns and missiles waiting again as they dove towards an arm of the 5,000-strong formation of Krogg ships. This section of the enemy flotilla was nearly separated from the main group, sweeping far out on one flank as it collected itself. Nonetheless, it was powerful, counting many Dreadnoughts and a number of Motherships.

The Larosian Carriers were being held back for now, so as not to sacrifice their precious fighters in the false retreat. Those vessels waited with the hospital ships and transports in the rear, ready to come forward and defend the fleet when the time came...

So this would be an unfortunately brutal first engagement.

Or not so *unfortunate*.

We have their range, sir.

Narosh leaned forward in his chair and watched the fleets come together in

his mind's eye.
Open fire.

Claw had never seen a Larosian fleet stream into battle. Genesis hadn't been a fair example — the Larosians had been pinned to a foothold by the Kroggs. This current battle was the sort that the Larosians were used to fighting, and it was spectacular in the most brutal way.

Lines of Warcruisers stacked into something of a wall, accelerating in excellent order towards the Kroggs who came on in clouds, their seventeen Motherships to the rear. There were over 100 Motherships in the system, most still sitting at home.

Move soon...

The Larosian wall fired in a sudden fountain of antimatter. The main guns of the Larosian ships were meant for close range, and Narosh liked to get very close to use them against the Kroggs. Unlike missiles, they could not be deflected, and against Krogg tissue they were brutally successful.

Now his Warcruisers transformed the space between the closing fleets into death. Narosh sat satisfied in his chair.

Further off on the flank, Novash's Battleship force ran down on the outer feeding base that had been the station of the Krogg ships now driving towards Sarah and Narosh's forces.

But these stations were expecting an attack, and massive spines of a sort the Admiral-of-a-Division had never seen began hurtling through space, catching unwary Battleships in their regular formation.

Divide to division echelons, engage the stations!

This group of stations appeared to be built around grazing ports, but there were no ships with them. The mobile units were doubtless already moving to engage Narosh or Sarah...

And no fixed defenses, no matter how powerful, would interfere with what the Battleships did best.

Breaking by echelon, Novash watched as the massive vessels decelerated and opened their forward missile tubes. They then began shifting vertically and horizontally, randomly moving as spines slashed at their ranks, and the missiles began erupting.

Larosian missiles were *very* well armed, and the ones carried by the Battleships had more than enough speed to compensate for the big ships' lack of momentum.

The weapons slashed into the first station without mercy, salvoes from thousands of battlewagons all at once, tearing the weapons base apart in a gory explosion. The counter fire continued from the half dozen other stations that had been clustered around the guard base, but only four Battleships were lost.

Then fourteen Motherships appeared.

CHAPTER 48

Caine watched the Krogg Motherships close with Novash's Battleships and for half a second he thought of sending some of his own ships to help the Larosian formation weather the inevitable storm of corvettes. The First Fleet was lying just seconds away by energy drive...

But of course he couldn't send any assistance without betraying his presence, and so he immediately dismissed the option.

Orion was sitting at anchor, just far enough back from the action not to be obvious to the Kroggs. The rest of the First was even further behind, out of sight while Varnon stood in for them with the ships of the Fifth. Telemetry coming through from *Flame* showed the Krogg forces in the orbital space around the Queen's planet to be holding station, though; 2,000 ships which easily outgunned the Earther Fleet that would have to dislodge them...

Caine looked at his chronometer and then glared back into the plot.

They'd have to move soon...

Pat gripped the arm of his chair as *Templar* turned over fast and spilled a salvo of missiles. The Posse was doing what it did best — mixing it up with Krogg capital ships. Lumbering Dreadnoughts couldn't keep up with the fast Battlecruisers of Pat's three squadrons, and even Krogg Destroyers were unable to close range with the hastily-moving Genesis ships.

The only thing Pat had to worry about now were corvettes... and none were in sight yet.

So he could focus on his job of drawing the Kroggs out of the center of the system...

Templar heaved sideways abruptly, a salvo of spines tearing viciously into its port armor. The Battlecruiser took the hit but swerved away from a follow-up volley, one of the other Battlecruisers from the Posse closing range and engaging the attacker. Krogg resistance was thickening.

Joseph Barron was untouched. The big, powerful Superdreadnought rained missiles on the Kroggs as they tried to close range, and four of its eleven fellows had been blasted to chunks by the venerable alien defenders, but *Barron* seemed to have good luck working for it.

All the same, Sarah wasn't relying too much on luck just now. She tried to keep her squadron further to the rear than she would normally prefer, recognizing the need to regroup after they all staged their retreat...

Joseph Barron seemed to lunge forward and then its decks shivered, another full volley of missiles escaping its tubes and sliding into space, hurtling down on a Krogg Dreadnought...

Sarah ignored the simpler operations of her ship's fighting process, instead focusing on the icons on the plot screen. The Fourth Fleet was pressing the Kroggs hard, but the battle was scarcely minutes old and the full weight of Krogg system garrison still hadn't quite come to bear.

Varnon was fighting in his usual style, though; the Fifth Fleet was hurtling out of energy drive in a fast fury of broadsides before disappearing again. The Earther Admiral was losing a handful of ships each time he dropped from and returned to energy drive — soon he'd need to back off or he'd risk more substantial casualties than were acceptable for this early stage of the battle. Besides, for all their determination, the ships of the Fifth Fleet weren't doing any significant damage to the Kroggs.

Indeed, inflicting significant amounts of damage in straight fighting was the province of her fleet. And they were doing that job well.

Narosh's Warcruisers slashed through the Krogg cloud like daggers, the Larosian ships' neat wall formation disintegrating into combat wings as soon as the two groups of ships came together. Big Krogg batteries mounted on Dreadnoughts tried to track the much faster-moving Warcruisers, but the Battlecruiser-like ships were too speedy to be caught easily by turreted fire.

Krogg Destroyers moved in large swarms to counter the Larosian infiltration, and spines and neuro pulses from those smaller ships began to tell... *Lycrotar* shuddered, but its shields held against the sting of small Destroyer spines. One of its fellow Warcruisers, however, shattered under the lucky shot of a Krogg Superdreadnought.

Larosian antimatter guns continued their rapid, point-blank fire, and the space around most of Narosh's division turned into a storm of mutually destructive breeds of atom. Krogg ships began to fragment, but at the same time their neuro pulses began to take a heavy toll.

And all the while, heavy Krogg ships remembered their old techniques for catching the bulging Larosian Warcruisers in the flank, and as the black Dreadnoughts and Superdreadnoughts swung round, two dozen Warcruisers were blown to pieces in a flash. The fighting did not cease — not yet. Narosh was going to press this for a while longer before he gave the order to break. He *had* to.

They would only retreat when the Kroggs were bloodied enough to want him dead.

And he knew he could whet the aliens' appetite for his death...

Novash's battlewagons noted the arrival of Motherships as the last of the stations spiraled apart in a bloody puff. The eyes on the new battle-Motherships were already opening, and salvoes of spines crashed into a handful of Battleships even as the corvettes began to rain outward.

This was exactly what Battleships usually *couldn't* handle on their own — what Warcruisers could only barely deal with when unsupported by fighters.

But because these were new anti-Earther Motherships, they were leaner and carried fewer and slower anti-gunboat corvettes. This subtle difference didn't entirely allay the plight the Battleships abruptly faced, but things could have been much worse. Indeed, with 1,800 ships in a rough wall around him, and with only 4,200-odd corvettes coming at him, the situation was not bad in Novash's estimation...

All the same, now wasn't the time to make a stand. He could easily lose too many ships for meager gains, and besides, he was *supposed* to flee.

The rest of the outlying stations could wait, for now the plan of retreat needed to be hastily implemented.

All ships withdraw at flank speed. Warcruisers deploy to serve as a rearguard screen.

Sarah watched the Larosian Battleships drop back in the plot, Novash evidently having ordered them to flee before the significant number of corvettes that were coming for him. That seemed as good a cue for her as any.

"Detecting corvettes closing our position, ma'am. About 1,500 at present... no, make it 2,000... more..."

The Kroggs weren't just playing at trying to drive her back — perhaps a good sign that there was no trap here. Still, that many enemy ships coming forward was a bad enough sign for anyone who had to try to battle them back without the support of boats.

"All ships, break action and retreat in chaotic disorder."

Narosh wasn't paying much attention to the other two forces hammering away at their own segments of the Krogg line on the hyper front, but he did catch a mental glimpse of *Shanavorus* breaking contact in the face of only fourteen Motherships. Under normal circumstances, the dishonor to Novash for ordering such a flight would have been immense...

That thought almost made Narosh smile.

Lycrotar shuddered against the strikes of more spines, and loosed another wave of missiles into a nearby Dreadnought at point-blank range. He'd lost over 200 ships so far... and his forces had killed at least as many Kroggs in that time.

But now it seemed good to withdraw...

Admiral-of-a-Fleet, there are now corvettes approaching from the rear of the Krogg force.

Narosh confirmed his decision to himself as he received the report, then he passed on the orders: *Very well, all ships retreat as per the plan.*

Corvettes began to overtake Pat's Posse as the three-squadron Battlecruiser group swerved away from the fighting... hundreds of the Krogg small craft clawed at the tail of the Fourth Fleet as it turned to flee their advance. Pat's eyes narrowed and he ground his jaw as three more of the Battlecruisers of the 446th succumbed to the Krogg bombardment in his wake.

"Get more counter fire on those bastards!" he half snarled, and the AI and the gunner obliged him.

Lasers sliced out against the corvettes, the entire Posse quickly moving to obey the instructions of *Templar's* battle computers.

The chaos really began.

The Fourth Fleet disintegrated in a sufficiently chaotic fashion, ships and squadrons scattering and redlining their drives to clear the sphere of action. Dreadnoughts and Destroyers, clearly of the faster breeds, hurtled after the human vessels, spreading out smoothly to hunt them across the breadth of their retreat. Superdreadnoughts clustered with the Motherships and churned along in their faster cousins' wake, spraying spines at the Genesis stragglers.

After only a few minutes of action, Sarah's fleet was down to 1,100. She watched as the last damaged ships that were too slow to escape the Krogg advance were swept up by clouds of black aliens, then her gaze came to focus on Liz's squadrons on the screen. The Fourth Fleet was all broken up and retreating in seeming disorder now, so it was left to Liz to get into the fight...

But not yet.

A squadron of Light Cruisers trailing near the rear of the retreating Fourth was abruptly overwhelmed by three Krogg Superdreadnoughts. A squadron of Genesis Dreadnoughts was dragged down by hundreds of corvettes...

Joseph Barron surged away from the fighting at the head of its squadron.

"Come on... come *on*..."

Caine's eyes didn't leave the main battle tank. His gaze was fixed on the black icons of the home fleet — the 2,000 Krogg ships he'd have to face in their entirety if some weren't drawn off soon...

They weren't budging.

Damnation.

"Come on, *move!*"

"Fast DNs coming starboard aft, down vector 133!"

Pat's head whipped around and he nodded. The debris from the last Destroyers that had attempted to serve as interdictors against the Posse was spiraling away from the rushing Battlecruisers. Only twenty-seven of Pat's initial force of thirty-five remained, and one was lagging behind...

The fast Krogg Dreadnoughts immediately snuffed out that lone straggling cruiser.

"*Shit.* Any sign that they're moving the orbital fleet yet?"

A pause, then, "None sir."

Pat ground his jaw and slammed his fist into the arm of his chair, "Squadron shift course to port forty-five, down angle seventy. Maximum speed…"

The three squadrons of the Posse rolled fast through space, trying to dodge the Dreadnoughts, and send them on another hunt… but the group of Battlecruisers seemed to have been marked by their alien pursuers. The Kroggs kicked after them, spraying fast spines into the rear of their formation.

"We can't engage that many Dreadnoughts, Pat, and they're going to overtake us…" Jessica Forbes, his Flag ArcColonel and longtime veteran of this war, made the comment quietly from over his shoulder. Pat's eyes shifted to her and he nodded quickly…

Some of the Posse needed to get out of this scrape… he'd have to buy them time. If only all the original Pirates were with him. Well the new ones would have to do.

"Pirates to come about 180, rest of the Posse break action… get a targeting solution on the leading bastard. Quick now!"

There was no question in the mind of any of the men and women on *Templar's* bridge as to whether they should obey, even despite the almost certainly suicidal order.

Gods help me, I've turned into Sarah…

"Firing!"

Templar's tubes flushed and then the Battlecruiser and nine of its fellows charged into the formation of seven Dreadnoughts, outmaneuvering the Kroggs' clumsy first volleys and trying to get around the alien capital ships before their spines could actually find targets…

Three Battlecruisers evaporated, armor slicing off their hulls as fire clawed them apart.

Four.

"They've got our range, skipper!"

"Helms go wild! Dance us!" Pat's roar was drowned by the thundering crash of a salvo as it tore through something beneath them.

Templar slid sideways but the bridge lights stayed bright. Whatever the damage to the ship, it could be dealt with later…

Another Battlecruiser disappeared from the screen.

This all started to seem familiar to Pat — he'd lost the Pirates once before, and here they were dying again. It made the Irishman angry.

Royally pissed, in fact. Not to put too fine a point on it.

His 444th paid so heavily, every *bloody* time…

Templar was hurled sideways again, and Dreadnoughts moved towards the battle group flagship, sensing its vulnerability.

Pat wasn't impressed.

CHAPTER 49

ArcGeneral Elizabeth Hastings was the matriarch of this Genesis Fleet, and as she watched it being picked apart piece by piece, she set her jaw and tried to ignore the itching in her regenerated leg.

The Kroggs weren't budging from their homeworld to give chase. Maybe she could press the issue if she hit their advancing forces at just the right moment…

Liz saw the Pirates double back, ending their attempt to flee the Krogg advance in order to buy time for the rest of the Posse. That was Pat, doing what he had to do to try to save his ships and getting ready to die in the attempt.

Templar was taking fire.

"Now!"

Graham's eyes hardened as he glared at his plot. *Pope Edgar Fitzpatrick* positively *lunged* into the fray, leading over 100 heavy Genesis capital ships from the Sixth Fleet against the now-scattered Kroggs.

The plot showed the icons of his Battleships closing fast with the various sections of the Fourth Fleet, squadrons from that Genesis group smoothly attaching to his flanks as he passed through them. The reassembly of most of the Fourth Fleet would take place further to the rear, but whoever he passed could join his ships if they wished, and any additions to his firepower were gladly welcomed.

All the more to win with.

Templar limped forward relatively slowly, significant damage having been absorbed in the Battlecruiser's engineering section. The ship's tubes — all intact — flushed another volley of Type 98s, and lasers from its upper quarter sliced outward, carving into a nearby Krogg.

But there wasn't much hope of escape in this case…

So Pat would go out with a *loud* bang.

"Ramming course… see if we can't kill something!" he barked.

No one replied for a few seconds and as Pat waited in his chair, that few seconds drew out to almost thirty. Sure, it was an unpleasant order, but it still needed to be obeyed…

Pat filled his lungs to bellow at someone to carry out his orders, but just as he was about to begin the verbal flaying, his eyes settled on the screen that everyone else had been staring at.

Leave it to him to overreact for once in his life.

Here came the entire Sixth Fleet to the rescue. His timing hadn't been too bad after all — had he been any quicker he'd have just gone kamikaze.

Well, his ship was in no shape to keep fighting, even if reinforced.

"Alright then! Signal *Guardian Preacher* that I need to transfer the flag!'"

The Krogg Dreadnoughts had been readjusting themselves to overwhelm the Battlecruisers of Pat's Pirates when Graham's first salvoes came in and shredded them. The human capital ships then drove straight on, moving fast to hit other scattered Krogg targets.

Claw marveled at the spectacle from *Flame's* bridge as Liz's group hurtled right in after Graham's to support Sarah's collapsing center. The unexpected addition of new Allied ships had briefly wrong-footed the enemy, and now the widely scattered Krogg fleets tried to pull back and consolidate, only to find Bill Wallace's cruisers harassing them most of the way.

Now it was up to Varnon to give the aliens a real headache…

"Out of energy… *now*, Master."

Varnia's smooth voice did her father proud as he sat next to her, though he was ignoring that proud paternal aspect of his psyche just now as he nodded to the Signal Officer. The Fifth Fleet appeared among the divided Kroggs in hundred-ship division formations, and like the Sixth they poured merry hell into the regrouping aliens.

Overextended and flanked, the Kroggs were fast giving up their advantage and their advance was grinding to a bloody halt.

But the home force wasn't committing to the fray yet — it still sat cautiously around Krogg 'A'.

Damn…

Narosh's orders reversed his fleet's retreat in such a speedy fashion that he didn't even recognize the change from flight to fight.

His Warcruisers had dropped back a long way under the 'threat' of corvettes — far enough to bring the Larosian Carriers into range. Some 130 of those Carriers, moving away from the transports and hospital ships, put *thousands* of fighters into space.

Some 42,000 fighters, in fact — each one too small alone to destroy a corvette, but in the massive swarms offered by numerical superiority, a nasty force. Wasps attacking rodents, they swept past the retreating Warcruisers and slammed into the clouds of corvettes. The Warcruisers turned, accelerated and dove back into combat in their wake.

The faster Destroyers from the Krogg force rushed ahead to help deal with the renewed Larosian assault, splitting around the fighters to make a stab at the Carriers. Narosh ordered two squadrons of Warcruisers into their path, then the Destroyers abruptly changed course, making straight for the hospital ships and transports in the rear.

Give chase, protect the hospital—

With no illusions that they might survive contact with the Larosian forces chasing them, the Destroyers set ramming courses and slammed headlong into the hospital ships. Earther transports lumbered to either side and slid into energy drive to escape the surge of kamikazes, but the defenseless Larosian medical vessels were easily overwhelmed before the Warcruisers could intervene.

And that again reminded Narosh of the true character of his enemy. Even if he didn't annihilate them all, he would kill these...

His blood *boiled*, in a way he had never felt before. It was as though he had new *instincts*. The Earther DNA may have changed him. It didn't matter.

The Kroggs would die.

Advance and fight! Death to them! All of them!

Novash's thin force of Warcruisers had played the role of rearguard long enough. These smaller ships lacked massive Carrier support, but each of the 1,800 battlewagons whose retreat the Warcruisers were covering did maintain a flying garrison of six fighters, and now was the time for him to reveal them to the Kroggs. Fighters began streaming from lumbering Battleships, and the entire heavy force reversed its course in a split second, antimatter from its guns filling space and ravaging the corvettes.

The Kroggs barely realized what was happening before the fighters slammed in.

Gunboats began fountaining from the ships of the Fifth Fleet, and Sarah watched with a great deal of satisfaction as the 2,400 small combat craft carried aboard the Earther vessels went to work against the clouds of corvettes.

There were endless streams of corvettes by now, but with the arrival of the claw formations of Earther boats, the Krogg small ships' attention was diverted from the conventional ships of the Fourth, Fifth and Sixth Fleets...

Joseph Barron remained untouched, leading the rest of Sarah's particular assemblage of squadrons back into the fray. The Kroggs were still consolidating and dropping back in the face of Graham's and Liz's advances, trying to get under the cover of the net of stations that guarded their inner system. Enough firepower could doubtless be spewed from those hundreds of stations to make life hell for a fleet...

The Kroggs would simply have to be crushed before they made it there.

"Range is optimum, ma'am."

"Open fire," Sarah's words were cold.

This was what she did so well.

Liz felt the rush. Adrenaline, a sharp mind. Everything she remembered. Everything she'd been meant to do.

Pope Gerald Windsor slashed through a Krogg Superdreadnought-Mothership formation with lasers blazing, the rest of the ships of the division following with fast, tough lunges of their own. The enemy formation came apart, most of the ships disintegrating under the unexpected surge of Genesis fire.

This moment represented a reversal of the momentum, to be sure, but Liz knew better than to assume it assured the longer-term victory. If the Kroggs were allowed to consolidate things would turn against the Allies again. The Krogg forces *had* to be kept apart...

Liz quickly checked the plot for signs of Bill Wallace, but his pennant was nowhere to be seen. That wasn't good.

Cruisers were needed to get between groups of retreating Krogg ships and keep them apart for as long as possible, but if Bill was dead or out of it...

She paused as long as she dared and frowned at the plot. A haphazard group of cruisers was already forming around *Guardian Preacher*, a junior ship in the 444th, and then Pat's pennant winked into life on the screen, centering on the Battlecruiser. Liz felt a smile coming on, and tried to suppress it.

This was beginning to feel like old times.

Just like old times...

Pat had changed ships many times in the past months, but to do it in the middle of the battle of the decade? Ye *Gods*. Well bloody fun, he had a fresh Battlecruiser now and the Kroggs were in split formations on the run. That was where the remnants of the Posse would come in.

"Get word to every cruiser you can, group with us or get between the Kroggs and their line of stations! We need to try to keep them from consolidating."

The Comm Officer on *Preacher's* bridge was nervous — she wasn't used to getting orders from the famous Pat Conroy himself.

The cruisers accelerated again, and lasers sliced out, harassing anything Krogg that came into range. The Kroggs began to slow as Battlecruiser and now Heavy and Light Cruiser missiles began to slash into their ranks. Too few Genesis ships were here to entirely stop the big alien move, but enough were in position to attempt to slow them down...

An unemotional Sarah ground her jaw and watched Pat's ships do their work, waiting for the best moment to strike...

"And... optimum again, ma'am!"

Without moving her eyes she nodded, "Fire."

Joseph Barron and the rest of the ships around it rained death on the Kroggs Pat had slowed.

The enemy started to retreat in earnest, Liz forcing them back from one angle and Sarah from the other, with Narosh and Novash renewing the most vicious fighting further down the line.

Now Caine. Now's your time.

CHAPTER 50

The First, Second, and Third Fleets hurtled into energy drive at 700 pls. It took them scarcely more than forty seconds to travel from their anchoring stations in the rear to their destination.

Aboard *Orion*, Caine watched the plot as it projected the data from *Flame*. The Kroggs hadn't shifted their home fleet out of position — they were clearly nailed to their planet, and rightly so. He'd have done the same. No committing of everything to the hyper limit when he knew what the Earthers could do.

Damn all, Caine could understand that logic, but he wished the Queen didn't, because it was certainly going to make his Navy bleed. But there wasn't another option.

The orbital fleet's 2,000 warships, 100 Motherships... they had to be dealt with *now*. And as *Orion* swept from energy drive in the space just off the planet Krogg, Caine was certain of that need.

"Run out the guns, port roll 100, up angle forty!" Forepaw was ordering sharply, and the entire Earther Navy appeared before the Flag Captain and his First Lord in the battle tank.

Caine took one breath as he watched, "Launch boats!"

The Kroggs were waiting for the Earthers, and spines were flying by the time *Atlas* and *Vulcan* had gotten their guns out. Fox watched the volleys coming in on the plot and bobbed his head to Mister Gunth, the Master, who threw *Atlas* into a maneuver away from the first salvoes. *Vulcan* followed closely, but *Sultan* was torn to shreds, along with ninety-six other Earther warships of various classes.

In one salvo.

But now the veteran ships of the line and frigates were moving, and Fox would do everything he could to make sure *none* of the rest of the spines hit home.

"Up forty-four, squadron break by division and engage by numbers," he said in a cool voice. "Roll us Mister Gunth, port broadside... *fire!*"

Atlas' broadside slammed into a Dreadnought which pitched sideways under the blow, then came apart when *Vulcan's* guns zeroed on it as well. The 74s surged past, weaving away in an intricate dance.

Agamemnon bucked as a neuro pulse scorched its shields, but Ursla scarcely felt it as the First Rate and the other troop-carrying ships of the line closed fast with the planet. They wouldn't launch until the orbit was cleared, but they needed to keep out of the hardest fighting to preserve the troops.

That wasn't to say they'd be out of it *altogether*.

"Adjust thirty-two port," Tigar commanded with his usual reasoned presence. "Starboard broadside... fire!"

Sixty guns flared from *Agamemnon's* side, and the Dreadnought for which they were destined never saw the shot coming. The First Rate then swerved around more incoming fire, and boats began hurtling from its bays.

Jardaw was calm as *Highlander* twisted away from a brutal salvo. One of his 58s was shredded by those Superdreadnought spines, the rest of his ships poured broadsides into the menacing Krogg ship until it died. They immediately found another one to shoot at.

Jax Furgus' 74s were keeping close to him now, and *Madrid's* broadsides were incinerating formations of Destroyers before they could close with the more vulnerable 64s of the escort group. The Carriers stayed within the pocket behind, and as Jardaw watched, they rolled into their spherical formation for point defense.

Draco Maximane wasn't keen on launching too soon... But the corvettes would be coming any second now, and the fleet would need his boats, so it was time to deploy.

"Sphere complete, sir!"

Getting the Carrier Group into a sphere simplified launch arrangements remarkably, and made point defense much easier. Now was the right time...

"Launch!"

Orion slammed past Superdreadnoughts, the First Rate's boats having launched and its carronades tearing Krogg flesh to pieces while its guns quickly cycled. Ships forced their way through the flagship's wake — other First Rates of the valiant 101st, and now frigates of Dran Nightclaw's elite 111th.

That panther Commodore had seen much action since Ursla had joined *Agamemnon*, and now would be perhaps the greatest moment for his 38s. They certainly did form the best cruiser squadron anywhere — the greatest ever assembled, exceeding the likes of even the intrepid Ami Cairn and Pat Conroy. Such was the grand cruiser legacy of Andra Ursla herself.

As the fighting intensified, Nightclaw attached himself to the best line squadron in any of the Earther fleets — not that of Fox Magnus, Ursla or even Jax Furgus, but the 101st Battle Squadron, built around *Orion* with well-known Captains like Esther Arbear and Lab Forepaw, and of course, with Caine himself at its head.

Thus, the Fifth Rate 38s and First Rate 100s of the two squadrons swirled through space in fluid crisscrossing arcs, the frigates laying fire into Kroggs wherever they tried to block the mighty capital ships, the ships of the line offering massive broadsides to their alien opposites.

The two squadron fought with a wordless, instinctive partnership in a deadly dance.

Caine observed the cooperation from the bridge of *Orion*, and he contained a surge of pride. Close cooperation like that made both forces stronger — strong enough to hammer the Motherships...

"I need gunboats to clear the corvettes from orbit. Four squadrons of 74s and four of frigates to form on *Orion*, prepare for strike against the orbital facilities."

Boats were pouring from *Engadine* and its fellows when that signal came from the flagship, and Maximane quickly passed it on to Trax Earon and the gunboat wing leaders. Thousands and thousands of boats now filled space — some from the fleet and many from his Carrier Groups. They met charging corvettes head on.

The Kroggs had been expecting this meeting of small craft, but then, so had the Earthers. Heavy neuro pulses batted gunboats aside, but gunboat cannon tore through corvettes in return. And the boats gave better than they got.

They slammed together in a weightless melee, but the pack instincts left in the Earthers made them even more lethal than the Kroggs. They weren't willing to lose this fight — boats supported each other, fought together, even when the crews had never even *seen* each other before.

Maximane watched the tide of boats hit the tide of corvettes, and within seconds the latter formation became entirely preoccupied. The two revolutionary forces were keeping each other busy so the capital ships could do their brutal work.

And that left Caine and his guns.

Maximane's jaw set and he watched as the First Lord began to shift fire to the orbital facilities over Krogg 'A'.

Garvin Jardaw held fast to his chair as *Highlander* bounced against a neuro pulse, but *Madrid* was there at the 64's side, Jax Furgus keeping close to his compatriot in Carrier defense. Conventional Krogg ships were trying to force their way to the Carriers, but the Third and Fourth Rates detailed to the defense of Maximane's force were determined not to let them through.

Not after all this.

Madrid swung around and presented its guns, hurling fire into a closing Dreadnought, pushing the aggressor back and away. *Highlander's* broadside clashed with a Superdreadnought, and three 58s helped seal that Krogg's fate.

It was all working very well — the defensive cordon was keeping the Kroggs back from the vulnerable Carriers while the boats focused on the corvettes...

Then Jax Furgus's flagship *Madrid* exploded.

Garvin Jardaw blinked in surprise but couldn't afford to pause.

Atlas accelerated to a position off *Orion's* starboard beam, Thena Venus'

Vulcan settling into formation to the big First Rate's port side. Fox wouldn't have Caine doing the hard stuff without solid help, so his 186th, fighting in tandem with Ami Cairn's 141st, was coming up to join the 101st and its accompanying 111th. Now twenty ships of the line and twenty-two frigates closed with the orbiting platforms that served as the Kroggs's last line of defense. Ships of the line above and below fought hard to keep Kroggs back as *Orion* led the dash, and the Kroggs began to drop back in futility.

The sheer ferocity of the Earthers' first strike had broken the aliens' organization, left them wrong-footed. Some edged back in confusion — others charged blindly for the same reason.

Orion approached the first set of platforms and Lab Forepaw ordered the First Rate over to lay broadsides against them. Spines were flung at the First Rate, but they were badly aimed and easily avoided. As *Atlas'* first broadside came to bear, Forepaw ordered the guns loosed.

The torrent of energy from *Orion*, never matched by any other ship in the fleet, seared into the upper atmosphere of Krogg 'A' with a roar, batting a defense platform aside even as the First Rate rolled and presented its next broadside.

Atlas, Vulcan, and the rest of the ships of the line joined the heavy cannonade, their guns shattering the platforms. Frigates swerved in close to the atmosphere and picked off swirling debris with carronades, loosing broadsides whenever appropriate.

There were plenty of appropriate moments.

Ursla watched the platforms fall one by one... it was slow work on the relative time scale of this attack, and she had a squadron of First Rates and another of 74s that could help hurry it up.

She looked to Captain Artemis Tigar as he stood next to her at the plot, "Take us in close, Artie. Clear the drop zone."

As the cat nodded and *Agamemnon* turned at the head of the 201st Battle Squadron, gunboats began to sweep past it in echelons, climbing to engage corvettes sent to menace the convoy. The Carriers moved within their defensive sphere, closing behind Ursla's group heading towards the planet.

Caine no longer focused on the platforms — those were being dealt with. So far 482 Earther ships had been lost, while 512 Krogg ships had been destroyed.

Almost even.

"Ursla signals that she's preparing to land General Grieve's force, sir," the Signal Officer reported over the rumble that filled *Orion's* bridge as it slid through the planet's upper atmosphere.

Caine turned from the plot and nodded, "Very good."

Now the real fun begins.

He determinedly ground his jaw and watched *Agamemnon* in the plot.

CHAPTER 51

"They're moving too fast, sir!"

Pat's fist collided angrily with his chair's arm and he glared at the ArcColonel of *Preacher*, momentarily wishing for his veteran Jessica Forbes, but ignoring that thought given the circumstances, "I don't *care* how bloody fast they're going, we have to get behind them!"

The ArcColonel nodded, then turned to his exec and helm officer, nodding to each of them. The Posse began to roll on *Preacher's* lead, accelerating away from Sarah's advancing forces as it tried to get around the scattered Krogg Fleet.

But the Kroggs *were* moving too fast, and for the most part Pat's cruisers could do nothing to slow them down. The inner sphere of defense stations wasn't too far ahead now, and the Kroggs were getting the chance to regroup — to put up a solid front.

And with a solid Krogg front and an Allied Fleet scattered by the advance, things could very quickly change for the worse.

Come on universe... I swear I'll bloody crush you if you bugger this up!

Novash's Battleships began to integrate with the edges of Narosh's Warcruiser armada as the two Larosian forces pressed forward to the defense stations. The Fourth Fleet was linking up with the Larosian flank at the same time, while the Kroggs were dropping back to the comparative safety of their perimeter of stations now that they'd managed a brief respite from the pressure applied by Allied forces.

Narosh wondered for just a second if the feigned Allied retreat had not indeed been a *bad* idea...

Whether it had or hadn't, some 37,000 Larosian fighters now scrambled forward, clearing the space between the converging battle fleets of corvettes and Destroyers that had been left to frustrate their advance. Gunboats from the Fifth Fleet were beginning to mingle with them as well, and in a symbiotic fashion, some Larosian fighters were even starting to maximize their Krogg-killing efficiency by attaching themselves to the more heavily-built boats.

But Narosh could see what the Kroggs were doing, and he had a good idea of what would come next. The Son had lead the Fourth Fleet-of-War against a similar wall of stations in his last battle, and it had nearly proved the end of them. Indeed, the Son had only been able to break one station, creating a sufficient breach to reach the Hive they guarded, and kill the Queen that hid there.

This time they faced more Kroggs and a tougher goal.

But the Earthers were surrounding Krogg 'A' itself. Perhaps the combined firepower of the Larosian and human ships could break through the inner station perimeter...

Battleships forward at maximum speed, alert the humans of our intent to lead the bombardment.

"Signal from *Lycrotar*... they're sending their Battleships to hit the stations up ahead, sir."

Graham nodded without letting his eyes drift from the plot screen. His capital ships were suffering, but not so badly as they might. Only fifty-six of 172 gone — modest when compared to the gruesome casualty average of the battle so far. The rest of the capital ships were in usable shape.

Those stations, though, were ominous. He'd been preparing to lead a move against them himself, but his ships could scarcely match the firepower of 1,800 Larosian battlewagons. And the Larosians had much more experience with these sorts of things...

"*Gerald Windsor* is still advancing against the stations, sir, should I repeat the signal to them?"

Graham frowned and his eyes shifted to the image on the plot of Hastings' flagship, "Yes, pass it on."

Liz's Superdreadnought and its section of the Sixth, plus whatever groups had joined on its flanks, were still closing fast in pursuit of the fleeing Kroggs. They had to be warned off.

"We're coming into range of those stations, sir."

Pat nodded in acknowledgement and frowned at the plot. The atmosphere on *Preacher* was even heavier than it had been on *Templar*.

Didn't change the tone of the battle, though... and this wall of stations looked too tough and closely-knit for the Posse to break or pierce on its own.

"Back us off–" Pat's almost dejected comment was cut off abruptly as the plot showed what could best be described as a machine-gun burst of spines ripping away from one of the stations, hammering towards his Battlecruisers.

It wasn't a traditional-seeming salvo: a flight of over 100 *massive* spines careening through space, and then a second, both from the same station. The Kroggs should *not* have had the ability to fire bursts like that...

"Gods wept... *Move us out quick!*" Pat came out of his seat as the spines closed on the plot.

Preacher was handy at the helm, turning away and kicking speed up to a hefty .97 cee. The Posse followed, managing to stay just out of the line of fire.

"Pass warning onto the fleet — those damned things are *loaded*."

Novash didn't notice the burst of spine fire as his ships were advancing against a far distant section of the inner station sphere. The Admiral-of-a-Division was most concerned with arraying his battlewagons in their wall formation for bombardment. They would all focus on a single section of this inner frontier, guarded against corvettes by the massive clouds of fighters now hurtling through space all around them...

Shanavorus and the few Warcruisers with the Battleship Division swept out of the way and Novash gave the order to begin bombardment, watching in his mind's eye as the Battleships closed slowly, shifting irregularly to avoid spine strikes.

Missiles screamed from tubes, and antimatter guns filled space with raw chaos, the shot angling straight for one station.

The station folded in on itself and exploded, and with that much ease the Battleships angled in to exploit the breach.

"Go back!" Chronos Claw nearly yelled his warning at the plot, then whirled fast to his Signal Officer. "Warn Novash, they've got to pull back!"

But it was too late, and Claw knew it.

The Kroggs, it seemed, had been well aware that a single station might prove weak, and so they'd laid their perimeter out with overlapping fields of fire. Their spine guns — or whatever was firing those machine-gun bursts of ship-killers — had great range, and the loss of one station therefore meant nothing. Fire from the four surrounding stations could turn the gap left by the first's destruction into a corridor of death...

Too late.

Warning coming from Flame–

Novash didn't have time to listen to the report, as the first *forty* Battleships in his division cruised into a scathing fire from all sides, and were torn apart in a damning hail of Krogg bone-and-acid spines.

Then the stations revealed their true range, pouring their spines in long bursts, raking the Larosian battlewagons despite their lumbering maneuvers to escape the barrage. Counter fire from Larosian missile tubes was shot down — spines were coming in such volume as to destroy the bulk of missiles launched and absorb the antimatter.

A wall of Krogg spines collided with the wall of Battleships, and the latter suffered immeasurably.

Pull back — quickly!

Novash wasn't one to panic. But this was the time to be fearful...

Three hundred Battleships folded. *Five hundred.*

It was unfathomable — and the retreating ships were still not beyond the range of the spines.

Seven hundred, sir... almost eight now...

Novash did not breathe, nor did he want to.

The Kroggs had been waiting for this. They had made the destruction of their outer stations *easy* to trick the Larosians — to set a trap. And Novash had fallen into it.

• • •

Narosh was stunned at the extermination of almost half the Battleship force. *Half.*

And many more were damaged.

The lumbering ships limped out of range, and now only the Warcruisers remained active and reasonably well organized. But the Krogg Fleet was pushing out to take advantage of that fact.

All Warcruisers, move to meet them! Remain out of range of the stations. Fighters, attempt strafing runs against the stations! Move swiftly.

Liz's heart felt as though it had stopped when the Battleships of the Larosian Fleet were torn up, because her Superdreadnoughts were already inside the envelope of Krogg fire when the images came in.

"Reverse! *Reverse!*"

Pope Gerald Windsor was lucky; the rest of the Superdreadnoughts in its squadron weren't.

As the ship writhed and dragged itself around at a painful .87 cee, those Superdreadnoughts absorbed the first streams of fire. *Windsor* rushed away, carrying much of the Sixth and the attached squadrons with it.

But thirty-four capital ships were left shattered.

Liz's mind was in turmoil — again, lulled into the trap, into the crafty defense of the Kroggs. The Larosians had paid dearly for it, and now the Kroggs were coming out to meet them again, having broken them up and shaken them...

That would go badly for the Kroggs, she'd see to it...

Despite Sarah's shock, the still untouched *Joseph Barron* was the first to empty its tubes into the Krogg Dreadnoughts that were moving out from their stations to counterattack. Much of the Fourth Fleet, hovering now just beyond the spine envelope, vented their tubes, and the long-range Type 98s dove headlong into the charging Kroggs.

Counter fire from the stations dropped off as the spine guns stopped firing for fear of weakening their own charge by hitting their counterattacking ships, so the human missiles slammed into the first line of Kroggs nearly unopposed.

Sarah's eyes followed them coldly on the plot. She nodded to her Comm Chief, who ordered the fleet advance.

The Kroggs clearly thought they had the strength to drive the Genesis and Larosian Fleets right out of the system. They must have believed this counterattack would break the Allies, because in launching it, they'd gambled on winning a ship fight and had managed to silence their own stations — the spine guns couldn't fire for fear of hitting their own ships, and that gave Sarah and about 1,000 ships the chance to do what they did best.

Strange that the Queen won't sacrifice these ships... they must be her last serious space forces...

"Concentrate on their mobile ships, but anybody who gets a chance, open up on those stations. If we can mask ourselves with their ships and get in close enough, we might be able to blow a hole through..." Sarah hoped her orders weren't too optimistic.

Joseph Barron swung into action.

With his meager force, Graham felt a bit inconsequential as he watched his sister move forward, but a swirling ring of Pat's Battle-, Heavy, and Light Cruisers suddenly formed around him. As Graham watched the plot, Pat's pennant blinked twice, and Graham recognized the dipping of the proverbial flag.

It was somehow absurd but appropriate that in the middle of this maelstrom Pat would signal the equivalent of a wink to his friend. Graham rather liked the idea.

"Flash my pennant twice, please," he said in almost comfortable tones, then he turned to his Comm Chief. "All ships ahead."

CHAPTER 52

"They walked into it," Forepaw's quiet voice masked his shock. The main plot on *Orion's* bridge showed the destruction of one half of the Larosian Battleship fleet in all its horror, relayed via *Flame* to the flagship.

Even as the First Rate's guns hammered another orbital platform — one evidently less well-armed than the stations which had ravaged Novash's force — the First Lord and his Flag Captain stared at the chaos.

Narosh said they'd be willing to die.

And so they did.

"That must be their fallback plan," Caine turned quickly to Forepaw. "If we hit here, they could isolate us with that sphere of stations, and if we hit from the hyper limit, they could draw us to it. It's perfectly placed..."

Forepaw nodded in slow agreement, "Orders?"

Caine looked back to the plot, his ear twitching as *Orion* rolled abruptly and its guns hummed. A shockwave sent tremors through the floor.

They had to secure this planet.

Had to.

"We destroy them here. We can't let any of this home fleet get out there to strengthen their stations. All ships try to keep them engaged *here*."

Forepaw nodded and turned to the Signal Officer to relay the orders.

Caine stared at the plot as more Earther ships winked out. And more Kroggs. They had hoped to simply crush the Kroggs by catching them between the two forces, but the *Queen* had foreseen their manner of attack.

She'd known, and she'd set the system defenses up to cope with their plan.

Damn her.

Now the fight in space would be as bloody in space as it promised to be on the ground...

Orion rolled and fired again.

Atlas and *Vulcan* were all that Fox could still see of his 186th. It seemed likely there were more of his 74s around, but for now only these two fought together, and to Fox, that was useful. Brutally so.

Atlas and *Vulcan* were veterans of Felix's old 301st. They had been together through gallant little actions like those at Galahad's Belt and the one with *Joseph Barron* when Sarah had gone rogue. They'd fought as a team then; they still did now.

Together they lunged into the center of a Superdreadnought squadron, twirling around each other and letting broadsides fly at such a speed as to deny their foe any hope of reply. The pair of 74s moved like frigates, and as the Signal Officer read Caine's orders to hold the Kroggs in place, Fox just barely processed them. His hand was perpetually on the edge of the plot while Mister Gunth, the grizzled Cruising Master, stood at his side.

Kroggs died.

Fighting in the elite ways expected of the 111th since Ursla's time, Dran Nightclaw led his ships against waves of Krogg Destroyers. The eight Fifth Rates of the squadron were untouched — elite among the elite, their guns hammered hard and thoughtlessly wiped Kroggs from the cosmos.

Garvin Jardaw didn't know what had come over him. As *Madrid* exploded, his mind cast aside any lingering doubt, and *Highlander* twisted quickly away from the blast, joining the fray even more closely with its smaller 58-gun compatriots. The ships of the line cut into waves of Dreadnoughts, and as Jardaw spoke, broadsides flew and smashed through the bigger Krogg warships.

The polar bear had been in this fight from the start, but he somehow felt he was only hitting his stride at this moment.

Well he had that stride now, he couldn't dwell on whether or not it had been with him from the beginning.

"Move us in closer to Garvin — quickly!"

Draco Maximane stayed on his feet despite the violent maneuvers being made by his leviathan of a Carrier. *Engadine* and its fellows weren't out of the fight — despite initial hopes, the Carriers couldn't be shielded completely from the conventional fighting.

To drive the Kroggs away from the planet would spell certain death for the Allies fighting further out at the sphere of stations, and to withdraw to energy drive would abandon thousands of gunboats to space.

So Draco refused to do either.

The Carriers had never been designed for fleet action — a major flaw, it seemed now, as their gunboat screens dealt exclusively with the many thousands of corvettes that filled space. *Engadine* had only forty active guns, and none were bigger than a frigate's.

With *Madrid* gone, the 74s assigned to aide Jardaw were leaderless. Despite their Captains' abilities, those ships couldn't coordinate as well with *Engadine*, and that left the Carrier Group in a difficult place.

But they hadn't lost too many... yet...

"The Carriers are going to get hit *very* soon," Tigar pointed to the sphere floating off Krogg, and Ursla nodded.

They were still waiting to launch the landers — they couldn't chance the drop until the area had been reasonably secured by gunboats. In the meantime, they kept a steady fire against the stations, trying not to reveal their plan to land troops by waiting in an obvious orbit...

There were some 1,400 Earther ships left in the area, and they were all doing what came naturally to them: fighting as packs. The ferocious, predatory tactics that turned the well-organized Earthers into the most vicious melee fighters that Ursla — and perhaps even the Kroggs — had ever seen...

But the packs were too absorbed to provide much support to the beleaguered fifty ships escorting the Carriers... and the Kroggs had *marked* the Carriers.

"We can't move to help them until we drop the marines," Ursla said with a grave finality.

Usually, this was when Savanna Felix would have come to the rescue.

The realization struck her, and she released a low growl. He was gone, and now Jax Furgus was gone too...

"We have to wait," she said again more quietly.

Agamemnon poured forth more fire.

"More Motherships moving towards the planet from the inner station sphere. They'll have enough corvettes to tip the balance against our boats, sir."

Maximane heard the words and saw twenty Motherships closing... and all he had now was about thirty Carriers.

"Anyone out there able to stop them?" Maximane turned to the Sensor Chief, and the cat shook his head in reply.

Maximane clenched his jaw for a second, then took a breath. It would be better to abandon the boats just briefly than to let them face the onslaught of more corvettes.

"Energy drive, signal the escort to follow us if they can."

"The Carriers just moved, sir!"

Caine frowned into the plot as the Carrier Group and eleven of its escort ships — including *Highlander* — accelerated into energy drive and sprinted out of the action.

Abandoning their boats...?

Oh. No.

"Get a line to Varnon, we *need* the Fifth to support Maximane right now!"

Caine's words were translated into actions almost immediately.

Almost immediately.

"We've knocked out three stations, ma'am..."

Sarah nodded, her eyes not leaving the plot. Her ships were lobbing Type 98s at the stations behind the advancing Kroggs, and the focusing of fire from hundreds of human Dreadnoughts and Superdreadnoughts had been enough to take a trio of the venerable Krogg stations out of the fighting. The destruction had opened a pattern that might create a safe path of advance if they could just get the fourth one out of the picture.

As Sarah's eyes narrowed, Krogg ships in the plot began to drop back around that crucial station. They saw the danger as clearly as she did — with the fourth station gone, she could break through the defensive sphere.

Perhaps they could run the breach anyway... No, even one station's fire was too much...

As *Joseph Barron* heeled hard to starboard to avoid a Superdreadnought's spines, Sarah gritted her teeth.

"Send to Admiral Broadpaw. See if he can take out that station for us."

Engadine reappeared after scarce seconds in energy drive, and as it did its light guns slammed back on their tracks, the thundering colossus of a ship emptying its broadside into the leading Mothership. The massive Krogg vessel was one of the well-protected new breed, but the surprising broadside was joined by many more, including three salvoes from 74s and eight from 64s.

The Mothership heeled to one side and came apart, leaving its fellows to begin their launch procedure.

Broadsides crashed hard into launch-eyelids — a stalling tactic to try to trap corvettes in their bays, if only just briefly. It paid off... carronade shots cut crucial relays and painfully jammed the doors shut as the Motherships swept close together to consolidate their defensive fire.

The Earthers' advantage here wouldn't last, and Draco knew it, but it was something... a brief opportunity. *Engadine* closed with one Mothership, carronades and bow chasers hammering into the Krogg vessel. For moments the Carrier went unchallenged, then a salvo of spines collided with its forward shields.

The protection held and *Engadine* fought back, its guns, though light, smashing into the Mothership again.

Draco gritted his teeth. If only he'd designed these ships with guns as well! It was a crucial weakness, he saw now, but reflecting on it was also wholly irrelevant. He'd meet the Kroggs with whatever he had.

As *Engadine's* carronades gouged deep into the Mothership, a spread of spines broke through the Carrier's weakened bow shielding and tore off the ship's forward quarter.

Highlander danced a surprisingly agile dance, sending broadsides in every direction, trying to wound as many Motherships as it could... but it was clear to Jardaw that the Motherships would regain launch abilities all too soon–

Engadine toppled through space just before the 64's bow, and Jardaw's mind abruptly ignored the rest of the fight.

Maximane...

A string of subsidiary explosions bubbled from the ship's shattered forward quarter back through the underside of its hull, and Garvin could see the engines die on the enhanced video feed to the bridge.

By the *Earth*...

"Move us to their aid — quickly!"

Jardaw's mind quickened again — time was of the essence now...

"Sir, three Motherships are getting ready to launch!"

The Carrier Group had no boats with it. A launch would be the end of them...

"No response from Admiral Broadpaw, ma'am."

Sarah scowled as six more of her ships were annihilated by the Krogg Dreadnoughts and Superdreadnoughts that were closing all around them. They needed to break the Krogg static defenses... what was Varnon doing that was somehow more important than that?

Damn...

"Orders to squadron, and whoever's with us. Break through the Krogg mobile forces and do whatever it takes to crack that last station at the gap," Sarah's words were cool.

ArcColonel Evan-Thomas ordered *Joseph Barron* forward, and two dozen Genesis capital ships followed their flag.

"Normal space... *now*."

Varnon was *very* proud of his daughter.

He was also still too involved in the battle to dwell on that, even as Varnia's smooth words drew *Algenon* and 278 ships — all that remained in action from his original Fifth Fleet — into normal space around the Carriers.

The situation immediately processed in his mind, "Signal the 517th, the 520th and the 577th to block for the Carriers. Everyone else, hit those Motherships."

The orders were dispatched by *Algenon's* Signal Officer and the fleet leapt to action, broadsides abruptly filling space. The Motherships preparing to launch were torn apart, their hulls overwhelmed by the tides of energy that crossed them simultaneously — and then Varnon's ships went to work.

Highlander slowed slightly as it fell into company with *Engadine*. Inertia was carrying the wounded ship towards the Krogg stations at a fast clip — soon it'd be in range of their scathing spine volleys.

Escape pods were already dropping from its sides — Jardaw had seen more than enough ships near death to know that this one couldn't be saved.

"Begin recovery, get some pinnaces out there *quickly*, get the rest of the squadron to assist where possible..." Jardaw's voice trailed off a bit and he got a strange sensation in the back of his mind.

"Signal from *Engadine*... coming in weak."

With a simple nod, Jardaw directed the message to the main plot, and Draco Maximane appeared, the holo slightly distorted but clear enough to read.

"Blown to hell, Garvin. Most of the bridge crew was wounded so I sent them and Ron Hobbes out in the one bridge pod we had working. Then it turned out I was cut off from the rest."

Jardaw blinked twice, "Any helm control?"

Maximane shook his head on the screen, meeting his former First Lieutenant's eyes, "All engineering offered me before I ordered them off was a two-second burst of energy drive, at about 450 pls. I can't disengage from the action."

All Jardaw could do was nod slowly, "We'll try to tow you then..."

"No... no, you'd just make yourself a target, Garvin. And I'm the only one left aboard. Not worth it."

The lion's face was grim but determined, and the signal dropout was worsening. Jardaw turned quickly to his Signal Officer, "Can you clean it up?"

The Lieutenant shook her head slowly and Jardaw turned back, "We're about to lose you, Draco..."

Maximane nodded, "Alright... it's been a pleasure to fight alongside you again, Garvin. You're a damned fine fellow. You go on and do well."

Jardaw couldn't quite believe what he was hearing.

"My love to my family, my luck to all of you... and tell the R&D folks that we need more teeth and protection for the next batch of Carriers..."

A bit of a sad smile crossed Maximane's face, "Well. I think that's it for the melodrama. I'll see you in–"

The picture abruptly failed, and the bridge was silent.

"–the next life... or whatever."

Maximane's ear twitched as the link cut and the signal transmission gear stopped humming.

Keying a couple of consoles to see if it could be brought back online, he only managed to get a message from *Joseph Barron* onto the screen. It had been sent to *Algenon*, but *Engadine's* array had picked it up too.

Well. That was it then.

Draco Maximane knew precisely what he had to do, so he left the communications section and paced across the bridge, passing the pair of burnt-out holo tanks, the weapons panels, and the sensor consoles.

He came to a stop before the helm, which thankfully remained intact, and the small guidance display marked the appropriate bastard of a Krogg station not too far ahead. They'd have *Engadine* in range momentarily.

But he had them in range now, after a fashion at least.

It had been many years since Draco Maximane had piloted a starship, but it felt like high time he got back into the practice.

Gently lifting the dead pilot from her seat, he took the chair, targeted the station with the navigational computer, and keyed the energy drive.

His mind flashed back to the days of commanding *Apollo* with Garvin as his First Lieutenant, to the first days of the Carrier program, to the renegade run that had nearly killed him... to Krogg 'B'.

To home. To his wife and daughter.

All that, all his life... it was to be traded now for the Earthers.

For his friends and fellows.

It was a good trade.

Jardaw's eyes were locked on the plot as *Engadine* painfully surged into energy drive.

He sat back and looked at the display, then watched the result as the mammoth Carrier came out of its energy state *inside* the Krogg station Sarah had identified.

It was as though a small star went nova as atoms tore each others' bonds apart.

CHAPTER 53

The orders to drive the 401ˢᵗ Battle Squadron towards the last station had by no means pleased Pat. He'd been keeping the ever-shrinking Posse near Graham's *Edgar Fitzpatrick* when the call came from *Joseph Barron* to go forward, and he'd immediately decided to try to get in front of Sarah again.

This sounded like her suicidal play for the day, and as always, he'd be there to keep her from dying if he could…

Damn you universe, I better be able to…

"Holy *shit!*"

Pat blinked and whirled on *Preacher's* ArcColonel, "Swearing on the bloody bridge, are we?"

The ArcColonel held up a tentative hand and pointed at the screen, but the shockwave buffeted *Preacher* before Pat could turn to see what was so incredible. The Battlecruiser — and every other ship in local space — was thrown backward by the massive concussion of a blast no one had even seen coming.

The Kroggs least of all.

Ships scattered, fighters and gunboats somersaulted haphazardly through space, the lights on *Preacher* flickered and then hummed back to life.

"What the bloody…"

"One of the Earther Carriers just rammed a station in *energy drive,* sir! Reconstituted *inside* the station!"

Pat slowed and his eyes widened, "Gods wept. Which one was it?"

There was a pause, then the word: *"Engadine."*

Gods.

Joseph Barron had been cruising directly towards the station when it blew, so the spear point of the ship's bow allowed it to pierce the pulse wave with a more stable ride than was the case for some of its peers. The Superdreadnought still bucked as the energy hit, but no damage was done. Krogg ships all around, though — caught at bad angles and with their less rigid organic hulls — were crumpled or torn out of the action.

"What was that?" Sarah turned to the Sensor Chief, who shrugged quickly as he keyed pictures up onto the main screen…

What looked like energy shot collided with one of the stations… and then exited energy drive — great *Gods.*

"It was *Engadine,* ma'am."

Sarah blinked. *Draco.*

•••

Graham was too busy to really think much about what had just happened. All he could see at this moment was an opening in the Kroggs' line — a real one this time.

The shockwave had not only managed to toss much of the fleet about, it had annihilated the station that Sarah had been seeking to destroy, and had knocked several more out of their orbital positions.

Leaving a modest-sized hole to be exploited.

"Signal all ships to follow us through that gap," Graham's words were cool, and *Edgar Fitzpatrick* accelerated ahead at a good clip, ships joining on its flanks.

Astonished, Liz watched the destruction of *Engadine* and tried to remember if she'd ever seen the like... no, she hadn't. So much for that line of thought.

"Signal from *Fitzpatrick*, ma'am, they're exploiting the breach."

Liz nodded slowly, turning to her Comm Chief, "Orders the fleet to go through — quickly, before the Kroggs can redeploy to stop us!"

Narosh's mind lit with the explosion — the bright vision of it actually forcing him to close his mind's eye for a short second — and then the gap it left in the Krogg defensive sphere fully registered.

His Warcruisers were still heavily engaged with Krogg mobile forces, however, and to try to exploit such a small breach with cruisers alone would be foolhardy. There was little hope of making a heavy push beyond the stations with only the limited firepower of the Warcruisers...

No, the Larosian Fleet would keep doing what it was most adept at.

Send to ArcGenerals Hastings and Manchester: we will hold the Kroggs here to clear the way for their advance. To all our crews: we must keep the Kroggs from closing the breach.

Shanavorus was already exploiting the breach when the orders to stand against the Krogg mobile forces came from *Lycrotar*, and Novash found that he had no desire to turn about. He'd spent much time with the Allies — now he felt almost obligated to fight at their side, no matter the risks.

Novash to Admiral-of-a-Fleet Narosh, request permission to accompany the humans. My squadron has already begun exploiting the breach, along with three more squadrons.

There was no response for a time, and on the bridge of *Shanavorus* the crew continued about their business, moving the Warcruisers forward after Pat's Posse.

Narosh here, Novash. I'm reluctant, but I defer to your judgment.

Novash almost smiled. *Many thanks, sir. We will see each other again soon.*

Indeed, I certainly hope that's so, my friend. Narosh's reply seemed laced with a collegiality that would have been foreign to him before his accident.

But that was irrelevant. Their minds parted and the seventy-odd Warcruisers under Novash's authority pressed on through the gap.

•••

"We have the Fifth on scope."

Sarah frowned at her screen and nodded — what was left of Varnon's force was pulling together and making a run for Krogg itself. The fighting was getting bloody there, so that was where the humans, such as they were, needed to make an appearance.

"Mark course to follow them–"

"Ma'am, coming down on us from–"

For the first time, *Joseph Barron* took a hard hit.

"Gods! A whole lot of them are dropping on us sir — *Barron's* taken a hit... superficial I think..."

Graham's eyes flew over his displays as they promptly changed angles to show him the arrival of the consolidated Kroggs that had been waiting behind the line of stations. So the aliens hadn't sent everything forward against the Allied attack... the ships that had remained unengaged had stayed out of the immediate area and hidden amongst the stations...

There were at least enough of them to slow the Genesis Fleet down.

"Tell Varnon to make for Krogg. We'll keep them tied up here," Graham's voice was stony, and then he turned to face the Comm Officer. "Send a general rally. What remains of us must come *here*. We hold them *here*."

Liz came through the gap into a storm of fire, and she knew immediately that their troubles weren't over. The Earthers would have to fend for themselves...

"Ma'am... strange ship seems to be departing the stations about seventy-six northeast of us relative to Krogg 'A'."

That was a surprise. Liz turned to her Sensor Chief, "What sort of ship?"

There was a pause, then the image came up on the main screen, "Looks like the ship from Krogg 'C', ma'am, based on the images the Earthers provided."

Krogg 'C'? Oh bloody wonderful...

"How fast is it moving?" Liz turned back to the Sensor Chief, and the woman's eyes narrowed.

"Only about .65 cee... looks like it's trying to get out of this zone unnoticed."

But it can go faster. And that means we have to warn the Earthers...

"Set course for the sun by way of Krogg 'A'. Move us as if we're trying to join Fifth. Don't tip it off that we've seen it..." Liz's voice was low.

This would be *so* much fun.

Liz clenched her jaw and sat.

All around, the Superdreadnoughts and Dreadnoughts of Genesis collided with the Dreadnoughts and Superdreadnoughts of Krogg. The once-enslaved and the once-masters...

Fitting, Sarah thought coolly.

Very damn fitting.

And she knew which side would win.

CHAPTER 54

"We have clear skies now," Artemis Tigar turned from looking over the First Lieutenant's shoulder, but Ursla didn't immediately respond to his comment.

She'd just watched *Engadine's* last run through the eyes of *Flame* and she was a little short of speechless. It had really come down to this...

"Launch dropships."

Beckett Lupus had dropped from warships many times — once even from a ship that was blowing up around him. He was too accustomed to the resulting sensations to worry about the trip down, he just closed his eyes and sat back in his seat, his mind already focusing on what he'd face on the ground. His hands tightened around his rifle, and the sword felt light at his hip. Next to him, Sergeant Major Howler, the veteran second from his old recon squad, sat in equal serenity. Lupus could feel his fellow Earther's calm confidence.

It was an awareness they shared — an awareness born of fights together since Antarctica, an awareness born of them being Earthers.

Though Lupus somehow felt that his role today wasn't to be as great as that of some others, he knew that Howler would make his job much easier.

One day the two of them would do this again.

He *knew* that, and because the 'knowing' didn't make too much sense to him, he decided to just focus on the landing.

Oh yeah, we're doing that now, aren't we? And I thought I'd given up being a comedian last time out.

Grieve's lander had been, by his order, the first to hit the atmosphere, and he sat tightly in his drop seat as the craft hurtled downward. It wasn't a smooth ride — not that he'd really hoped it would be. There were no set flight paths to the plateau, and they were under serious threat from the Kroggs that were humming about.

Three squadrons of gunboats were hurtling into the atmosphere with them — all that could be organized as an escort for the time being, but enough to keep any corvettes over the planet out of the way.

The boats swirled around them now, and as the first corvettes moved to interdict, the roar of energy cannon in the atmosphere thundered through the dropship. The corvettes weren't even able to close range, and that was definitely good.

There'd be plenty of close-in fighting on the ground.

• • •

Orion found its way to *Agamemnon's* side, with the 111th appearing close behind and *Atlas* and *Vulcan* coming around the planet to meet them. Then the last five frigates of Ami Cairn's 141st, and *Hibernia*, Esther Arbear's First Rate of the 101st joined them. It was no coincidence these ships had found each other. Those who fought so well together — some of them the living heroes of their fleets — banded together and fought their enemy.

Caine was taken aback by Maximane's sacrifice, the loss so brutal and yet so necessary. But in the din of such a massive action, the First Lord couldn't allow it to slow his thoughts at all...

The overall battle was disordered — a huge melee that left the Earthers barely in control of the orbital space around Krogg. Barely enough to send Grieve on his mission. Barely enough for a little — and *just* a little — breathing time...

"We've got the Fifth Fleet coming in... and about seventy Warcruisers. They're joining action at the far end — 241 by 136 by 177," Forepaw's assuring voice turned Caine to the main battle plot and he nodded.

Shanavorus and *Algenon* were leading the strike — two more ships that *felt* like they needed to join this group of elite combatants. Caine couldn't say why... perhaps it was instinct.

Whatever it is, we need it now.

"Take us over that way — we should help them break through. If we can get them in safely we can assemble a good orbital defense until the Fourth or the Sixth can make it here."

"Down angle forty-four, port guns...*fire.*"

Varnia's commands were slow and deliberate, but damned if they didn't make *Algenon* fight smoothly. Sitting next to his daughter, Varnon let himself withdraw ever so slightly from his duties — just for a second — to be enormously proud.

Fleet commanders had little to do at this stage, the squadrons would mostly handle themselves... but hang on a moment, some orders from him were indeed required right now, "Signal Officer, all ships angle towards the planet Krogg 'A'. Try to form a solid perimeter around it."

Grieve cast a quick glance out the window of his lander as it slid into the atmosphere. As far as he could see, space was filled with bright flashes and hurtling bolts of energy. The void all around Krogg 'A' was filling with destruction...

As his boat rocked heavily and dropped into the lower atmosphere, Grieve looked away. That wasn't his fight. Never had been, never would be.

His fight was on the ground, and this time he would have to win a war. No Kroggs, however strong or determined, would stop him on his ground.

And any *ground* was his ground.

He was a soldier.
Grieve's mind settled.
Completely.
No more worry, fear, misunderstanding.
I'm a soldier. Damned if I won't win as one.

Caine felt a twinge of something in the back of his mind, like a voice that he couldn't quite hear... but he ignored it.

His fleets were fighting the way they always fought, but the Kroggs would keep attacking as long as they had any hope that the Earthers could be stopped, or so long as they thought that they could at least seize the initiative.

Caine had to take that hope away from them. He had to prove there was no way the Earthers could be stopped, even if there were, in reality, many ways...

"One gesture..." Caine said softly to himself. "To show them they've lost..."

Forepaw's ear twitched and he glanced at his friend, "Come again, Setter?"

Caine's head turned, "They'll crack. *Soon*. We've just... we've got to do something..."

A frown formed over Forepaw's brow — the fighting remained fierce...

"Up twelve by ninety, port guns on that Superdreadnought," Forepaw turned away as the plot marked another target, then looked back at Caine. "We're very heavily engaged."

Caine nodded slowly, "But it won't be about us for much longer, Lab. The Queen has to *know* Andros is landing, and that's going to make her desperate. She'll have to face him on the ground, because we'll have broken this fleet."

There was a surge of confidence in Caine's words, and Forepaw raised an eyebrow, "How?"

No answer came.

The icons on the battle plot flashed through Caine's mind.

Frigates danced brutally with Destroyers, ships of the line hurled their shot into Dreadnoughts. Gunboats and corvettes traded fire. Grieve's landers made their way to the ground.

The Kroggs fought with passion and anger and hatred, intangibles the Larosians didn't quite grasp, but ones which the Earthers knew all too well. Whatever guidance the Queen gave them, then, they remained primal creatures at their core.

That was how Caine would have to beat them. That was what all this had led to. Not a squadron gun duel, but a *vicious* and *terrifying* fight.

The Kroggs needed to be confronted with something they'd never seen — something that would cause instinctive and extreme fear, and break the discipline commanded by the Queen, driving them to flee.

The Earthers had to spark that greater fear.

"They only have 1,100 ships left, with Varnon we have... 1,400," Caine quietly examined the plot.

Then something he'd read once about a great human Admiral, Nelson, came to mind. That human had once defeated two ships, each one greater than his, by *boarding*.

There were marines on every Earther ship out here. Good, strong marines. Determined crews.

And the Kroggs wouldn't know what hit them.

Caine nodded slowly and straightened himself, "All ships... close for boarding."

Forepaw's head swivelled abruptly towards the First Lord, even as every member of the bridge crew unconsciously froze in place. The pause that seemed to last for an eternity really lasted little more than a few seconds.

Caine's amber-gray eyes were resolute.

"We want them to run, Lab. So we put them to the sword. We're mad enough to board *them*, board *Krogg ships*, and no one's tried it before, I expect. So that's how we break them."

Forepaw nodded very slowly, and Caine turned to the Signal Officer, "Fleetcomm."

The entire Earther Navy, despite the intensity of the battle, heard the words Caine had to say.

"We have to *break* them, and to do that we must board them and finish them face to face. They won't run from anything less."

Boarding.

"We've never done it before, so they won't expect it."

Those ships that first realized what was being asked began to close on unsuspecting Krogg victims. Marines all across the fleet were snatching swords and rifles from racks, checking comms and shield belts, and rushing to airlocks. Crew members who could be spared from their stations were heading to arms lockers.

"Marines stand by to board; crews, arm yourselves. A great human Admiral once sent the signal: *engage the enemy more closely*. Let's get *damned* close. Let's carry this day."

There were no words among the fleets' crews. Earthers across all the surviving ships of the Navy were preparing themselves for something they had never conceived of...

But they believed it would work... because it had to work.

Trusting his instinctive knowledge that this was what had to be done, Caine smiled at Lab Forepaw, his old dear friend, and closed his eyes.

Opening them after a moment, Setter Caine nodded, "My friends, don't doubt it. We *will* carry this day. Now, *to arms!*"

For a very long second there seemed to be no response from any of the crews, but then it came: the roar. From the crew on *Orion's* bridge, from throughout *Orion's* hull, and then from everywhere in the fleet.

"It's time the Kroggs *faced* us," Caine locked eyes with Lab Forepaw, and his friend and Flag Captain smiled and nodded slowly.

Below decks in *Orion*, files of bear marines roared their determination as they sprinted to locks, and crew members joined them. In every ship in the fleet, the crews erupted in a grand, rumbling chorus of anger and determination.

"All able ships, *board*."

The channel closed after Caine's last word, and the Kroggs battling hard around Krogg space were suddenly faced with something inconceivable.

Frigates, ships of the line, First, Second, Third Rates, *sloops*... Earther vessels dove towards the living hulls of the Kroggs, their guns still firing at ships and corvettes.

Counter-spines and neuro pulses tried to drive the Earthers back, but most reached their targets.

Only 700 Earther ships tried to close for boarding. Only 694 of the 1,100 remaining Krogg ships were bound by grav tractors.

That left only 400 Krogg ships unmolested by boarding Earthers, and Varnon was suddenly in amongst them with more ships, gunboats whirling through space around his 74s, blasting apart corvettes.

Ursla, standing on the bridge of *Agamemnon*, couldn't quite believe it.

A boarding action, in the tradition of navies long, long past.

She nodded to Tigar as he grappled *Agamemnon* to a Superdreadnought, then she took a shield and a long sword from the bridge arms locker.

"I'm joining the marines at 'B' lock. Look after things up here, would you?"

He nodded simply.

CHAPTER 55

The dropship hit the red ground hard, kicking up a cloud of dust.

Grieve was on his feet immediately — as were the rest of the marines on the craft. He had a good section of 2/54th on this dropship, many of them having volunteered, in full understanding, to go with him.

These were the very best troops. Anywhere.

"Ramp dropping... *now!*"

Grieve was already moving to the bow of the ship where the broad disembarkment ramp lowered smoothly to the soil. The clay-like ground gave briefly under the heavy metal door, then held it.

"Number Four Company, with me!" a Captain from the battalion called over the building rumble of other dropship landings, and the first files of Earthers quickly descended the ramp.

"Follow me, Captain," Grieve addressed the black bear, and she nodded in reply.

Closing his grip tightly around his rifle, Grieve gestured forward with his free hand and then ducked out the door and skipped down the ramp. His eyes quickly took in the alien — *very* alien — planet. The sky was lime green, the soil a brown-red. The air was the sort that Earthers breathed, but there was a... a *lack* of odor. The world itself seemed *dead*.

The plateau was as projected, and they were right where they needed to be. The black writhing palace stretched to the sky on the far side of the plain... only about half a kilometer away. It was an ugly thing, shining spires reaching up into the sky like horns, a liquid black life that felt nearly toxic to look at.

Well, with luck, he'd be inside it soon.

"Engineers, deploy the line," Grieve turned away from the palace. "First and second battalions of Second Guards, form firing line along the right. Fourth Guards and 2/54th, form to the left. Gillian, get your people between. Torallis, form your Stealth Guardsmen by line and stand by."

Grieve began walking along what would be the perimeter as he gave the orders, and marine engineers skidded to a halt all along his route, laying down their shield generators and keying them active before rejoining their platoons. All around the perimeter — even facing the open cliffs — they extended the shield line. If any corvettes slipped by the boats, they'd need that insurance.

Now the Earther marines swept from their dropships together, the 2,000 feline, canine and ursine infantry of the famed Guards Brigade of the Heavy Division. They dropped to one knee just behind the shield perimeter, formed in ranks two-deep, leveling their rifles and keying off their safeties. Two companies from each battalion stood to the rear as reserves. Pulsars came out along the line — ten per battalion, making a daunting forty on the ground. They spread out at intervals, setting up firing arcs against an enemy that'd probably be impossible to miss anyway.

Gillian Hodge and her Genesis marines came forward, the Commandant waving them to the gap in the line between the Earther battalions. She'd come down with only 1,100 marines of her own — the formidable 1st Marine Regiment — and now she put half into the gap between the flanks of 2/Second Guards and 1/Fourth Guards, then formed the other half behind to wait in reserve.

Standing behind her firing line, she took a few seconds to absorb the foreign place and briefly examine the spire, then she turned to Grieve and nodded to him.

Grieve glanced from the line with that nod, just as Lupus and his old squad arrived at the General's side. Sergeant Howler's eight-Earther team was nominally part of the 2/54th, but they tended to move exclusively with Lupus, and the Colonel didn't mind at all.

Quite frankly, scanning this horizon, Lupus was rather glad to have his reliable old squad around. They'd been in and out of dangerous situations many times before.

Lupus looked up at the General, "I'd comment on the weather, but how the hell should I know if this is a nice day by their standards?"

Despite himself, Grieve chuckled, "I don't like it much. The brigade's deployed though."

Lupus nodded as the Larosians began filing out of one of the landing craft. They'd been moved to the 74 *Thunderhead* for the drop, and for the sake of ease, Torallis had agreed to drop in Earther craft. Now, the 155-strong unit of the Larosian elite warriors formed themselves into a perfectly ordered line, five ranks deep and thirty-one files broad. Torallis, at their head, examined the sky.

There was no doubt in the Captain-elite's mind about his mission today — nor should there have been. He didn't have second thoughts or worries, he was a Guardsman, and he did his duty. Today that would mean his death. And that was acceptable.

Guardsmen, stand prepared.

For the first time, an abrupt, painful dagger shot through Torallis' head — he felt as though something powerful was trying to grip his mind, perhaps to crush it. The Queen...

But the Genesis ore that lined his helmet seemed to be doing its work — it was the mineral the Kroggs had used for centuries to mask their presence in the Genesis system, now it would work against them in the final moments, provided the Queen wasn't strong enough to bypass its scattering effects as they neared her location.

The Stealth Guard drew their swords from their back sheaths and held them point down in their right hands, not yet switching them on.

Torallis turned from them and walked to the clustering of Earthers around Grieve, "We're ready, Andros."

Grieve nodded to the Larosian, then turned to Lupus, "They still haven't come out to meet us..."

Lupus blinked, "You *shouldn't* have said that."

Grieve frowned as he began to feel the very slight tremors and hear the hissing, even over the sounds of marines and engineers moving back and forth around him. All eyes along the firing lines fixed on the spires of the hive, and Grieve turned to see precisely what was drawing such attention.

Small black Krogg forms were coming out of the hive, running towards the Allied position.

Within seconds there was a wave of Kroggs.

And a flood.

And a torrent.

There was a hissing roar as thousands — *tens* of thousands of Kroggs *filled* the width of the red plateau with blackness, and then advanced at a run. And behind them the blackness persisted, because *more* Kroggs were coming out of the palace. Many more.

"By the Earth."

"Praaxus' soul."

Grieve's mind reeled for seconds. He could have brought the entire Earther Marine Corps along and they'd still have been outnumbered. But today it wasn't just a matter of numbers, they had to draw out the Kroggs, and then punch through.

Gillian slowly drifted back from her line, and turned to Grieve, "You want to go through *that?*"

Looking down, Grieve nodded, "We *will* go through it."

The Commandant looked up at Grieve's resolute eyes, let out a deep breath, then extended a hand, "Good luck."

Grieve took it and nodded, "Thank you. And keep the fire up, we can't let them overrun the shield."

She nodded to the General, and then offered separate nods to Torallis and Lupus, returning to her anxious regiment. Genesis marines weren't as well suited to dealing with Kroggs as Earthers or Larosians, but they were quite useful for pouring on fire. And that was exactly what they'd do today, with Earther-built rifles and as much vigor as they could muster.

Grieve watched her go, then glanced down at Lupus and deftly covered his headset microphone, "Don't let her get too ambitious today. I think she and Graham have a road to travel."

The Colonel smiled briefly and nodded, "Alright."

Despite all the Kroggs filling the clearing, Lupus was remarkably calm. He'd never seen this many, but he knew they wouldn't best him.

The aliens would lose this day.

"You going immediately, then?" Lupus glanced back up at Grieve, and the General nodded.

"No point waiting. Volunteers front and center. Leave your rifles."

Two hundred and fifty Earthers withdrew from the Earther lines. As they slowly left their places, their friends patted them on their backs, thanked them for volunteering, wished them well, and said their goodbyes.

Those 250 Earthers had, when informed of their objectives before the attack, offered themselves for this veritable suicide mission because they knew it had to be done, and they felt it was their time and place to die. Those who remained on the line were no less courageous, they simply knew their place was on the plateau, and that they weren't meant to fall in the spire.

There was no bitterness either way, and as the gaps opened in the ranks they were closed by troops rushing up from the reserve companies. An air of camaraderie saturated Grieve's instincts.

Lupus looked up at Grieve a last time and offered his hand, "Get there, Andros. I know you'll do damned well."

Grieve smiled, handed his rifle to Howler, and then took Lupus' hand in both of his, "I know you'll stand, Beckett..."

Something gnawed at the back of Grieve's mind.

"What I do today isn't even going to compare to what you do one day, I think. Always look to your front, my friend. You might well save us all in the end..."

Lupus frowned for a second, not sure what the General meant, but he placed the words in his memory, smiled and nodded a bit sadly, "Whatever you say, my friend. We'll stand today."

Grieve nodded one last time, drew back his hands, turned and bobbed his head to the volunteers and to Torallis. The 250 Earthers were forming a rectangle around the Stealth Guard now, taking up pre-determined positions, swords in hand.

Checking the shield on his arm, Grieve drew his own sword from his hip sheath, and with a final look to Lupus, left the Colonel and the elite recon squad.

"This is Colonel Lupus," the wolf said into his microphone as Grieve went to the volunteers. "Brigade, stand by to open fire."

Grieve took his place at the front of the box of Allied volunteers, casting a glance over his shoulder at the few ranks behind him and at Torallis, whose Guardsmen stood in the center.

"Volunteers, activate shields. Tortoise-Phalanx."

The custom-built shields hummed to life, rectangular and for all intents and purposes, interlocking. The marines on the outer edges of the box held their shields out, touched their edges together, and formed a solid energy perimeter.

Those on the outside were all large bears, and now they slid the tips of their blades through slim gaps provided between the linked shields. A bristling Roman tortoise formation appeared behind the Allied line, and Lupus watched as it came to life.

Grieve was in it, front and center, his shield humming, his sword ready.

"Gillian, I need a gap in the line to advance through, please."

The Commandant heard the request through her earpiece and immediately nodded, "Captain Collins, Captain Murphy, C and D Companies make a hole!"

The Genesis troops scrambled aside, and the giant tortoise formation began to edge forward towards the perimeter shield.

Lupus turned his eyes back to the plateau.

It was a sea of black, surging and rushing, with the Kroggs of the Queen's personal guard only a hundred meters away…

Closing fast.

The tortoise edged its way towards the shield, and the Kroggs sprinted at it from the other side. As far as Beckett could guess, the Queen wanted to drive the Earthers off the plateau before they had a chance to do anything… but so far, no Krogg force had ever faced a full brigade at one time, and certainly not a brigade deployed in two ranks behind a shield. That sort of concentrated fire probably hadn't been seen at all since the Antarctic Plains.

Hopefully it would be enough to stem this tide.

Lupus took a deep breath and clenched his jaw. He'd read about Lord Kitchener at Omdurman in 1898… he could only hope concentrated fire by line was as successful today.

No, there was no hoping. The Earthers would stand.

Lupus' mind steeled at that thought, "Guards, 54th, at eighty meters… open *fire!*"

Hell was loosed.

CHAPTER 56

Caine passed the marines waiting at the lock and stopped at their head. He nodded to the Captain who was leading them, then drew his sword from his hip and saluted. The marines, armed with swords only, saluted back, raising the guards of their blades to their faces and then down in a perfectly synchronized motion.

"I'll be going in with you," Caine said simply. "Actually, you'll be going in with *me*."

The marines nodded and Caine turned to the airlock hatch. This was his idea, and he was going to make sure it was carried out properly. He tapped his first shield belt to life, stood ready with his sword, and waited.

Lab Forepaw had the Superdreadnought he wanted in his sights.

"Down forty... stand by grav tractors..."

Orion moved with the ease of any Earther ship, and even as the Superdreadnought tried to turn to present its spines, grav tractors latched on. The Krogg vessel was stopped dead in space by the larger First Rate, and now *Orion* hauled the ship roughly to its side. The locks made contact with the hull, and smaller grav tractors pulled tight to the living exoskeleton.

"Hit the cutters, all boarders to the locks," Forepaw gave the commands as he pulled a sword from the arms locker, and the Master repeated his orders. Forepaw turned to his First Lieutenant, "You have the bridge, I'm joining the flight deck party."

The Lieutenant nodded.

The airlock seemed to hum as energy torches on its outside — nominally used to cut open alloy hulls in the case of an emergency docking — sliced through the Krogg Superdreadnought's thick skin.

As an appropriate-sized hole was made and the atmospheric shields mounted on their airlock's exterior sealed the crossing, the light inside *Orion's* lock went from white to blue.

Caine keyed the hatch open and leapt across the gap, landing in front of a Krogg soldier.

He worked in silence, his blade flicking up one-handed and decapitating the warrior before it could react. There were dozens more though, and he advanced on them fast, the marines letting out a roar as they leapt to his side.

• • •

Agamemnon held fast to a Superdreadnought and the hatches were flung open, Ursla leading the first party of marines across. She carried the longest sword currently manufactured by the Earthers — one about half her height — and the Krogg corridors, surprisingly, were high enough that she didn't need to crouch too much.

She'd half expected to have to fight on hands and knees.

Now her big sword took a massive swing, cleanly slicing through the torsos of the two soldiers running to face her.

She'd fought like this before, but this time she was using a sword instead of a bayonet, and this time, there was no need to hold back. The Kroggs seethed from the inner decks of the Superdreadnoughts, and they would get no mercy.

Not if they fought her.

And fight her they did.

The marines swelled in the passages behind her, their Captain already barking orders. From many access points, the Earthers were storming aboard, spreading through the ships and dealing death.

And the Kroggs were learning to fear.

Fox preferred mobility, and was inclined to keep *Atlas* out of the boardings, but a Dreadnought had picked on *Vulcan* a bit too nastily, and *Atlas* dropped on the live ship from above, airlocks finding hull space and cutting through.

As a small fellow — a *fox* — Fox had no illusions about being able to defeat a Krogg soldier hand-to-hand... so he was holding the hilt of his short sword rather tightly.

He reached the nearest airlock just as the marines swung the hatch open, and he followed in their wake as they stormed across the gap.

Caine would not be stopped. Not after all that had happened.

He'd never focused a great deal on the sword in his past training, but today something more than practice was driving him on. Launching forward in quick movements, he wielded his sword one-handed like a saber, and the Kroggs that tried to get in front of him fell, their corpses slowly being absorbed into the deck of the ship.

Behind him more marines entered the black, fleshy hull of the Super-dreadnought and drove back further defenders, then spread outward. But it was Caine who led.

The 'deck' beneath his feet felt fleshy. It was part of the inners of a *living* thing. A breed of thing he killed frequently. At least this way he got to isolate the killing to those who truly asked for it, not to the ships that served as their mounts.

Caine's mind wasn't working logically so much any more, he realized.

Thoughts weren't coming in the patterns he was used to.

He suddenly understood how Ursla and Andros and Beckett Lupus had all felt on the ground.

And the release of direct conscious control over his actions satisfied part of him. It also greatly disturbed another part of him, but he would deal with that later. Right now he had to put fear into the Kroggs, and the way they were reeling, a straight push to the Telepath of this ship would do that.

"The Telepath — we need to get to the bridge, it should be forward. We kill the Telepath and they'll lose cohesion. This ship'll be useless."

Ursla's words were coming in loud growls, even as she was hacking through a soldier. She wasn't even thinking about swinging her meter-and-a-half blade, she just *was*. And the marines behind her were standing and waiting.

"Whatever you say, ma'am. We're following you."

Ursla nodded and made another effort to press forward.

Caine wasn't the most ominous-looking Earther of all time, but his glare was cool and laden with determination. His blade was flying faster than the eye could follow, cleaving through all that stood before him in short, economical motions. Its force, and the focus with which he drove forward, caused some of the soldiers to become afraid.

And that fear grew, not just in them but in the Telepaths, the only beings on the ships with any form of higher intelligence. This manner of face-to-face *intimidation* was something the Kroggs had never — *never* — seen used *against* them. No one had ever been so desperate as to bridge the gap of space to fight Krogg soldiers by hand.

No one *chose* to board a Krogg ship.

Except for the Earthers.

Fighting in passageways, swinging their broad swords and outmaneuvering soldiers, they blazed trails into the cores of Krogg ships.

And though the Telepaths sent more warriors to stop them, the soldiers were shocked, at the very basic level of their understanding. Soldiers thought little, but they had always understood fear.

They'd understood *inflicting* it, that is.

They'd never themselves faced much of it, except for the fear of their overseers.

Now, though, even as they cut down one Earther marine, another seemed to come on. They were unstoppable and lethal, vicious predators with skill and technology, and a single goal on every ship.

And Caine led them.

"We're near the bridge, I think, sir!"

Caine nodded to the marine Captain fighting at his side, and just as he took the head off another soldier, gestured towards a long corridor to their left, "That one, perhaps. We should be far enough forward, and there are a *lot* of soldiers here."

The Captain nodded, his marines pushing forward into a dark, black-decked clearing with him. Caine pressed ahead as well, and in the slightly broader intersection, the Kroggs tried to push back.

A handful of Earthers and Caine fought against dozens of Kroggs, and at last, the numbers began to tell — the soldiers began to succeed in their attempts to drive the party back.

The Kroggs' fear shrank just a little.

Prematurely, to be sure.

"*Orions*, with me!"

That was Forepaw, and from another direction a party of *Orion's* crew, brandishing swords and wearing shields, surged to bolster the small party of marines.

Forepaw found his way forward, and suddenly Caine felt him at his side. The Flag Captain's sword was in one hand, a pistol was in the other, and he nodded to Caine, "Not easy, eh?"

"You'd be surprised," Caine hammered his way into the corridor protected by the soldiers, and Forepaw and the *Orions* followed.

"They're trying to protect a corridor here ma'am, and we've only got six with us. You have my signal?"

"I do," Ursla's personal intercom unit, nominally for use on a ship when away from comm panels, also had a handy homing feature. It showed her that the marine Captain who was talking to her now wasn't too far away, and he'd found the bridge.

"To the left up here!" Ursla called back over her shoulder, swinging her sword again. The marines, with nothing to do behind her, simply nodded.

"Maybe we'll get into it when the corridors get wider and she isn't killing them all for us," one of them suggested.

Caine stopped at the door as his crew cleared the Kroggs from the hall behind him. He paused for a few seconds, looked for a hatch control, gave up quickly, and nodded to Forepaw. The pistol whined, and after a few shots at close range, a hole formed.

Swords then sliced through the door, their atom-wide blades tearing at the strong tissue of the Superdreadnought, slicing out from the hole and dragging around the fleshy plating as they attempted to carve a proper hatch.

The smell was truly unpleasant, but the door finally began to flop and peel away like a flap of skin.

And inside, the Telepath of the ship realized the measure of this defeat.

The Larosians would never have managed this, but these Earthers had.

And the Telepath sent out a warning to all other Krogg ships that these Earthers would board their ships and somehow *win*.

Caine was the first through the hole in the hatch, and he made his way directly to the Telepath. Some soldiers left on the bridge as guards tried to intervene, but the *Orions* overcame them. Caine recognized Forepaw and the Flight Deck Chief keeping pace with him, and the Krogg Telepath stared at them with an inexplicable glare.

"*Beasts!*" it spat in the language of the Genesis humans.

Caine eyed the alien coolly, "Surrender this vessel."

The Telepath's eye narrowed, its fang-like teeth bared. It was not as physically forbidding as a soldier, but it had the advantage of a mind. One that could summon power, or invade other minds.

The Krogg's mind lunged outward at the Earthers, meeting nothing but emptiness.

Even now the Earthers could block their thoughts. The telepathic organs were there, the Krogg could sense them, but something in their Earther blood made their minds impenetrable.

And that hideous thing in their blood suddenly snarled back at the Krogg's mind, and attacked it. Laughed at it, goaded it, mocked it... proclaimed its destruction... The Telepath's mind had no chance to respond as attacking thoughts clawed at it. It was worse than facing a Larosian telepath...

The Telepath's mind died.

Stumbling backwards, the Krogg fell, and suddenly the Superdreadnought lurched, nearly knocking Caine over before righting itself. The ship slowly moaned, and comm units among the *Orions* chirped.

Forepaw drew his, "Forepaw."

"They're all running, sir, the soldiers don't seem to have any fight left in them."

Forepaw glanced at a somber Caine, "The Telepath must have released them."

Returning his comm to his pocket, the Captain stepped slowly over to the Telepath and crouched, "What do you suppose killed him?"

Caine shook his head, "I have no idea... Let's clear the ship, it isn't a threat anymore."

CHAPTER 57

Grieve was about to reach the Guards Brigade's perimeter shield, passing the Genesis troops as they began to pour fire through the field. Just as the first rank of his tortoise was about to push their shields through, however, they paused at a new roaring sound coming from high above.

Grieve looked up and listened, certain he remembered the sound from somewhere, but it was louder than anything he'd heard on fields on other planets.

"Beck, what's going on?"

Lupus hadn't been able to watch the battle between *Flame* and the Destroyer over Pat's base camp after *Bishop's* crash, but Ernile Cuttar, one of the wolves still with Howler's squad, had been a major participant, and he immediately recognized that noise for what it was — the sound of energy shot cutting through the upper atmosphere...

Corvettes crossed the sky abruptly, coming from the horizon behind the palace — a dozen of them, lining up for a strike on the plateau.

Then a trident of black specs dropped from space behind them, and the sky thundered even more loudly as energy cannon sent blindingly bright waves of shot into their rear.

A new voice came over the comm, "This is Trax Earon above you General. I've got four squadrons with me and a good look at your situation. Should I put fire down on the Kroggs?"

Grieve blinked, "Volunteers halt!"

He'd forgotten that slight advantage — too long fighting without it, too focused on the grittier parts of the job to come.

"By all means, Captain Earon! This is Colonel Lupus commanding the brigade position; try to collapse the exit points from the palace they're coming out of, if you can. And put a hole in that citadel for the General."

A rumble from Lupus' rear grew louder, "Copy that Colonel, get your heads down."

The marines on the line, hearing the conversation, crouched a little lower as they fired, the Kroggs coming very close now, surging over the last twenty meters of open ground towards the shield. Pulsars sliced through tides of them, concentrated rifle blasts from the tightly-packed ranks battered down more.

As the aliens came closer, Beckett's eyes narrowed and he finally got a good look at his enemy. Each had six arms as compared to a regular Krogg soldier's four, and red trim lined their carapaces, looking almost like spattered blood. Each one of these Queen's Guards was two and a half meters tall, and every one of them *hissed*. Or roared. Something.

The sight of them was disturbing to the Earthers and it terrified the humans. Both groups of Allied marines seemed to fire faster as the aliens came closer.

Kroggs were falling in heaps on the red clay, and then the rumble from above became deafening. Cannon thundered in the distant sky, and shot slammed hard into the masses of swelling Kroggs.

There were screams as each shot wiped away dozens — even hundreds. Fifteen energy bolts cleaved through the open plateau on the first run, and then the second salvo nearly disintegrated the upper spire of the palace, tearing clear holes in its base and knocking many of its horns over the steep cliffs that backed it.

As the two squadrons of boats raced away to recharge, the complexion of the ground action seemed to change. Grieve's tortoise-box formation had a bit of breathing space, though thousands of Kroggs still flooded the field.

"Captain Earon, Grieve here, I'm advancing out. Keep up your strikes but avoid hitting me, would you?"

"Understood, good luck."

The marines on the line kept their fire hot, and had the pulsars not been literally vaporizing most of the falling bodies, a ridge would have grown before the perimeter. Lupus ignored the sheer gruesomeness of the spectacle, and with his old squad, moved himself to the back of 2/54th's line.

"Volunteers, forward."

Grieve's commands were simple now, and they would stay that way. He edged up to the shield perimeter, took a breath, and stepped through it. The one-way shield let him pass, and at a steady, carefully measured pace, he moved with the front rank of the tortoise as it advanced.

Almost immediately, Kroggs slammed against the shields of the marines holding the outer layer of the tortoise-rectangle, but the big bears held back the determined aliens with all their strength, stabbing back at the Queen's Guards with their swords through the narrow slits. As C and D companies of Gillian's 1st Marine Regiment fell back into line behind the advancing formation, their guns began destroying the Kroggs that tried to crush the tortoise.

And the gunboats cruised in again, vaporizing hundreds more Kroggs, and shaking the plateau.

Grieve ground his jaw; the Battle of the Antarctic Plains had looked like hell. This... well, this *was* hell. He leaned into his Larosian-style shield, pushing the Kroggs before him with sheer weight and muscle.

They had to get to that palace. It would be exhausting, but they had to.

And they would.

So Grieve pressed forward a bit harder, "Let's pick it up, half-step."

The Earthers in the formation moved faster, reaching a gap in the tides of Kroggs where the first boat run had demolished so many.

"Quick step now…"

Grieve watched through his shield as they accelerated even more, and he watched the Kroggs as they came forward towards him again. The roar of boats overhead came suddenly, and energy shot disintegrated the edge of the cliff to the left, knocking hundreds of Kroggs over the side.

The palace took more hits.

Kroggs slammed hard into the front and sides of the volunteer tortoise. Swords stabbed out against them, but the Kroggs remained persistent. They tried to crush the Earthers with muscle, but the hordes of guards weren't quite coordinated — their sheer mass could have broken the Allies if all on the plateau had immediately worked toward that outcome, but there was too much chaos in their ranks. And the bears on the outsides of the formation were bolstered by their comrades within.

Bone blades couldn't penetrate these big shields — they were taller than the Kroggs, and the Earthers in the center were using theirs to form a roof. But Grieve knew the protection of these seemingly invulnerable shields wouldn't last. He leaned hard forward, his shoulder — protected by a traditional Earther shield — crackling as it pressed against the Larosian one. The tortoise forced its way through the dense Kroggs by sheer strength, and the Earthers ground down on their jaws as they fought to maintain their pace.

They'd covered half the distance now, about 350 meters of the 700-odd to the palace. The Kroggs were getting thicker. But there had to be a finite supply of Queen's Guards, and as the gunboats tore into them and long-range fire from the lines of the Guards Brigade cut them to pieces, the Kroggs kept dying by the hundreds.

It was so much worse than Antarctica.

Safeties had been on at Antarctica, and thousands had survived.

There would be no such luxury here.

Grieve ignored that reality — this was gruesome, but it would save lives in the long run.

And it would fulfill the Earthers' promise. That thought gave him strength and he pressed on harder. Kroggs banged angrily against his shield, their blades bouncing off it as they tried again to kill him. His sword thrust through the slim gap between his fist and the shield of the marine next to him, and he stabbed Kroggs out of the way as best he could. He had to step over some dead, but most were vaporized by the cannon shot.

The tortoise had disappeared into a writhing sea of Kroggs, but Beckett could hear Grieve in his ear. There was no problem yet, though the Kroggs were no longer paying much attention to the Earther lines. And at longer range, the marines' fire was much less effective.

Another boat strike sliced the Krogg tides apart as they tried to reach Grieve's position, and the Kroggs who had begun to slow their charge at the shield turned, pressing back into that writhing horde towards the tortoise. Most were gunned down as they ignored the Guards Brigade, but still more pressed the General's party, and open ground appeared before the firing line.

Open ground that created an opportunity...

Lupus made a decision, "Engineers, deactivate the forward perimeter and move it ahead 100 meters. Guards Brigade, pull up the reserves and advance everyone in close support. Gillian, your marines should hold a reserve line here."

The orders went over the comms, and engineers leapt from the ranks to grab the shields. Firing stopped, and then, led by one of Lupus' counterparts, Lieutenant Colonel Garnet Wiskar, the Earther battalions came from their kneeling position and sprinted forward, rifles spraying any Kroggs who so much as turned to look at them. The gap to their new position was covered in a very few seconds, and the marines of four elite Earther battalions dropped to their knees again in a slightly less orderly line, firing at whatever presented itself.

"Beckett, let my marines move up," Gillian appeared at Lupus' side, and he turned to her.

It struck neither of them as odd that the commander-in-chief of the Genesis Marine Corps was taking instructions from a relatively junior Earther brigade commander.

"Andros' orders, you stay out of too much danger. We'll need a reserve line when we pull back, so get your regiment laid out in good order to cover us when we do. Get some more shields from the dropships and deploy them."

Hodge eyed Lupus for a second and then nodded, turning to her officers.

Lupus bobbed his head forward and Howler's squad followed as he sprinted after the Guards Brigade.

"Only a hundred more meters," Grieve almost growled, and the Earthers in the formation grunted in agreement.

The formation was beginning to cave quite noticeably under the ever more coordinated pressure. Queen's Guards pressed on all sides, and the box of Earthers contracted.

Fire against the Kroggs thickened as the brigade settled into its new line 100 meters beyond its original position. The Kroggs began to take notice of that larger force again — perhaps this box of Allied troops was a diversion, as it did seem rather a pathetic offering for the Queen. The main advance might come from the four Earther battalions...

Perhaps...

Nope, that's my job...

Grieve leaned harder into his shield.

Lupus stood behind crouched Earthers as they poured energy into thick Krogg waves, and he raised his own rifle as the Kroggs slowly began to turn on the new perimeter.

"Keep the fire as hot as possible," he ordered into his comm, but the marines were well ahead of him, their triggers held perpetually down as they swept the Kroggs.

And then in a sudden change, the Kroggs turned almost entirely on the perimeter. *All* of them.

The aliens surged forward, through the shot of one gunboat attack and a second, their new focus hopefully giving Grieve an opening to the base of the citadel...

Beckett's eyes narrowed behind his rifle sight as he tried to determine just *why* the Queen's Guard was suddenly so interested in the brigade. The Queen must have decided Grieve was a feint, and that a battalion advance was the plan...

Ramming into the marines' shield perimeter, the Kroggs began to drain the copious, interlaced energy of the Earther shield generators. Fire sliced them apart, but by sheer weight they began to warp the field.

Lupus kept shooting even as he paced behind his troops, the energy from his rifle tearing at the warriors he faced. They kept pressing, blood thirsty and determined to kill those they thought were *really* coming to kill their Queen

"Main shield is buckling here, sir!"

Lupus' head turned just in time to see one of the humming — *whining* — generators *stop*.

The shield for the section dropped, pulsars swinging to try to keep the Kroggs back from the breach. The fire of two dozen of those powerful weapons seemed to have little effect: the Kroggs just kept pressing.

"Sling rifles — to swords, and fall back to the reserve line!"

The Kroggs weren't as thick right at the base of the spire. The palace was badly shot up, and the tide of Kroggs from its flanks was beginning to slow. Boats were hammering fire into those who still came, and for the most part Lupus had them deceived... for now. The Queen probably believed, rightly, that Grieve's small party could not have any explosives that could hurt her from the surface... she couldn't believe that the volunteers alone would be trying to enter her palace.

By her standards, that was probably work for an entire brigade, if not a division.

Grieve needed to take advantage of her mistake, "Break formation. Enter here."

The columns of the tortoise broke apart immediately, what Kroggs there were around being set upon quickly by the thus far unengaged Larosians of the Stealth Guard. The Earthers took a few seconds to recover, and Torallis came to Grieve's side while the elite silver-armored warriors sliced through the Queen's Guard.

"If we enter here, we should be able to go directly down through the spire to the Queen's chamber. The way should not be confusing; as you recall — all passages lead to the Queen..."

"But this time there *will* be Queen's Guard all around," Grieve agreed. "We'll get there."

Torallis nodded, and as the 400-odd Allied marines and Guardsmen bunched at the spire's base, some of the Kroggs began to take notice of them and turned back. Only some of them — not enough.

A number of the Earthers went out to meet them, determined to hold the entrance to the spire and give the rest of the volunteers time to get below. Grieve watched about two dozen take on this task, and one of them called to him clearly, "Go sir, we'll hold them as long as we can."

Grieve took a silent breath, looked up at the alien sky, and nodded, "Volunteers, lead the way."

They filed into the broad corridor that descended shallowly through the plateau, and behind them gallant bears of the Earther Marine Corps fought to their gruesome, brutal deaths at the hands of the Kroggs.

CHAPTER 58

Caine found his chair on the bridge to be somewhat comforting, as did Forepaw.

"Master, let's get off this Superdreadnought, best speed."

The Signal Lieutenant had stayed at his post, "We have reports sir, the Krogg are easing off a bit. Some of the ships in this vicinity are actually running. Admiral Broadpaw has ships after them broadcasting orders to surrender on every frequency they figure might get picked up."

Caine paused thoughtfully and turned his chair. It had worked.

"Any word from the Fourth or Sixth?"

The Signal Officer shook his head, "Still fighting out there."

Tensing his jaw for a second, Caine made his decision, "Marshall what you can of the First and Third. Send to Ursla to hold Krogg 'A', we'll go help our Allies."

"Aye, sir."

Sarah didn't pay much attention to the boarding actions. They were far across the system, and matters at hand were a bit more pressing. In company with *Edgar Fitzpatrick*, *Joseph Barron* turned and surged again, missiles slamming into a Krogg Superdreadnought that'd been trying to run down on the pair unnoticed.

With Pat's Posse in company, these two Genesis capital ships were inflicting significant damage within their sphere of influence, but the Kroggs kept coming. The humans were running out of Type 98s again.

"Reports coming in from most of the fleet now, ma'am, over 200 ships are back to firing Type 92s," the Comm Officer made his report in a grim tone, and Sarah mentally winced.

Reduced to type 92 missiles again, the Genesis Fleet would lose its parity with its foe. The Kroggs would be able to dictate the fight from ranges the humans couldn't touch…

"Signal Narosh, we're going to have to back out soon if we can't break them. Ammunition running low."

Narosh's Warcruisers were suffering from a similar problem. Missiles were not necessarily the Warcruisers' primary weapons, but they remained important elements in the Larosian arsenal. Now the magazines on most of the Fourth Fleet-of-War's vessels had been emptied.

It was to be close antimatter fighting then... while the Kroggs grew more spines to bombard them with from long range...

The Queen had to be destroyed... that was the *only* thing that would stop the Kroggs once and for all.

Energy drive signatures, sir, two Earther fleets approaching... 600 vessels.

Graham's eyes hurt from staring at the plot — the Kroggs *wouldn't* break, no matter what they were hit with...

"That's it sir, we're down to 92s."

Looking up at *Fitzpatrick's* ArcColonel, Graham's voice was coarse, "Laser range then. We'll give the bastards something to think about–"

"Earther ships, about 600 coming in, sir!"

Preacher took a salvo of spines in the bow.

Pat was standing at the main screen when the ship went sideways under his feet, and he smacked the deck with an angry grunt.

"Gods bloody damned hell sonofa–"

"Systems going down! We're dead in space!"

Only seventeen other Posse members were left, and in the interests of survival they needed to maintain full speed, even as *Preacher* tumbled off in another direction.

"A couple of Destroyers are coming in... lost them, sir — secondary sensors are offline!"

"Get them back!" Pat came to his feet and knew he'd feel the bruises tomorrow.

If there *was* a tomorrow...

Oh shut it...

"Okay, I think I see something... bigger than a Superdreadnought... it's coming over us!"

Preacher suddenly shuddered, and the bridge was deathly quiet.

The comm crackled, "Problems, Pat?"

It was Caine's voice.

Pat looked up at the speakers in the ceiling and opened his mouth to say something. He just didn't really have any words to come out.

Orion cradled the wreck of *Preacher* under its hull, pulling it close with grav tractors while pinnaces slid out of the flight bays to dock with the maimed Battlecruiser.

All around, Kroggs fled from the First Rate.

No fight — as soon as the Earthers closed and a few of the ships of the First and Third Fleets approached their foes with the clear intention to board, the Telepaths of the Krogg vessels recognized the danger that was coming for them.

In a very predatory fashion, the Earthers had just proved themselves the 'alpha' killers in space — Krogg instinct, even in the Telepaths, was clear enough under the circumstances.

It told them to run.

Narosh had seen Kroggs run before, but never for seemingly no reason. Six hundred Earther ships were important, but they couldn't easily break the defensive sphere of stations. Why run?

Sir, I believe the Earthers have boarded *Krogg ships and captured them in hand-to-hand combat. They may have broken the spirit of the Krogg lower ranks.*

Narosh wasn't sure who passed the thought into his mind–

Natosh, sir.

Ah, Natosh put the thought in his mind.

Reliable then, no matter how unlikely it seemed.

All ships, pull back from action range. Make reports of ammunition and damage.

As brutally as it'd begun, it ended.

Sarah was still clutching the arms of her chair.

She watched the Kroggs run, turned questioningly to *Joseph Barron's* ArcColonel, and Evan-Thomas pointed at one of the secondary screens. A screen that showed a 74 unlatching itself from a Dreadnought, presumably having carried the Krogg ship by boarding.

"*Edgar Fitzpatrick* on the comm, ma'am."

Sarah blinked, "Put it up."

Graham appeared on one of *Joseph Barron's* forward bridge monitors, his face weary but his eyes steeled.

"The Earthers put some damned fear into them, eh?"

Sarah was still frowning at the image of the 74 — *Atlas*, by the looks of it — rejoining the fleet.

"You've seen those images of them boarding?" Graham pressed a bit impatiently.

Sarah nodded, "It'd scare the hell out of me."

Graham's forehead creased and he nodded in agreement, his mind strained, but still quite tactically capable, "Still don't want to close on the stations though. Seen Liz lately?"

"The stations will probably hold until... Liz?" Sarah paused, "I haven't see her lately — she's not around here?"

Graham frowned and looked off screen.

His frown deepened, "Hang on, on the long-range scopes. *Gerald Windsor* just bypassed Krogg 'A'... she's following a ship headed for the star."

Sarah's eyes widened slightly, "Get Caine!"

"It's seen us."

Liz Hastings nodded slowly, "Increasing speed?"

"Slightly... looks like... yes, making .87 cee now... climbing."

Gerald Windsor had shadowed this thing slowly for quite some time now, and it seemed that keeping pace with the Krogg suicide ship had been a very good idea indeed.

"Accelerate to flux, let's get ahead of it."

Pope Gerald Windsor accelerated to a little over light speed.

Caine had let some tension go when the Kroggs had broken, but he knew better than to relax entirely. And as the telemetry from *Flame* passed into *Orion's* plot, he realized a *lot* depended on Liz and *Gerald Windsor*.

"Get word to any ships nearby to go to her aid, just in case..." Caine's voice trailed off as Forepaw leaned forward and pointed out something in the plot.

"What are *those* five?"

By the Earth, there wasn't just one Krogg ship sprinting for the star.

Of course the Kroggs hadn't just sent one. If they were going to lose, they'd go out with a bang. Made sense. So they'd hidden six bomb ships in their defensive perimeter — the one perimeter that they were fairly certain couldn't be destroyed outright.

And now the Queen would position those ships to take the system hostage.

There were too many Allied survivors floating in pods, marines on Krogg, and boats in space without energy drive to make abandoning the system a real possibility. Caine wouldn't lose that many Earthers, Larosians, and humans to Krogg bitterness.

Atlas and *Vulcan* were moving in tandem again when the signal arrived.

Fox hadn't ended up doing all that much on the Dreadnought he'd boarded — the hard work had been taken care of by the marines. Now that he was back on his bridge...

"*What?*"

"Six, sir."

"*Lovely.*"

A few eyebrows went up but Fox was too far ahead of himself, "Send to Thena to stick with us in *Vulcan*. See if Ami's nearby and check if she's got any frigates left to send along. Mister Gunth, think 600 pls is out of the question?"

The grizzled Cruising Master, standing at the helm, glanced back over his shoulder with a smile at the Commodore.

Fox nodded, "Good. Go to it, Master. All crew back to action stations."

Novash had known something was up when *Gerald Windsor* had hurtled past the planet, and with the introduction of the Earther boardings — something Novash had never conceived of, let alone understood — *Shanavorus* had seemed a bit superfluous. He'd ordered the rest of the Warcruisers to help clean up and secure the orbital space around Krogg 'A', and now he was redlining the drives of his flagship to try to keep up with Liz Hastings' pursuit.

He had just realized what Liz was chasing when Caine's warning arrived, and while the Krogg ship leveled its acceleration at .9 cee, *Shanavorus* had peaked and was now holding .92134 cee.

The Larosians, as a rule, liked to work in precise numbers.

Now those numbers needed to pay off.

We may reach them in time, sir... but we cannot be certain.

Novash nodded to himself.

Liz's eyes widened as five more ships appeared on her display — *Flame's* scans were coming in again, after a period where the sloop's signal had been masked by the planetary body of Krogg 'A'. And they showed things to be infinitely worse than Liz had realized.

"Stand by to decelerate, we're going to need to take out many more than we expected–"

"Incoming!"

Just as *Gerald Windsor* dropped from its low-level flux, the ship it'd been chasing veered towards it and exploded.

The blast wasn't that powerful, but with armor offline and the state of flux still partially in play...

Shrapnel sheared through much of the Superdreadnought, crippling its generators in an instant overload.

The impact was barely felt on the bridge, but the tumble towards the star that followed immediately was obvious. Liz lurched from her chair as the grav generators lagged.

So the Queen was determined that at least one of her ships reach that star...

"They took the hit hard, skipper. They're on a collision course with the star."

Chronos Claw had sat out of the fighting for long enough. He'd been back and forth a dozen times over, keeping his eyes on the battle. Now he was close, and there were *five* of those Krogg bomb ships closing fast with the star.

"Take us to one of those things and drop out of energy drive. All hands to the guns."

Flame surged towards a bomb ship.

Shanavorus changed course fast, and Novash ordered the drives pushed much, much harder. The acceleration nearly shook the ship apart as it hit .94 cee, but the extra burst of speed was sufficient to gain range on one of the Krogg bomb ships... if only one...

Target confirmed, sir!

Fire!

Missiles leapt from *Shanavorus* and their speed multiplied thanks to the velocity of the Warcruiser that dispatched them. Novash's ship angled for another Krogg bomb as its first target exploded in a bright flame, but there was no time to reach it...

"Missile separation... skipper, they just blew up our target!"

Claw frowned. That didn't often happen — the ship *Flame* had been about to hit had been destroyed by an abrupt salvo from *Shanavorus*... Oh well.

"Target another one!"

"Aye..."

Gerald Windsor stabilized just enough for Liz to come to her feet and see a star growing large in her view screen.

So that was it then.

Her heart fell as she realized that all this, her chance to *lead* again, was going to kill her.

"We have range on one of those bomb ships ma'am. Four tubes are in action with 98s. May I fire?"

Liz blinked and glanced at the gunner, "Fire."

Maybe they'd get one after all.

"You've got to be kidding!"

"No sir, *Windsor's* missiles just hit it."

Claw was starting to see this as not funny. Twice *Flame's* targets had been picked off... and the last three bomb ships were getting awfully close to the star they were seeking to destroy...

"Got the next one selected sir!"

"Go!"

Flame came out of energy drive abruptly, and the bomb ship didn't expect an interruption this close to a star. The sloop's broadside — small though it was — slammed into the Krogg vessel, and then the sloop rolled hard and unleashed a second salvo. A carronade shot finished the bomb ship and *Flame* returned to energy drive...

"Two to go!" Claw's voice showed some relief.

"Uh. Sir."

Vulcan went from 600 to 60 pls in the blink of an eye, and its port guns were already running out when the bomb ship realized it had company. Thirty Earther energy cannon flared and the Krogg vessel disintegrated.

At the very same time, Ami Cairn's frigate *Inferno* dropped from energy drive over a different section of sun, and the 38's starboard broadside crossed a small gap and batted the last bomb ship away from the star's corona, a follow-up from the port side battery smashing the Krogg vessel.

Commodore Cairn let out a long, relieved breath as she sat back in her chair on *Inferno's* bridge, and her Flag Captain, the redoubtable Bartemius Stowt, smiled as he sat next to her.

"Don't think we've saved a day quite this big before," he glanced at Ami, and she smiled in return.

"No, Barty, I don't think we have."

Fox let out a very long sigh as he watched the bomb ships blow to pieces, "And that's that. Andros won't have to worry about the Queen holding us hostage…"

Mister Gunth cleared his throat conspicuously.

Not immune to subtle hints, Fox looked over, "Yes Mister Gunth, I haven't forgotten. We in position yet?"

"Matching vectors now."

"Pods would get pulled into the sun at this range, ma'am. We've got about ninety seconds until we melt."

Liz nodded slowly, taking a deep breath and trying not to contemplate just how it would feel to die when *Gerald Windsor* was swallowed by a sun.

Well, if she was going to die, she had to talk to someone first.

She turned to the Comm Officer, "The antennae still working?"

The ArcLieutenant nodded.

"Patch me in to *Joseph Barron*."

Sarah was watching the drama at Krogg 'A's sun play out on her screen. There was nothing she could do except get ready to run if the Allied ships converging on the Kroggs out there failed to destroy all the bomb ships. But that wasn't an issue now…

"Signal from *Gerald Windsor*, ma'am."

Frowning, Sarah nodded, "Put it on."

"Audio only…"

The speakers crackled, "Sarah? Sarah you there?"

"Yes."

"Good… I need to tell you some things. We'll melt in a minute so listen… okay?"

"No."

There was a pause.

"What'd you mean *no*. I'm about to *die* here."

"No. No you're not."

Liz scowled on her bridge, "I'm looking at a nice, *bright* star here, Sarah."

The sound of a throat being cleared came over the speakers.

"Listen, I've got half a minute left, let's not argue."

There was another pause, then muttering, followed by moderately frustrated words from a familiar voice, "Look, I can't think of anything gallant or witty to say, ArcGeneral, so oblige me by pretending I said something extremely clever."

Liz stood confused for just a moment at the interruption, and then *Gerald Windsor* was abruptly caught by two 74s' grav tractors.

Sarah smiled to herself as she watched from half a system away. *Atlas* and *Vulcan* caught hold of *Gerald Windsor*, and as *Shanavorus, Inferno* and *Flame* closed to serve as escort, the six ships began to draw away from the star.

Standing on *Orion's* bridge, Caine felt a weight — *two* weights, actually — lift from his shoulders. No threat of the Queen eliminating the system, no loss of the head of the Genesis Navy.

All that was left now was for Grieve to do his job.

And if at the beginning of this day Caine had been asked what one part of the operation he had absolute confidence in, it would have been Andros Grieve's attack.

The General would win this war for them all.

CHAPTER 59

The Earther volunteers and Larosian Guardsmen pushed hard and fast, forcing their way down the single broad corridor that descended in wide spirals to the depths of the hive, dying in ones and twos as they went.

Grieve had to lead from the rear this time because he *had* to get to the Queen. He didn't quite know why it had to be him personally, he just knew it did. And somehow his volunteers also knew he was the one who had to make it the whole way.

As the corridor filled with Queen's Guards, Earther and Larosian warriors fought with the utmost skill, and the force drove deeper into the palace. The Kroggs were by no means weak, and their determination slowly overwhelmed the volunteers' shields, but each Earther and Larosian fell only after exacting a heavy price.

Grieve stepped over the fallen, silently thanking them as he pressed on. His very best were dying at his feet; he wouldn't see their sacrifice wasted.

The corridor through which they were driving had grown wide and high so the Queen's Guards could exploit their many blades in broad swings, and the Kroggs took full and effective advantage of that fact. But at the same time, the red-trimmed foes were forced to deal with large Earther bears and elite Stealth Guards.

Neither side would retreat.

All had in some way pledged to fight to the death — and as cliché as the phrasing might have been, that was precisely what they would do.

The volunteers battled deeper.

Beckett Lupus' rifle was slung and his sword was drawn in less than the blink of an eye. Grieve was forcing his way into the Hive, but here on the surface the Colonel was fighting a rearguard action to give his marines time to make it back to Gillian Hodge's reserve line. Lupus and his squad and the entire brigade were at blade point, falling back as the gunboats realized that the perimeter shield had given way and intensified their pounding of the red ground covered by black Kroggs.

The surging masses of Queen's Guards continued to close, and the Earther marines faced the challenge steadily as they dropped back in good order. Pulsars gathered clumps of sword-wielders around them and kept up a vicious fire, moving towards the rear more quickly so as to help anchor Gillian's line. The rest of the brigade — now about 1,500 of the most capable Earther marines in the service — let their blades fly.

Despite all the carnage around him, Lupus knew that he and Howler wouldn't suffer death here. Graxton, however, fell and she didn't get back up. Ernile Cuttar went down too, but he got back up, albeit missing an arm.

Then Beckett Lupus was targeted by some Queen's Guards who must have noticed and comprehended the significance of his rank bars. He watched the aliens choose him, and he stopped retreating as they came forward. The Krogg ranks were thinning now. The gunboats were sweeping the plateau clean, and Grieve was drawing the reinforcements away. Lupus could at last see open plain on the other side of the sea of aliens... but that was still a long way off.

Nonetheless, he got the feeling that maybe — just *maybe* — the Guards Brigade of the Heavy Division could break the Queen's Guard.

Such a turn of the tide would almost certainly draw enough of the defenders away from Grieve.

"Guards Brigade, choose your ground and stand as you can," he said in abrupt, hard tones, and the Earther line stopped dropping back.

Beckett picked his spot on the ground.

The Kroggs came at him but despite their formidable speed, they suddenly appeared brutish and clumsy to Lupus. He consciously knew they weren't, but his instincts were seizing control of his actions, in a more complete way than he recalled ever having happened before, even in battle.

As the first arrived on his chosen killing ground, Lupus leaned aside and avoided a massive swing, then swung his sword through the back of the attacking Krogg's head, putting him down. He didn't realize he was roaring.

Earthers all along the line were roaring back at the hissing Kroggs now; bears and wolves and cats hurled themselves into the midst of the Queen's warriors with a ferocity that wasn't their custom. Some kodiaks literally hefted the Kroggs overhead and pitched them into files of oncomers. Tigers slid through entire clusters without being touched, and then sliced the larger aliens apart from their flanks. Wolves picked their ground and fought together, the way wolves always did.

And Guards on both sides died.

Shields failed, Earthers fell by the hundreds. But over a thousand Earthers stood fast.

These were the mighty Guards Brigade: the Second Earther Guards, the Fourth Earther Guards, and the second battalion of the 54th foot.

Damned if they wouldn't break the Kroggs somehow.

A Krogg came in fast, trying to take Lupus with blades on three levels — knees, waist, and head. The Colonel swung his rifle off his shoulder with one hand and shot out the Krogg's eye; the alien fell, pitching to the left.

Howler was at his side then, with the rest of the old squad save Graxton. Even Ernile Cuttar had a sword in his one hand. Together they stood their ground, and the Earthers on their flanks stood and bathed in the blood of both races.

• • •

Torallis stayed close to Grieve, but the Allied ranks ahead were thinning.

Warriors of both races were dying in great numbers — only sixty remained, if that many. Torallis could feel the presence of what he had to assume was the Queen. She was laughing at him, her great power penetrating the scattering zone of his helmet, mocking him and trying to make him doubt.

It wasn't, however, slowing him down. Nor was it slowing his Guardsmen — these Stealth Guards were the elite of the Larosian elite, and they fought proudly next to their Earthers comrades. Swords slashed, thrust and flashed dimly in the ever-darkening tunnel.

"We must be close," Torallis' voice reflected no consternation, and Grieve nodded.

"We're almost there."

The ranks were growing so thin... but the volunteers fought on, steadfast and determined. The soldiers pressed forward, each fighting long brutal minutes before falling under Krogg blades. Some lasted longer, some didn't.

Slowly the resistance before them ebbed, and as the presence in Torallis' mind grew, the opposition in the corridor abruptly halted. Before the Captain-Elite or the General could question why, a call beckoned them to the front of their force.

"Sir."

It was one of the forty-four remaining volunteers — twenty-nine Earthers and fifteen Stealth Guardsmen.

Grieve answered the volunteer, "Problem?"

"Corridor is empty right up to a door ahead."

Grieve paused, "Approach with caution."

The battered group edged forward, and in the minds of the Larosians, something dark loomed ever larger.

"We're very near, Andros," Torallis said in low tones, gently lifting his sword to the ready position.

Grieve did the same, and nodded, "I think so too."

This had to be it — the Queen's chamber at last.

"The brigade has stopped falling back, ma'am."

Gillian Hodge nodded as she watched the khaki-clad Earthers stand their ground, roaring defiantly and fighting a significantly superior number of Kroggs without support. Pulsars were anchored twenty meters back, hitting whatever they could, but the Earthers seemed all but overwhelmed.

"Enough of this," Gillian Hodge turned to her officers. "We go forward fast. Set up fire positions to support the pulsars. Let's fix bayonets."

The officers nodded almost eagerly. They'd get into the thick of this fight at long last — do some good.

As the orders were called out, the 1st Marine Regiment broke from its long line into a series of platoon-sized units, each of which began sprinting forward and fixing bayonets. Some stopped as they reached the pulsars, then hefted their rifles and opened energy fire on the Kroggs. Others — more elite or at least more eager — pressed forward to support the Earthers themselves.

The bayonets fixed to the human rifles were built to the same pattern as Earther swords — they had atom-edged enhanced blades that had long been proven equal to the task of breaking Krogg carapaces.

The rifles lacked a bit in reach when compared to bears with swords, but Gillian remained confident in the elite men and women of her tough 1st Regiment. She rushed forward with them, a company behind her, and as she closed with the Earther line she angled right for Lupus' squad.

Beckett Lupus' rifle fell to the ground and he took a second sword from a fallen cat nearby. With two swords, he bent slightly at the knees and his eyes narrowed. No Kroggs around him could mistake the danger he now represented as he stood unassailed and stared at his foes. The warriors of the Queen halted their attacks on him, meeting his gaze instead, as their own primal instincts recognized the danger.

Reluctant to rashly assault such an opponent, the Kroggs before the Colonel began to drift back slightly, and his now-steeled eyes pressed them back even further. The entire Guards Brigade seemed to be instinctively following Lupus' menacing example, offering silent promises that nasty things would happen to the Kroggs who pressed this attack.

For the first time these Queen's Guards responded to a threat with concern instead of arrogant dismissal.

Howler moved to Lupus' side, and the wolves of the squad stood next to their Sergeant. They shed their rifles, and with the exception of Cuttar, hefted their swords in two hands. Up and down the lines, the two sides drew apart, staring each other down in a silent contest, waiting perhaps to see who would be the first to lunge.

But perhaps there would be no movement; the Queen's Guard at last had a foe they *believed* might be able to match them. A foe to be *respected* — how remarkable — respected enough to stop their bloodlust even briefly...

But the bloodlust was rekindled immediately as a foe *not* to be respected arrived on the scene.

Sixty humans burst past Lupus, bayonets on rifles and a determined cry raising among them. For a second Beckett didn't realize what was happening — and then he watched the uncertain Kroggs he faced mark the easier targets.

Humans were torn apart by the dozens.

Bayonets stabbed outward, but Kroggs with six singly-bladed arms had better reach and coverage. Determined, courageous humans were literally ripped to shreds; sixty eviscerated in mere seconds as they closed gallantly to fight alongside their Earther friends.

Heads rolled on the field before Beckett Lupus, along with parts of human anatomy that were beyond civilized description. But more of the men and women of 1ˢᵗ Marine Regiment still threw themselves forward, yelling their determination.

"Get back!" Lupus was calling suddenly, and Earthers up and down the line took up the cry.

The humans, however, had come to save their Earther friends, to buy them time to retreat. They threw themselves at the Kroggs with abandon.

Beckett Lupus spun away — he'd promised Grieve that Gillian Hodge would be saved...

There was Gillian, coming right for him, "Get to firing positions — back off!"

The charge had been moving too fast for her to realize that it was ending in slaughter — she was barely seconds behind the first wave of her marines when she saw the first head roll past her in the opposite direction. Hers were elite humans, acquainted with fighting Krogg soldiers... but the Queen's Guard must have been even more formidable than Gillian had realized.

It was slaughter. The air before her seemed to fill with red mist, and Gillian realized she'd gone one step too far...

She had to fix it.

She caught sight of one of her officers, fighting desperately to avoid the blows of a Krogg... she leveled her bayonet and charged.

Lupus knocked her out cleanly with an elbow to the chin as she tried to pass him, then waved two Genesis marines who'd managed to back off from the fighting to grab her.

Then the Colonel turned to the Krogg line, and he saw over 300 humans — the brave and loyal, hardened troops that had fought the Church on the Plains of Antarctica — die.

Anger writhed inside him.

The Kroggs, finished with the humans, began to turn back to their Earther foes.

Scarce seconds earlier the battle had seemed to be a silent standoff. Perhaps they expected it to stay that way.

But it didn't.

Because Beckett Lupus felt an almost alien *burning* in his blood. He didn't know what it was, but it fired his instincts, and it fueled his anger. Every Earther up and down the line felt the very same sensation, as if a great voice from their blood was crying out.

Kill them.

And as the human bodies fell in pieces to the red clay of Krogg 'A', the Guards Brigade of the Heavy Division of the Earther Marine Corps listened to the demand.

The roar was deafening as they savagely launched themselves into the Kroggs.

The door was blown open by small energy charges, and the remaining forty-four volunteers rushed in.

Grieve was last through, and he stood at Torallis' shoulder, quickly looking over the great room.

For a moment he felt triumphant, but then the absence of the Queen struck him, as did the presence of what must have been hundreds of Queen's Guards.

"We are near! I can *feel* it, Andros!" Torallis' words were sharp, the pain in his mind filling them with an acute immediacy.

Grieve's eyes narrowed as he saw what looked like a door on the far side of the chamber.

"On the far side. It *has* to be."

Torallis forced his mind to clear and nodded towards the hatch.

"To that door!" Grieve roared, and the Earthers acknowledged with what could only be described as a collective snarl.

They rushed into the swelling Kroggs before the aliens could prepare to meet them; the Larosians moved swiftly with their comrades, Torallis making his last command a verbal one.

"We must clear that door! Die well, my friends!"

Grieve's long blade swung fast and hard, and the Earthers ahead of him massed and forced the Kroggs aside as best they could. They began to fall in ones and twos, then in greater numbers.

But missing limbs or stabbed through, the Earthers fought until they fell. And they died only after they had done all the damage they could.

The Kroggs tried to crush them, to force them back, but those still carrying the special tortoise shields pushed the Queen's Guards aside until they were killed from behind.

The Larosians took up the rearguard position, fighting behind Grieve and Torallis to keep them safe from the closing Kroggs. In the great hissing din of the chamber, the roars of the Earthers marked exclamation points, and the volunteers forced their wave through the cavern in a bare minute — giving no time for the Kroggs to reorganize.

Only six of the party concluded the trip — including Grieve and Torallis. And the last four volunteers forced the Kroggs back as the two great leaders worked the last door.

The Kroggs had never witnessed the sort of fury Lupus unleashed, at least not from anyone but themselves. And worse, their Queen was summoning them in panic, so they tried to turn and reach the palace, to help protect her.

But Lupus wouldn't let them go. He couldn't. What drove him was too strong, and it controlled him even as his mind seemed to retreat in disembodied shock at his own ferocity.

"*Don't let them escape!*" the spite and venom in his voice was clearly recognizable, and not a single Earther on the line seemed to waver in spite of its decidedly un-Earther character.

Something powerful... something *hateful* flowed through their veins...

But what is it that can do this to us...

Overhead, a squadron of gunboats laid fire into the front files of the retreating Kroggs. To the rear of the alien horde, the Guards Brigade seemed to leave none alive.

Beckett Lupus knew he wanted to kill every last Krogg he saw, to fill it with terror and eviscerate it as it might a victim. To become worse than–

What the hell is firing in my blood? What am I doing? I cannot let this continue...

Beckett slid to a stop on the red plain, and his swords slowly lowered as he regained his self-control.

As the Earthers hacked into the Kroggs, he looked up and down the lines and watched the Guards Brigade deliver a spectacle of a slaughter which was not in their nature. He could feel something inside him demanding he continue it, but he firmly rejected such a notion.

This could not be allowed any longer.

"Everyone back off. Let them go... I don't know what we're doing. Stop now, everyone..."

As the marines slowed their advance, then stopped all across the plateau, they experienced similar feelings of bewilderment. Sword tips dropped to aim at the ground, and deep, gasping breaths were taken to try to recover faculties that had somehow been wrenched from them.

Something told Beckett, however, that this wasn't the time for reflection.

"Let's collect the wounded and get back to the dropships. We'll need to get off the surface soon."

He hoped for Andros.

The door burst and Andros went through first, followed immediately by Torallis.

As the last two volunteers fought back the throngs of Kroggs on the other side, Grieve drew from his pack a shield generator, set it at the door, then keyed it on. The energy barrier wouldn't keep the Kroggs out forever, but it would buy time.

Then he turned to face the Queen, and his heart seemed to stop for a moment.

He'd been expecting a giant thing, with malicious spines and fangs, a great gleaming eye and other grizzly features.

What he saw was barely taller than a child. With a single eye, a black, unnatural carapace, and an enlarged head. There were no spines, no blades.

This was the Queen.

Torallis approached the thing with his blade leveled, but stopped, his mind filled suddenly with the image of the creature's face, with its cackling voice...

Fail-fail-fail-fail-fail-fail-fail-fail-fail-fail-fail-fail-fail-fail-fail-fail-fail-fail-fail-fail-fail-fail-fail-fail-fail-fail-fail-fail-fail-fail-fail-fail-fail-fail-fail-fail-fail-fail-fail-fail-fail-fail-fail-fail-fail-fail-fail-fail-fail-fail-fail-fail-fail-fail-fail-fail-fail-fail-fail-fail-fail-fail-fail-fail-fail...

Torallis' blade dropped from his hand and he grasped his helmet, his hands forcing the now-useless protector off his head and pressing at his temples. *I will not!*

"Torallis!" Grieve moved to his friend's side and turned the Larosian to face him.

The Larosian's eyes were shriveling, silver blood oozing from every opening...

"I will not *fail*..."

The Larosian fell to his knees...

Weak-weak-weak-weak-weak-weak-weak-weak-weak-weak-weak-weak-weak-weak-weak-weak-weak-weak-weak-weak-weak-weak-weak-weak-weak-weak-weak-weak-weak-weak-weak-weak-weak-weak-weak-weak-weak-weak-weak-weak-weak-weak-weak-weak-weak-weak...

Torallis' body began to convulse, and Grieve put steadying hands on his armor, "Hold on Torallis..."

"We..." the Larosian struggled with his words, "...*die* anyway. *Win! Honor... Praaxus... Me.*"

Die-die-die-die-die-die-die-die-die-die-die-die-die-die-die-die-die-die-die-die-die-die-die-die-die-die-die-die-die-die-die-die-die-die-die-die-die-die-die-die-die-die-die-die-die-die-die-die-die-die-die-die-die-die-die-die-die-die-die-die-die-die-die-die-die-die-die...

Torallis' body convulsed one last time.

He fell forward against Grieve, and the General crouched slowly, looking at the mangled remains of his alien comrade. Silver blood smeared his uniform, and he gently laid Torallis on the spongy, fleshy ground before standing and turning to the Queen.

The meter-high creature looked at him with her eye, and hissed through a tiny mouth at the base of her head.

"*You beast... mind shielded.*"

The words didn't seem to coordinate with the mouth movements, but they echoed through the great conical chamber nonetheless. Grieve spared a glance at the room — the nerve center for the Krogg war effort, perhaps a magnifying chamber that projected the Queen's thoughts out to the stars...

Grieve's eyes shifted back to the alien and his head tilted sideways as he listened.

"*You fight like us but savage and thinking. You destroy my plans. You ruin my fun.*"

Grieve let a small smile cross his face, "I'm glad to hear that."

"*But you are more evil than us. Your blood is a plague... it screams at my mind and is powerful...*"

"Getting better with the English, are you?" Grieve knelt and picked up Torallis' sword.

"*You do not know how much death you bring. Your blood is the destroyer of so much...*"

"And your mind is the destroyer of so much more."

The Queen backed away as quickly as her short legs would move her, and for a second Grieve considered lopping her head off.

But that wouldn't necessarily kill her.

Instead he reached over his shoulder and pulled a second silver box from his pack. This one wasn't a shield.

"You act so righteous, you believe you are good and that your conviction is good for you and for all. But you are no different than mine. We are as you, as determined and as sure of our rightness."

Grieve responded somberly, "Trying to say that we're wrong and you're right? May be true, but all things being relative, I don't much care. If we're wrong for trying to save our home and to right *your* wrongs, fine. My job is to fulfill our promise. To get rid of you."

"Spare me and I will help you fight your blood!"

It had been too long and bloody a day for Grieve to listen to desperate pleas.

He took a deep breath and looked at the Queen, "You've killed so many, and you'll kill so many more."

"No! Spare me — destroy my minions but not me!"

She really was a coward. In the end, a pitiful little coward.

"You didn't spare Savanna Felix. You didn't spare Torallis, or his savior. You didn't spare my marines. Or *anything* you touched, but for humanity. And that was just so you could use them. That was *you*, not your minions."

The Queen hissed angrily, and stamped her feet on the soft ground, *"You are a fool! Your friends died in fools' traps, and now you will die! And I will die winning with the death of so many of yours! You will die, all on this plateau will die! You may have thwarted the destruction of my star, but I will kill many of you more! And then your race will have to come to terms with the blood it holds all alone. The evil! I am nothing next to it!"*

Grieve smiled sadly, "That's it, keep trying."

On the plateau above, Beckett Lupus' earpiece suddenly began picking up on the conversation, as if something had patched him in. He didn't know what... perhaps it was transmitting through Grieve's microphone...

Something told him to get off the plateau — was it in his ear or his *mind*? Well the brigade was boarding the dropships now anyway.

"Get ready to lift off — everyone get aboard quickly!"

Goodbye, Andros.

I should give Beckett time to run... in case she truly will destroy the plateau.

"How can you cope with being what you are? A savage pretending to be civilized?" the Queen was petulant now, and Grieve turned away from her. The shield was beginning to fail.

"You are the greatest contradiction, the worst being, a traitor to what you hold dear!"

Grieve's microphone was still broadcasting, and the telepathic energy permeating the Queen's chamber — the very energy that let her order her fleet — must have carried the signal into space, because it reached *Agamemnon*.

A chill filled the air of the First Rate as the Queen pontificated, and the signal from there was broadcast to all ships in the system.

Sarah, Graham, Liz, Pat, Narosh, Novash, Fox, Chronos, Varnon, Varnia, Garvin, Artemis, Andra, Labrador, and Caine all listened.

The minds of the Earthers twisted at the scathing accusations.

On *Orion*, Caine's dark brooding bubbled up.

Lupus' marines carried the last of the wounded to a landing craft and the ramps came up as quickly as they'd dropped. With boats forming above as cover, the craft lifted off — far lighter than when they'd landed.

Grieve felt them leave.

He couldn't explain just how that worked — perhaps it was a residual effect of the telepathic power of the company he was in.

It didn't matter.

He looked carefully at the silver box in his hand, the energy charge, and opened the lid to the control panel. He just needed to hit the red button.

He turned to the Queen, and the short thing hissed at him one last time, *"You throw your lives away against me! I am nothing next to you! You traitor savages will be the death of all! I hear your blood talking, I know the enemy that is in you! Let me live! Or be a fool! And lose!"*

Grieve blinked two long blinks, and then looked into the Queen's eye.

"We don't lose, you see. We gave our word that we would end this war. And that's what *I'm* going to do. At its source. And nothing you can say will change that fact."

Grieve offered the Queen a reassuring smile, and he heard the shield behind him give out. Kroggs forced their way in through the blasted doorway, and Grieve stood still.

"You see, Queen, it's got nothing to do with what's in our blood. We do what we say we'll do. And we do it our way. That's who we are."

The Queen glared at him as her Guards stormed into the chamber.

Grieve nodded to the Queen, "Whatever else you say about us, that's what we do."

Grieve remembered home, and his friends and family.

And he knew the Queen was wrong.

Because the Earthers were now as they always had been.

And that put him at peace.

He pushed the red button.

In silence, the fleets of the Alliance observed a massive flash as the energy charge mingled with the power of the Queen's mind, and a crater three times as wide as the plateau appeared on the surface of Krogg 'A'.

CHAPTER 60

Andros Grieve's last words echoed all through the fleets of the Alliance, carried by a force no Comm or Signal Officer could quite explain.
But it didn't matter how they spread, just that everyone heard them.

Sarah listened and blinked away tears, though she wasn't sure she should hide them.

Graham stared at the image of the planet and then closed his eyes against the burning. He had no idea what to feel.

Liz frowned as she listened, letting out a breath and nodding very slowly. Then she stared at the floor of her wrecked ship.

Pat stood with his hands behind his back and stared at the planet, because Andros Grieve was right.

Novash felt some surge of sentiment, and he bid farewell to his old comrade. Then the telepathic shock of the Queen's destruction hit him — a raw force of telepathic energy that locked him in his seat.

Narosh and his crew extended their minds in salute, then they too were driven to sit by the telepathic shockwave.

Chronos Claw was stunned, as was his crew. *Flame* sat quietly in space, and everyone aboard was silent.

Atlas was hollow as the words came through the speakers. Fox sat up straighter and stared directly into the plot.

Garvin Jardaw thought of Draco Maximane and knew the words to be true.

Beckett Lupus stared out the dropship window at the planet and slowly closed his eyes.

Varnon placed a reassuring hand on his daughter's arm and silently bid farewell, trying to accept the fact that another dear friend was lost.

•••

Artemis Tigar looked at Andra Ursla, and they stood without speaking on *Agamemnon*'s bridge.

Lab Forepaw patted Caine on the back twice and let his head hang for a second.

"Stand down from action stations," the Flag Captain then turned to the his First Lieutenant, and *Orion* relaxed.

The battle had ended... the fallout needed to be dealt with... in time.

The Krogg stations of the inner defensive sphere had surrendered immediately after the death of their Queen. Leaderless ships returned from their flights, and huddled together with the captured ones in space near Krogg 'A'. Allied vessels collected life pods and combed through the wreckage that littered space.

Pat found his way to *Joseph Barron*.

Sarah didn't know he was coming, and she was sitting at her desk trying to remember if she knew how to sleep when the door chime rang. But she'd already been talking to Graham, so who was at the door...?

Pat.

When Sarah answered the door she was still in a state of stunned silence. She couldn't think and she certainly couldn't feel.

So Pat came in and they simply sat on the couch until somebody remembered how to do some of that thinking and feeling. Talking followed that a few hours later.

When they did at last begin to speak, it was the first very small step to recovery.

Liz boarded *Agamemnon*, the nearest flagship to her towed wreck of a Superdreadnought. She wanted to talk to an old friend, and Andra Ursla was the best she could ask for.

For her part, Ursla was just as much in a state of uncertain disbelief.

When the ArcGeneral knocked on her door, the kodiak Admiral answered and found the start of a smile. They got some fish and ate in silence.

Chronos Claw boarded *Atlas* and shook the hand of his old commander. Fox felt better for the company. The two old comrades went for a drink in the mess, to toast the memory of great Earthers, great humans, and great Larosians.

Novash set *Shanavorus* alongside *Lycrotar*.

We've both survived this trial, he suggested to his senior as they communicated over the short gap between their ships.

Narosh acknowledged. *We have.*

•••

Caine sat alone in his cabin, trying to focus.

But it wasn't working.

His mind wanted to escape the gravity of all that had happened, to go home and to leave this war in the past. He wanted to go live in peace again... to make sure Andros' death was for a good cause.

The knock came at his cabin door during this slow escalation of Caine's short thoughts. He actually didn't hear it, he only noticed when the door opened on its own and a somewhat slumped figure stumbled through.

Caine looked up without interest — his mind not much caring about his immediate surroundings... Then he caught sight of Graham's face, and he waved the younger Manchester to a chair.

Graham sat silently.

The younger Manchester's mind was in turmoil — because he was good at fighting ships, because he missed the dead, because he believed Grieve, because he worried about what he was.

And because after everything they'd been through, he didn't *know* what he was.

Caine was good at sorting out those problems, or at least he always helped with them. Like Varnon did, like Andros had... like so many Earthers could.

Savanna Felix aside, it had been Caine who'd helped him at Gibraltar, when he'd been at his worst, with Sarah gone rogue and the universe in shambles.

And so he looked at Caine's face. Into the wolf's eyes.

They were empty. Caine looked back at Graham with a blank stare, and wondered if the younger Manchester could help sort out the difficulties.

Graham's head sagged, and he flopped back in his chair, staring at the coffee table.

Caine's eyes found the same spot.

"Well, he was right."

Caine blinked slowly at Graham's words.

"Andros was damned right, you know."

Caine looked up slowly and Graham rubbed his eyes for a second.

"You lot are what he said. You're the best of us. The most balanced of us. Neither too good nor too bad."

Caine's eyebrow arched involuntarily, "But we could be either."

Graham winced and tried without success to lean forward, "You *could*. But only if you *let yourselves* be. And say all you like, I know you lot better than all that. Everything you did today, you did to save lives. You keep that in mind when you judge — it saved my homes, your homes, and *Krogg* homes, of all things."

Caine tilted his head.

"Yes indeed. You didn't blow up the planet or some bloody thing, did you? You accepted the sacrifices to do the job right. To do what you said. Just like Andros said," Graham's mind was beginning to lag again. "So now *I* need to figure out *me*."

Caine cocked his other eyebrow, "Ursla and I already figured out humans, I think."

Graham looked at Caine, "Have you indeed?"

"Yep. 'The human equation', we called it. You're all determined to suffer and not to trust your own goodness because you're cynical. And 'the alien equation', well that says the aliens can often make no sense to anyone but themselves... and 'the renegade equation' — that one's Andra's — found that the Freetowners understood us more than most of the Genesis Fleet, because they chose to reject the cynicism."

Graham cocked an eyebrow, "So which one applies to me?"

Caine looked up, "You're Graham Manchester. None of them."

A long blink allowed Graham to absorb that one, "*What?*"

Caine took a deep breath, "Graham, look at all you've done. You're not average, and you're not identical to your sister. You're well-rounded, and you're a leader."

"So I fit nowhere?"

A smile crept over Caine's exhausted face, "You *can* belong wherever you want, Graham. You've done every job in this fleet except marine, and you're in love with one of those. You can handle whatever's handed to you, and that carries a certain responsibility with it."

"Eh?" Graham did lean forward this time.

"You can't just sit back, Graham. You learned the last lessons about how to take control when you found out about Savanna. Now you just need to get used to the idea. You can do *anything*, Graham, just *do* it."

"So I feel awful now because...?"

Caine smiled weakly and got to his feet, walking past the young human and heading towards the fridge.

"There are more than enough dead for one thing. And because you're like me," he patted Graham's shoulder. "You're dead tired, and you've got a conscience backed by a large amount of awareness. Only fools want as much responsibility as we have."

"Fools and *great* humans and Earthers, perhaps. So we've got demons to fight, then."

Caine nodded and poured two glasses of water, then returned and handed one to Graham.

"We all fight our demons, Graham. I just can't tell you how to win yet."

Graham let a sad smile cross his face and then raised his glass, "To Andros, and everyone we lost."

Caine raised his glass as well.

"Indeed."

They drank.

CHAPTER 61

It took more than a little time to recover.

For two days, the feeling within the fleet remained tense — Krogg stations surrendered and Kroggs ships were drawn together and put under guard, the search for Allied survivors intensified, exhausting every ship that had some cruising power.

Fleets that had been committed solely to destruction only days before became rescue formations, and thousands of survivors were pulled from pods drifting through space, or from pockets of atmosphere on demolished ships.

Jax Furgus, true to his reputation, had managed to survive, though he was missing a hand — *Madrid's* loss made something like seven ships shot out from under him in just two years. He announced his intention to retire as soon as he was helped aboard the 74-gun *Illustrious*.

Graham, retreating to his cabin for hours of contemplation, finally emerged in a personable fashion — capable of standing upright and speaking — and after a day of rounding up ships to form a hospital squadron for the wounded, he happened across Gillian Hodge. They both needed reassuring, so they talked for hours.

Just like Pat and Sarah, who regained speech capabilities some four hours after the latter's arrival on *Joseph Barron*. Then they promised to spend a *lot* of quality time together after rescue operations were completed and they got things sorted out.

Graham was beginning to realize that, with all the misery they were really going through out here, he wanted his relationships to be more than idle sport. He didn't have time to waste on being heartsick, he wanted to spend time with the woman he loved.

He nearly said the 'M' word, in fact.

Serious things, then.

After her meal with Ursla, Liz found her way to *Joseph Barron* just as Sarah and Pat were parting company. Pat was returning his flag to a Battlecruiser again and Sarah was trying to piece together what was left of her scattered fleet. With so much movement going on in order to rescue survivors, the latter seemed an impossible goal. Sarah capitulated and sat down with Liz for a few hours.

• • •

Fox and Chronos finished their toasts and went about the business of locating survivors, *Flame* finding over sixty pods and *Atlas* and *Vulcan* locating some seventy more. Finding the provisions for ship repair to be inadequate, Fox then rendezvoused with the Earther transports that were reordering themselves after their hasty flight during the battle, and got the mobile fleet yards unloaded. Commissioning each of the repair bases would take a few days, but once done, the fleets could patch up their wounded for the long cruise home.

Varnon and Varnia enjoyed their cooperative command aboard *Algenon*, and as the Fifth Fleet was the only one approaching organization at the end of the battle, they took it upon themselves to pen the Krogg ships that had surrendered into a small quadrant surrounding an unprotected feeding station.

Narosh and Novash met aboard *Lycrotar* to account for their losses and make provisions for the carrying home of the injured. Their hospital ships had been destroyed, leaving the wounded from the wrecked ships without any care. It was decided to divide them amongst Warcruisers of the fleet, as unfortunately few of those elite ships had survived.

Ursla and Tigar set about trying to reorganize the fleet. Casualties had been high, and the scraps of the fleets that had gone in all directions during the action needed time to pull together and rebuild administrations. Officers needed to be promoted to fill gaps, the trip home needed to be considered.

Such reorganization as Ursla contemplated was nominally Caine's job, but a matter of slightly greater concern dominated the First Lord's mind. As the decision to spare the Kroggs had been his responsibility, he now elected to sit across from three surviving Krogg Telepaths and Warlords, and deliver to them the terms of their surrender.

The terms of their *survival*.

So with Lab Forepaw to his right, Colonel Beckett Lupus to his left, and the remains of Howler's squad of marines standing behind them, he sat at the table in *Orion's* main briefing room. His eyes narrowed as he looked across the tabletop at the pair of Telepaths and the Warlord who seemed to lead them. The former pair seemed particularly terrified of him — and of all the Earthers. They probably knew precisely what Grieve had done — the Queen's link to them had likely proved enlightening. So they had put someone of nominal lower rank, a Warlord, in charge of speaking to Caine.

Without the commanding influence of their monarch, and in the presence of the Earthers, whose minds were invulnerable to them, the Kroggs seemed quiet, docile, passive. That was why neither Larosian nor human delegates were present — there would be *no* leverage for the Kroggs in this meeting.

This trio had been summoned off Krogg 'A' and out of the surrendered fleet — they had been selected by their few thinking peers to meet the Earthers.

Where Krogg soldiers and ships lacked the mental abilities to act on their own, Telepaths and Warlords were capable of thought, though they seemed hardly as formidable without the overpowering direction of their Queen.

The question remained, however, as to how they would react when Caine delivered the terms.

At this point, nothing about their demeanor suggested they'd become too violent.

Nor should they — Caine had conceived of these terms of capitulation in consultation with Ursla, Liz, Sarah, and Narosh the day before, and while they were only provisional, they would be the basis for the status of the Kroggs once ratified by the governments of the Alliance, and particularly by the Earther Consulate.

The leading Warlord fixed its eye on Caine, "You *ssummmoned* usss."

Oh *typical*. The hissing 's-thing'.

Caine nodded slowly and looked at each of the aliens, "I have terms for your surrender. Your Queen is dead, and we understand that to mean that your war effort is *dead*. We have no quarrel with you if you do not intend to pursue further aggression."

The Kroggs stared blankly at him, and Caine felt slightly unsettled at having three big eyes peering at him instead of six average-sized ones.

"You mean not to *exterminate* usss?" the Warlord's head tilted awkwardly.

'Exterminate' came in what seemed a sharp nasal hiss — like nails on a chalkboard. Caine almost flinched.

"The Larosians would *exterminate* usss," a Telepath said quickly, glaring at Caine.

The First Lord paused and glanced first to Forepaw, who shrugged, and then to Lupus, whose eyebrow was arched.

"Well, sorry to disappoint you, but we're letting you live, under a certain number of conditions."

Telepathically, the Kroggs muttered in surprise and interest, then one hissed, "What are we to do alive without our Queen?"

Caine laced his fingers and laid his hands on the table before him, "You'll have to learn to live on your own, make your own decisions. From what I'm told, you're not *unintelligent*, you Telepaths and Warlords, so we expect you to take control of your population."

"To breed a new *Queen*?"

The aliens seemed to make words they wished to emphasize painful to hear. Had they been trying to be intimidating, they could certainly have pulled it off...

"*No* new Queen, or we *will* wipe you out."

The Kroggs again muttered to each other telepathically.

"What *then*?"

Caine took a breath. He'd hoped they'd have a revelation, but it seemed unlikely this would happen after so long being dominated...

Lupus cleared his throat, "You're going to have to figure that out yourselves. You get to do whatever you want, within certain restrictions."

There was a look of understanding among the Kroggs. Maybe. On the Krogg face, that could have been confusion as much as understanding...

"*We* control?" the Warlord waved his arms to encompass his two fellows.

"We're not putting you three specifically in charge," Caine said cautiously. "Any groups with the ability for rational thought will do fine. Choose leaders and stick with them. And we'll remain in control out here, supervising everything you do."

They hissed in what Caine hoped was understanding.

"You understand, then?"

"Our caste shall rule... we understand."

Caine blinked. Alright, that went better than it could have.

"What ruless must we rule by?" another Krogg hissed, and Caine nodded, tapping the holo tank at the center of the table active.

The Kroggs lurched back in surprise as the Krogg system filled the table in blue light. A red sphere surrounded Krogg 'A', with only three million kilometers clearance around the outside of the planet itself.

"You'll be required to release all of your warships, to let them graze on the stations that are left, and to live without your control. They reproduce on their own?"

"They release *eggss.*"

Caine cocked an eyebrow, "Indeed. They get to go about their lives on their own. You and your people are to be restricted to this sphere, and you are not to have more than ten small ships capable of interstellar travel, or *any* ships capable of combat. You will not attempt to birth a new Queen, nor will you develop any weapons. You're to try to develop your race however you see fit, but not in a way that could threaten us or any other living species."

The Kroggs paused in mild surprise, "No conquest? We are not slaves of war?"

Caine frowned, "Pardon?"

One of the Telepaths hissed in surprise at Caine's lack of understanding, "In old timesss, when many Queens fought, the *defeated* would become soldiers of the *victor*. They would conquer in the name of the new Queen."

"Nope. None of that," Caine sat back and re-laced his fingers. "As I said, we'll be leaving a significant force here to make sure you abide by the rules, and we'll be maintaining our station at Gibraltar. Your leadership will be required to make regular contact with our in-system commander, and you must be ready to allow inspectors at any time. Remember we had the ability to find your Queen this time — you won't be able to hide anything from us."

That last bit was a complete bluff, but he didn't want a caste of Kroggs who had been fighting wars for millennia to get any ideas. This was going to be hard enough as it was.

"Our *stationsss* will be abandoned?"

Caine nodded, his ears slowly adjusting to the emphasis shrill, "Yes. Are they self-aware?"

"*No*. Flesh only. They serve but are not thinking. Food for our shipsss if nothing else."

"Well then when you free your ships, the stations will be taken care of."

"They will be *eaten*."

Caine nodded, "Yes. Now, is this acceptable to you? Confinement and reorganization — you understand?"

The Kroggs passed thoughts to each other, "We understand. As the vanquished we *ssswwearr* loyalty to you, Queen."

Caine blinked twice, "Not *quite*."

So it would be a bit of a long meeting after all, but it was much better than genocide. And maybe the Kroggs would prove productive one day...

Well, that might be a stretch.

CHAPTER 62

Orion's upper officer's mess was cluttered with Earthers, humans, and Larosians. At long last, the atmosphere seemed to have lightened.

The Allies had won a massive war, and they'd gotten enough things organized in the twelve days since the final battle's end to have time for Pat to pull together another spirit-lifter. No one else seemed to have the Irishman's knack when it came to these things — most had by now credited it to good celtic blood on his part.

So *Orion's* mess buzzed with life as high-ranking officers from every fleet drifted, drank, and celebrated the culmination of the campaign.

Despite being the planner, though, Pat wasn't the host.

"Come *on* Sarah, girl! Stop pecking at it!" Pat shoveled another forkload of fish into his mouth and chased it with an intoxicating Earther beverage called 'apple juice'. It looked like liquor — but wasn't!

Sarah raised an amused eyebrow at the emptying plate next to her and then looked contemptuously at her own serving, "Why do we have to have *food* at these sorts of things? I thought we were supposed to mix, celebrate... be *happy*."

Pat swallowed, "Food brings happiness, Sarah! It's a fact of existence — look at Novash!"

The Larosian was across the room enjoying a piece of chocolate cake — something undertaken with great reserve after numerous scans by the medical department to ensure it was safe for him to consume. He did look happy...

"But I'm *not* hungry Pat..."

"Like bloody fun, you're just afraid to eat in front of so many people!"

Sarah scowled, "Now that's ridiculous!"

Pat grinned, stopping his fork in mid-lift, "Is it? Go on then."

He dropped his fork and sat up straight, watching her.

With an amused expression, she took a bite, and then proceeded to eat more, stopping between chews, "See."

Pat shrugged, "Got you eating, didn't I?"

She frowned for a second and then elbowed him. He chuckled and continued to eat.

"Take it easy on my brother-in-law to be, Sarah!"

Sarah paused as she was lifting her fork and looked up with a frown. Graham was standing there with a grin as broad as his mouth would allow, Gillian on his arm, "Congratulations big sister..."

He put a hand on Sarah's shoulder and looked to Pat. The Irishman's glare chilled him, and Pat cleared his throat, "Hadn't gotten *that* far yet, Graham. Thanks."

Graham's grin faded to a nervous smile... "Oh. Well. Y'see. Well. Um..."

"I think I need to go over there, Graham. Come along, would you?" Gillian, well acquainted with Pat, knew when to retreat.

Indeed, retreat was a word she had been forced to come to terms with after the problems on Krogg... and her chin still hurt. She didn't want to think about what she'd seen. For now she gently pulled Graham away.

Sarah's head slowly turned to Pat, and the Irishman laid his fork down and wiped his mouth with a napkin.

"By the way, Sarah, I've got a question for you..."

"You believe you can trust them, Setter?"

Narosh stood beside Caine, looking out the mess windows at the reorganized Earther First Fleet. Numbering 511 ships, the First was almost in good enough shape to permit the cruise home...

Caine sighed and shrugged, turning away from the window and taking a drink of water before facing the Larosian, "I really have no idea. They seemed receptive enough, but I'm still leaving a couple of fleet divisions here. I'll be sorting that out tomorrow or the next day... I think I know who'll volunteer. With luck the Kroggs will see the writing on the wall."

Narosh tilted his head and also took a sip of water, noticing to himself that he seemed to savor the taste and smoothness of the liquid more than he had before his accident, "What writing? Where is the wall?"

Caine paused and then a smile spread across his face.

"What?"

The First Lord chuckled and patted the Larosian on the back.

Fox Magnus sat across a table from Ursla, with Chronos Claw sitting on his right and Artemis Tigar facing the Commander of *Flame* from Ursla's side.

"So I hear there's to be a permanent station set up here," Fox leaned back in his chair slightly, and Ursla — already well back in her seat — nodded.

"We'll be leaving about 200 ships and some stations here to begin with. If the Kroggs follow the rules, we'll probably pull much of that back to Gibraltar in time."

Fox took a long sip of water and frowned, "Looking for volunteers?"

Ursla nodded absently, "Probably the best way to do it. A lot of people want to get home."

"Mmm," Tigar nodded.

Claw and Fox looked at each other, and mischievous smiles spread on their faces as their eyes met. Open space with 200 ships, some Kroggs to keep in line, and prospects for the unknown. Somehow that sounded appealing...

They looked back to Ursla and Fox grinned, "Sign us up."
Tigar chuckled, "You youngsters…"

"Dad!"
Varnon looked up abruptly as his daughter stopped in front of him. He put on an innocent face and tugged the napkin out of his collar, "What?"
Varnia leaned over his plate, "You keep eating like that and you'll be dead before you're 150."
Frowning, Varnon heaved a sigh. He reluctantly pushed the plate away and Varnia picked it up, "That's better. Have some fruit."
She turned and walked away, and Varnon tucked the napkin back into his collar. He leaned over in front of Forepaw, "She's worse than her mother."
The Flag Captain smiled and then frowned as his plate was removed to Broadpaw's safekeeping, "Mind if I have this?"
Lab Forepaw arched his brow, "I don't suppose it'd matter if I said I did."
Varnon grinned and shook his head, and Forepaw chuckled, "I'll get more before your daughter comes and takes the rest."

"Garvin!"
Jardaw, standing out of place in the corner, almost flinched in surprise as Jax Furgus called to him and came over, holding a glass in his single hand. The polar bear offered a small smile to the one-handed Rear Admiral, and Furgus extended his hand to–
Oops, stub, not hand.
He looked down at it with a frown and then looked up at Jardaw, "Hmm, guess no handshakes for a while."
Jardaw smiled a bit, "No, I suppose not…"
"Ahh, brighten up, Garvin. Draco really wouldn't have wanted you to be glum."
Jardaw stiffened a bit, but nodded. Then he drank some juice and laughed with the one-handed Furgus.

Liz marveled at Novash's capacity for cake.
"So you're still not full?"
The Larosian tilted his head, "Full? It would take rather more than four cake pieces to completely fill me, I think."
"Really?"
The Larosian bobbed his head in a nod, "Yes… my estimates provide my stomach with the capacity for about thirty-two pieces of this size — accounting for processing time, of course."
Liz frowned, and Novash tilted his head, "Is that a problem?"
For all her time with the Alliance, Liz had never spent much with the Larosians. This brief encounter seemed to be as telling for her as her first meal with Ursla had been. She recalled that conversation with Andra, when the bear

had thought her to be 200 years old... bah! Well, now she'd heard of Earther drugs under development that could double human lifespans and youthfulness and such... yes, under *development*.

But no Earther drug provided for thirty-two pieces of cake.

"No..." she said finally in answer, "just wish I could eat that much... Wait a second, will you get fat?"

Novash's eyes seemed to glaze even *more* silvery for a second, "Fat?"

Liz closed her eyes and shook her head. *Grass is always greener on the other side...*

Novash tilted his head, "What does that mean?"

Liz smacked her forehead. Damned telepaths.

"Well *pardon* us," Novash smiled.

Lupus arrived a bit late. He'd been toasting the memory of Private Graxton with Howler's squad, and now, in *Orion's* marine mess, the Guards Brigade officers and NCOs were having a similar gathering to the one happening here. As senior Earther marine in system, he'd been invited to both, and so he'd spent time with his marines first.

Now he walked right into Graham and Gillian, Graham throwing back quite a sizable glass of apple juice as the Colonel saw him.

"The Earthers say this is as close to alcohol as they get... why don't I feel better?"

Lupus stopped in front of the couple, "Probably because it's unfermented fruit juice."

Graham stopped in mid step to avoid hitting the wolf, and his nose went forward into his glass, "Dammit..."

He put the glass down on the nearby counter and wiped his nose with the back of his hand, "Beckett, how are you old fellow?"

Lupus shrugged, "Alright I think, you?"

Gillian cleared her throat, "Mister Tact here just congratulated Sarah on her engagement."

A surprised look crossed Lupus' face. The Colonel had been fighting alongside both Sarah and Pat since before Antarctica... usually their intentions seemed obvious enough to him, but he'd missed this. Though it was inevitable, wasn't it, that they final marry, since they'd survived...

"I didn't realize..."

Gillian smiled, "Neither did she, before *he*–" she elbowed Graham lightly "–*told* her."

Lupus paused, then grinned, patting Graham on the shoulder, "Swift move. Well done."

Graham smiled mockingly and bobbed his head, "Oh *thanks*..."

"So it was a figure of speech, then."

"Precisely!" Caine grinned at Narosh and the Larosian smiled slightly in kind.

"Meaning can be very hard to discern without telepathy, it seems," Narosh continued, drinking.

Caine nodded, then caught sight of Lupus at the door, "Aha. That's everyone — I've got to do the toast. Hang on Narosh..."

The Admiral-of-a-Fleet nodded, and Caine moved to the center of the windows, "Alright, attention everyone... come on..."

Officers put down forks and stood, shedding napkins and the like. Everyone gathered around Caine in a semicircle, Narosh standing on his flank.

As his comrades steadied themselves, Caine glanced around to ensure glasses were in hand...

"Well, this isn't all just about the food. We've come a long way and we've lost quite a few friends. Right now I want to mention five officers from among us, commanders who had been with us for a long time..."

The room turned respectably somber — though noticeably not sad. The time for grief was passing, now was the time for remembering... as best those two could be separated, they would be.

Caine pressed on, "First, to Bill Wallace of the Genesis Sixth..."

There were nods of agreement — the ArcLieutenant-General's ship had yet to be found... in its entirety.

"And to Draco Maximane..."

Jardaw nodded and sighed, as did everyone.

"Our dear friend Savanna Felix..."

There were greater nods and sighs. Felix hadn't seen the last battle, but he'd probably saved it with his sacrifice.

"And then Captain-Elite Torallis, of the Stealth Guard..."

Narosh and Novash drew themselves to full height at the mention, and Earthers and humans who knew the Captain straightened as well.

"And of course, to Andros Grieve."

"Indeed," Varnon spoke up.

"Hear hear," Liz raised her glass.

A rumble of agreement washed over the group.

"A toast to them," Caine said, raising his glass. "Our brave friends."

Each officer raised a glass, "Our friends..."

They drank, and then the glasses came down and eyes turned back to Caine.

"And, of course, to all those whose names we didn't know. Those who have fought for us all this time, and died in service of our mission out here. We owe them as much, if not more. So this one to them, our brave fellows who will not return home with us."

Caine lifted his glass high again, and all assembled matched him, "To our brave fellows..."

They all drank, and once again the glasses came down, and Caine drew the attention of all assembled.

He looked over the officers for a second — some he'd counted on since the first day, some he'd met only recently. But all of them were to be trusted. They were the best...

"Well, that's all I can think of... anyone else need to say anything?"

Pat looked at Sarah, and Sarah looked at Pat.

"You tell them," she said with a bit of a smile.

"Why me? No, *you* tell them."

"No, it was your idea..."

"Yes, but it was *your* fault..."

"How do you figure that?"

"Oh *I* don't know... that whole love thing maybe."

Caine cleared his throat, and the two looked up quickly, only to find all eyes directed their way.

"Something you kids would like to share with the group?" Liz was the first to get a word in.

Pat and Sarah looked at each other and frowned...

"Graham!"

All eyes turned to the junior Manchester, and he stood frozen. Gillian nudged him, and he sighed.

"You've all met my *brother-in-law to be*."

There were cheers, and a toast.

CHAPTER 63

The affair didn't end for hours, but when things finally began to break up Pat and Sarah left to figure out what to do with engaged life. Liz grinned as she watched them go, finding herself next to Varnon.

"Feel like I'm watching my daughter, though Pat's almost like a son too..."

Varnon flashed an amused grin, "Scandalous."

Liz elbowed him, "Watch it, your little girl will probably find an appealing canine any day now."

Broadpaw chuckled, "Un*likely*... where is she, anyway...?"

"Why... isn't that her over there, talking with Lab Forepaw?"

Varnon's expression grew instantly serious.

Another Flag Captain? Nah.

Liz chuckled.

"You're sure you don't want any support?"

Narosh shook his head, and Novash spoke, "We appreciate it, Setter. But we must do this ourselves."

"You won't take the Genesis route home?" Graham frowned at the aliens, but Narosh shook his head slowly.

"We need to collect the Battleships we left on blockade, and trying to take a shortcut might send us into the hands of the plague when we cross into our own galaxy."

Graham nodded slowly, "I suppose so. Well, drop us a line any time..."

Narosh paused and read the meaning of the figure of speech from Graham's mind, "Right. We should agree on a way to identify official traffic, shouldn't we?"

Caine nodded slowly, "A code phrase, perhaps... something identifiable as yours. To make sure the quarantine isn't broken."

Narosh paused thoughtfully, then approximated a smile, "*The writing is on the wall.*"

Caine cocked an eyebrow, "Works."

Novash paused quizzically, but then read the meaning and context of the wall comment from his senior's mind.

Graham frowned but Caine leaned towards him, "Tell you later."

"Ahh... right, sounds good!"

The four officers stood for a few seconds more, then Narosh extended his hand, "We will go then... may fortune favor you both."

He shook Graham's hand as well, then Novash did the same, "Goodbye Setter, Graham."

"We'll see you again, I think," Caine said slowly... "Don't ask me why I know. Good luck."

"Indeed!" Graham stepped back after Novash's hand withdrew, "I know you'll find a way to cook that plague."

Cook it? Narosh read Graham's mind again...

"I hope you are right," he paused and looked between the two again. His blood seemed to itch a little, and he bow-nodded, "Goodbye."

Novash did the same, "Be *seeing* you."

The pair turned and exited the mess, and Graham and Caine glanced at each other and smiled, then Graham followed them out.

Jardaw and Furgus found themselves in conversation with Fox and Claw...

"Staying, you say? That sounds interesting," Furgus said with a bit of a frown.

Fox grinned, "Think of the fun, Jax! Whatever goes on will start here... probably!"

Furgus chuckled, "If I were thirty years younger... well, no, if I had *one* more hand, I might sign up. You kids have fun."

Fox chuckled and patted the Rear Admiral on the back, "Yeah, you too 'old fella'."

Jardaw, with a bit of a serious face, looked between Fox and Claw, "Where do I sign up?"

Tigar left to warm up *Agamemnon's* pinnace while Caine drifted to where Varnon was talking Ursla's ear off–

"Do you think Lab likes her? I mean... he's never shown much interest in romance before, but he's never had time to really relax... You think, I mean... is he... you know..."

"He's a *puppy*, Varnon. Stop worrying, Varnia's a grown-up now," Caine interrupted, and Ursla grinned.

Varnon cocked a suspicious eyebrow, "Easy for *you* to say."

Caine chuckled, "Don't worry, I'll get mine when Phealan grows up. Meantime, you go pry your daughter away from my Flag Captain — I'll be needing him to run the ship in a while."

Varnon left his fellow Admirals with a determined step, and Ursla and Caine chuckled in his wake.

"Poor guy," Ursla grinned.

Graham and Gillian were just on their way out when Lupus left, and they caught up to him in the hall as they walked towards the lift.

"Beck," Gillian's hail brought the Colonel around, and he smiled.

"How's the chin?"

Gillian winced a bit, "Tender."

Lupus 'hmmmed', "Yes... sorry about that."

Gillian's face sobered and she looked at the wolf, "Why'd you do it, by the way?"

The Colonel paused and Graham looked between the two, "What sort of question is that?"

Lupus opened his mouth and closed it, then opened it again, "It's a wise one... One of the last things Andros asked me to do was to keep you out of harm's way... said the two of you might have roads to go down."

Gillian had to try to keep her jaw up, and she looked at Graham, who frowned, recalling a conversation with Grieve in the observation lounge over *Algenon's* flight deck. The thoughtful bastard had been looking out for the two of them even while he'd been preparing to save the universe.

"Well..." Graham swallowed.

Lupus nodded, "I think the lesson is not to let him down."

Graham and Gillian nodded slowly.

"Thanks..."

"Yeah... thanks..."

"We'll see you later..."

The pair slowly passed Lupus, and he sighed, a strange thought crossing his mind. He'd managed to save both of the Manchester's love lives — that'd definitely go on the resume.

"I should be in their wills," he muttered with a grin, then paused and looked at the ceiling, "And you too, Andros."

He paced off, unaware that Varnia had been watching with interest from the door as she waited for her father... Lupus certainly did seem to be an interesting character...

"Colonel!" she called, "Wait up..."

"So, Lab..."

Forepaw raised his eyebrows at Varnon, "Yes, Varnon?"

Broadpaw paused... cleared his throat, "Well, Lab... what are your intentions with my daughter?"

Forepaw blinked, and slowly frowned.

"Um. Well, when I get promoted, I want her to take my place on *Orion*..."

Varnon's eyes narrowed, "*And?*"

Forepaw smiled curiously, "And *nothing*, Varnon. I'm not looking at Naval officers for myself, really... I'd like to settle down with a botanist. Or a doctor."

Varnon's eyes opened again, "Oh *good!*"

He patted Lab on the shoulder, "Glad to hear it. Don't have to give you a beating."

Forepaw chuckled, "You think you could take me on?"

Varnon shrugged, "I couldn't take Beckett or anything... but I could handle you..."

He turned to look for his daughter...

"Hey, where'd she go?"

Forepaw frowned, "I wasn't paying attention actually."

Ami Cairn and Dran Nightclaw were passing Varnon while talking about frigate-related topics, but hearing Broadpaw's question, the former Commodore stopped, "You say you were looking for Varnia?"

Varnon nodded immediately, and Cairn bobbed her head towards the door, "She just left with Beckett Lupus."

As the Commodores moved off, Varnon's face blanked.

"You said you didn't think you could take Beckett, right?" Lab chuckled and sipped his water.

"There an arms locker around here?"

EPILOGUE

The Larosians had left the day before, and now the Earther and Genesis Fleets were packing up to do the same — save for 200 ships under the command of Fox Magnus and Garvin Jardaw, who had volunteered to stay behind.

From *Atlas*, the former now oversaw the final Krogg abandonment of the fortresses, and watched the first of the ships be set free. Those ships weren't all that sure what to do without telepathic yokes on them, but slowly they found their way to food, and eventually into some sort of social groups.

A few 74s watching the process seemed to have been 'adopted' by some of the ships — it seemed that despite years of war, the Krogg vessels had little concept of animosity... without their masters manipulating them, at least.

The rest were slowly being set loose, and the perimeter zone around Krogg was being laid out. Fox was enjoying it... and he had a feeling that things might just work out here.

Pat's Posse had, at last, been reduced to just 'Pat's Pirates' again, Pat had turned command over to his XO for the cruise to Gibraltar, and Sarah had turned total fleet command over to Liz. Now they enjoyed some quality time on *Joseph Barron*, and tried to get themselves out of the pattern of stress that had been so devastating.

It wasn't *that* hard, it seemed.

And of course, their decision gave Liz a chance to command the fully assembled Genesis Fleet — such as it was — for the first time without a Church overseer. It felt good, and in order to chaperone the two 'kids' of hers, she elected to fly her flag from *Joseph Barron*. As the Genesis Fleet began to accelerate into flux drive, she was happy.

Graham was happy too, and beginning to feel remotely like himself at last. Even though he hadn't given up command of a major chunk of the fleet for the cruise home, flux travel tended to leave time for relaxation and recreation. And Gillian was making the passage home on *Edgar Fitzpatrick*.

Good things all around.

For some reason, Beckett Lupus was feeling alright too. He still sparred with Sergeant Howler, and since he was making passage home on *Algenon*, he'd have plenty of recreational time.

Varnon, however, was very *unhappy*.

In a fatherly way.

But Varnia, ultimately, was very *happy*... so Varnon was secretly — top secretly — happy for his daughter.

Forepaw felt more relaxed on his bridge, though that wasn't to say he was less himself than before. He was still the Flag Captain, and even though he knew promotion was likely to be close to immediate when he got home, he wanted his ship to run smoothly.

It ran *perfectly*, as always.

And in a tradition that had developed unofficially in the years since the humans had reached Earth, Caine sat in the main observation lounge in *Orion's* upper hull, and watched his ships preparing to leave.

He heard Ursla come in and sit down, but didn't turn to face her right away.

"So this is it then... the last time we'll have a meeting like this after a battle?" Ursla leaned back in her chair and looked across the table. Caine slowly turned and frowned.

"You know, I wouldn't mind if it was... but it won't be."

Ursla cocked an eyebrow, "You really think the Kroggs are going to stir up trouble?"

Caine steepled his fingers in front of his chin and looked thoughtfully at the table, "No... no, I just have this *feeling*."

All Ursla could do was shrug, "Either way, this war is done. So I can give this back to you."

Laying the picture of Elandra and Phealan on the table, she smiled, "You earned it."

Reaching out and picking up the image, Caine felt a smile form on his lips. He'd see them soon. And he'd be going home with the same principles he'd left with.

The same ideals he'd started this whole journey with.

He wasn't the same — no, too much had happened to leave him unchanged. He'd seen too much. Done too much.

But he hadn't betrayed himself... and for that he was happy.

Earthers had died in this war, but they'd died as they'd lived. They'd chosen to join, they'd chosen their fate... and that wasn't just a mind-settling generalization. It was the truth.

Ursla knew exactly what he was thinking.

"You hit it on the head when you addressed the fleet, you know. Just as Andros did with the Queen."

Caine looked up from the picture slightly perplexed, "How do you mean?"

Ursla smiled, "We do what we say we'll do. And we do it in a way that reflects *us*. That's what this whole thing's been about. We've kept our word since we vowed to protect Earth... since we promised to help the humans restore Genesis. And we've done whatever was necessary to make good on our promise."

Thoughtfully, Caine looked back down at the picture.

"Wasn't easy," Ursla leaned back in her chair, "and we lost a lot of people. But every one of us was obliged to do as was promised. Everyone agreed to that by being with us instead of leaving. We kept our word. We didn't violate our principles."

"And we bled to do it."

Ursla nodded in agreement, "Yes we did."

Caine gently laid the picture on the table and looked across at his friend, "That seems to be our lot in life, doesn't it?"

Ursla smiled, "What, doing what we say we'll do, no matter the cost? Following our principles, being ourselves? All that?"

It took Ursla just a second to realize exactly where Caine was going — what *equation* this was adding up to.

She smiled, "It does sum us up. I suppose you could say it's the..."

Caine held up his hand and matched his friend's smile, "Don't you steal my thunder..."

He thought back to a morning on a pinnace before he'd taken over the fleet, and a conversation with Ursla just before she'd left for Genesis, and another after the battle there, and the last one after Gibraltar.

The universe made sense some days.

"That's the *Earther* equation."

They smiled.

POSTSCRIPT

Transcript of Setter Caine's Inaugural Consular Address to the Earther People, Ten Years after the conclusion of the Krogg War.

Good day to you all — and thank you.

I've taken my seat as First Consul, effective this morning at 09:00, and I may now speak on behalf of the Consulate, fully and with their support. You know me — I am a Navy Lord. I have been for a long time, and I was during the Krogg War. I've played a role in the fighting that we've done, and now it's time I play a role in the peace we've made.

For seven hundred years we expected the humans to come, and they have. They've fulfilled the promises left to us in the documents of their forefathers, and we've extended to them the friendship that would maintain the safety of Earth. Now their question is settled, as is that of the sanctity of their new world. We've stopped a scourge that once terrorized the galaxy, and we've done so without the betrayal of our morality.

We've conducted ourselves with honor and dignity, and we've reached the natural end of the plans we established so many generations ago.

Now we face a challenge of a wholly different kind. We've stood together for centuries, with a very clear, unified goal — to protect our world. And we've succeeded; our determination and our loyalty to each other have carried us through the most dire circumstances imaginable. And we've *won*.

All that remains is to choose our next path, and that, I believe, may be the most difficult task we've had to face in all our time together. With that I mean not to slight us as a people — as you all so well know, we've stood together through burdens that would have overwhelmed many of Earth's civilizations. I refer only to the unknown nature of the future — the new journeys we face have not been mapped out: there are no ancient logs to tell us where we must go, or what the threat to our home will be. We face a challenge: this time we face the future with complete blindness.

And I believe we are *ready* to do that.

In our centuries together we have not been stagnant. Our time has been framed by consistencies, but it has also been marked by growth. We are not the same beings who emerged from our parent species seven centuries ago. We are not even the same people who met the humans on the Pluto Orbital Plane. We have been to war, and we have fought it on a scale that had not been conceived of before it came about. We *chose* to join a battle in the name of good and at the obligation of our word, we followed through.

It is something we have *always* done with each other, always *intended* to do when we met others, yet as the humans so fervently claim, things cannot be proved until they're tested. I must admit that I now understand their point — it is not a matter of giving a simple oath, but of committing to it.

That is something we have done.

That is something we have done *well*.

As Earthers, we have not strayed from our morals, in spite of what we've suffered. Our costs have been great, and many have paid with their lives. Many have suffered for our resolve, but they have not — and we should not — doubt the resolve we've shown.

Now it's a matter of choosing a new course for that resolve.

The direction we take will define us in the centuries to come — it will shape the lives of our children and our grandchildren. And none of us can honestly claim to know where that future will lie. We must trust our judgment, and trust our instinct. These decisions will not be made lightly, but I can assure you, as you can assure yourselves, they will be made wisely.

We've never been an impetuous people. We are determined, but not careless. This time the choice we face may be uncertain — our path into the future lies behind a shroud that we cannot see past. But we advance into the darkness of time with the strength gained from our struggles, and our resolve to remain true to who and what we are.

Our character has not changed, nor will it. Not fundamentally, not in a way that matters. We will grow as we reach out into space; we will not betray ourselves. Understand that as you look up at the stars at night. Be certain of that as you watch them flutter by.

We go into the universe with the same spirit that holds us so tightly to our home. Challenges will present themselves, and we will *overcome* them. It is nothing new to us, it is something we accept. We cannot fear it, and we understand that.

The time for our decision is at hand. We will make it. And we will be right.

If we aren't at first, we'll *make* it right — because that is what we do. And that is what we believe.

It isn't a simple matter of principle, it is a matter of *fact.*

As Earthers, we are to chart our new course together.

I look forward to the journey.

Thank you all.

APPENDIX A: CHARACTERS

Here we are again, new book and new list of characters. By now we have plenty of Earthers, humans and Larosians running around doing a lot of different things, so hopefully this list can help you if you have questions about who's where and why! By the way, you're probably going to hear that a lot of these people are the very best, the most elite, the most spectacular, etc. I guess that's why we've been following them for this whole series!

Broadpaw, Varnia — Flag Captain, ENS Tonnant
Savanna Felix's Flag Captain and Varnon Broadpaw's "little girl" (a designation she tolerates because her dad doesn't seem to care that she technically shouldn't be called a 'girl'), Varnia is one of the Earther Navy's rising stars — and for her skill, not her family lineage. A cool combat commander who has a penchant for making the right calls at the right moments, she's moved from commanding a gun deck on *Orion* straight into command of *Tonnant* and Flag Captaincy of the Third Fleet without so much as a hiccup. Felix is lucky to have her; she's got a bright future ahead.

Broadpaw, Varnon — Admiral, Fifth Fleet
Perpetually witty (if not always funny), Varnon remains perhaps the most light-hearted of the Earther flag officers. He's proud of his daughter, happy to be away from the dietary restrictions imposed by his wife, and even more pleased to be at the head of the newly-formed Fifth Fleet, a fresh formation built up of the newest Earther ships out of the yards and crewed primarily by the survivors of the many destroyed ships the war has seen. After the war he's thinking about Consulship, but he wants to make sure he and his daughter survive unscathed before he starts getting too far ahead of himself.

Caine, Setter – First Lord of the Admiralty & Admiral, First Fleet
Setter Caine remains the patriarch of the Earther Navy. His guidance has carried the war to its final days on the Allied front, and as his ships blockade the Krogg systems it will be left to him to decide how the Allies should end the war. He's tired, he's worn, and he's not so sure of himself as he once was, but those who call him the greatest Earther ever to live may not be far wrong. History will decide — there's much more for him to do yet. His flag still flies from *Orion*, the ship from which he's commanded since the very beginnings of this war.

Cairn, Ami — Commodore, 141ˢᵗ Flying Squadron
Ami Cairn has become well known thanks to her coverage in the Genesis Free Press. A fine frigate officer with an excellent fighting reputation, this white wolf is definitely on the track to promotion. One of her more notable credits to date is the development of spatial charges as viable Allied weapons. She flies her flag from her 38-gun frigate, *Inferno*. Thanks to Wes Prewer for his continued contributions with this venerable canine.

Claw, Chronos — Captain, ENS Flame
The intrepid skipper of the diminutive *Flame*, this cat remains one of the best scouting officers the Earther Navy has ever seen. Having been Fox Magnus' First Lieutenant in *Flame* during the Genesis Campaign, he's come a long way to get command of a reconnaissance squadron for the blockade of the Krogg home systems, and as one might expect, he and his ship are both doing splendid jobs on the front line. Watch for his almost-inevitable promotion after the war.

Conroy, Pat — ArcLieutenant-General, Pat's Posse (Battle Group)
This Irishman probably needs no introduction. Despite having been through more than his share of drama since the Church mutiny, he's managed to keep his head level and his mind focused... and he's in love with Sarah, despite her issues. He's tired of the war, to be sure, and is strongly considering retiring and writing histories of human-Earther interactions. Having talked to Caine about conversations with Ursla, he's decided that if he goes that route, he'll call his first book *The Human Equation*, because it sounds dramatic and seems an apt enough choice. Plagiarizing bastard. With his original 444ᵗʰ Flying Squadron (Pat's Pirates) destroyed when *Bishop* was lost, he's been given a new 444ᵗʰ plus two additional Battlecruiser squadrons, thus creating 'Pat's Posse'. He flies his flag from *Divine Templar* with Jessica Forbes as his ArcColonel, but he misses his old *Bishop* daily.

Cuttar, Ernile — Corporal, Special Recon Squad (attached 2/54ᵗʰ)
Just a reminder that Ernile's cool name (pronounced 'Urn-i-lee') was sourced from a British First Lord by the name of Ernle Chatfield. Sorry, I really like him so I keep bringing him up. And of course he's a top-notch wolf in Howler's squad, destined to do some great things, so remember his name!

Felix, Savanna — Admiral, Third Fleet
Savanna Felix is perhaps the most self-assured of all the Admirals still with the blockade fleet. Despite having begun at a desk, he's weathered the storm of the war with the most resilience of his fellows, and he's almost found himself in the role of morale monitor. He remembers exactly why he's in the war, and why the Earthers have fought so hard for so long, and he's not afraid to remind those who've been too worn down to keep focused. And, of course, he's still a razor-sharp combat officer, flying his flag from *Tonnant*, 80.

Forbes, Jessica — *Flag ArcColonel*, Divine Templar
Jessica Forbes survived the destruction of *Bishop* as well as the illness that hit the crew after their evacuation by *Atlas* and *Vulcan*. She has remained with Pat Conroy as his trusted right-hand officer. A skilled combat commander, she's glad to be nearing the end of the war, and looks forward to retiring to a Genesis that she hopes will be much more open than the one she grew up in. At present she commands *Divine Templar*, the 444th's new flag-Battlecruiser.

Forepaw, Labrador — *Flag Captain, ENS* Orion
Though he takes no credit for it, and though he manages not to be obvious about it, Lab Forepaw is one of Setter Caine's greatest supporters. While the First Lord grapples with the deeper questions that might change the destiny of his people, Lab quietly keeps his dear friend on course, all the while making sure *Orion* and indeed, the 101st Battle Squadron, are in fighting trim. Since the death of Kella Felar at Gibraltar (and the total transfer of tactical command of the First Fleet to the First Lord), the extra paperwork that comes with running the force has gone to Forepaw's desk, not Caine's, and the First Lord may not even realize how many minor details are looked after by his trusted friend. Lab Forepaw is an extraordinary officer, a fine Earther, and a future leader who Setter expects will be greater than he himself could ever be.

Furgus, Jax — *Vice Admiral*
Jax Furgus is a cat, but he seems to have been issued more than nine lives. Having had so many ships shot out from under him that he has actually lost count (or at least he says he has), Jax remains one of the best Earther fighting Admirals, consistently getting into the nastiest sections of the big battles and turning the tide, even at the cost of his own ship. He looks forward to retiring, and has been looking into having an old-style shotgun and rocking chair produced so he can sit on a porch and heckle passers-by in the good old style. Lately he has a 74, *Madrid*, for his command. It would be in poor taste to guess how long that'll last once the shooting starts… but come on, you know you're wondering.

Grieve, Andros — *General*
One of the greatest soldiers the Earther Marine Corps has ever seen, Andros Grieve is coming off the triumph of the Avalon and Amaratsu campaigns (which were going on while Gibraltar was being menaced and after), and is preparing for a dangerous mission in Krogg home space. He's under no pretense that the fighting will be easy if he's tasked with assaulting the Krogg homeworld, but he knows — and frankly everyone in the Allied fleets know — that he's the best one for the job. One way or another, he intends to see this war through to its end.

Hastings, Elizabeth — *Commander-in-Chief, Genesis Navy & ArcGeneral, Sixth Fleet*
Liz Hastings is as much the matriarch of the Genesis Navy as Setter Caine is the patriarch of the Earther Fleet. She built the professional fighting force that,

despite its technical handicaps, has managed to make major contributions to the defeats suffered by the Kroggs thus far, and now she's looking forward to getting back to front-line command. She's finally satisfied that her old nemesis, Harvey Bingham, has truly changed his ways, and so she's willing to leave the Genesis system with her Sixth Fleet to play a fighting role in the end of the Krogg War. She's a leading candidate for the civilian Presidency that Bingham is promising to create with his reforms after the war ends.

Hobbes, Ronax — *Captain,* ENS Engadine
Ron Hobbes serves as Draco Maximane's Flag Captain aboard *Engadine*. An experienced ship commander, he moved from 74s to the purpose-built Carrier at its launch, and proved an excellent boat officer during the period of the Battle of Gibraltar. He remains with his ship, and continues to disagree in Carrier doctrine with Commodore Tom Locke, who heads the Second Carrier Group.

Hodge, Gillian — *Commandant, Genesis Marine Corps*
One of the most experienced soldiers left in the Genesis Marine Corps', Gillian is in fact the commander-in-chief of that service, overseeing its employment in the campaign against the Kroggs. Having begun her rise to command at the head of *Bishop's* marines during the mutiny against the Church, she's gone on to support Andros Grieve in his strikes over Genesis, and to fight a number of small actions on the front. She took a romantic interest in Graham Manchester for a while during the period of the Gibraltar incident, but he proved a bit too emotionally unpredictable for her given the wartime climate, so she backed off at least for a while. In any case, Gillian commands 184,000 Genesis marines, which seems rather more important at this stage than her relationship with Graham.

Howler, Cadmus — *Sergeant Major, Special Recon Squad (attached 2/54th)*
With the promotion of Beckett Lupus to officer status, Cadmus Howler was made up to Sergeant Major and put in charge of the elite eight-wolf recon squad that has earned a spectacular reputation beginning with its first engagement at Antarctica. That squad has remained at its old commander's side, Colonel Lupus having attached it as a special force to his current command, 2/54th. The combination of elite squad and elite battalion is a bad one — for the Kroggs, that is, as it's rather good for the Earthers.

Jardaw, Garvin — *Commodore*
Garvin Jardaw commands the escort group that looks after Draco Maximane's Carrier Groups. With his flag flying from his veteran 64 *Highlander*, this polar bear has turned a force of aged 64s and even near-ancient 58s into a sturdy protective force. Though he isn't fully settled into his Flag Rank yet, Garvin is benefiting from the friendship of his old Captain from *Apollo*, and he ultimately wants to retire from the service — as soon as the war is finished.

Kandam, Karl — *Commodore*
Karl Kandam's 236th was one of the first Battle Squadrons to engage Krogg forces in Genesis space, but during the great battle of Genesis and in the weeks of campaigning afterward, both he and his squadron were too badly shot up to keep pressing forward. As such, he was assigned to take command of the Gibraltar stations, and after commanding them through the Gibraltar action, he has become a fixture of that system. After the war he'll probably be staying with them for some time.

Karr, Farley — *Captain, ENS* Diadem
Still in command of the converted Carrier *Diadem*, Farley Karr is one of Draco Maximane's most experienced Captains, and often is called upon by Maximane to offer advice and consultation on Carrier problems. After the war, he looks forward to retiring, though he enjoys interstellar travel and is considering options that might keep him in space.

Lazarus, Celia — *Senior Medical Technician*
Presently stationed aboard *ENS Orion*, Celia Lazarus is an up-and-coming medic, destined soon to be certified as a doctor and put in charge of a medical staff of her own. This wolf actually worked as an intern with Elandra Caine for a few months at Fengate Hospital in Australia after the Battle of the Antarctic Plains. Her experience treating wounded Earthers and humans convinced her that her medical aptitudes were better suited to helping combat casualties than working in a lab, though; she's rather handy around a multi-phasic spectral scanner unit... or whatever 'MPSC unit' stands for.

Locke, Tom — Commodore, Second Carrier Group
Commanding *ENS Monarch* during the time of the Battle of Gibraltar, Tom Locke proved himself an exceptional Carrier officer, and earned promotion to head the Second Carrier Group once it was assembled. He holds command of that unit until it can be integrated with Draco Maximane's First Carrier Group, at which point Locke will move to the Vice Admiral's right hand. He and Captain Ron Hobbes disagree regularly about preferred Carrier doctrine.

Lupus, Beckett — *Colonel, 2/54th Foot, Guards Brigade of Heavy Division*
Beckett Lupus might be said to be the greatest fighter and most elite soldier in the Earther Marine Corps, well on his way to post-war command of the Corps, once Andros Grieve retires. Having jumped from Sergeant Major to Major after the *Bishop* incident, he's distinguished himself in various planetary actions since his return to the fleet, and with his squad remaining at his side, he was given command of one of the most elite regiments in the service, the 2nd Battalion of the 54th Regiment of Foot. Indeed, he has even seen that unit integrated into the Guards Brigade of the Heavy Division, which he has been appointed to command, despite his rank of Colonel.

Magnus, Fox — *Commodore*
The ever-dapper commander of the 186th Battle Squadron, Fox is one of the chief squadron commanders in the Earther Navy — no mean designation considering how battle-hardened the force is. Flying his flag from *Atlas*, he's approaching the end of the war feeling somewhat exhausted. Still, he's determined and one of the best ship-handlers around. He'll probably be First Space Lord one day, presuming the Admiralty reorganizes in order to create that rank...

Manchester, Graham — *ArcLieutenant-General, Sixth Fleet (Capital Ships)*
Graham seems to have come a long way from the guy who fainted when he first saw Ursla. Having commanded boats at Gibraltar, he's now been put at the head of the capital ships of the Sixth Fleet, a testament both to his ability to adapt to new missions, and to the dire need for Flag Officers that Liz Hastings seems to perpetually face as the casualty lists grow longer. The younger of the Manchester siblings, he's flying his flag from *Pope Edgar Fitzpatrick*.

Manchester, Sarah — *ArcGeneral, Fourth Fleet*
Sarah's had a rough ride through the war, what with her personal life only surfacing in full form since the beginning of the war, and her old unresolved issues impacting her command style. She's probably the best fighting fleet officer humanity has seen since Horatio Nelson, and almost appropriately she seems to have foibles in kind with that great Admiral. Her command of the Fourth Fleet can hardly be faulted for its military merits — hers is the most formidable human fleet ever to see action. Hopefully she'll find what she needs in her personal life to settle down, because otherwise the end of the war won't be much of a relief for her.

Maximane, Draco — *Vice Admiral, Carrier Groups*
The originator of the Carrier concept, Maximane has become the commander of the First Carrier Group on its blockade station between the Krogg home systems. Having previously commanded the 74 *Apollo* with Garvin Jardaw as his First Lieutenant, he's a skilled combat officer, and has since become the chief Carrier tactician. He and his wife Hera have a daughter who Draco elected to name Minnie. Minnie Maximane... that's Draco for you. Anyway, he flies his flag from the CVA *Engadine*.

Narosh — *Admiral-of-a-Fleet, Fourth Fleet-of-War*
Narosh was the Captain who served as the Son of Praaxus' right hand during the campaigns against the Kroggs in the Larosian galaxy, and he has since become one of the most renowned fleet commanders in the Larosian Navy, with his elite fighting Fourth being sent on the most difficult missions. His determination to end the Krogg race as retribution for the death of the Son is pronounced and perhaps slightly out of character for him; the Son did indeed once warn him not to become too much like his enemy. In any case, he commands his fleet

from the Warcruiser *Lycrotar* — the same ship that once served as the Son's command vessel.

Novash — Admiral-of-a-Division, Fourth Fleet-of-War
Having been the first Larosian to meet with an Earther (after Ursla managed to save his Warcruisers from the Krogg trap at the Genesis corridor), Novash has become one of the most empathetic Larosians in their fleet. He appreciates Earther culture despite its peculiarities, and enjoys working with the hairy, oversized, non-telepathic creatures, no matter how un-Larosian they might be. He remains one of the very best officers in the Larosian Navy, with his flag flying from *Shanavorus.*

Nightclaw, Dran — Commodore, 111th Flying Squadron
If you had to name the best cruiser commander to fight for the Allies in the Krogg War, or even in the battle against the Church, you might consider Pat Conroy or Ami Cairn or Andra Ursla herself... but after all of them you'd have to decide on Dran Nightclaw, because he *is* the best. His frigates are the most elite in the war — a bane to Kroggs and an asset to whatever command they're attached to. Dran is still his usual cool, collected self, and his instincts have not dulled over the war. He remains aboard *Cerberus,* 38.

Sandpelt, Lang — Lieutenant, ENS Flame
First Lieutenant and chief engineer of the diminutive little *Flame,* Lang Sandpelt has become recognized as one of the young rising stars of the Earther Navy. Though he has a long way to go before he hits flag rank, his skill will likely see him in command of large groups of ships before he knows it.

Stowt, Bartemius — Flag Captain, ENS Inferno
The redoubtable Captain of Ami Cairn's flagship, Barty Stowt is an agreeable bear with a great deal of experience in ship-fighting. His exploits and wit are known in the fleet, and have been popularized by the Genesis Free Press. Originally created by Wes Prewer, he's a fine Earther and a welcome actor in the final siege of the Krogg systems.

Tigar, Artemis — Flag Captain, ENS Agamemnon
Sitting always at Andra Ursla's right hand, Artie Tigar is an excellent skipper and a very apt tactician. With a track record for sniffing out traps, he's become a trusted partner in his Admiral's strategic planning. His sense of humor keeps things light and even, while his fine leadership abilities keep *Agamemnon* running in top form. Definitely a star of the future, Tigar looks forward to seeing an end to this war.

Torallis — Captain-Elite, Larosian Stealth Guard
Torallis is known widely as perhaps the best Captain-Elite in the Larosian Stealth

Guard, with combat skills beyond any of his peers, and telepathic discipline that would likely impress the Son himself. Having stormed an empty Queen's Hive with Andros Grieve in the Genesis system, he looks forward to the opportunity to finally assault the real Queen of his mortal enemy race. He is prepared to die in the venture, and perhaps even expects to, but this hardly dissuades him; duty and honor must be upheld, and so he must help kill the Queen.

Ursla, Andra — Admiral, Second Fleet
The great commander of the Second Fleet, and Setter Caine's right hand, Ursla is one of the bedrocks of the Earther Navy. Despite her fatigue, her mind remains one of the best for fleet tactics among the Earthers, and she'll be instrumental in finishing the Krogg War. Perhaps more important than that, she's Caine's best friend on the front, and if anyone can keep him steady despite his weariness, it's her. She flies her flag from the 150-gun *Agamemnon*.

Venus, Thena – Captain
Skippering the 74 *Vulcan*, Thena Venus is one of Fox Magnus' elite skippers in the 186th Battle Squadron. For many months they were divisions mates in Felix's 301st Battle Squadron, and there they became partners in crime. She also happens to be a fox, so her sense of adventure matches well with the former sloop commander.

Wallace, Bill — ArcLieutenant-General, Sixth Fleet (Cruisers)
Bill Wallace has been out of the limelight since his Heavy Cruiser, *Darymanis City*, was saved by Ursla's 111th during the defection from the Church. That incident introduced Audrey DeBrooke, now a head of the Freetown Colony, to popular awareness, but unlike his counterpart Bill has stayed with the fleet, and due to the enormous casualties among Genesis flag officers, has risen rapidly to flag rank, being given command of the cruisers of the newly-minted Sixth Fleet. He has a wife and young daughter back on Genesis, but because of his distaste for the Church his is a 'common-law' family, off the legal marriage books at least until non-Church weddings are made legal by the Bingham Chancellery.

APPENDIX B: THE EARTHER MARINE CORPS

The Earther marines have blazed a rather glorious trail through the *Equations* novels, seeming to show up at just the right time with the right mix of firepower and strength to break their enemies, and forcing whatever enemy they face to retreat or die. In *The Earther Equation*, the marines play an even more critical role than usual, so we thought it'd be a good idea to explain, if only briefly, just what about the EMC makes its troops so formidable, and how it is set up and organized for the war it's fighting.

Introduction

First of all, you already know the main reason that Earther marines are so elite: they're Earthers. Tangling with an intelligent, well-armed and instinctive humanoid bear... well, that's not a good prospect for anyone. If anything, the latent predatory skills inherent in all Earthers are of even more use to the marines than they are to the members of the Navy; while the Earthers can translate their instinctive bonds into excellent ship and squadron cooperation, the wolves of a recon squad can operate seamlessly together as if they were a classic wolf pack.

But the Earthers would probably be the first to explain to you that instinct alone doesn't win wars. Common sense and organization have always figured large in the success of military formations — from the Romans facing barbarian hordes in the first century BCE to the British facing determined Mahdist opposition at Omdurman almost 2,000 years later, organization and discipline have always been crucial to military success.

So how precisely is the Earther Marine Corps organized, and what mission was it designed for? The EMC is a force meant to fulfill two needs for the Earthers: it serves as both a standing land army and as a specialized naval strike force. What's the difference?

The Standing Army

The concept of a standing army is perhaps surprisingly not a universal one — in medieval times, for instance, neither nations nor standing armies existed. The advent of organized Westphalia-style states led to the creation of permanent standing forces of soldiers, usually embodied in armies of the state. Everybody in Europe seemed to have one by the eighteenth century, and twentieth and twenty-first century nations certainly have them.

But the Earthers actually don't have an army.

That's right, technically speaking, the Earthers have no army, no professional land-only fighting force. What about the marines? Good question... oh wait, there I go again. Sorry. But in answer to that question...

The Earther Marine Corps is actually a sub-branch of the Earther Navy, with the Navy being the senior service and the Corps General Staff thus technically being junior to the Admiralty. That's a wildly different scenario than what you might find in Britain or America in the twentieth century, where there was always and Army which existed as an autonomous organization within the military.

How this is important to the way the marines and the fleet interact will be dealt with in the next section; for now let's look at how the lack of a standing army has created one half of the marine corps' military role.

Essentially, perhaps obviously, the Earther Marine Corps has been designed in such a way that, if a situation demands, it can deploy as an organized ground force not unlike an army group. Specifically, the corps has been laid out in such a way that its units could be deployed on a battlefield with coherent ease.

Logically it might seem that all marine corps should be so disposed. However, if you look at the Royal Marines as an example of a combat force you find that it's not always the way things go. Best way to explain is to use a couple of examples.

From the 1750s, there were about fifty companies of Royal Marines organized into three divisions... meaning that the biggest tactical unit in the service was a company (probably between fifty and 150 men), whereas in a standing army of the time, the unit of maneuver was a battalion of 500 men or so, or even a regiment of 1,000 (for those with background in this period of military history forgive my glossing over the details!).

That disposition reflected the role that the Royal Marines were intended to play in war — a role I'll get into in the next section — but I think it's pretty clear that as a land fighting force at that time, the Royal Marines weren't organized well for fighting pitched battles, because that was what the British Army was for.

So getting back to our topic, the Earther Marine Corps has no Earther Army opposite it, and as such it can't overlook the possible need for its forces to fight large pitched battles. Indeed, you might recall that the first real action the marines got into was the biggest in their history to date: 50,000 marines were on the field... ice... at Antarctica.

Think about that for a moment... 50,000 marines organized into companies of 50 troops would mean coordinating 1,000 separate units to fight that battle. As you probably recall, there wasn't *that* much chaos on the Earther side that day.

So how is the EMC organized to allow for pitched battles then? Divisions are divided into brigades which are made up of battalions which are made up of companies... and then 'regiments' are actually not field formations, but administrative units.

Essentially, each regiment is made up of two battalions, but even if those two battalions are part of the same brigade and they fight alongside each other, they don't take orders as a 'regiment', but as two separate battalions. It's a bit confusing, so if you're slightly lost (as I often am) just realize that 1/54th and 2/54th (the first and second battalions of the 54th regiment) are essentially connected to each other only in name and pride.

So that's how the organizational structure is laid out to allow for major battles. At Antarctica, Andros Grieve was able to rely on the divisional structures of First (Light), Second (Heavy), Third, Ninth and Twelfth (reserve) Divisions to help organize his attack on the base; he was commanding General in charge of the army, and his five Lieutenant Generals took his deployment orders and set their divisions up to adequately meet his needs. They in turn passed orders down to Brigadiers, and Brigadiers to Colonels, and so on.

Much less confusing than General Grieve ordering 1,000 Captains around, I think, even if everyone involved did happen to be an Earther.

So hopefully that demonstrates how the organization of the Earther Marine Corps is designed to meet the Earthers' strategic need for a land battle force capable of fighting pitched battles. If it doesn't... well, take my word for it.

But what's the second role for the EMC, then? Well, there are no specialized support formations. In a standing army in modern human history, a division has every kind of support formation wrapped into it, from artillery to full medical units, engineers and logistical supply units. Not the Earthers. They're made up of combat formations only, with specialists like engineers being integrated into companies and required to fight as regular infantry until their abilities are needed.

What's that mean? The Earther Marines Corps has no independent staying power as a land combat force. And that, despite the compromises made to allow the corps to serve as a land army, indicates the primary role of the corps...

The Projectile of the Navy

Sir John (Jackie) Fisher, the British First Sea Lord on two separate occasions during the opening decades of the twentieth century, overseer of the original *Dreadnought* battleship project, and architect of the Royal Navy that would fight the First World War, once stated that a nation's army should really be a projectile of its navy. Now that statement was not fair to the British Army of that time, which (in contrast with the common misconceptions about First World War combat) was an exceptional military force. But the claim does work very neatly when describing the Earther Marine Corps.

The primary job envisioned for Earther marine units comes in the strike role: they're meant to arrive in a system carried by a squadron of ships, to be landed against an enemy installation and to be withdrawn as soon as the fast strike is complete. Think of how Andros Grieve hit both the Krogg installations on the surface of Genesis and the abandoned Queen's Hive. Fast in, fast out, with a minimum of forces traveling light and hitting fast. Major Colin Brawn of *Atlas* did the same in bringing his and *Vulcan's* companies down to save Pat

Conroy's *Harbinger Bishop* survivors. Don't forget Colin Brawn, by the way; he's a rising star.

So you can guess why the EMC doesn't have a major army-style logistical support network — no staying power because according to their doctrine, they don't need to *stay* at all. They go in fast, kill the bad guys, blow up their bases, and get out.

And indeed, this is the way much of the Krogg War (that you haven't seen, at least not yet) has been fought. A Battle Squadron arrives in a system with a Krogg base, it sends its eight companies down to take out the installation, the marines do the job and are withdrawn, usually within hours.

What happens if things get more drawn out? Well, the Avalon and Amaratsu campaigns that Andros Grieve was fighting while Gibraltar was being menaced and after (and which you'll hopefully read about some day!) are fine examples. The extensive Krogg presence on these planets led Grieve to rally a brigade — the elite Guards Brigade of the Second (Heavy) Division — and to stay and besiege them for about seven weeks. The demands for a lengthy operation there thus forced the EMC units involved to draw on their army-style organizational structure, fighting as a brigade.

But didn't I just say the marines have no staying power? I did, but they don't need it, because remember, the Earther Marine Corps is a branch of the Earther Navy, so guess who provided a steady stream of supplies, medical support, and everything else a ground force would require to stay intact? Yep, the Earther Navy.

So in itself, the Marine Corps lacks the mechanisms to remain in ground combat for extended periods, but because it is a branch of the Earther Navy, it's expected that it will always be able to rely on the fleet to supply those supporting elements it lacks. Should the fleet lose orbital superiority this policy could, of course, prove a major liability, but that's why the fleet doesn't insert marines into a situation until the Flag Officer on scene is satisfied that orbital control has been achieved.

It's worked well enough so far.

Conclusion

So that's how the Earther Marine Corps works. A branch of the Earther Navy, it has the ability to fight pitched ground battles, thus replacing a more traditional land army, but is at its best as a fast strike force.

Ultimately, though, remember what I said in the introduction: Earther marines are Earthers first. You stick them in the middle of a fight, no matter what their organization, and they've got a solid chance of getting out of it.

Well, unless they're storming the Queen's Palace on Krogg 'A'. That's more complicated...

THE
EQUATIONS NOVELS

The Earthers evolved after humans were driven from the Earth by an intelligent bio-weapon dubbed 'Omega'. They are faster, stronger, smarter, wiser, *better* than humans, and they are the only hope for the survivors of the human race as an interstellar war between two great alien powers absorbs the galaxy. But all is not as it seems, and the humans and the Earthers face challenges that overshadow the wars of alien empires and threaten to destroy their civilizations...

The Equations Novels by Kenneth Tam

Book One: THE HUMAN EQUATION (Oct 2003)

Book Two: THE ALIEN EQUATION (May 2004)

Book Three: THE RENEGADE EQUATION (Dec 2004)

Book Four: THE EARTHER EQUATION (July 2005)

Book Five: THE GENESIS EQUATION (July 2006)

Book Six: THE VENGEANCE EQUATION (July 2007)

Book Seven: THE NEMESIS EQUATION (July 2008)

Book Eight: THE DESTINY EQUATION (July 2009)

The Equations Novels are complete, but there are spinoff series and new stories in the Earther universe still to come!

For more information, please visit
www.earther.net

ABOUT THE AUTHOR

Born in 1984 in St. John's, Newfoundland, Kenneth Tam holds both a Bachelor's and Master's degree in history from Wilfrid Laurier University in Waterloo, Canada. His MA thesis examined the creation and operation of the Caribou Hut, a hostel for Allied servicemen in St. John's during the Second World War.

In 2006, Kenneth received a prestigious Canada Graduate Scholarship from the Social Sciences and Humanities Council of Canada. He was also awarded a Balsillie Fellowship at the Centre for International Governance Innovation during 2006-07. In that capacity, he worked for Mr. Paul Heinbecker, Canada's former ambassador and permanent representative to the United Nations. He presently serves as a Communications Consultant for Kitchener–Waterloo's federal Member of Parliament, Peter Braid.

Since releasing the first *Equations* Novel in 2003, Tam has promoted his books across Canada, speaking with junior and high school students, delivering writing workshops, and doing book signings at bookstores and Iceberg-organized events. He frequently appears as a guest author at science fiction events across the country.

Kenneth is a partner in Iceberg Publishing, the company he and his family started in 2002. He has authored many of the company's existing titles, and is also responsible for graphic design, including the company logo, website, banners, advertisements, and other marketing materials. He acts as a primary contact with printers and suppliers, and is also key in new author development and recruitment.

He remains very lazy about writing his author bios. When they told him to make this one longer, he mostly copied and pasted it together from the Iceberg website, www.icebergpublishing.com.